Spymaster Allegro

Roger Bensaid

Published by New Generation Publishing in 2017

Copyright © Roger Bensaid 2017

First Edition

The author asserts the moral right under the Copyright, Designs and Patents Act 1988 to be identified as the author of this work.

All Rights reserved. No part of this publication may be reproduced, stored in a retrieval system or transmitted, in any form or by any means without the prior consent of the author, nor be otherwise circulated in any form of binding or cover other than that which it is published and without a similar condition being imposed on the subsequent purchaser.

www.newgeneration-publishing.com

New Generation Publishing

The Plot

Major Rodney Brown, invalided out of the army, finds himself in a section of the British secret service that deals with matters that do not fall neatly into the remit of either the Foreign Office or the Home Office or that neither of them wants to deal with.

This second Major Brown adventure takes him and his team from the streets of London to Somalia. While his nemesis Brigadier General Tsygankov forms his team in his dacha to bring havoc to the UK using the IRA. They travel to Afghanistan, Moscow, Split Libya, Ireland, France, Canal du Midi and Toulouse before setting foot in the UK and Southern Ireland and setting up a mission devised by General Tsygankov to cripple a major arm of the British Army and Major Rodney Brown.

The Author

Roger Bensaid spent 24 years in the army and a further 17 years in the gas and oil industry before becoming a specialist consultant for 10 years that took him to many of the world's conflict zones, often in support of the services he has the highest regard for. When asked why he did it, he said, "To give something back."

He spends much of his time now painting and writing.

Acknowledgements and Foreword

This 2017 revised Spymaster Allegro, would not have new been published at all without again the heroic editing effort and support of the David W and an Editor from New Generation Publishing for this revised 2017 edition. A special thank you to Susan Marshal. All who, unlike me, can tell a comma from a full stop and where a capital goes and does not! I will get there.

So why did I write a sequel and planed a third, now completed? Well, like the reason for writing the first book, it's complicated, but with different drivers. To prove something to myself, certainly, that I had more than one book in me and as a discipline, it's hard work. Mostly of all I think for myself, the family and friends. Three books in this first series sound about right?

For their input and help, and my thanks to Kate for putting up with my mental absence at times when I was deep in thought among the plots.

Roger 2017

My Motivators

"Get on and do it, never give up. Focus on the barriers to achieving your mission, innovate, improvise, and overcome. Just get it done!" Bob (plays the head of SO13 Anti-Terrorist branch, he insisted on being promoted in this one.)

And wanted me to add the following again : must be getting soft in his old age but to those who know, thank you from me and the rest of the country.

"We are the pilgrims, master, we shall go always a little further; it may be beyond the last blue mountain barred by snow across that angry or glimmering sea." Extract from *The Golden Journey to Samarkand* by James Elroy Flecker, 1884.

"If it's under the bridge it's gone; only the next step counts, so step carefully." Pat (plays one of the Brown SIS team.)

"The only ones truly free of the daily struggle, strife and war are dead." Apologies to Plato.

Dedicated to my father, a retired warrior.

Narrator

The events of August 1988 are as related to me by General Carl Tsygankov KGB Spymaster, retired, and Major Rodney Brown, retired British SIS by the Volga in Southern Russia in the autumn of that year. All characters appearing in this work are fictitious. Any resemblance to real persons, living or dead is purely coincidental.

Contents

SPYMASTER

Chapter 1	AFTERMATH	1
Chapter 2	AFGHANISTAN SIX MONTHS BEFORE	5
Chapter 3	SAIED	29
Chapter 4	SAIED TRAIL BY COMBAT IS BORN	37
Chapter 5	LONDON BRIGADIER ROBINSON AND MAJOR BROWN	40
Chapter 6	THE RUSSIAN MISSION	47
Chapter 7	MAJOR BROWN	51
Chapter 8	CAPTAIN SERVO'S SPATNEZ EXECUTES HIS PLAN	55
Chapter 9	THE BIRD TABLE	64
Chapter 10	TSYGANKOV AND POLYAKOV	73
Chapter 11	BRIGADIER ROBINSON'S BRIEF	80
Chapter 12	THE TSYGANKOV DACHA	84
Chapter 13	THE ROBINSON MEMORANDUM	90
Chapter 14	MOSCOW	97
Chapter 15	THE QUARTERMASTER'S ENFORCER	100
Chapter 16	THE DACHA TEAM FORM	104
Chapter 17	SCOPE AND TRUST	107
Chapter 18	TSYGANKOV'S DINNER NIGHT	112
Chapter 19	MAJOR BROWN CLEARS HIS DESK	117
Chapter 20	TSYGANKOV AND CARLA	120
Chapter 21	TSYGANKOV OUTLINES THE MISSION TO THE TEAM	124
Chapter 22	THE JOURNEY TO SOMALIA	133
Chapter 23	TSYGANKOV TALKS TO SERVO AND CARLA	142
Chapter 24	THE EX	147

Chapter 25	TSYGANKOV TALKS TO VASILY	155
Chapter 26	THE HOSTAGES	158
Chapter 27	TSYGANKOV AND SAIED	164
Chapter 28	RODNEY GETS THE GO	166
Chapter 29A	TSYGANKOV SEES HIS TEAM OFF	169
Chapter 29 B	RODNEY GETS HIS TEAM ON THE ROAD	172
Chapter 30	TRAIL IN SPLIT	180
Chapter 31	THE BANKER	188
Chapter 32	CARLA AND SERVO	194
Chapter 33	VASILY	200
Chapter 34	SAIED'S LIBYAN MINI ADVENTURE	205
Chapter 35	THE Q SURVEILLANCE TEAM	210
Chapter 36	THE FBI AND SO14 MEETING WITH BRIGADIER ROBINSON	213
Chapter 37	SAIED'S DAY OUT WITH THE LIBYAN SECRET SERVICE AND THE IRA	218
Chapter 38	VASILY	229
Chapter 39	THE FBI MAN	234
Chapter 40	- SERVO CARLA AND THE IRA	243
Chapter 41	MOULD AND SHARKY AND THE AVERY'S TEAM	263
Chapter 42	RODNEY DIRECTS	271
Chapter 43	VASILY	276
Charter 44	ROBINSON AND RODNEY	287
Chapter 45	THE RUSSIANS	294
Chapter 46	- MAINTAINING THE ZERO	302
Chapter 47	GAME	310
Chapter 48	- RENDEZVOUS	329
Chapter 49	THE ACCOUNTANT	336
Chapter 50	THE WALLOP SAFE HOUSE	344

Chapter 51　SET 361

Chapter 52　MATCH 370

Chapter 53　ALLEGRO 397

Players in this Story:

(*And I need to remind you, the reader, it is only a story – to while away your free time but also to amuse "players" and my long-suffering "friends and acquaintances". All characters appearing in this work are fictitious. Any resemblance to real persons, living or dead is purely coincidental.*)

"*The beginning is the most important part of the work.*"
Plato

The Russian Cast:

General Polyakov – Director 1st Directorate KGB

Brigadier General – Carl Tsygankov, The Spymaster Deputy of the 1st Directorate KGB

Brigadier General – Shabarshin, Spymaster Deputy Designate of the 1st Directorate KGB

Colonel Pavel Gorsky – KGB Operations Afghanistan

Major Carla Kazimira Tskhovbova

Captain Vasily Vladimirov KGB Intelligence Officer Afghanistan

Captain Vladimir Servo – Russian GRU Special Forces Spetsnaz Alpha Group – Officer

Jean (Salomon) Saied the Contract Mercenary to General Tsygankov

Tamara and Mac Szukaj – Tsygankov's housekeeper and her ex-airborne Special Forces engineering husband, Tsygankov's dacha engineering estate and maintenance manager

Captain Jean Paul – skipper of the *Harlequin*

The British Players:

Brigadier Robinson Director ex-Guards of the Secret Services "Off Piste" Section

Major Rodney Brown ex-SAS – Deputy to Brigadier Robinson, Chief Intelligence Officer SIS

Major James Collins - Serving Ordinance Officer,

Mr Reid ex-SAS/Ordinance, Senior Field Operations Agent Intelligence Officer SIS

Patrick Jones ex-RMP/Fire Service (Resources and Planning) Intelligence Officer SIS

Graham Swain Agent ex-Ordinance (Coordination Field Admin and Logistics) Intelligence Officer SIS

Andrew Harrison ex-Oman Forces Officer (Weapon Traffic Contract and legal Specialist) Intelligence Officer SIS

Ms Jane ex-Special Branch/MI5 (Communications and Intelligence Specialist) Agent SIS

Mould ex-INF Operations Agent Intelligence Officer Field SIS

Sharky ex-INF Operations Agent Intelligence Officer Field SIS

Fred Jones ex-Guards Watcher Field Agent SIS

Lewis Jones ex-Guards Watcher Field agent SIS

Dr Jules Christian – Department's Forensic Scientist and Man Friday SIS

Mr John Brown Investment Banker and Money Laundering Specialist on loan from the Bank of England

Mr Avery Special ops trainer and field operative director

Captain Freire Howell-Speed – Royal Signals

The Third Parties' Players:

Major Igor Surgun – KGB
Robert Coveney – S013 Ante Terrorist Branch
Q – General Quartermaster and Instigator, Real Irish Republican Army

Liam – Chief of Operations for Q and the Enforcer

Joe and Ian – IRA Technical and bomb makers

The Mujahedeen – Insurgents' Camp in Pakistan

Simon – Somalia Warlord Sub Clan Tribal Chieftain

Alex – Dakota pilot Somalia.

FBI – London Liaison Officer Carol Winsor

Chapter 1

AFTERMATH

Major James Collins in his dream state let out a silent scream and grimaced, jerking his body awake and into a world of pain; shifting his body posture carefully to help ease the most acute of them. His consciousness secretly dreaded the nightmare scenario where he was maimed and damaged. Collins gingerly moved each limb and appendage in turn. He found feeling in all his limbs and digits, stiffness too. Satisfied he was bruised but whole, he blinked forcing his eyes open to scan his environment; his vision was slightly blurred, but he instinctively knew, somehow, he was in the Gosport Naval Hospital, "Perhaps it was the dark blue sisters and their staff naval nurse uniforms," was his thought. He could see them hazily in the background around the ward on urgent busy business attending to others.

His brain would not, could not, immediately understand the reason why he was there and in pain. Then he remembered the flashes, explosions, screams and shouts before the memory of shadowy figures deepened and he again slipped back into the blackness and oblivion.

Much latter he woke again, muscles stiff and hurting; he grunted as he tried to sit up to make sense of the images of the briefly glimpsed carnage and chaos that had come to him in his dreams. His movement and involuntary grunt attracted the attention of a bedside nursing sister who sat silently watching him.

She sedated him quickly, for he was to remain in a semi coma, that way for overnight it should help his injuries heal and to a point where the pain would be reduced to a manageable level. "Sleep well major, you were luckier than you know." The nurse looked down at her sleeping charge and checked his drips and other instruments. He would not wake now until the morning when, emerging in the semi coma, she and the doctor would check him again and send him back to sleep. As an afterthought she smiled to herself, "Not a bad specimen for his age."

At thirty-five James was a career soldier who had served in most of the places open to him. His first marriage had failed and he blamed himself. He had spent simply too much time away on unaccompanied tours and every time he had returned he was in some way changed by the experience. He and his wife had grown apart, no longer enjoying each other's company until little was left of the shared joined-up life they had hoped to share. Perhaps if he had tried harder, but in the end he had felt there was another. They drifted and he took the step to move on so both could have another chance.

The sister collected her belongings and handed over to the night sister and left for the day. In the corridor leading out of the ward a stocky man of average height, five-eight to nine, in his late thirties early forties leaned heavily on a walking stick, his blond mousey hair greying at the temples was carelessly groomed and it fell over his forehead almost to his eyes. He had a few cuts on his tanned face but otherwise seemed fine. It was his hazel eyes that arrested her and she felt she had to ask. "Are you all right, do you need anything?"

The man smiled disarmingly, gaining the trust of the nurse. "No, thank you sister, just wanted to know about Major James and if he would be alright?"

"You're a friend of his perhaps? Looks like you were caught up in the same incident," the sister was not suspicious of the man, just curious.

"Yes a friend. He saved my life once, I think so yes, interested in his recovery." Major Brown, Deputy Head of the most secret group that worked between the Home Office's MI5 and the Foreign Office's MI6, the SIS, gazed without blinking deep into the sister's eyes.

She felt her soul was being searched and averted her gaze disconcerted. "He is going to be fine, he was lucky, badly bruised, a few minor burns and cut about, torn muscles, somewhat deafened, surprisingly only mild concussion, no latent collapsed lung from the blast etc. Got all his limbs, fingers and toes, lucky and they work. But," she said suddenly forcefully to regain the high ground, meeting his gaze, "he will need a day or three to mend; he is going to be sedated, off and on, for at least another day, perhaps two, so why not come back to see him Monday morning. I will back be on duty then. If he is receptive I may give you a minute or two with him, helps to have a friend at a time like this to tell you all is well." With that and a smile she swung on her heels, bobbed hair swishing with the movement, her dress swirling around her long legs as she continued on her way, her shoes echoing down the corridor.

"Sounds good," Rodney called after her and turned and limped his way following the sister. "What a beauty, lucky James." Her stride was long and brisk; hips swinging, the sister soon outpaced him leaving him alone with his thoughts. "Ah for the energy of youth, where the fuck did mine go? Or is it like James, simply sleeping?" He grinned to himself. "Besides that dark-haired beauty of a sister Lt Commander Rank has to be in her late thirties maybe more, hell, there will be less than few years between us." It had taken time for him to get over the loss of his Valeria at the hand of the Russian Spymaster Brigadier General Tsygankov. "Perhaps it is time to return to the world, don't think Valeria would mind too much?" He moved his head from side to side as though weighing up the options. "Hum, you only live once or so they say." Unexpectedly he thought suddenly of Tsygankov. "Was Tsygankov one of those people who simply existed to bring chaos to the world or just another misguided soul? I wonder what new evil scheme he is up to these days, although," Rodney thought ruefully and then, "he should be long retired and amen to that?" Why Tsygankov had been brought to his consciousness at this time he did not know. He shuddered and then erased the Russian general from his mind.

At the exit to the hospital two of the key agents in Rodney's department, Mould and Sharky, waited sipping coffee from plastic cups. They looked up as he approached them. "What's this? Why are you two gentlemen not back at the site sorting it out?"

Mould held up his hands in innocence. "It was the old man's orders. We are now your minders 24/7 until this mess is sorted and the entities behind it we can be confident is not going for a quick revenge attack while we are clearing up."

"No way! Do I want you two heavyweights cramping my style; I have just seen the most interesting woman in a long time! Thank you anyway?" Rodney was half joking, half serious.

As Rodney turned to leave, Sharky rolled his eyes, his lean face tightening into a grimace as he gripped Rodney's arm. "It's like this, boss. The old man reasoned that you, we, others or someone else were among the targets, not just the event itself, and you know that," Sharky said quietly. He released his grip but held his leader's arm and waited patiently. Sharky realised he'd have upset Rodney if they had in anyway been responsible for the incident that could have killed or maimed and ruined others' lives.

"That makes no sense, Sharky; I was rather hoping we had got them all, in fact we know we did?" Rodney frowned and shook his arm free, he felt momentarily angry and he was not sure who with. "I am sorry Sharky, just a bit pissed off at the moment, not thinking straight; I can see the old man's logic, even in this case I think he may be being too cautious. Time will tell." He had been angry and was already and immediately regretting his remarks.

Mould and Sharky exchanged glances.

"Accepted boss, and you will want to know that the old man is sending down Reid and Avery's man to watch over Collins until we can get him back to his own lines." Sharky's lean six-foot wiry frame relaxed along with his facial muscles.

Mould matched Sharky's height but was the rounder of the two with a bullet head, and added in disgust, "Good, now you are on board. We got one part of the organisation, true enough, but not who was ultimately responsible and behind the blast so we still may have a job to do."

Rodney looked at the ground and then his mood cleared, "You're right. Clearly the old man is concerned, therefore so should I be. Come on then, your first duty as my 24/7 minders is to take us somewhere for a burger and beer and bring me up to date with what the hell is going on and where we are with our own clear-up."

Chapter 2

AFGHANISTAN SIX MONTHS BEFORE

The exceptionally tall Russian bent his bony head and looked out of the window of the giant military transport plane as it circled Kabul Airport. He could appreciate the Afghanistan landscape; it was in its own way he thought, quite beautiful. As with any country it had diverse geographic areas. In Afghanistan's case it was a harsh, high, hilly and mountainous environment interspersed with deep valleys, and uneven desert vista to the south. Melt water fed and flowed from the high country, the water runoff forming rivers, streams and potentially dangerous waddies.

He had recently read a recent operations situation report somewhere that a big waddy had burst its dammed-up banks creating a massive flood that spilt an engagement between the Afghans and the Russians just at the right moment. The rush of water allowed the Russians to withdraw without losses. "Perhaps Mother Nature loves us after all," he mused and grinned to himself.

He had been to Afghanistan from time to time over the years for one reason or another and in particular preferred to visit Kabul in its winter months, with its cold spectacular near distant hills, framed by even more distant mountains far more than the sweltering heat of the Afghan summer. The climate in the warm months was hot enough in the high summer to melt the glue holding the soles of your boots; no wonder the Afghans loved their sawn sandals, he had reasoned at one time or another.

Tsygankov thought it a conundrum, the contrast of the suffocating blistering summer heat and the winter where most of the country was as cold as charity. How could anyone exist comfortably and cope with such extreme temperature differences? He glanced at the cold mountains through the window of the aircraft and shivered into his Russian greatcoat wrapping it involuntarily tightly round his broad shoulders.

Brigadier Carl Tsygankov, a Deputy Director of the First Directorate KGB was, at seventy, still active and, he thought ruefully, on his swan song mission before he would be forcibly retired along with the Old Russia. He had retired more than once after he led the assassination of Gipsy and his daughter Valeria, but was pleased and flattered that the KGB kept calling him back for more and more spells that seemed to get longer every time for this reason and that.

Certainly most Russian senior officers rarely retired of their own volition, but he had been lucky, he was good at what he did and his skills were in short supply, so he was torn between the twin imperatives of feeling useful and getting on with life at his pace. He knew his field experience was sought after even at his age, for few could rival his record. The truth of the matter for him at this precise moment was that he preferred to work rather than spend his time overseeing the final few weeks work on his dacha.

The dacha and his land had been under major renovation for 18 months. It was all but finished and he needed a break from the builders and the mess, and he had been assured the builders would be gone within the fortnight along with the skips. But not for that matter the traffic on the Volga, which fascinated him as it plied the great river and which he could observe at close quarters from the cliffs or from his private beach of "his Island," as he thought of it.

It was also a simple equation, he had unfinished business and needed to be where the resources could be gathered, allocated and the opportunity now available gifted to him by the KGB which would enable him to close it out.

For his retirement, the dacha he had set up for himself was on one of the smaller islands half an hour north of Astrakhan in southwest Russia. True it was an idyllic spot from his point of view; few neighbours and a half a dozen hectares, some laid to vines, a mixed fruit orchard, a small lake and spare land to develop. The plot was bounded on two sides by the escarpments and the third a beach leading to the riverbank of the Volga. High stone dry-wall ringed the land and the wall in particular that went from one side of the escapement to the other side of the island made the plot private and defendable. A glass house and large orangery he had had constructed was a luxury he wanted to make the best use of his estate. He had such plans for his home.

Unexpectedly he had been given the chance to settle an old score for one last time. His retirement plans could wait awhile.

His pale, almost translucent skin, stretched as it was on his face, gave him with his thin sparse hair a skull-like appearance, yet he was not an unattractive man. He pulled a glove on to the scarred hand with its frozen tendons, a gift from Major Brown's man. He smiled despite the memory. Revenge, he believed, should always be taken cold and be totally unexpected; it motivated the natural driving force in him.

Tsygankov also knew in his heart that he had to get this mission completed before the KGB was re-formed, he feared a much lesser entity as would also be the New Russian Federation. He was well aware of the growing differences between Gorbachev, a rising star, and the Chairman of the KGB, General Viktor Mikhailovich Chebrikov. The Chairman had been in the post since 1982 and was a veteran of World War Two where he had served with distinction as a battalion commander and an engineer. Chebrikov's resistance to change and intransigence coupled with now poor sight made him vulnerable to the coming regime. Tsygankov also knew of another general; General Koskov, who was to be given the unenviable task of the Afghanistan drawdown, leading to withdrawal probably in two to three years' time. All this and the whispered rumour that Gorbachev seemed to favour the West, possibly to the point as future best friend and the current American President's possible successor did nothing to allay Tsygankov's feeling of an era passing.

Tsygankov unexpectedly and uncharacteristically felt himself brooding; he was not looking forward to Kabul City itself, where he hated to see the poverty of the poor. Most of the population had nothing and lived mainly in fear if they didn't belong to the right tribe or gang. As in any society there was the rich and powerful. In the case of Afghanistan he felt the differences between the rich and the poor were indecent. Was it any wonder they turned to anyone who could assure them simply of survival for themselves and their family, which by definition would mean being under the protection of a warlord. The matter that the cost to the individual was high in the context of liberty and social wellbeing as much would be demanded of them, the demands were nevertheless secondary to life itself. "We," he thought, "simply had not given the populace any alternative but to seek security elsewhere."

He was old enough to know the horrors of the Second World War and now specifically in Afghanistan the toll of dead and maimed young Russian soldiers to date, running as it was into 1986. What a waste of men and money on both sides. He favoured the gladiatorial settling of accounts between two or several protagonists these days, not the whole of a country's population. He found himself annoyed. He felt the simple answer as far as Afghanistan was concerned was to split the country into its major natural tribal regions, despite it being a country in name since the late 18th century, make each tribal region a country in its own right and get rid of the accursedly named Afghanistan forever!

"The British failed long ago, twice, as we will in our turn," he thought depressingly. "You can't beat an ideology or have a rational argument with a bigot or ideologist. And after us, who else? We have been here in one shape or another for over 30 years, admittedly only since 1979 in earnest but what have we achieved in Afghanistan – nothing but failed aspirations. It is truly the *"Bear Trap"*. He suddenly thought, "I seem to remember telling my old General the Chairman of all Russia just that," he mused, his lips curling into a semblance of a smile, what a night that was to remember in the chamber of the Chairman with Polyakov and Chekov the traitor.

"The British what a troublesome race they are?" he thought to himself. "Not only do I owe them for Chekov, I owe them for finding my mole Batteney and for finessing an old friend, Guks when he was the Russian KGB resident in London two years ago to make way for his deputy to take over, Gordievsky the traitor," he mused. "Such a small people now on their sea-surrounded island. How did they get to have such a reach?"

On the other hand, Tsygankov thought reverting to his preference for the colder weather. "After the winter of course, many of the public spaces and the better of districts in this fertile area all around Kabul with its verdant vines, flowering and abundant fruit bearing trees was a paradise and it thronged with birds." He was well read and could vaguely recall a description of Kabul and its old Palace written up by a young British Officer Lieutenant Alexander Burns, who Tsygankov considered was at least on par with the famous Lawrence of Arabia. Burnes writing around the 1832s Tsygankov remembered; passed through on a great game spying mission with three other companions working from the East India Company. Their mission was to discover what overland routes the Russians could take if they were to lead an army to overthrow the British in India. Burnes had cemented friendships not only with the powerful Ranjit Singh, the ruler of the Punjab whose army at that time would have given the East India Company a run for its money, but Dost Mohammed ruler of Afghanistan, and on Burnes travelled via the river Oxus to Bokhara where he won over the Grand Vizier Koosh Begee. Tsygankov wondered if today's young officers would fare as well as the Russian and British men in the great game in the 18th and 19th centuries in desperately hostile environments and peoples. He thought probably they would, as he never ceased to wonder at the innate instinct for survival of men in whatever situation they found themselves. "Ah the Russian and the British, what a game we were involved in; for nearly a century, the British to protect their Jewel in the crown, India, and Russia to annex central Asia. Of course due to the proximity we clashed"

He had to admit he admired the British in a way. One thing he was aware of was that the Chinese were currently a headache to their security services and that their focus was split. With an embassy staff and "hangers-on" of five thousand, the Chinese had also salted some three thousand students in many of the UK's educational and research establishments. There were other Chinese too, feeding back from diverse sources not limited to the British armed force courses they attended. He found it inexplicable that the British were currently making Sikh extremists their highest priority, "Foolish Director, it will fizzle out." He almost felt like helping the British to re-focus their attention on him. He laughed at and to himself. "For certain the British would be lucky to have any research and technical stone unturned and shaken inside out by the Chinese when they had finished sucking the country dry." This final thought gave him little comfort, for he felt the Chinese could teach his people a thing or two and it didn't sit well that another hunter, the Chinese was on his hunting ground. After all am I not in the words written of Abu Nidal like him, "The evil spirit of the security services."

The aircraft's large jet engines roared, reversing the thrust, and the aircraft slowed, quickly sitting on its nose before the brakes came off and it coasted forward. It gracefully turned into the terminal area, but still the turning G of the aircraft pressed him against the seat. The other passengers around him stirred, eager to be free of their restraints and seat, eager to disembark after the long flight from Moscow. He expected to be met and hosted by the local KGB officers, some of whom he knew well. He also knew and got on with the GRU officers responsible for Military Intelligence at home and abroad as well as the Special Forces he was expecting to meet as well.

He was fully aware the GRU ruled the roost in this part of the world, where fortunately, perhaps in Afghanistan, "it was a brother's in adversity thing," the normal antagonism and competition between the KGB and GRU was stilled and cooperation here between the two directorates was as good as it got at this time. Much of the credit for this state of affairs, he counselled himself, was down to the Army General in Command of the Theatre and the KGB colonel in post his long-time friend Pavel. Unlike Pavel, who boasted a large family, Tsygankov had never married. As he moved on in years this was a disappointment to him, it just seemed he had always been too busy to form any permanent attachment. There had been lovers over the years but he had failed to find that special person that he could feel totally comfortable with. "Ladies approaching 7ft were thin on the ground," was his ready excuse whenever the matter of being unmarried arose.

Whilst he was looking forward to hearing first-hand how the course of the war was going, his visit would however, he felt, be short and he might have little chance to see the operations on the ground, but harboured the hope off doing so. "Perhaps a quick round-robin trip on a Hind Helicopter into the combat zones might just be possible." He was quietly determined that he would get the GRU or KGB to set a flight up for him if they could.

***

Earlier that morning in Kabul, an hour before dawn, Captain Vladimir Servo, Alpha Group, GRU Spetsnaz and his troop of Special Forces turned right off of the "Russia" road, down street number eight to the south corner of the bisecting road. Here they clambered down from their armoured BMD-1 airborne Special Forces vehicles and made their way on foot to the corner of street nine. They fitted their night vision goggles and attached silencers to their weapons. Their target was the nest of terrorists, they had been advised, were eight new Arab insurgents newly arrived in Kabul after completing their training in one of the main mountain training camps.

The insurgents, the Russians had been told, were forming up in a house on the northwest outskirts of Kabul city before being blessed and deployed into the wilderness of the country. There they would be split up and added to existing mujahidin cadres, to reinforce them, in order to replace the wounded and fallen.

The two-storey house, three houses down street nine and on the left, was set in the middle of a crumbling high-walled garden enclosure. The Arab squad inside the house had been given up to the Russians by a Mujahedeen informer. The Mujahedeen were culturally different to the Arab incomers and many found their arrogance offensive. They felt that most of the Arabs lacked battle experience in the context of Afghan operations and were a risk to them and their fight. They were no respecter of the Afghan feudal system, where power politics between the tribes of the Mujahedeen warlords and elders was a constant block to a unified resistance to incomers, whatever their motives.

The Russians had practised the assault on this particular house all the previous day in a mocked-up building within their barracks, so everyone of the thirty-six man Spetsnaz troop knew exactly what he was going to do at the target building.

Eight men peeled off to secure the four corners of the compound on the outside of the walled enclosure. Two men went silently either side of the front gate, the only entrance to the compound. Eighteen men infiltrated as quietly as was possible over the wall to the rear wall of the house. The rear of the house was windowless.

Four men had remained with the armoured vehicles leaving the Captain and three men, who were to make entry through the gate after dealing with the two guards they knew would be dozing in the compound's shelter to the left of the entrance gate.

The overflying of the property the previous day had confirmed that whilst the enemy guarded the gate, there was no show of any guards or lookouts on the roof or in the compound. Clearly the enemy felt confident and had opted for concealment as a philosophy.

The building with its two floors had two shuttered windows on each side of each floor and side doors on the ground floors. To the front of the house a large shuttered window was constructed either side of the main door. The grounds were strewn with litter among yellowed straw winter grass.

Captain Servo took a deep breath, winding himself up for the assault, and let out the breath slowly. Ready to go, he paused and did a final check of his kit and drew his pistol. He eased the magazine out of the gun and checked the bullets and silently pushed the magazine firmly back into the pistol and cocked the weapon, screwed the silencer on and set the safety catch to off. "Ready to go, go now," his mind screamed at him. "Do it now!" With his free hand he pressed his section radio presell switch once.

The attack force, receiving the click through their individual headphones from the task commander, first move was to alert the eight corner men who manoeuvred themselves into a position so they could cover the top floor windows. They raised their weapons and took aim on the upstairs windows.

The Captain and another soldier at the same time were hoisted to the top of the wall and with silenced pistols dealt with the two slumbering guards.

The team of eighteen men now free from any fear of discovery, streamed silently down the sides of the building leaving two men at each ground floor window on the sides and to the front of the house. The remaining six men formed up by the front door.

Then the two clicks issued into their earphones that seemed in the heightened adrenaline atmosphere coming within seconds of the first.

Earlier before they left their camp their captain had warned them, "I want them all alive!" Vladimir Servo had warned his men. "Okay, damaged maybe, wounded maybe, but alive. They must be alive enough to have a chance of full recovery. No excuses." His men had received the news in silence. They all knew how difficult that order would be to comply with a fanatical dedicated ruthless enemy.

With the second click received, as one, the Captain's forces made entry through the windows and side doors throwing ahead of themselves the stun grenades and tear gas. The front door locks were blasted with heavy shell shots from two short-barrelled shot-guns. The shot-guns bucked in the men's hands bruising the area where the thumb met the palm and first finger. They took the pain, it could be sorted later. The six men then burst into the hallway heading for the stairs, throwing tear gas and stun grenades left and right and forward, up onto the top landing and then into the open doors of the bedrooms.

There were ten not eight of the enemy within the house; those that surrendered were cuffed with electrical ties; those few that resisted or still had the presence of mind to reached for their weapons were clubbed into submission or shot in the arms and legs before they could effectively react and return fire.

The captives were hustled roughly out of the house and onto the open compound ground close to the front gate and had their arms plastic-cuffed behind them. Those few that could not walk from the rooms upstairs under their own steam had been rolled down the stairs and kicked into a crawl into the compound rather more than they were carried to join the other lightly wounded or simple shaken insurgents. It was not a time for kid gloves, both the attackers and the attacked were pumped up, the adrenaline was still running high in both parties. All were breathing heavily but it was Servo's men that recovered first and sorted out their racing hearts.

Servo's men let their training take over, moving quickly and taking up a defensive to deter anyone foolish enough to object to the presence of the soldiers and the confiscation of the property and its occupants.

A large troop open-cargo carrier drove up to the front gate protected front and back by two armoured cars. "Right listen in," Vladimir Servo shouted. The men fell silent. Only the groans of the captives mingled with the near silence of the dawn. "Get this lot patched up and into the truck. But not just yet, I need to have a look at them. Regardless I want them back in at headquarters within the hour." He turned to his second in command. "Take two squads. One squad is to collect any spare arms and ammunition. The other squad to look for intelligence material maps whatsoever. You have ten minutes." He beckoned over two of his men, "Set the charges; I want this building flattened so it can never be used again. First take the two dead sentries from the gate and place them in the house. They can be buried there. You have eleven minutes. Go!"

Vladimir Servo turned his attention to the captives and drew from his breast pocket a coloured photograph. The photograph was a few years old but good enough. The man in the picture had intensely dark eyes set in a doe-shape eye form. He had regular features and short dark hair. A shaped chin and a smiling mouth which matched the laughter lines around his eyes. All these distinguishing features Captain Servo took in; including the fact the man had more of a European look than Middle Eastern. He was good matching people to photographs. He had to do it more than he would have liked, more often than not on dead bodies.

He walked down the line of captives eliminating them as he went. He walked to the end of the line and motioned for his men to take out two possibilities. He consulted his notes again. He read "average height, slightly stocky in build, fit and strong". One man fitted perfectly. He motioned for the other man to be put back in line.

He stood stock-still in front of the picked man and looked unblinkingly into the man's eyes. When he was sure he had eye contact he said quietly in halting English with a heavy Russian accent, "Good morning Jean Saied, and welcome back?" The man's eyes flickered down and left minutely and the man's body barely tensed but it was enough.

***

Tsygankov's rank and seniority gave him much envied privileges, including the front seat on the aircraft enabling him to be the first off the aircraft. Once at the foot of the aircraft steps he was met by a young KGB officer, who unsmilingly saluted and waved Tsygankov impatiently to a waiting car but he said nothing, the young officer was obviously under stress. The officer saluted again; and, as the officer closed the door on the brigadier, the captain informed him, "The driver will take you to your accommodation. I will make sure your belongings get to you immediately, Comrade General, and of course the colonel will meet you there in an hour. He regrets not being here but I was told there has been an incident at the barracks this morning and the colonel is sorting out the matter." Without any further explanation the young officer moved quickly off to meet and greet other disorientated and bewildered passengers disgorging from the aircraft onto the icy, cold, windswept and snow-covered runway.

Once Tsygankov was settled in the car, the driver pulled smoothly away and passed through the numerous security airside and airport checkpoints. They left the last airport security gate and negotiated the chicane fortifications, in place to slow down any attacking vehicle and to prevent a bomb ram raid.

As they drove round the airport exit roundabout, Tsygankov gazed up at the military icon that served as a warning and seemingly a work of art on the centre of the road circle. The icon was a demilitarized MIG fighter jet propped up at an angle of 60 degrees as though pointing to the stars. The icon was both, to the layman's eye, arresting and a powerful symbol of Russian Technology in its own right, leaving an abiding memory for those who noticed it, probably more than any other in Kabul. The icon was the first thing of note and the last they saw as they entered and left the country.

Immediately on leaving the "MIG" roundabout, the car drove down a wide road where waiting armoured fighting vehicles pulled in front of them and others secured their back. The fighting vehicles would be the escort to the staff car all the way to its destination.

Tsygankov noted the protection he had been given and was impressed, before noticing the driver rank for the first time and the escort in the front seat. "Gentlemen even at my advanced age and exalted rank I don't normally rate a captain driver and a captain minder, maybe one but never not two?" he said lightly.

The driver and the minder both laughed, "It's this way, General," the driver explained to Tsygankov. "The Colonel said if a hair on your head was harmed, he and I," he tapped the minder on the shoulder, "that is we, would be here for at least another year, if not forever. So we thought why put our future in somebody else's hands when we had so much riding on the outcome."

The minder smiled silently at his partner's explanation adding, "And the boys in the armoured vehicles are mine and they have had the same message, only in their case from me."

"Interesting? I would probably have done the same if I thought it may help me to leave on time. So who do I have to thank for this first-class service? Except the colonel of course."

The minder spoke first. "Captain Vladimir Servo, Alpha Group, GRU Spetsnaz Special Forces, at your service Comrade Brigadier General." Tsygankov could both sense and see the physical strength of the younger man. Servo would be a formidable foe to come against by any measure. Probably a touch under six feet, Servo was broad at the shoulders and heavy-chested, just enough to be considered stocky. Dark brown haired curling at the sides, a little long was Tsygankov's first thought but Servo had a winning smile that would disarm more senior officers that had the balls to criticize him for that.

Tsygankov was an expert at reading people and knew that although the man's clear, frank, hazel eyes were coupled with an open, friendly, smiling expression; they could not conceal the world-weariness of someone who had seen and experienced the horrors of war. Nor could the man disguise the alertness only found in a wild animal as he appeared to casually survey the route and the surroundings. Tsygankov was reassured and felt that whatever the country might throw at them on this journey they would survive.

The driver followed on. "Vasily Vladimirov, Captain KGB Intelligence Officer."

"Ah yes Vasily, I have heard of you. A product and member of the 5th Directorate responsible for assassination and mayhem outside our borders, you seem to have come to the right place but you must have upset someone to have pulled this particular posting." He chuckled and changed the subject. "I believe you have my product in safe-keeping for me; but more of that later. Tell me Captain Servo, was it you and your men who were involved in the assault in December 1979 by any chance?"

"Indeed yes. We were part of Operation Storm-333. I was a bit younger and greener in those days, not long out of the Special Forces training school, certainly leaner and fitter than now; although I must say picking up your product this morning, I would say I felt as good in a minor way. As for Operation Storm-333, which took place on the 27th of December, is the day I felt we invaded Afghanistan proper and took it over, no longer pretending to be in an advisory capacity as we had done for what 30 years? We took out Hafizulla Amin and put Babrak Karmal in his place as head of the Government, he was a bit of a disappointment as you will know. At the time they thought him a better bet than Hafizulla, who was destabilizing the country; Hafizulla I am told executed anyone who disagreed with him no matter their status or so they say – medieval was how he was once described to me. Karmal for his part is now the deputy of the ruling party and seems to have found his niche, for how long who can say."

Servo continued in a slower more reflective tone. "When we attacked that December we captured the Tajbeg Palace in our stride, they say that, that attack was one of the most successful Spetsnaz operations in its history, I would not like to comment but it was a pretty swift, and with its clearly defined mission, a breeze as they say. We did lose some men including my commander. It was difficult as some of us were dressed as locals and as ever there is confusion once the bullets started flying." He slowly shook his head from side to side, reliving the assault and its aftermath. He snapped out of his revelry and added. "As you will know the palace is now the headquarters of 40th Army Group and where you will be staying during your visit."

Tsygankov leant forward in his seat to make himself heard, "Well Servo, from what I understand of 'Operation Storm' and the man who dreamt up the Special Forces from which you're Spetsnaz Regiments derive, Mikhail Svechnykov and of course the grandfather of the Spetsnaz Special Forces, Starinov would have been delighted. Incidentally I and Ilya Starinov met during my own early training years. I know he would have been very proud of you and your men, of that I am sure. More than that in some ways not only that his beloved Spetsnaz did so well but it was exactly the sort of operational he would have envisaged them excelling in." Tsygankov was quite serious.

"That's very interesting, with our current role out here sometimes the original purpose of Spetsnaz and the reality of what we are doing on the ground seem to blur our intended purpose. Thank you General for your generous words." Servo was a little embarrassed, he was beginning to realise the General may have more sides to him than he had been led to believe.

"I can understand that Servo, once a campaign matures it changes shape and we all find ourselves doing things we never thought we would be involved in or feel others should be doing them and they became everyday routines, it part of the soldier's lot to be infinitely flexible and adaptable." Tsygankov chuckled. "Can I know what incident the colonel was caught up in? Not that I expected him to meet me himself at the airport."

Servo looked at Vasily before answering. "Nothing serious, the General thinks the colonel may have been sorting himself out after a particularly nasty boil on his neck got the better of him. A visiting ranking KGB officer I think, Major Putin?"

"Ah I see, a boil indeed."

Vasily cut in before Tsygankov could dig deeper, it could wait, the colonel would tell him later if he wanted to. "I had Captain Servo bring your product to the palace sir, courtesy of Captain Servo and his men. The colonel thought, as he also stays at the palace, it would be the safest and most preferable location to stay in. We hope that that is acceptable to you, General." Vasily swivelled his gaze from the road and locked eye contact with Tsygankov via the driving mirror without turning his head.

Tsygankov met Vasily's gaze, this younger man intrigued him, barely thirty if that. He nodded confirming his agreement. Vasily immediately detached his gaze and concentrated on the road that, as they left the city, got more and more rutted and potholed. Vasily had a slighter frame than Servo, with slightly Slav features that would have allowed him to blend in with the locals, which Tsygankov felt he would have had to do from time to time. Like Servo, Vasily had longer hair than a regular soldier and in his case it was thick, midnight black and straight as a poker. Vasily's dark serious eyes were a mirror to the General in which he could judge the man's experience and maturity and Tsygankov felt he could also rely on this man too.

Tsygankov cut away and turned to look out the car windows at the desperate plight of the beggars and equally poor quality of life of many of the street sellers, all humanity here was shivering in the cold wind and snow flurries. Mostly the men were dressed only in their ragged trousers, coats and head rags, and old or liberated, whole or bits of military uniforms were worn by some; the women added shawls. A few more prosperous individuals littered the populous, probable servants of the powerful and wealthy. They were properly protected against the weather with warm quilted coats or furs drawing the envy and notice from the people around them. These people had money to barter for goods, and the stall-holders vied for their custom. Young boys and youths jogged, pushing rickety wooden wheelbarrows along the road or pavements transporting goods to and from, for the same stall traders.

The third world shacks lining the road were covered in tarpaulins. These were stretched out on metal skeletons, occasionally wood, to form shops and stalls as covered spaces. Many stalls were additionally supported by adjoining corrugated iron or cement block out-houses. The traders' constructions lined the wide road on both sides along the pavements. The road, which was the main route out of the city, hosted the stalls almost without a break for a good kilometre or more.

The kerb stones protective barrier lining the road was mostly broken and missing in places. The trees on the area between the road edge and the street sellers' stalls and the shacks had lost all their lower branches. The lower branches that could be reached by the population had long ago gone, broken off or cut down to be burnt to supplement the scarcity of heating materials for cooking and warmth.

There was a thriving black market trade in heating stolen oil, mostly bartered from the army as downgraded aviation fuel or old engine oil that had been filtered and centrifuged to get rid of as many impurities as possible. If it could burn it would be put to use. Fuel was precious, all of which had to be brought into the country at great cost in both life and currency. Contraband trading went on, not only for fuel but just about every material thing needed to support the population and it was rife, though few could afford it easily. On the stalls could be found anything you could conceivably want in varying quantities, from food to Kalashnikovs, which were hidden from the view of the police and soldiers. To be bought or traded along with food fuel and white goods were cheap cigarettes and sunglasses flashing in the bright sunlight. Similarly the second-hand tyres, with a little tread remaining, to bright cooking pots, glinting as they swung from the skeleton spars of the stall structures, were for sale. And on other stalls melanges of vegetables, fruits, meats and spices. In various places mountains of huge watermelons were stacked like colourful pyramids.

All this Tsygankov took in at a glance, only once did he smile at the Afghan who manned a petrol-driven compressor by the side of the road. The Afghan would for a few coppers start the compressor and blow up the tyres of any vehicle that needed air. Around him were a motley selection of funnels and sealed clear plastic tubs containing gas oil and motor spirit for sale. Most of the plastic tubs in size varied from 5 to 25 litres and were stained yellow from much re-use. A few empty water or fizzy drink bottles had been pressed into service and had also been filled with motor spirit. Tsygankov supposed these smaller bottles were used for the refuelling of motorbikes or scooters, "Must be Service Station Afghan style," Tsygankov mouthed.

There were numerous blocks of flats set away from the road and they too seemed to be, in general, grey and tired, not unlike parts of his native Russia. These anonymous faced flats reminded him of those he had seen on Sakhalin Island where it seemed to be 20 years behind the times and stuck in the 1960s. The flats, even though they were at a distance and with a fresh fall of snow now mostly slush, had a depressing effect on everything around him.

Turning to the horizon his spirits were at last lifted as the mountains stood out dazzling white in the sunlight. They were, he thought, amazingly beautiful, and the greyness of Kabul was forgotten for a moment.

They rode on in comfortable silence; the vehicle heater was efficient and on full blast, keeping pace with the outside chill. Tsygankov from previous visits knew they had some 16 kilometres more to go, and probably as many check points to get to the Palace, and had his fingers crossed that the journey would be uneventful but was ever watchful taking his cue from the two captains. If civilian vehicles approached from behind they were blocked. If from the front, the armoured vehicles shepherded the vehicles off the road and allowed the General's car to pass using the armoured vehicles to shield them. As they passed, the shielding armoured vehicles drew forward and the rear guard vehicles took their place. Thus the convoy well practised in these manoeuvres quickly reformed its shape.

Only once during the trip did they come under fire, albeit ineffectively when a few spent, small arms bullets rattled the car and bounced off the road around them. Tsygankov was not worried, he judged they had been fired from over a kilometre away and were not a threat to them; he was more amazed that some shots were on target, and said so to Servo.

Servo shook his head. "They never give up harassing us. Any chance they get. Those shots were probably loosed by a couple of men spraying a couple of magazines into the air and hoping the cone of fire would hit something, or someone? Don't know if you have experienced it, a spent bullet falling out the sky at a million to one can still take an eye out or stick into exposed skin if the round falls sharp end down and sticks in and that, whilst not life-threatening, is painful."

This morning traffic was light and the General viewed the side of the roads littered at intervals with burnt-out vehicle carcasses or others bombed and shrapnel-damaged. Cars and trucks, twisted and torn apart into alien sculptures. "Why," Tsygankov thought, "doesn't someone clean up this mess and recycle the scrap metal." He chided himself. "Foolish thoughts, the Afghans have more important matters to see to – like staying alive."

Half way to the destination they passed a group of a dozen or more armed Afghan tribesmen sitting on the side of the road. A few of the tribesmen stood and rattled their weapons at the convoy, whether in a salute or threat the military party would never know or care.

The Afghan tribesmen then re-joined the others hunched over a wood fire sitting in a tight circle for warmth. They fell silent, their long rifles resting over their knees, looking up and staring as the convoy swept past. They were lean men in warm padded coats over ragged clothes, faces mostly hidden with soiled head cloths wrapped round the head, neck and shoulders, leaving only their eyes and noses exposed. The General noted in passing the way the breeze whipped at the ragged garments making the shawls of the women whip around their faces, and loose tails of the men's head covering, flutter like fairground bunting. There was harshness to the countenance on the Afghan men's faces and the resignation to the way of life on the faces of the women. But it was above all the yellow of the eyeballs, opium-stained and sharp features that eventually arrested Tsygankov's full attention. "My God, they are hard men, every one of them," shocked, his thoughts travelled on, "certainly they would be more than a match for our young inexperienced conscripts, more so when these Afghan warriors were fired up on drugs or were ideologically driven."

Several of the women fussed around the fire with kettles or tea pots and blackened cauldrons of traditional Afghan food that steamed in the clear cold air. Tsygankov suddenly felt hungry. These women he noted were swathed, head to ankle in many layers of cloths giving the appearance of thick bulky clothing. They wore soft sheepskin coverings around their shoulders against the chill and warm skin Afghan boots on their feet. They were better dressed and protected against the harsh environment than the poorer wretches in the city. "Hill people," was Tsygankov's concluding thought.

"On our side I trust?" Tsygankov questioned, turning away from the scene and raising his eyebrows.

Vasily laughed, having caught the playful inflection in the Brigadier General's voice. "Yes and no sir. Yes, they are on our side if we pay them enough to give them security and weapons. A few people even ideologically supportive of us and the government cause, but God help them if we ever leave they will be hunted and cut down like dogs. Even so in the context of the ordinary Afghan people as a whole no they are not, and will turn in an instance, from a friendly smile cut your throat for a rouble or pair of boots or more likely if they are told to."

He paused for a moment to concentrate on his driving, wrestling with the steering wheel and narrowly avoiding a deep pothole. "That's probably unfair, but the truth is, they are ultimately under the orders of their immediate tribal commander who in turn, for the most part, is answerable to the tribal elders. The elders themselves too can be influenced or pressurised by other factions. The regional warlords for example. It is a complicated affair. It means under the limitations of all that hierarchy, the Afghan's personal freedom and life choice is not his alone. In general, and as a consequence, it is difficult to trust the Afghan alongside you in a fire-fight. Because you know full well his loyalty can never truly be given one hundred percent to you, a Russian outsider. His allegiance deep down, in the very core of his very being, belongs not to us but to others. So on balance, I think as a nation they are not on our side and furthermore nobody bloody else seems to be either. I sometimes try to rationalise the Afghan behaviour and I keep coming back to the same question, which is the bottom line as far as I can see, are we any different? Is anybody? It just seems to me that like their brutal mountains, the situation is starker here in Afghanistan than anywhere else I have been or known."

"Lonely for you then Vasily, situation normal, as they say." Tsygankov joked, lightening the mood. The two younger men laughed, they had not expected Tsygankov to have a sense of humour.

They knew the skull-headed man with the claw hand only by reputation. They had understood that he was mission focussed, operationally experienced, widely travelled and both ruthless and some said amoral, with only one mistress, the KGB. They could only assume that as he was far from the office he was off the leash.

Tsygankov for his part had decided he needed these two officers to help him later and would woo them as needs be.

"Tell Vladimir and me where you think we are in this Afghan adventure and about the players in this drama culled from your distilled experience of the place. On this, your second tour I take it, as an intelligence officer," invited Tsygankov.

Vasily smiled. "Yes second tour, seems I am not flavour of the month in the directorate back home as I volunteered for my first tour which did not go down well with my boss. He thought my volunteering would set something of precedence in the directorate group and anyone including him might be called upon to serve here. Just in case, as soon as I finished my first tour after getting back, they made it clear I should get my laundry done and pop back for another stint."

Servo laughed. "Don't believe a word of it Comrade General. He is good at what he does and the colonel asked him to stay on. It is true they did send him home for a couple of weeks to do his laundry and get some more kit."

Tsygankov's thin lips curled upwards. "You two make a good double act. I shall enjoy your company on this trip. Now Vasily please let us get back to the evaluation of where we are in this war."

Vasily frowned. "Where to start, Comrade General, is the first question? Perhaps we should go back in time to Vladimir's operation in 1979. Shortly after that invasion and at the Afghans' request we are suddenly an occupying force, full stop. All pretence of supporting the Afghan government as a benevolent benefactor is now seen by all parties as a sham. Even later bringing in the Muslim brigades from Russia's Eastern States to fight with fellow Muslims against the Mujahidin does nothing to placate anyone. And there have been problems with them as you know. But statistically our Muslim brigades in the context of desertion breaches in military law and discipline are not dissimilar to ones for our Slavic brigades. The Americans are upset and continue to beef up their interference in various ways, trade embargoes, and aggressive insertion of CIA-led special operations operatives mostly covert. And some limited in-theatre operations with a few British Special Forces thrown in for good measure, probably because of American pressure to get the Brits to show they are still their best friends and allies. It has been rumoured that the British interference is limited to training and arming the Mujahedeen with surface-to-air hand-held missiles from the American arsenals. Then again Islamic religion doesn't tolerate communism for a start, so the Americans can also play that card against us at every chance they get. I personally think it will backfire on the Americans, as the Islamic extremists don't seem to tolerate anybody else either!" He laughed at his witticism.

Vasily then paused for a moment to gather his thoughts. "The Afghans have been at each other since 1779 or thereabouts. Even before that, they were tribal and fiercely so. Their warlike culture has relevance to the present day. Unlike us, who will one day retire to our home and live out our lives in relative peace, they never retire from the fray till the day they die. Think on that, which may be a warning to all for the future, don't get involved if you are not going to stay the course and that could be for generations to come, are we that prepared for that scenario in a land with useful but limited natural resources? Economically it doesn't make sense. My personal view is that the old stand-and-fight wars are over; it seems now to be hit and run, ambush, mine, booby trap anything that wears the occupier down piece by piece until his will or that of his country is sick of the losses and cost and wants out. We seem to me to be approaching a tipping point in this Afghan adventure, will it be flight or fight?"

The captain continued to brief the General. "There have been to date, nine major offences since 1979 by us to unblock the supply routes and winkle out the enemy. This attrition on both sides goes on without remit. Our attack helicopters get in amongst the enemy in the hills and mountains doing tremendous damage and still they come against us. It is and always will be a difficult war when you can't bring the enemy to a decisive battle. Even driving those enemies when we can into killing zones does not halt them." Vasily looked up. "Ah we are about to enter the palace." Vasily was forced to slow his car down in order to match the decreasing speed of the escorting front armoured vehicles that were now approaching the final checkpoint.

Tsygankov looked up at the palace sitting like a citadel on its own hill. It was certainly impressive and he could imagine it in better times; without the fortifications and the soldiers' huts, the barbed wire, pickets and paraphernalia of war, the palace would have been a pleasing location to visit. It had been repaired well and showed minimal signs of damage from the assault in 1979; a few spotting of small arm fire around the main door was all Tsygankov registered.

They drove him through the checkpoints with ease; it seemed the two captains were well known and the winding drive to the front doors of the reception area was seen. Here officers and soldiers entered and left through the huge entrance doorway, busy with their own tasks. Vasily turned to Tsygankov, "Captain Servo will take you to your quarters and wait there with you until you are ready to see the colonel while I return this vehicle to the vehicle lines."

Entering the palace their identities were checked by armed guards. Captain Servo then led the Brigadier up to the third floor and down a series of corridors, hung with Afghan traditional tapestries and paintings, to his room. "The colonel's room is next door to the left and Vasily's and mine are on the other side of the colonel's."

Servo fished out a key from his pocket and unlocked the room pushing open the door for Tsygankov to enter. "Sir, please to check out your room to ensure it is acceptable to you." Servo stood back and Tsygankov surveyed his accommodation.

Tsygankov strode across the large room to the bay window overlooking the entrance and in the near distance the heavily fortified main entrance. Scanning the room from left to right, he thought it had probably been previously a drawing or ante room of some sort with its ornate fittings and furniture. His eyes rested on the extra-long metal military bed. The bed was out of place; incongruous in its utilitarianism was his immediate thought. A large copy of a picture of the Chairman hung on the wall over the bed, and large Afghan tapestries on another. On the marble floor thick rugs were strewn around, "Thank you Captain. This room is very acceptable." He ran his hand over the small double knee-hole antique desk set in the bay window. The wood top showed its age; highly polished it could not disguise it had been well used over time. He wondered briefly how many generations would have worked at it; many would now be long dead and forgotten. He turned to face Vladimir and with a wave of his hand indicated they should leave, "Let us, Captain Servo, go and meet the colonel. You can tell me on the way about the capture of Saied." Tsygankov straightened his uniform and carefully placed his high KGB peaked hat on his head. Despite his 70 years he was upright and the hat took his height to well over two and a quarter metres. With his great coat thrown casually over his shoulders he was an imposing figure, dominating the space around him.

As they retraced their steps towards the first floor and the KGB operations area Servo related the morning raid. Tsygankov was impressed and said so. Servo briefed Tsygankov, reporting that, "Saied has suffered no more than flesh wounds in his leg and shoulder along with a bruised jaw from a blow designed to subdue him. He resisted and my soldiers had no option but to stop him. They said he was quick. They described how as they entered the room he was out of bed, rolling, grabbing his AK and cocking it all in one motion. Pretty impressive, hate to think the damage he may have done if he had not been disorientated by the stun grenades. He has admitted he is Jean Saied. I think it was the mention of your name, General, and that you were coming here to see him that may have had something to do with it."

Tsygankov nodded his head. "Could be. I am particularly interested in how come he is alive when both the Israelis and the South Africans claim he was assassinated." Tsygankov looked down at the Captain. "Can we go and see him after I have presented myself to the colonel?"

"Of course we can General; it will be my pleasure to escort you, I am at your service while you are in Afghanistan," Servo confirmed as they approached the part of the building on the first floor directly above the ground floor main entrance.

Both men now approached the two intricately carved, massively tall, doors in dark wood and to the right of the first floor landing stairwell. The doors mirrored the front entrance doors in size and design. These doors were guarded by KGB guards; two standing in front of the doors very alert, Tsygankov noticed as they moved to intercept him and another at a table at which they now halted. Captain Servo flashed his identity card at the desk officer. The desk officer carefully checked his list and nodded to the two heavily-armed guards restricting access to the inner workings of the KGB. Only then did the desk officer stand and salute Tsygankov. Satisfied, the guards then pushed open the door into the vast ornate space that housed the nerve centre of Afghan KGB operation. The KGB operations room itself had probably been the ballroom in times past, Tsygankov thought.

His next impression was one of hectic activity; staff officers were holding sway in their discreet desk areas with their attentive personal staff. Briefing boards and marked maps ringed each staff officer's cell in the room and to the left, in one corner of the room, was a signals troop with a fully-equipped communication centre. A closed-off section of the communication centre in the form of a large metal container with its own guards was the cypher and secure communication room. The troop was busily receiving and sending messages and couriers could be seen signing for dispatches. Despite Tsygankov estimating that there were close to two hundred people in the room, it was not overcrowded. Despite the activity level the room was almost quiet, just the low deep hum of human activity and commerce, giving great credit to the architect who had designed it for size with a two-storey height to its ceilings.

The deceptive quietness was broken as Colonel Pavel Gorsky looked up from one of the desks in the central aisle and roared to the room in a voice guaranteed to break the concentration of anyone who had not seen the Brigadier enter the room. "Stand up." The room came to attention. Tsygankov waved them back to work.

The Colonel's round and craggy, ruddy face with its many times broken crocked nose, lit up in a massive smile as he moved quickly down the room to personally greet Tsygankov. The Colonel grabbed the General's arms with his spade-like hands and looked up at Tsygankov. The Colonel was himself just over two metres tall but he always marvelled at his old comrade's great height.

What the colonel lacked in height he made up for in bulk and width. Not that much younger than Tsygankov, he too had been called out of retirement to run the KGB operations and its intelligence centre. As to his nature, he was no great respecter of rank, all knew and none took offence. His masters and peers had long ago given up any hope of charming or changing him.

"My dear Comrade General, it is so good to see you." He let go of Tsygankov's arms and took the General in a great bear hug. Standing back now he put a hand round Tsygankov's back, while his other showed the way they should move. "My God, I never thought to see you here, it has been far too long. Come let's go to my office and discuss your visit." Turning to Servo, he told Servo to wait outside his office as they would need him shortly and he added, "No interruptions, whatever. Not even if our beloved KGB Chairman Viktor Mikhailovich Chebrikov wants me personally." He winked at Servo. By then he was gently pushing Tsygankov through the thong of curious onlookers who fell silent as the two officers walked through their ranks. Tsygankov inwardly smiled as the silence gave way to whispers and then a general chattering, building in volume until it was cut off as the two officers closed the door to the office on them.

"My dear Colonel Pavel you do seem to have surrounded yourself with talent and found yourself a comfortable niche in this inhospitable country." Tsygankov chided him and threw his hat spinning it onto a spare chair. Colonel Pavel Gorsky, apart from Lieutenant General Polyakov, was one of the few people Tsygankov had ever felt any true respect and warmth for and it showed. Perhaps it was because both Pavel and Polyakov were the antithesis of himself, he had often wondered.

Pavel simply smiled adding. "As for talent, don't I always tell you Carl, if you have gathered together the staff that is better than you, cleverer than you in every way, your life is made all the more easy and you get to sleep easily at night? Am I right or am I right?" He puffed out his cheeks. "As for comfort, no complaints; not bad but it's a bit restricting looking at the same wallpaper every night. Mind you, can't complain about the food either. I do love some of those local dishes they do in the mess, like, Lamb Chopan Kebabs and Mirza especially. We will have some this evening if not for lunch. But for now," he said, reaching into his desk cupboard for a bottle of vodka and flourishing two shot glasses which he filled to full. He offered a glass to Tsygankov who accepted the tumbler, clicking his against the colonel's before they both drained the glasses and the colonel refilled them.

Pavel pressed on. "Now tell me all about your retirement home and how you are doing." He paused eyeing his friend. "But that can wait until dinner, as I suspect you would rather get on and see your man we have downstairs. Anything you want to tell me?" Pavel was fishing and he knew Carl knew he was.

Tsygankov shook his head slowly sipping his drink. "Excellent vodka," Tsygankov remarked before adding, "I genuinely don't think it would be in your best interests to be involved in this one. Except to say I would be grateful, subject to the time my task takes here in Afghanistan and my negotiations with him, if Captain Servo would take him under his wing going forward and get him well and fit for me, before sending him to me in Moscow, if needs be."

"That is a big favour, my friend. True Servo is a good choice and would, I know him, do a good job for you; but remember he is no KGB but GRU. I think I need some assurances that your man will not return to wreak vengeance in Afghanistan before I were to speak with the GRU boss. Not that that will be a problem, we get on just fine." He picked up the Vodka bottle and shook it by the neck. "We are old drinking comrades from way back."

"That will not be a problem." Tsygankov looked at Pavel steadily to assure him and was he felt believed, not that he didn't expect Pavel to ask the same question over and over again in one form or another.

"Good then. It was a double stroke of luck for you by the way. Vasily you have already met. He has a long-standing relationship with a Mujahedeen Tribal Elder who hates the Arabs even more than us. He lost a son who was with an Arab group who were careless enough to attack a group of Captain Servo's men. Vasily was around and took the dear son back to the elder for burial. They bonded, so now whenever a new Arab group arrives that the elder is aware off, the elder contacts Vasily direct. So that was the first stroke of luck. Vasily, once tipped off, then tasked his team to use a couple of their local informers to shadow and photograph the group before they went to ground. They were also asked to find out where the Arabs were holed up. Checking the photographs of the Arabs we got a 'photo-fit match' with your man who had a flag in the system, the rest you know." Pavel re-applied his efforts to his drink.

This short break gave Tsygankov time to wonder again, as he often had in the past, about the efficiency of some of their intelligence systems and KGB databases. "Why was the flag not removed when it was reported Saied was dead. Just as well the famous KGB duplication of effort that could at times lead to mistakes of this sort was alive and thriving," was his private thought as he finished his vodka, draining the glass and upending it on Pavel's desk. He saluted Pavel and picked up his hat, smiling at his old comrade, "Well I had better relieve Servo from his door sentry duty and go and see my man to make absolutely sure he is who we think he is." Tsygankov stood and replaced his hat. "I look forward to seeing you later and for that feast you promised!"

The colonel stood, "Carl one last time, are you absolutely sure there is nothing I need to know?"

"My old friend, trust me, no. How could there be for I am not here and was never here?"

The colonel roared with laughter. "Blessed are you, my old spymaster. But even you have to admit you are getting a little old for this game. Despite your deniability it's going to be hard to explain, who was the tallest man, most of the garrison had ever seen wandering around the palace?"

"Speak for yourself Pavel, on age I have at least another year in me." And he paused. "You are not far behind, as for the tall man he is a ghost from the past, one of many I should think that walk the corridors in the small hours." With a wave and half bow he discharged himself from the colonel's office leaving Pavel shaking his head in mock despair.

Chapter 3

SAIED

Captain Servo escorted Tsygankov down a broad corridor; on its walls were a fine collection of watercolours depicting Afghan scenes and local life. Despite Tsygankov needing to see Saied, he stopped at a few of the paintings to appreciate them. Servo waited patiently and felt compelled to explain to the General that a decision had been taken some time ago for political correctness and good will to the Afghan people to try to show the palace as it was before 1979.

At the end of the corridor to the palace's west wing was a winding stairwell that led to the cellars of the palace. They descended the wide spiral marbled staircase with newly whitewashed walls into what previously had been a large wine cellar and below stairs staff complex. The complex was awash with light and the guards and prisoners in the cellar enjoyed a constant year-round temperature of around fourteen degrees, night and day.

The cellar had been converted into a secure jail and several multiple double rows of cells. The cells had been constructed to hold comfortably around three hundred prisoners. Important ones were either held indefinitely or sent to Moscow. The other short-stay prisoners were there simply for processing; some would be found guilty and shot, some released and some handed over to the Afghan governing regime. There was a low murmur from the prisoners, some were in prayer, and some were in mental or physical anguish, all voices seemed to be muted, like in the ballroom, by this cavernous underground space.

Guards and servants, of whom there were many as far as Tsygankov could make out, clearly saw to the captives' needs and the impression he thought to himself was one of a well-ordered disciplined organisation. Tsygankov had expected the facility to smell like an unmanaged urinal, overlaid by unwashed bodies like he found in the KGB Moscow detainee cellars, but it was in complete contrast to that fetid atmosphere, here the air was fresh.

The guard commander asked for Servo's identity papers even though he knew him and Tsygankov suspected the charade was for his benefit. Servo took the minor irritation in good humour. "Need glasses now to see me and recognise your favourite captain do you Corporal?" Servo chided him.

The guard commander simply raised his eyes to heaven and said wearily. "I take it, sir; you want to see the prisoner calling himself Saied – the one you brought in earlier?"

"Yes in one, and the General wants to speak to him privately too," Servo demanded openly.

The guard commander looked up at Tsygankov and determined the General was not a man to be messed about, "Then follow me please. We do have interrogation and interview rooms down here and I will have the prisoner bought to you so you can speak to him in private as quickly as possible."

The guard commander led them to a room with a metal door that would previously have been used as a tasting and blending room. Tsygankov looked carefully round the room for eavesdropping equipment, raised his eyebrows knowingly to Servo. "No bugs here, General, the room is clean," Servo confirmed as they settled themselves in the interview room.

Tsygankov removed his hat and sat at the table. The table was metal and bolted to the cement floor. Servo stood with his back against the door. When the door opened five minutes later the prisoner Saied was shuffled in, his legs and arms shackled. The guards pushed Saied into a chair opposite where the General now sat. The guards padlocked the man's arm shackles to a ring in the middle of the table.

Tsygankov studied the man for a long time. He had not changed much, a little grey at the temples and thinner perhaps. He smiled before he spoke to Saied in English. "I am perplexed I was told the Israelis with the South African BOSS had eliminated you in the Lebanon. How is it you seem to be very alive and sitting here in front of me, Saied?"

Saied lifted his head and looked at the General, meeting his eyes without fear. "Then I can't be who you think I am or I must have had nine lives, and after today I must be down to seven."

"Saied," the General grunted tiredly, "Please don't mess me around. I would know you if you were in the most elaborate disguise. So pause, think and consider your circumstances, they are not good, whichever way you look at it."

"Excuse me, General, forgive my flippant manner, but I needed a moment to orientate myself. Your actual presence is a shock to me, even though the captain said you were coming."

"I do hope it will be a pleasant one as far as we are both concerned. Now not to prolong this, so we can move on, tell Captain Servo and myself how the Israelis and the South Africans got it so wrong? You are supposed to be dead. I really am fascinated to hear your story." Tsygankov lent back in his chair.

"What I set up for them was a simple deception. I needed some space after the mission in Guatemala and I was equally also sure someone would want to come after me as soon as they could, and I was right. God, but the South Africans were pissed off with you and me! Anyway I got a double, well someone of similar features and stature to become me while I waited to see if I was a dead man walking. I gave him documentation that proved he was me. I left a trail to his door, not immediately obvious to everyone but one the Israelis could follow and lead in the South Africans. They followed up quicker than I had expected; no sooner had I organised the subterfuge then they were on to my decoy and had killed him before I could react. After that, I thought if they think I am dead then I am home free. I had some money, not a fortune mind you. I did think about some plastic surgery to change my appearance but I reasoned I was small beer as you would say," Saied reported without hesitation.

"On another matter Saied, where did the money go that was supposed to be paid over?"

"Ah well, I reasoned that nobody in the African mob really deserved it and you had the device so were not too bothered about it. There was a lot of it; I took what was due to me and a little more for expenses and a hedge against old age should I make it. The rest is in an offshore trust account and a small annuity goes to each of the dependants of the men from the South African missions that were afterwards murdered. The dependants get their annuity each month according to need." Saied waited for Tsygankov to either laugh or ball him out. He did neither.

"How very honourable of you Saied, it still wasn't your money to play with?" Tsygankov was calm if not inwardly amused.

"Well it seemed like the right thing to do. The fund now has investors. They put their money on before moving it elsewhere and pay a small percentage for the privilege. The fund is growing quickly and should see the dependants right for their lifetime at least."

"I think we will move on and forget the money is actually ours, shall we? So far so good Saied, I believe you, but how in the name of all that's logical did you end up in Afghanistan preparing to have a go at your past paymasters?" Tsygankov was still a little perplexed by this turn of events.

"That's even simpler. Money was being offered, not that I needed it, but perhaps, more so for the excitement and challenge, I think any mission would have done, just wanted to be active. True, I worked in Asia mostly training others for a number of years to keep my hand in and as an assassin but needed to work my way back home. Afghanistan seemed a good halfway house. I think you can understand that." Saied grinned. "And also I think perhaps for a career move." Servo laughed and Saied looked at him for the first time. "Yes well my captain, even in my shadowy profession as a mercenary, gun for hire assassin, call it what you will, there is a hierarchy and that means pay bands just like your army and more important recognition by your peers. I expected to show them I knew what I was doing, unlike most of the poor deluded recruits I met, many who had never even seen a gun before they were fed into the pipeline only to be spat out into the training camp. There they met hell, they were disorientation disenfranchised and had no idea where they were and who was training them for what." Saied paused. "I did not think you would employ me again General, so that ruled out the possibility of any more Russian pay cheques. I reasoned Africa was a little hot for me so I changed my name and when I heard they were hiring for this war, I joined a group of hopefuls at an Iranian forming-up centre for potential hopefuls not too far from the Afghan Pakistani border. We were batched and kitted out then we were marched off to training camp just inside Pakistan. It was a forced brutal march and we lost a few who could not take the pace. But we were fit at the end of it." Saied gave a gesture of surrender as best he could in his shackles.

Tsygankov gave a mirthless chuckle. "Well as you're dead, let's keep it that way shall we?" He motioned to the silent guards standing at either side of Saied to leave him and Servo alone with the prisoner.

When they were alone, Tsygankov beckoned over Servo and leant forward and whispered to Saied just loud enough for the three of them to hear. "Think carefully Saied, take your time, do you want to work for us again in another place?"

The Russians saw the hope in Saied's face blossom and fade. "How should I answer you? How will you trust me if I say yes I want to work for you, which I do?"

Servo's English grasp was rudimentary but he followed easily what Saied was saying and remarked to the General, "He has made a good point, how do we trust him?"

Tsygankov said seriously, "Normally I would have said we buy that trust with money, although in Saied's I am not sure money is solely the prime motivator and after finding Saied in Kabul, well I think we would need a demonstration of his loyalty and bloody quickly too."

The room fell silent for several minutes, each man thinking up a scenario that would serve as a test.

Servo had an idea and broke the silence. "How far from the Afghan border was the Pakistan training camp you were in, Saied?"

Saied looked for a moment at Tsygankov who nodded. "I would say no more than a few kilometres; the border an area if not disputed, is not policed by anyone, hence it was an ideal location. When I say border I mean east of the 'Durand Line', the line the British fixed in some bygone era. So on one side of the line is Afghanistan proper, the other side the Pushtan lands and then Pakistan itself."

Servo addressed himself to Tsygankov. "It would certainly be a coupe for us to neutralise that camp and a blow to the enemy." Servo tried to keep the enthusiasm out of his voice.

"Hmm," Tsygankov was interested, he stroked his bald head with his good hand, standing he stood over Saied, "Tell us about the camp," before resuming his seat.

Saied leaned forward, "First a little history for you, my General, I learnt while I was in the camp. When the Russians arrived in Afghanistan the people of the border regions as ever porous, in particular, rose against the Russians, as they valued their autonomy. In fact this eastern region called Nuristan, called itself the Islamic Revolutionary State of Afghanistan, or Dawlet. A General called Issa rallied the Nuristan people to raise a 'Jihad' against the Soviet Army when they arrived. He was not long for this world and was soon assassinated. The area, and in particular the camp I was in, is now ruled by an anti-Soviet warlord whose name is Mawlawi Afzal. He came to the camp while I was there and gave a moral lifting rant at us," Saied paused to allow the information he was passing to sink in.

Servo prompted after a pause. "Go on this is interesting."

"Okay, the camp itself. It's over the other side of the Durand line on a reverse slope facing east. Clever when you think about it. It cannot be seen by the Soviet patrols and helicopters unless they cross the border. The hillside is honeycombed with caves in which we lived and were trained in; arms, survival, patrol section tactics, IED laying, all the usual." Saied paused to allow Servo to join the conversation.

"A difficult target to attack then, by any measure you would care to think off? Even accepting that, it is going to be hard enough to get to in the first place." Servo was thoughtful.

"But not impossible and there are many ways in which it is very vulnerable." Saied warmed to the possibility.

"In what way is it vulnerable, Saied?" Tsygankov questioned.

"For a start it's isolated 10 or more kilometres from any village or reinforcements. The only way in is by a single track. The track is narrow and in the valley with a small river to be crossed so any stores including water from the river along with everything has to be carried a few hundred metres up the hill to the camp, so it has few reserves. It is guarded, true, but only in the camp area, manly I suspect to stop the recruits wandering off or changing their minds until they are formed into cadres and have formed brotherly bonds. Secondly, the permanent training cadre is only low platoon strength. I counted no more than 30 fighters including the admin and logistic staff that ran the place. The recruits number around 50 at most at any one time and spend some 4 to 6 weeks in training, longer if they are useless or unfit. We recruits were based in the four upper caves and the cadre occupied the five caves at the lower reaches of the hill. Thirdly there are shoulders to the hill, so movement left and right is very difficult; it would be a stiff and dangerous climbing exercise to get round the shoulders which are sheer rock faces in places. Last but not least whereas the cadre is armed, the recruits don't get their weapons until they leave." Saied paused for questions.

"Fascinating, do you think you could spot the camp on a map and or aerial photograph?" Servo could not now disguise his interest.

"Definitely, remember I walked out of there and all the way to Kabul. It's not a journey you would forget." Saied smiled warmly for the first time.

"We need to clear this upstairs but I would say it is a way in which the trust I had in you previously could be re-established." Tsygankov turned to Servo. "Would you please arrange for Saied to be placed in solitary confinement? We can't afford for him to be got at in any way. Would you also arrange for the doctor to see him again and get him in the best possible shape within the next 12 hours?" He turned to Saied, "I take it those scratches you received this morning are not debilitating enough to stop you taking part in any operation?" He remembered how physically strong and resilient Saied was a few years earlier. He was nevertheless gratified to see Saied nod to confirm his willingness to join the operation.

Saied added nevertheless, "The injuries look worse than they are and painkillers will take care of the aches and pains."

"Good. Captain Servo, please sort out Saied. I am going to talk to the colonel and would appreciate it if you joined me at lunch?"

When Servo stood and let the General out of the interview room and closed the door, he turned to Saied. "The General knows you; I don't, so you need to persuade me why I should give you air space."

"That's going to be difficult sitting here, word are just words. Nevertheless understand me, my only enemy is the Israel State not the people most of whom I have respect for, despite our differences. I blame the State of Israel for what they did to my family and Palestine. You could argue that as the Russians are no great lovers of Israeli State either, we have that at least in common. I am by definition a soldier of fortune and I go where the money or glory is, to enable me to survive mostly. I have my bounds nevertheless and there are some things I will not do for money. There is no work for me back home and the Israelis had a price on my head or did, but now to them I am dead."

Servo grunted.

"I will prove my allegiance to you and the General in the field in combat. I have no loyalty to the Mujahedeen and the fanatics that are created out of irrational hatred. The recruits I was with out there at the camp were no more than cannon fodder. They were for the most part misguided; admittedly there were a few that were out for revenge or family honour but not many. The cadre I despised were feeders on the bodies of others. Some fanatics, true, and they practised a brand of Islam which for the most part I did not recognise or want to be associated with. I am a Muslim, proud to be one but I despair at the high jacking of my peace-loving faith for greed, power and an excuse for the worst atrocities you can ever imagine. The innocents that die in the name of faith and as a consequence of faith grieve me. I have killed many but in all truthfulness they have all been combatants in one form or another."

Servo gazed at Saied who now had his head down. "Look at me Saied."

Saied raised his head and Servo could see in his eyes only a deep sadness, no sign of cunning or deception.

"Saied, if they permit it, we will go to the mountain together and destroy this camp for insurgents. I will be guided by my gut and trust you, do not betray that trust." With that Servo hammered on the door and beckoned in the guard commander. Servo arranged for Saied to be locked away from the other prisoners and for the doctor to revisit him to attend to two flesh wounds in Saied's arm and leg. "Tell the doctor I want this man made fit for battle in the shortest time possible, tomorrow latest. For now on treat him as a Russian soldier, take off the chains for a start." Saluting he left the guards to carry out his orders.

Chapter 4

SAIED TRAIL BY COMBAT IS BORN

Tsygankov was pleasantly surprised that the colonel was energised by the opportunity to hit, not only behind the lines but to take out an insurgent training camp. Less so that he was going to have to refer the mission upwards. "I am just going to clear this with the boss, Comrade General-Lieutenant Igor Rodionov, he has had a rotten time to date and a little victory like this would be a little tick in the box for him before he hands over to General-Lieutenant Viktor Dubynin in a few months' time."

"Is that really necessary?" Tsygankov queried. "Can't we just do it?"

"My dear Carl, this is Afghanistan not some back street punch-up, although I sometimes wonder. It will be fine and with the General's blessing I am quite confident the GRU commander will rubber-stamp the task. We will get the resources we need. We need approved resources quite a few. Going to need Servo's men and fighter bomber aircraft and three Hind helicopters at least. You and I know Rodionov for what he is, but he is a champion of the military and any reason for him to show its worth to the state will be of great interest to him."

"Okay Pavel, you know your business better than me. I would prefer that my name was not raised as I am too old for medals."

The Colonel chuckled as he picked up the phone. "As ever my dear, I seem to remember you telling me you were a ghost and were never here!"

Tsygankov could not repress a smile, "In passing, Carl, I saw Vladimir Putin as I came in. I thought he was serving in the East German, Dresden office?"

"Putin? Oh yes he is here investigating some mismatch in the personnel intelligence files between here and Dresden; think it's deeper than that, could be opium traffic related." He tapped the side of his nose conspiratorially. "He has promised to debrief me before he flies back at the weekend just in case there is an issue in my section we need to sort. He is a clever man this Putin, probably the most intelligent man I have ever met. Almost scares me." The colonel was serious.

"He is certainly spoken of well, a hard man by most standards, I met him a few years ago and I would like to reacquaint myself with him on the way to lunch, if that's alright with you?" Tsygankov sought confirmation giving the colonel his due.

"No problem Carl, but a word of caution, I think he is a dangerous man. He is going far that one." Pavel was half serious half joking.

"I do hope so, we could do with some young blood, or you and I are still going to be in harness when we are in our wheelchairs. So while I can still walk, I am off to lunch with Servo. See you there; after you have seen General Igor, with good news I hope; my fingers are crossed for you."

"Trust me Carl as I trust you; Igor will jump at the mission." Was this a veiled warning to him Tsygankov wondered as he made his way out of the colonel's office.

***

The lunch in the officers' dining room in the palace was an eye-opener for Tsygankov. Although he had been to Afghanistan on numerous occasions, mainly pre-1979, he had never been to the palace before. The dining room was not a disappointment with its Eastern gold and silver ornate features, paintings and tapestry hangings. The polished dark mahogany dining room tables were long, fully forty metres long and two wide, Tsygankov judged, and there were five runs of them with a raised head table for very senior officers and the their guests. The chairs were finely crafted and upholstered but many now showed wear from the constant use by the soldiery.

For lunch the table, the fifth run, had been laid to a buffet with silver plates and tureens of local and traditional Russian food. The local Afghan waiters were busy replenishing the vessels as the food disappeared in great quantities on officers' plates who selected from the numerous dishes on offer.

He was introduced to the military key players and a number of local enthusiastic Afghan supporters of the Russian efforts. He thought of his own project and then of the Russian mission in Afghanistan. Gazing round the faces of the people in the dining room, he wondered idly how it would be, if this body of mission critical people ceased to exist. Chaos in the military and the country he thought would be bound to result at least for a time. Some would be difficult to replace except over time. There would be a vacuum in specialist professions and trades.

Along with Servo he shuffled in the line to collect a plateful of food for his starter. He sat at a table with the two captains, Servo and Vladimirov, waiting for the colonel. The mess waiters served them drinks and on Servo's recommendation they had chosen the local food and it looked very appetising to Tsygankov; if it tasted as good he would not be surprised as the aromas from the steaming food made his juices flow.

As they began to eat their starters, they saw the colonel threading his way through the throng of officers. He stopped briefly to acknowledge some or nodded to others. As he joined them he simply said. "We have the boss's blessing. Now let us eat drink, but not too much, and be merry for this afternoon we will be busy. The boss wants it sorted yesterday latest, well tomorrow morning anyway as everything we plan seems to get leaked." With that he raised his arm for service. He added turning to Servo, "After lunch, back to Saied, get him a uniform make him a lieutenant, airborne insignia of course." Then he dropped his voice to a whisper and leaned in to the group so as not to be overheard, "Then get him to the map room and let's fix the exact spot of this target. A plane already in the air has diverted and is overflying and photographing the area Saied already indicated, so we should have the pictures shortly, at any rate in time for our meeting. If we need more it will be arranged. Captain Vladimirov, I want you to get him papers to support his rank and etc, etc." He stopped whispering and his voice rose to its normal booming level. "Now let's eat!"

Chapter 5

LONDON BRIGADIER ROBINSON AND MAJOR BROWN

Robinson stood at his favourite spot in the office. With his hands in his pockets he lounged in the bay windows space, looking down at the snow falling from the sky. The snow fell in large gentle flakes onto the people and the traffic, adding to that already settled overnight. He smiled not out of malice, which was not his nature, but amusement as a couple of ladies clung to each other to avoid an icy patch on the pavement. The traffic was heavy, filling both sides of the boulevard and particularly slow-moving this morning, he thought. Amazing how a little adverse weather seemed to snarl up the country.

The pigeons ever present at the close of day had just returned from their breakfast foraging and were nestling together for warmth on the broad windowsills outside the bay. He glanced down at them, his flock as he thought of them. The pigeons cooed and squabbled at and with each other as they landed and sought out their individual favourite spot. Settling now, they fluffed their feathers against the cold and pecked idly at a few missed crumbs Robinson had fed them yesterday. "I think I might buy some proper pigeon mix for them today. Got to be better for them than my cast-off sandwiches crusts and other muck I feed them with." Having made the decision to buy pigeon food he returned his gaze to the street below.

By standing well into the bay and looking to the left he could just see the Houses of Parliament and on the far south bank of the Thames the Circus. A better view from this new office than the old view from Northumberland House and probably all in all the location was as convenient for his team. Close enough to get to those he needed too without too much trouble. At the same time far away enough from those whom he had to suffer, for them to have to think twice before taking up his time. He caught himself staring into the far distance but could break away.

Rodney found him there when he entered the room, the Brigadier continued to stare out the window. He gave Robinson a few moments to notice him and when he gave no sign of doing so he said gently, "Penny for your thoughts, sir?"

When Robinson turned round at last, he was smiling, "I was considering my retirement just for a moment, no more than that so don't get excited, amongst other things." Rodney laughed. "And I was thinking about an old Green Jacket friend of mine and his baptism of fire in a little reported engagement in Brunei."

Rodney hesitated and then said ruefully, "Brunei? Yes I know it well, however..." he said with feeling and tapped his old wound, "I don't see you ready for your slippers just yet, sir, far from it." He swept his unruly hair out of eyes. "I did read some time ago the report on the battle for the bridge in Brunei. Quite a trial for us I seem to remember at the time. Is that the baptism of fire your friend was involved in?"

"Quite right Rodney, what a memory you have. Yes it was, he did well and got his majority not long after or at least early. Often wondered why there was no one ever felt there was book in it. Had it written about, you see?"

"Perhaps when you do retire it might get a chapter in your memoirs?"

"Could be Rodney, could be," Robinson mused.

"Anything else on your mind you want to share in particular?"

"Yes the IRA."

"Thank goodness that is not one for us." Rodney said lightly in the hope that it wasn't.

Robinson sat down at his desk and tidied the few papers on it into the file tray. The desk was now completely clear. The ritual clearing of the desk was a sign to Rodney that the Brigadier was ready to concentrate on work. Head down rather guiltily, thought Rodney, he mumbled before clearing his throat: "Quite, ordinarily of course you would be right. But in truth, what's really occupying my mind are the IRA and its offshoots, full stop. I would surmise, I am really delaying the need to address the IRA decisively with diversionary rambles through the past and so on."

Robinson gazed up at the large portrait of the Duke of Wellington in its smoke-stained antique gold frame, hanging over the black marble fireplace, before frowning and settling further down his desk chair. "Rodney, to pre-empt you I know it is not our traditional area and the home office et al would be appalled if they thought we were interfering without their sanction. Nevertheless, my gut and others see trouble ahead. The patterns of things have changed over there."

"Would you care to expand on that, sir?" Rodney was already working out how he could divert the boss from this dangerous and unexpected interest. First he knew he had to let the boss talk it out so he sat back patiently and waited.

"Let's see Rodney if I can't unsettle you. Firstly consider the dreadful event on the 5th of January 10 years ago. The Kingsmill massacre near the village of Kingsmill in South County Armagh, where gunmen stopped eleven Protestant workmen travelling on a minibus, lined them up beside it and shot them. The Catholic workmen were left unharmed. One of the shot men survived, despite having been shot 18 times. A group calling itself the South Armagh Republican Action Force, whoever they are, claimed responsibility and said the attack was retaliation for the killing of six Catholics the night before. What we had was a string of tit-for-tat killings."

"Yes but that was a while ago now. The really bad years 68 to 75 seem to be behind us?"

The Brigadier waved at Rodney for silence, "Let me finish or my thought will become disorganised. Tit-for-tat is traditional, nothing sinister in that. Think I need to pace this one out," Robinson untangled himself from his chair and stretched. "Let's have spot of tea while I pontificate." From his pot of tea on the radiator to keep it warm, he poured two black cups and handed one to Rodney. "Secondly, as part of the policy of 'criminalisation', the Government ten years ago brought to an end the Special Category Status for paramilitary prisoners. This was seen by the paramilitary leaders as a serious threat to the authority to them inside the maze, quite apart from being a propaganda blow. The relationships that had existed between the prisoners and prison officers since that time have been seen to deteriorate ever since.

"Not quite following you, sir?" Rodney still had no idea where the boss was going but didn't like the sound of it. Robinson ignored him and continued on.

"Thirdly and significantly, last February a bomb weighing 20 pounds was found in a small case at Oxford Circus station, it was however defused. This is the first known attack on the underground since 1973. And before that 1939 was their last effort on the underground. And I might remind you last March a bomb exploded on a Metropolitan Line train at West Ham station. The bomber possibly took the wrong train and attempted to return to his destination. However, the bomb detonated prior to reaching the city of London. He then shot one man and killed the train's driver, who had attempted to catch him. He bungled a shot at himself, and the police arrested him. Add to this on the 16th of March, on an empty train thank goodness. That train was severely damaged by the bomb at Wood Green station. The train was about to pick up fans from an Arsenal football match, but the bomb detonated prior to arriving at the station, injuring one passenger standing on the platform."

"Escalation perhaps but still some time ago, expecting some recently?" Rodney still was not sure why the boss had picked on this subject.

"It's the pattern, traditional escalating violence, bombs and mayhem zeroing on the mainland, but traditional none the less, if there is such a monster, Rodney, coupled with other rumours and innuendo I pick up at the Joint Intelligence Group meetings. The violence is changing and one of our own has disappeared. He has failed to report in for his monthly debrief twice now." Robinson hung his head in anger. "He had been undercover for three years and penetrated a cell. I fear he will have been treated as an informer and will already have gone missing, forever."

"I see, but that doesn't make it a matter we should involve ourselves in, or does it?" Rodney was still fishing, he was not sure where the boss was going with this but it was unsettling even so.

"I think so, and so does the PM and the bosses of both SIS 6 and 5 and MI, Military Intelligence too." Rodney groaned out quietly, and Robinson ignoring him went on, "Primarily because of the latest developments which I will now use to clearly demonstrate my point."

Robinson stopped his pacing and leaned his back against the desk. "They feel they need an organisation, that is how, they say, 'off-piste' and that description fits us to a tee." The Brigadier swept his arms from their folded position into a mock ski push-off. Rodney had not seen him so animated for a while and could not help grinning. At times like this the old man looked half his 70 years of age. It was the "rush of adrenaline from going to living on the edge," something every old soldier knows well.

Robinson laughed seeing Rodney grinning. "Got your attention at last. Thought you were about to fall asleep. The American FBI, God love, has recently foiled an attempt to fly out of Boston to Ireland the following armaments that were destined for the Real IRA, Redeye SAMs for God's sake! M-60 MGs, M-16 rifles, MP-5 SMGs, bulletproof vests x 11. Now we have that mad ship captain bringing in a shipment from Libya no less. The intelligence indicates the whole of the consignment could be in excess of 150 tons of arms: AK-47s, SAM-7s (reported), Semtex, RPG-7 rocket launchers, Taurus pistols, plus other stuff. He will be stopped well before he gets here, never fear."

Robinson rushed on. "Rodney, think for a moment about the shape of the arms listing and the uses for which it could be put. This arsenal, if it had hit our shores, would have changed the shape of the terrorist envelope we are used to dealing with irrevocably. Can you think the unthinkable and horror of terrorists having the capability to launch a missile capable of bringing down a civilian airliner, and further that plane crashing into a centre of population like London? Imagine a missile-hit on some prominent building or structure at a stretch, parliament the heart of our system of government? Rodney we need to help."

"Ah now we have it, we have been tasked!" Rodney could not hide his grin although he felt a beginning of an icy chill envelope him.

"You might say that, I can't comment. As you know from time to time the PM herself and the other two and myself have a working dinner in the PM's dining room. Just the four of us, but this time there was a fifth member who joined us for pre-dinner drinks before disappearing back to his province. The fifth member was the Minster for Northern Island no less and he brought the chief of Military Intelligence with him."

"Do they all share your gut feeling? And how did this land on us?"

"In a word Rodney, yes they did! Not only them but Military Intelligence also claimed to speak for the Assistant Commisioner of the SO anti-terrorist branches. You know only too well that our department's remit is to be a bridge between the SIS Home and the Foreign offices, not just that, but to help other agencies where we can. Specifically we get involved where a problem doesn't sit well with the others for some politico-esoteric reason or just on a whim."

Rodney glanced briefly at the portrait of the Duke of Wellington hanging over the fireplace. The Duke seemed to be looking down at him, expecting him to do his business. Somehow the portrait symbolised, for the department, a constant reminder to both Robinson and Rodney that whatever they were involved in, the Duke would not countenance failure.

He wondered what the Duke would have done today to sort out the problems in Ireland. "So, sir, is this a whim or esoteric mission?" Rodney asked quietly, feeling suddenly resigned to a mission he knew was coming and one for which he had no enthusiasm.

"It is all of those things," the Brigadier said lightly, still pondering the problem. "Our involvement is to be low key, we are to be invisible. It is not to disrupt the work going on in the other two services or other branches. Like Special Branch, Military Intelligence SO this and that etc. But we can pick their brains. And the Americans, specifically the FBI, not the other mob CIA, one can never be quite sure whose side they are on from day to day. We will do this task under the guise of other business, got it?"

"When do we start? I take it you want full team participation as required. We will need to clear a few current operational missions off our plates first. I could wrap them up in a few weeks at worst."

"Tomorrow will be soon enough." Robinson had a smile playing on his lips and his bushy eyebrows were raised challenging Rodney to say no to him. "Don't misunderstand me. You know peace negotiations in the province, are as ever are on-going and we don't want to screw them up. We need to focus on the hard line splinter groups and their suppliers."

Rodney didn't bite and Robinson was forced to say more. "I do want the full team but I also have at this time no idea where to begin, so I thought we could have a 'bird table' meeting in the morning."

"Don't think the team are up with the 'new speak'. Will tell whoever is available we are going to 'brainstorm' a problem standing up around your desk." Head bowed scribbling in his notebook Rodney allowed himself a smile; he could feel the boss frowning, trying to determine if Rodney was having a laugh at his expense. "And sir I suggest as always we start at the beginning." Rodney looked up at his boss, clearly heading for 70 but didn't look it, tall, slim at the waist and broad at the shoulder. Ex-guards and didn't he let the lesser being know which regiment was the best. For all that, he was an extraordinary man who led from the front and fiercely protective of his staff.

"Very amusing Rodney, anyway that should do, it will be a start nevertheless. Think it is time for a whisky, don't you?"

"Do we have a budget for this OP, might need some additional funding?"

"Yes Rodney we have. So whatever you need or want I will get, now that whisky I think."

"Sir, please make mine a double, yes I know it is not yet eleven o'clock but I have a feeling a hangover will help me focus and at the same time numb me ahead of time to some of the crazy ideas that are bound to be put forward at tomorrow's 'bird-table' by our boys and girls. In the meantime Brigadier, there are a few signatures needed and matters to discuss now."

Robinson unusually said, "Oh bollocks, thought you had forgotten all about that." Striding to his drinks cabinet he poured the "amber liquid" as he put it.

The drinks poured, both men toasted the Duke's portrait. This moment was special between the three of them, Robinson, Rodney and the long-dead Duke. It was also a silent contract, agreement and commitment to carry out the wishes of State as best they could.

"He might have said I like to think if he had thought of it first," Robinson said holding his glass up to the portrait, "if you can hold your calm, be yourself, in success or disappointment against the false face of both, then you will likely win through when times get tough and be a man, my son."

Then they got down to work.

Chapter 6

THE RUSSIAN MISSION

Colonel Pavel had found a planning room on a second floor KGB suite of offices that would enable them to bring in Saied without him being seen by the curious eyes or the colonel's operational staff.

Tsygankov and the colonel entered the room, they thought first but found a GRU Major leaning on the table, arms folded. He came to attention and saluted them both. Well under two metres but broad chested, flat stomach and clearly very fit. His muscles had rippled under his shirt as he came to attention. Unlike the captain's, the Major's hair was short and dark, thinning on top.

"Colonel." The Major acknowledged Pavel who he knew and turned to Tsygankov. "General, may I introduce myself Major Igor Surgun of the GRU and Servo's boss for my sins." He had a confidence, energy and enthusiasm about him that Tsygankov found pleasing. "My boss sends you both his regards and luck for the mission. He is very happy to be supporting this venture which he thinks is just the thing to stiffen the troops; he asked after mission if you would both take a drink with him?"

"Major Surgun, I am very happy to make your acquaintance. I saw Putin before lunch and he is much taken with you. His recommendation augers well for your future I am sure. Like Servo, are you alpha group too?

"No my General, regrettably VDV Airborne trained only. But one strives to keep up with the men. With men like Servo's, I think I need an Olympic medal." Surgun laughed at his own joke.

"I don't know about an Olympic medal but after tomorrow who knows." Tsygankov smiled carelessly waving his hand in the air.

At that point Servo's party arrived.

Six men were shortly sitting round the room's large table with paper and maps spread out in front of them. Tsygankov took one head of the table and the Colonel the other, the two captains sat on one side of the table. Major Surgun sat between them and Saied on the other side by himself.

No-one was in doubt, including Tsygankov, that the Colonel was the chairman and would lead and control any discussion and planning.

Saied looked a natural in the Russian uniform, he could have been wearing it for all his adult life; apart from his dark hair and eyes, his light skin would have led an outsider to take him for a European, not quite Slavic but at a push, true tanned but otherwise possible if not Slavic, Latino.

"Saied," the Colonel began. "Tell us what you told Captain Servo about the training camp and then orientate us to its location and the approaches, its features and the terrain, begin please."

Saied showed no sign of nervousness and began strongly. As Saied went through the details in a logical order and speaking English carefully, choosing his words to avoid words that he imagined a few of the Russians would not understand. Important points he repeated until the table nodded their understanding. Vasily took detailed notes and Servo scribbled down possible ways of attacking the target and a shipping list of the resources he could foresee he would need.

When Saied signalled he had finished, the colonel thanked him for an excellent briefing. He then asked for comments and questions.

Surgun began. "To add to Saied's briefing we know the way to the border directly from the target, is hills and mountains with valleys. If we fly along the spines of the mountains we should avoid most missile strikes or at least have a chance of avoiding them. The mountain spine this side of the border and for a kilometre either side there has been a little activity from time to time, but it is normally not heavily patrolled by us or them and we have never had an engagement or contact within a five-kilometre envelope of the area. The enemy's traditional crossing point in this area is a good seven plus kilometres to the north. In this country that means several mountain ranges and valleys. Accordingly if the force time on target is short, they should not be able to deploy in time to attack the airborne force on its way to the target or on the way back in any great numbers."

"Sounds fine in theory but we will employ some insurance just in case." The Colonel turned to Servo. "Add to your battle plan a few Hind attack helicopters to protect your ingress and egress route."

Servo nodded and scribbled in his book adding the colonel's additional and welcome advice.

Saied commented, "The Mujahedeen still hate and fear the 'Hind' they call it the 'Shaitan-Arba' or Satan's Chariot."

The colonel interrupted smiling at Saied. "They may call it 'Satan's Chariot' we call it the 'Crocodile'!" He added, "Because of its bite and once it has you it doesn't let go."

Saied returned the colonel's smile with a grin. "True, Colonel, a crocodile does have tough skin and it is difficult to shoot down a Hind with small-calibre weapons with its titanium armour. You will understand the Mujahedeen travel light, on foot or by donkey and horse, so they normally cannot carry heavy weapons that could damage the Hind. But as you know, the Americans have attempted to even the fight and supplied the Stinger missile. The missile is effective and you have lost craft to them. In the insurgent camp we were shown a training weapon set-up during our course. On our journey to Kabul I did see at least one Stinger set up at the border crossing we took. The band of Mujahedeen that guided us to the hills overlooking Kabul had one with them too." He paused. "Of course they only expect the Hinds to fly in the day. They travel mainly at night and believe the night belongs to them. If you want to defeat them eventually you need to fight at night too. Psychologically, what the Stinger Missile has done is show the Afghans that an army with high-tech weaponry can be vulnerable."

Tsygankov stirred in his chair, smoothing his hands over the table attracting attention. "Thank you for that insight, Saied, an interesting perspective for me at least."

Servo refocused the meeting nodding to Saied. "Good stuff. Now, I would like to see the aerial reconnaissance pictures of the target to confirm my understanding of the ground to confirm my plan. From my Map recce, and study of the contours in the area, which I carried out with Saied earlier, and general area photographs available to us, I would confirm to you that Vasily and I agree with his suggested route to the target."

Servo paused to ensure he had the baton before continuing. "Now between the border and the target, the approach mountain continues until it drops sharply in height becoming a hill of some three hundred and fifty hundred metres in height above the river and then it splits forming a 'Y'. The 'Y' between its shoulders is a distance of around four hundred metres. It is a definitive and manageable killing ground. The points of the 'Y' curve forming shoulders to the hill. In other words, the training camp is in the re-entrant. On the other side of the river the ground climbs again." He paused. "The target area is mainly scrub with a few small trees around the shoulders and boulders strewn around. In places, on the other side of the river, trees are plentiful until they peter out on the higher slopes. Saied tells me they have erected stone protective walls in front of the cave entrances. Importantly the caves are, reported by Saied, not as deep as they may have been, the deepest only penetrates some 40 metres into the hillside and only a few are tunnelled into each other " He paused again. "Saied has confirmed the training area is not mined, which makes movement easier; conversely this time of year there may be some snow and ice to contend with on the hill."

Servo stood and addressed the men at the table, "I would like to show you all the target area and way to the target on these maps, and then outline the battle plan that I would like you to consider?"

Chapter 7

MAJOR BROWN

As the Russians listened to Captain Servo's battle plan it was approaching lunchtime in London.

After his meeting with the Brigadier and with the knowledge of the new task coming his way of that he was sure, Major Brown returned to his office and sat heavily in his high-backed chair. "Fuck," he exploded; the last thing he wanted was for his team to tangle with the IRA, real or otherwise.

He sat and jotted notes on his yellow pad. They formed a series of questions to which he diligently began to jot answers. Each set of answers and questions would form an approach or way forward for his team to follow.

That the Brigadier wanted a brainstorming session in the morning stirred Rodney to fall back on his military training and the British military passion for acronyms. He mumbled them to himself. "The 5 p's: piss poor preparation and planning equals piss poor performance." He smiled to himself. "Conversely, proper planning and preparation equals perfect performance." He thought back again. "If you can't measure it you can't manage it." Well this was one task he felt they needed to manage so he had better dream up measurement criteria.

Finally he allowed himself a little slack, frowning at a principle he had learnt as a soldier and had never forgotten. "A soldier must actively anticipate the commander's and the enemy future intentions!" Well, he thought ruefully, that principle needs polishing off!

Question one he jotted down: "If the IRA campaign is changing its shape, in Northern Ireland, who is creating that change or who or what is causing the most change?"

Question one supplementary he added: "Is the change an internal organic evolution or externally driven by a third party or ourselves?"

Answer one internal: "The early years' atrocities were claimed by the South Armagh Brigade, (Note to self: It is understood that they saw themselves as an IRA within the IRA and many veterans or their descendants were members of the old Republican Army. Some of their activities do not appear always to be sanctioned by the IRA Army Council – Out of Control.)."

Answer one supplementary: "If we focussed our attention on them as the most likely group to use the heavier weapons and explosives if they reach them. What do we know about them that stands out?"

At this stage Rodney decided he needed to have a late lunch to get the sugar levels up and flick through a few files to get some background.

Back at his desk he noted adding the following against his answer. "The South Armagh Brigade of the Provisional Irish Republican Army (IRA) was organised into two battalions, one around Jonesborough and another around Cross-maglen." He glanced at the name of the supposed commander and decided to commit it to memory rather than write it down. But he noted the initials down "T(S)M", to remind himself of the name later. He then noted that, "The South Armagh IRA saw themselves as an 'independent republic' within the republican movement, retaining a battalion organizational structure and not adopting the cell structure the rest of the IRA had been forced to adopt after repeated intelligence breaches and failures."

He then made brief notes of the brigade's activities. Seeing it written down he was appalled at their successes against the security and civilian population. He noted: "Over 150 security forces killed and more than 50 civilians to date and a fist full of their own. The brigade was also credited with over a thousand bombs and equal number of shooting. This terrorist mayhem had taken place all within a ten mile radius of Armagh. The brigade was known to travel outside the area and had a reputation for smuggling over the borders. The brigade was known to have active members on the mainland and in the Republic. Even so, their numbers are smaller now than in 1976 and their support remains undiminished. Clearly since the Army put up the towers overlooking this troubled part of Belfast it has made matters harder for them."

Rodney sat back and looked at his notes. He saw a traditional organisation working at what it knew best and focusing on its core business but would evolve, so he reasoned an offer from a third party to support or for a favour would be a difficult sell. Still, he reasoned, because of their high activity rate and the fact that brigade commander was thought to be a member on the main IRA council, he noted that they were to be on his "A" list for discussion. It was also rumoured that MI5 had a mole on the council and that they jealously guarded his identity, so no help there he thought.

Answer two to supplementary question one: "What legitimate third party do I think could affect change in the IRA writ large including the brigade? For the good it might be the Republic or the Americans for ill could be the other Americans or," he thought a while, "it could be the Libyans or some other Middle East Country or even the Russians making mischief, although traditionally the Russians and IRA had not been natural bedfellows. Could be a dissident group or individuals working out of Southern Ireland where many members of the IRA had moved for their own security."

Rodney paced the floor and then returned to his pad and wrote, "Follow the money!" and then he wrote, "Follow the communications."

Answer three to supplementary question one: "Are we forcing the pace and creating change in their organisation and activities."

Answer has to be yes; as an example, the criminalisation of IRA detainees, the erection of the lookout towers, informers' better intelligence, even the very effective special division of the FBI set up to counter the paramilitaries and certainly they had had some spectacular success and on-going peace talks.

He wrote down. "Communications to and from the brigade and who communicates with them, say in the context of the Libyan consignments." He sat back looking up at the high ceiling with its ornate plaster and the decorative rose from which a single light bulb was suspended encased in a plain MOD issue yellowing light shade.

He leant forward over his notepad, adding, "Follow the money! Follow the consignment. Follow the Quartermaster who must be the one man who will know where and why the arms are being procured and who will use them for what."

"Find out what they have promised the Libyans in exchange for the weapons. Above all follow the money!"

He wrapped up his office feeling pleased with himself; he had an entry point that was the main point! That the mission may change shape, even go in different directions that did not matter, the important point was to start.

He imagined the game of "Snakes and Ladders" and this mission he was sure would have its own share of two steps forward and three back, it would be no different. He locked his files and other stuff away in accordance with the dictate to leave clear desks of any information that could be an advantage to a third party.

Rodney had an early dinner appointment with James Collins in the Sherlock Holmes public house and Mould and Sharky would also be there to celebrate James' posting to Middle Wallop as a Staff Officer. The pub was a popular meeting place just over the river from Waterloo station so could be easily accessed. It was their favourite meeting place and the staff knew them. When they had grouped in the crowded noisy bar they grabbed their drinks and headed upstairs to the restaurant.

The four men had remained in contact and friends since the mission in Cyprus and Belize, it seemed to them years ago. Mould and Sharky both long time married had a leave pass for the night from their long suffering wives and were going to make the most of it.

Chapter 8

CAPTAIN SERVO'S SPETNAZ EXECUTES HIS PLAN

The Russian Commander Afghan Forces had not retracted his gift of resources even when the demands for material grew and Servo got everything he asked for and more.

Servo had kept his plan simple but it did depend on the air force coordinating its forces. He worried about this, and expressed his concern to the colonel. So to ensure everyone was following the script, the colonel insisted he was going to sit in the force operations room and tweak the air support commander as necessary. Servo was pleased at this development as it was a crucial matter for the success of his mission. He now felt with the colonel at the helm that part of the mission would at least go well. The operation was called "SABZI" Afghan for spinach. Vasily had thought this mission name up as most people knew Servo was called "Popeye" by his men, many of whom had tried to out arm wrestle their captain and all had failed. Servo took the reference to him by showing barely a lift at the one corner of his mouth showing a gold filling.

The force assembled on the runway at Kabul pre-dawn. The wind and snow-swept runway hosted flurries and small drifts of snow that settled on a parking area with its thick carpet of morning frost.

The men on the airfield stamped their feet and banged their hands together to get the blood flowing. Servo was alert despite the fact he had spent most of the night with the colonel and Air Force, tasking cell to make sure that his plan was fully understood, pouring over the new aerial photographs with them and hammering home the importance of the timing for the various sorties. In the end the colonel kicked him out but not unkindly; he knew Servo's attention to detail was to mitigate the risks to his men. "Servo leave this to me now. I was organising parties like this before you were born. So fuck off and get some sleep, you need the rest before this morning's sun rises." With that he put his arm round the younger man's shoulders and led him from the operations room. As he closed the door on Servo he called after him. "Good luck Servo. Give them hell!"

The Spetsnaz troops filed purposefully onto the squadron area where the seven Russian Hind helicopters sat silent and menacingly, waiting for them. This is what Servo's men lived for; a well-planned operation with the tools to do the job. Soldier humour is universal the world over and could be heard above the whirling rotors and roar of engines as they started up. Five of the Hinds were the new modified variant with shortened helicopter blades and uprated engines.

Each of the five uprated Hinds normally carried a complement of four crew and eight soldiers, but today they carried ten to enable Servo to put fifty men down onto the target. The Hind pilots had conferred, done their calculations and finally agreed that with the short foray into the mountains they would not run out of fuel carrying the extra men. Servo hoped they were not joking.

Servo's company commander, Major Igor Surgun, would command the other two Hinds to protect the Ingress approach to the target and see them safely back. He would be the aerial link between each aerial weapon platform and the field commander.

Behind the Hinds already running up their engines and carrying out last minute checks were two bombers and a flight of five fighters.

Much as the colonel had advised, against it Tsygankov got his way to travel, with the company commander in his Hind. Tsygankov had put his hand on the shoulder of the colonel and told him, "My dear comrade Colonel Pavel, at my age any excitement is welcome and I would think a flight in a Hind would seem to qualify don't you think?"

The colonel could only shake his head in disapproval and added, "Foolish man, you will get yourself killed or have a heart attack or something."

The Hind's rotors were now powering from idle and running up to speed and with all the men embarked they lifted off as one. The noise was tremendous and a new light flurry of snow whirled in the aircraft lights. They climbed into the dawn, with just the hint of the new day's light showing over the tops of the mountains.

The flight time to the target was a little under an hour. They initially flew south until they were out sight of Kabul to fool the ever watching enemy then turned north east.

Tsygankov was seated in one of the crew seats and had a panoramic view of the mountainous country as the sky lightened. On the ground in the valleys it would still be bible black. His crew earphones cut out much of the engine noise, but it was still loud and the gentle vibration and beat of the rotor were felt through his long frame. After a time the hypnotic effect of the machine lulled him and he relaxed.

As they approached the border, the company commander's two helicopters broke off and patrolled the mountain spin looking for the enemy. Servo's flight flew on.

***

As Servo's leading Hind reached the zenith of the mountain they hovered for a few moments as the two bombers flying low down the valley turned, unloading their heavy load of bombs on the target and peeled away to the north gaining height before turning for Kabul.

The explosion and resultant shock waves from the bomb run seemed to shake the mountain and the five Hinds danced and swayed as a result of the initial blast shock waves and following heated thermals.

Over the border Tsygankov saw the sky light up for a moment. His thought was only, "So far so good." Tsygankov crossed his fingers for luck.

The captain of Servo's flight came through on the radio, shortly after the shock waves passed by them. "All flights one minute to target. Green for go on my count."

The flight captain counted down. "40, 30…"

For Servo's group, the training camp approached fast. "Weapons tight, ropes out ready," Servo's voice came over the airwaves and was relayed into Tsygankov crew earphones.

As the noise of the explosion began to fade, Servo's three Hinds dipped their nose and headed down the mountain over the camp hillside and swung 180 degrees into the river valley, pulling up facing the caves of the training cadre. "10 seconds, 5 seconds, green to go." The flight captain and his helicopters steadied their aerial platforms.

"Go! Go! Go!" Almost as one, one after the other the Spetsnaz force slid down the ropes to the ground taking cover in the rocky slope. Even so, Servo was the first on the ground with his Chalk. Saied followed him, and was determined to become his guardian for the ground fight. Servo checked the remaining other two Hinds had discharged all their men.

The two other Hinds followed Servo's group immediately behind but then swung higher up the hill to face the upper caves holding the insurgents recruits. In essence, the men from these two helicopters because they had less distance to travel were on the ground at the same time as the three groups led by Servo.

There were some shaken and wounded enemies appearing now at the lips of the cave, shouting and pointing at the hovering helicopters. Servo's men froze.

At the same time Servo confirmed all men had landed, to the helicopters' captains. As one, the five Hind helicopters then poured continuous accurate cannon fire into the caves with pinpoint accuracy and each helicopter danced from the recoils and as the spent runs tumbled from the guns onto the silent Spetsnaz below. Some of the Spetsnaz men cursed silently as the hot spent cartridges fell and found bare skin here and there or when the hot cartridges heated through their combat clothing.

After the initial thirty-second burst of cannon fire, the Hinds steadied and carefully fired their rockets into each of the cave entrances, as they had been allocated on the battle plan. Then they gave another burst of cannon fire for good measure.

"Stop! Stop! Stop!" Servo radioed to the helicopters. "Alpha Troup go!" Servo's force had waited for a micro second for the silence after the rockets had exploded and the buzz of bullets ceased and the order to "go" had been given.

Now, as they neared firing to suppress anyone foolish enough to pop up his head from the cave entrance, the initial headlong rush slowed and they shook themselves out and began moving tactically, using fire and movement giving each other covering fire. They made their way cautiously the last two metres to the cave opening. Still maintaining a steady battle rate of fire from their automatic weapons and throwing, the fragmentations, grenades ahead of them.

Speed into the caves was the key and the elimination of any remaining enemy before they could organise, hunker down and hold up the attack. They all knew that was the danger and were focused to ensure that did not happen. Each of the Spetsnaz soldiers were seasoned by war and knew that in spite of the welter of ordinance, the bombs, rockets and the strafing, some of the enemy would have survived. They may be wounded, deafened and disorientated but any surviving enemy would have his adrenaline running high for a fight or flight.

Back in Kabul, before the raid, Servo had held out to Saied an AK assault rifle and five-charged magazines, holding eye contact for several seconds. "I give this weapon to you to use this in trust."

Saied simply replied, "It is well placed, my Captain." And he gently took the weaponry, checking its function and clicking home a magazine. With a smile he said to Servo, "A good gun this one and one I will use well today I think."

Servo led his team to the left of the cave the other two teams to the centre and right. The two Russian bombers had decimated the stone walls protecting the caves. Some of the cave entrances were also badly damaged and just about everything else that had been standing. Flying rocks, stone and splinters had entered the cave and created havoc among the insurgents on the bomb run. The ground around the caves was now liberally strewn with debris, human and every form of enemy material.

Although the ground was broken and cratered, the going for the Spetsnaz was good and the ripped-up ground meant their boots got a good grip as they moved forward.

Fires had been started by the attack and carried the sweet smell of burnt flesh mixed with the acrid billowing smoke of burning kerosene spirit. Escaping gas screamed and ignited, escaping from holed cooking and heating bottled gas. Some bottles driven by the escaping gas danced and snaked over the ground like mad grounded rockets. Servo's men could not only see but taste the destruction.

From the caves a few men re-emerged; deafened, dazed and disorientated survivors covered in blood and dust, most were wounded badly. Some of the enemy cried for mercy or help. Behind them a few able ones still had fight in them. These men let rip with their weapons, mowing down their own men who were blocking them from getting a clear shot at the Russians.

The Russian Spetsnaz troops in their turn made short work of these men with fragmentation grenades and well-aimed shots. The fight was one sided enough to momentarily sadden even the most hardened Spetsnaz soldier, until they remembered the hell the enemy had unleashed on the Russians elsewhere and the innocent Afghan population. It was a massacre as with the troops in the top caves who had quickly and dispassionately dispatched the recruits. The top group cleared the caves they were responsible for; collecting any intelligence they could find, and were making their way down the hill to the waiting Hinds just as Servo's teams entered the lower cave complexes.

Saied took the lead and led Servo and his men into the cave entrance of the leaders of the training camp. The cave entrance gave way to a spacious rocky interior with its high roof which came together in a cathedral-shaped dome. The early morning light now established sent streamers of light throughout the chamber from several natural rock formation ventilation and light giving holes in the walls high up in the dome. In the streamers of light, dust swirled. The smell was of human occupation mixed with cordite. Broken furniture crates, food and the paraphernalia of man littered the floor. The enemy in the chamber were checked, all were dead.

To the rear of the cave chamber were two large tunnels. They picked their way towards the tunnels cautiously moving over the chamber floor strewn with its twisted metal weapons, furniture and broken bodies. For a moment they stood to one side of the entrances, appreciating nature's work when the sound of firing from the tunnels within reached them.

Servo was galvanised into action, he indicated two of the team stay and secure the entrance to his right, threw fragmentation grenades into the tunnel, waited for them to go off then led the remainder of his team down the left-hand one. The Servo team laid down a continuous fire, men swapping point position as their magazine emptied for another to give the previous point man a moment to change empty for a full magazine.

The tunnel narrowed and then gained width and height bending to the right. Saied now took the lead, went low and peered round the corner. A burst of machine-gun fire erupted from the tunnel at him. Pulling back he motioned to Servo for a grenade. Servo passed him two. Saied pulled the pins, held them for the count of three and then tossed them into the tunnel towards the gunmen. As he did so the machine guns opened up again and he again had to pull back into the shelter of the bend. Chips off the rock face showered him and two shards spinning in the trajectory cut him cross the forehead and cheek drawing runs of blood.

When the grenades went off, two of Servo's men followed the explosion and burst past Saied into the tunnel with their machine guns on full burst. Saied followed in and then saw the men standing over three enemy men.

The tunnel went further back and linked with the other tunnel being guarded by the two Spetsnaz. Not wanting to get shot by accident, he left the team to clear up and with Servo went back to the main chamber. The two Spetsnaz men were dead, throats cut.

A machine gun opened up at them from the right-hand side of the cave. The shots were ill aimed and Saied could only roughly push Servo to one side and down, opening up at the same time with his AK cutting the enemy down who had been intent on a suicide attack against the Russians.

The rest of Servo's team came running out of each of the two tunnels, intent on joining the fire fight but only in time to see Servo getting up from the floor where he had been pushed in order to shake Saied's hand. "Eh men, we have a new recruit I think, saved my life. It does look like it is all over," he commented bitterly, thinking of the two dead men. Turning to his team he ordered them to get the two dead Spetsnaz men back to the helicopter. The remaining team noticed the two men for the first time, and their cut throats, and were angry.

Servo took Saied with him to check the other caves were cleared and team commanders.

The team commanders were clustered together in the shelter of one of the cave entrances and came to the alert as Servo approached. "Report," commanded.

Each team leader had the same response. "Caves and area clear."

"Casualties?" Servo asked. There were a few walking wounded but only the two men in Servo's section had been killed. "Enemy tally?" one team member reported and a total emerged of ninety-one of the enemy. Servo simply said, "Good job, now get yourselves on board. I want to leave in two minutes from now!" He looked at his watch, they had been on the ground for 35 minutes. Much too long, he thought to himself.

Servo's Hind was the last to lift off as only two Hinds could land and load at the same time. The formations of the five Hinds were able to reform as they reached the top of the mountain.

Servo called his commander. "Job done, call in the fighters and burn the place." He paused and checked with the Hind captain. "Crossing the border in one minute, wait out." He looked at the Hind captain who gave him the thumbs-up. "Zero Alpha, we are across."

Tsygankov heard the exchange and gave a sigh of relief. He had become tenser as the minutes had passed the half hour mark. Just then a cry from his Hind captain came through his phones. "Missile incoming."

The Hind was hovering on the spine of the mountain and spun to the right, dropping down the far side of the mountain.

As the missile curved over the mountain seeking to reacquire them, the captain drove his Hind hard upwards under the telltale trail of the missile popping over the spine with feet to spare and down the off-side of the mountain. The missile turned again and powered itself towards the mountain spine. Its on-board computer was still vectoring the new course to its target when it struck the top of the spine exploding in a brilliant flash and sending out a shock wave that Tsygankov felt rock the Hind. "Neat trick, Captain," a relieved Tsygankov said to himself only to be thrown against his seat as the Hind swooped onto the insurgents' missile fire position.

The captain of the aircraft had seen the flash as the missile had been launched and was busily ordering his gun crew to get ready and at the same time released his missiles against the target.

They were joined by the other protecting Hinds and together they strafed the area and small-arms fire directed at them soon died away.

The two Hinds regained the spine as Servo's fleet passed over them heading for Kabul. Just before they turned to follow Servo, Tsygankov saw the resulting fireball from the target and then the black smoke as the fighters went in and napalmed what remained of the insurgent training camp.

He looked at his watch, at this rate they would be back in the mess for lunch. He was suddenly desperately hungry and his mouth was parched, his throat dry. He found he was chilled to the bone but at the same time was bathed in cold sweat. He could only think it had to be the adrenaline rush he had experienced at the time of the missile attack and the follow-up counter attack against the Mujahedeen fighters.

He half listened to the traffic on the radio as they approached Kabul airport, but his mind was racing on to the next phases and the difficulties he could expect to encounter if he was to win the game he was about to set in play.

He now had Saied to work with and he needed the Arab as he could go into the murky areas of the terrorist world if need be where he could neither compete or was young enough to take the pounding and pressure of an agent in play. Tsygankov would resource and pull the strings as and when he needed to.

***

The welcome from the colonel was enthusiastic, he told them the Commanding General of the 40th Afghan Army was delighted and acknowledged the success tempered with sadness at the loss of two of his beloved Spetsnaz. All were aware that the Spetsnaz forces and other Special Forces along with the Hind helicopters' crews with their high moral were his balance for a largely disinterested and the patchy low morale of the rest of conscript Russian Army.

Major Surgun and Captain Servo acknowledged the colonel's congratulations but Servo soon excused himself as he needed to go and see that his troops were fed and their kit had been sorted and made "ever ready" for the next patrol or call out. He was not looking forward to writing up his report but he needed to do it, while the operation was still clear in his mind. But before he left the gathering he generously praised Saied to the gathering for saving his life in the cave. The gesture was typical of his leadership style which brought him the respect of his peers.

Later that day Tsygankov and the Colonel were closeted in the Colonel's office. "What now, Carl my old friend, are you going back immediately with your man to Moscow or would you like some more fun?"

A flicker of a smile curled on the side of Tsygankov's mouth. "Today, my dear Pavel, I realised I am too old for fun at the front. I did enjoy the feeling of being fully alive but I know my limitations. I have trouble bending and breaking into a trot these days, how the hell could I throw myself about as your young pups have to do to stay alive!" He chuckled, a rare event for him. "No, Pavel, no more of your fun thank you. However I would appreciate lunch and more local food." He paused. "As for my return to Moscow I need to talk to you later when I have my thoughts in order, so if you can put up with me for another night, I thought I would fly back tomorrow."

Chapter 9

THE BIRD TABLE

Rodney groaned as the alarm clock shrilled at him. He had drunk and eaten far too much in the Sherlock Holmes pub with the others the previous evening and he just hoped they were suffering as much as he felt he was. Struggling out of bed he wandered into the kitchen diner. He rested his hands on the kitchen counter, trying to clear his head. "Tea," he forced himself to get the kettle on and his mug ready. A glass of orange juice later and he was feeling brighter. He made his tea and took out the large frying pan. "Greasy spoon breakfast should sort this lethargy," he mumbled to himself. He took out a tin of beans and shook them in the frying pan. Moving them to one side, added mushrooms from a tin followed by a couple of sausages, a tomato and slices of bacon. As the beans cooked reducing the sauce and the remainder sizzled, he set the table and made the toast, buttering it liberally. As the breakfast came to its conclusion he moved the concoction to one side of the pan, stacking the mushroom and sausages and the rest on top of the beans before and cracking two eggs into the pan.

   He sat with his breakfast at the table, eating thoughtfully and feeling hungry; to his surprise he cleared his plate. "When in doubt eat," he smiled to himself.

   His top fourth-floor flat, several blocks down river from Tate Modern, overlooked the Thames and St Pauls was almost directly across the river from him. He liked the location and the amenities surrounding him. A keen cook, the Borough Bridge spice market was a favourite of his as was the Wellington Boot Public where in the back room he could always find a low stakes game of poker going on and the food was good. Great early morning walks on the Thames South Bank to work when the air was clear and clean. In the evening he would, more often than not, stop and explore a gallery at the Tate Modern of which he never tired.

A shower and shave, dressed for the city, Rodney looked at himself in the hall mirror. Apart from a slight reddening of one eye he thought he looked bright enough. Now he thought, "Wind yourself up, Rodney, for Bird Table game, it is going to be fun." He didn't quite believe that, so put on his scarf and overcoat leaving the house to walk to work. Glancing at his watch he realised he was late and his normal stroll along the South Bank was not going to cut it. His options to catch up time were the underground out of London Bridge or taxi. He wanted to be in on the beginning of the meeting.

He chose the underground. The underground was as ever busy and Rodney had to stand. This gave him the opportunity to observe his follow passengers. It struck him as it always did the diverse rational and cultural mix of the London inhabitants. He thought about the staff in his office and the monoculture nature there. "Maybe I need to talk to the Brigadier about bringing in some other people from different ethnic backgrounds, MI5 had?" He was deep in thought when he arrived at his station. Sighing he concluded, "The Old Man will not go for it. He has his small team of hand-picked old soldiers like me. I can't see Robinson changing his spots at this stage of his career."

He was hustled in the crowd and saw a pickpocket bump a lady punter and another slip his hand into her bag just in front of him. Instinctively he chopped the accomplice's neck and the man went down like a stone in the press of people as they, as if a shoal of fish, moved on and side-stepped the prone figure. Rodney swung to his right, grabbing the pickpocket's hand out of the lady's bag. Twisting the man's hand into his wrist until he heard a satisfying crack, he followed up with a quick chop at the man's neck as the man doubled over in pain. Leaving the growing mayhem behind him Rodney, unnoticed, continued calmly to the exit feeling pleased for dealing out swift and measured summary justice.

Rodney waved his badge at the security guards as he entered the entrance foyer. One held the door open for him while the other stared woefully out of his reception cubical. The man in the cubical suddenly sparked up and called after him. "Got any jobs going upstairs, Major, for us old soldiers?"

Rodney knew it was not just a throwaway request and both the security men, ex-Welsh Guards, had seen time in Ireland, Falklands and other parts. They were still relatively young men. He tried to let him down gently, not wanting to raise hopes. "Not currently I'm afraid and anyway your efforts keeping us safe while we chase paper are really important to us." He stopped; both the heads of the guards had gone down. "Bollocks." He looked at them knowing exactly what sort of feeling was going through their minds. So he said seriously, "Do me a favour, you two let me have your CVs and I will take a look. No promises and no disappointments. Fair enough?"

"I knew you were a diamond geezer, Major. That's good enough for me and for Mac a chance is all we need. Eh Mac!" the man in the cubical uncoiled his six-foot frame and came out and shook Rodney's hand. "CVs to you tonight, sir."

Rodney nodded and took the stairs to his floor. "So much for my last great idea, I wanted to try to create a greater ethnic diversity in the office team. Perhaps I can the next time?" He laughed at the thought. "Mind you I guess the Welsh could be considered a minority ethnic group." He convinced himself that he had gone part way to achieving his aim.

***

He found the staff clustered in a group near his office. "Eh boss, we got a mail from the Brigadier calling us all to a 'Bird Table', meeting in ten minutes. That is all about now. What on earth is a Bird Table meeting?" Sharky was voluble as usual, while the other looked sheepishly on.

Rodney shook his head. "Simple, it's a very short meeting, without chairs, standing round a table to brainstorm an opportunity." He could see they didn't believe him. "I am not joking; it is the new thing in management speaks." Graham eyed him sideways, frowning with a question forming in his mind. Reid looked at him as if he was daft, some sort of Martian. Jane, Sharky, Andrew, Mould and Pat went into a huddle.

"And where is this meeting to take place?" Graham's distinctive and deliberate public school voice while he polished his glasses vigorously cut through the hubbub.

Rodney looked at him with disbelief. "The meeting will be held in the Brigadier's office, where else?"

"Don't think so, the Brigadier called in, he is going to the dentist and said you were to hold it."

"Oh good? Thank you very much, boss. Right then, we will hold it in the boardroom. Listen in; Mr Reid and Pat get in two flip charts and two stands ready. Andrew and Sharky organise the tea and coffee for all, not Earl Grey thank you. Graham, white pads for all, pens and marker pens three colours."

Jane questioned, "What about me?"

"You Jane can set up the digital movie camera. We are going to record this historic event for the Brigadier to view later."

"And what about me, what do I do?" Mould demanded.

Rodney fished in his pocket for a twenty-pound note and the change from buying his train ticket. "Egg and bacon sandwiches all round." This brought a cheer from the team dotted around the floor carrying out their tasks. "Listen, meeting in half an hour or when the food arrives, whichever comes first."

Rodney left the team in a high activity mode and entered his office. He felt suddenly knackered again. He sat heavily into his chair. "My dear leader," he rubbed his face and ran his hands through his overlong mousey hair. "This is your idea of payback on me for questioning you last night on this new venture, I know you so well. Dentist I do not think so." Rodney hauled himself out of his desk chair went to the metal locker and took out his notes from the night before and went to copy them. One copy of the notes for each member of the team, he had decided. He checked his watch against the large white MOD issue clock on the wall, ten to nine.

He found the team sitting and chatting merrily in the boardroom sipping tea and coffee and the flip charts ready and the team's stationery in front of each of them. His steaming MOD white china mug of tea awaited him in the chairman's place at the head of the table.

The digital camera was set up on its tripod to cover the room and was ready to go.

Rodney sat down in the chair and supped his tea. He was still hoping the Brigadier would appear to sort the issue. After a while, as the room quietened, the permanent cadre looked to him for leadership; he considered them as a group and as individuals. He hesitated too long.

"You all right, boss?" Sharky sensed Rodney's reflective mood. The room looked expectant. He immediately forgot about Sharky's question as Mould stormed into the room, arms full of bags holding the food. With a flourish Mould slid each person's supplies to them across the table.

"Fine, thank you for asking and your genuine concern for my welfare," Rodney said sarcastically to himself.

When they had finished their food Rodney got up and went round the table putting a copy of his notes face down in front of each of them. "Let's get on. Don't turn them over yet." Rodney returned to the power position at the head of the table but didn't sit. "Jane please switch on the camera."

Rodney faced them and began, "First stand and move your chairs back." He waited for them all to shuffle to their feet. "Thank you, apparently you are supposed to be more alert and forthcoming if you're standing rather than sitting. Well, we shall see if you're all normal?" That throwaway got a laugh. "The situation is that we have been asked to look for something which has not been defined or quantified. The reason is that upstairs believe the IRA are changing and not for the better. Question one is, why the change? They have or will have at some time, what we might consider to be serious armaments to take on the security forces or the population at large. They may be more viscous, if they were ever anything else, in their war against us all. They may go for bigger targets, more dramatic. Question two is why are they tooling up for bigger and better targets? Perhaps to stoke up a more horrific demonstration of terror. Our task without disrupting or interfering with the present effort by our sister organisations, is to come up with something new that may make more sense than it does now, if it is true, what they believe. He paused for them to take in what he had said.

The room was strangely silent as each member thought through what they had heard.

"The question is where do we start?" Rodney asked. "Now turn over the papers I gave you. You have exactly ten minutes to read, digest and discuss among yourselves." There was much rustling of paper and mumbling. Rodney knew they would all feel as he did; this task was off the wall and not their part of their ship. He knew they would soon realise, as he had last night, anything they could do to bring an end to or mitigate the terror in their own backyard had to be as important as chasing shadows around the world.

Rodney went and got himself more tea from the pot and poured drinks for the others and spilled a tin of biscuits on to the table.

"Okay, times up!" Rodney called the room to order. "We shall form two teams. Mr Reid takes Mould, Sharkey and Pat. Jane you have Graham and Andrew. Teams address yourselves to the flip charts; one per team and each member of the team in turn write on it key words that come to you that relate to this task; no issue if team members duplicate each other at times. Two minutes. Go!" Rodney timed two minutes exactly. "Stop now. Still standing at the flip charts, hone the key words and I want two columns, one is possible start and routes into this task. The second list is possible individual's titles and or organisations that will be important to us. Ten minutes, go!"

Rodney left the room and he was pleased to feel a tangible buzz even excitement in the team. He went to the Brigadier's office and knocked. "Enter," he heard the Brigadier call.

Rodney opened the door to find the Brigadier holding a meeting with the minister responsible for their section. "Minister, forgive me I had not realised the Brigadier would be engaged at this time. We thought he had an emergency dental appointment and we thought we should check if he was back and well enough to work."

The Minister looked surprised, and Robinson furrowed his eyebrows at Rodney and Rodney knew; he knew he had dumped on him. "Serve you right, you old bastard," thought Rodney maintaining a bland expression.

"If you were back we just thought, sir, you might want to join the team; we are just about to start the analysis phase from the bird table exercise?" Rodney explained. "But that can wait. I need to get back to the team and apologise again for disturbing you." He withdrew closing the door quietly.

"Interesting, your deputy clearly knows you well," the Minister chuckled. "He has your number you know. Now I must get off. Don't forget what we discussed, we are very concerned with this supply of arms to the IRA and their future intentions. By the way, I have approval for the extra budget you asked me for; spend it wisely, you know the Prime Minister is as ever thrifty and will want it accounted for properly."

Robinson's reply was not what the Minister was expecting. "Do our best, but we are running a few operations that were not in budget so should think they will soak up the extra before we get to this one. Mind you, it might be prudent to double the pot now. As ever it's difficult to go back for more once committed to a course of action. Just a passing thought, Minister?"

The Minister studied Robinson for a moment as he stood to leave. He could not tell if the Brigadier was serious or pulling his leg. But seeing the Brigadier's serious expression he decided on balance he most certainly was. "I'll see what we can do, if you come up with the goods."

"We will have something on paper by tonight."

"Sounds fair. If you do that I'll get the money, deal?"

"Deal," replied Robinson suddenly standing, bolting out of his chair, he quickly crossed the room and smiling offered his hand to the Minister.

The Minster took the hand offered, grinning, but somehow deep down he felt he had been mugged by a wily, wiser and older fox.

***

Robinson saw the Minster leave his office and then walked down the corridor to re-join the team. Entering the boardroom he was pleased to see the team engrossed enough in the task not to notice him at first.

The room was throbbing with each of the teams arguing for their point of view. "Stop, stop," Rodney called laughing. "Right, next phase. First Jane's team present first please. Tell us what you think?" Rodney noticed the Brigadier leaning on the doorframe to the room. "Sir, please come in and share with us for the next phase of the bird table exercise." Rodney vacated the chairman's chair and offered it to him but he declined and sat next to Reid, picking up a copy of Rodney's notes. He looked at Reid's jottings and the flip charts but said nothing, his grey eyes focused on Jane as she rose to address the meeting.

Jane's short fair hair suited her oval face and she had startling amber eyes. Jane was average height for a man but tall for a girl. She was an attractive addition to the Brigadier's team and the rest of the team felt protective towards her. In her mid-forties, she had poise and confidence. An ex-special branch officer and latterly five years in MI5 gave Jane the knowledge and experience to compete within the group.

"We agreed in our team that any shift in the activities of the IRA is a consequence of organisational maturity, learning and a shift in the resources they are now able to obtain. This is not to diminish the efforts of our security services that mirror the advancements in knowledge and intelligence as well as initiatives that limit the enemy's activities." Jane paused and struck her team's flip charts. "We consider the acquisition of odourless Semtex, missiles and a flame thrower to be an escalation. We think that to limit or eliminate further arms shipments of these types of weapons is a number one priority. In a word, starve them of hardware. We think that to understand who is driving the new weapons on the IRA side we need to get that intelligence from the suppliers. We know that primarily the suppliers are at this time Libyan's visa to the Middle East, some small fry suppliers and through their American supporters and we need to get at them. Any questions?"

Rodney broke in at this point. "Can we hold off on questions until we have Mr Reid's report?"

Reid got to his feet taking his flip charts with him. He held them up for all to see. Reid's stocky frame, lived-in-face with its crooked broken nose and short black hair gave him a formidable stance. Smartly dressed in a city pinstripe suit with an out-of-fashion striped shirt and white collar, he could have been a banker. His black eyes told another story. His voice had a Scottish tinge to it but barely noticeable until he emphasised a point. "Right, all of what Jane said we agree with. What we would like to add to the other team's efforts are some ideas as to where we start. We would like to talk to the FBI anti-paramilitary team, I am sure they have an informer or informers and we should talk to them too. Secondly we should get GCHQ to do some eavesdropping for us. For example," Reid emphasised the word "example" and his Scotch's heritage arose in the diction. Rodney and the Brigadier exchanged a look, they knew Reid was warming to the mission, "conversations between this ship's captain that's shipping arms from Libya, our side are probably doing this already but we should see if there is another angle we can milk. All conversations between the IRA Quartermaster and his links and then follow the links to the arms or other players we don't know as yet exist. Lastly we need to think about how we neutralise the Libyans as arms suppliers. This may involve parties above our pay grade. But there are things we could consider. This leads me on to our next point, and one Rodney from his notes thinks important and so do we. Follow the money!" he went to sit down and changed his mind. "We are not shrinking from one of the primary questions as to why the IRA appear to be evolving. Jane discussed that but I forgot to emphasise that we should not forget other traditional enemies that would do us harm if they could, using the IRA resources to do so. Thank you."

"Considering the amount of time you have had to review this unusual request for us I am impressed. I confess when it landed on my shoulders I was unsure where to begin." The Brigadier was clearly pleased with their efforts and they all sat up. "I would like the team to spend some time until lunch now on the execution phase and who does what. Rodney, I would like you with the team to have a Q&A session and then to put together a plan I can put to the Minister and the other heads of services. I think that would the best way to ensure we get the support from the others and the budget we will need if we are to make any headway. I am going to send out for lunch for you all, so you can work through. My meeting is set for four this afternoon so I would like a fair draft to take with me." Robinson looked round the room, only Rodney was frowning as Robinson knew Rodney was already computing how they could make the deadline. "What would you all like; fish and chips, Chinese or Indian, my treat?"

Chapter 10

TSYGANKOV AND POLYAKOV

The First Directorate of the KGB had been busy for weeks now and the pressure was not letting up, everyone knew even at this stage that Gorbachev would in a year or two be the man who would open up Russia. There were worries too about the rise from the threat of growing overt worldwide terrorist groups and dictatorships.

General Polyakov, the Director of the First Directorate had just had a stormy meeting with the Chairman of the KGB Chebrikov. Polyakov had the greatest respect for the chairman with his unbending loyalty to the state but he would not bend to the coming new dawn and this caused Polyakov much grief.

It was well advertised, the battles between the chairman and the new order. He had thought good and hard about who would replace the chairman because for sure he was on his way out. There was only one possible successor in his mind that would satisfy all political factions and that was Comrade General Vladimir Alexandrovich Kryuchkov. "So," thought Polyakov, "I had better get on with him."

He was worried about the spy Ames who had lasted despite the investigations by the CIA and was now to be based in Rome. The man was reckless and not discrete but lived a charmed life in the context of evading exposure. He was concerned that the Manhattan Project had been declassified last year and the KGB involvement hinted at. That along with the advances in the West surveillance and eavesdropping and decoding resources worried him, at least the Verona Project run by the US for breaking and decoding Soviet intelligence traffic up until it was overtaken in 1980 with better systems had been within limits mitigated.

His mind flipped back to the interview with the chairman. He had been trying to get over to him the need to rationalise some of the departments to cut out duplication and improve efficiencies. The Chairman had squinted at him; he had poor eyesight and began to lecture Polyakov. "When will you learn, Polyakov, we are not going to reduce anything. Would the GRU? I don't think so and they are forever lapping at our door. What do we stand for?" When Polyakov didn't answer him, he said, "Don't know? Well let me remind you. We are the Komati Gosudarstvennoy Begopasnosti, known and feared as well as admired in equal measure worldwide as the KGB and we have been since 1943. Our task is to keep our borders safe and you can't do that with thin air. Primarily this involves; intelligence counterintelligence, operative investigatory activities, running agents legal and illegal, physical security not just of the borders but institutions, including the Central Committee. Well?" He stared at Polyakov.

"Well sir," Polyakov started.

"Well sir! Nothing! What, Polyakov, it means to me in summary is simply this. We have to be as big an organisation as we are, to manage all our responsibilities and be bigger and better than our enemies in every regard including the GRU. So no you may not implement your plans!" The Chairman's voice had risen to a shout and he thumbed the table as he stood up from his desk. "Go back to your Directorate and focus on the threats to us, not this crap." He shot Polyakov a last look and suddenly a glimmer of a smile creased his face as he sat down and said in a calm voice. "Nice plan Polyakov for all and that in a perfect world well, nice try, but my dear general just not now not at this time or sadly one to come I can ever foresee." He waved the General out of his office before bending close to the desk to read documents through his pebble glasses.

He was feeling rebellious as he entered his own office. His Secretary Galena and sometimes mistress had been with him for fifteen years. Galena sensed his smouldering anger. She let him brood in his high-backed black leather chair, swung round so he could stare out the window and think. Galena moved round his large bright office sorting files and tiding his desk before laying out the documents he needed to attend to this morning. She opened his diary on today's date and when she was sure all was ready for him when he calmed down, Galena quietly left the office to make him some coffee. The responsibility of the directorship had changed him she thought, hardened him in many ways but he still had that aristocratic way with him that endeared him to most but worried others, as they were never sure how he would react to a situation. The other directors in the KGB were wary of him and that was not a bad thing Galena concluded.

Only when Polyakov heard Galena bring in his coffee did he swing his chair round and look at her. He thought she was still a very attractive woman at fifty, well curved and above all, he thought, smart and always elegant.

"Good morning Director."

"Good morning Galena." He was smiling now and she knew he had his equilibrium back. "So what do we have today that can't wait?"

"The various papers in front of you need signing. A ten-minute job, no more." She pointed to the diary. "Also General, Tsygankov is booked in to see you."

"He is back then, good. Galena I think I will go to see him; I am in need of space and it has been a while since I visited the working heart of the Directorate. Give him a ring and tell him I will be down to see him in half an hour or so."

Once he had signed the various letters and orders he donned his high peaked hat and carried the documents into Galena's office. He placed them on her desk and bent and kissed her cheek. "Would you consider having dinner with me tonight, I fancy cooking something special for us both?"

Galena looked up at him and standing, straightened his hat, lightly pressing her body to his making him feel the stirring of an arousal. She stood back. "Now that is promising." She sensed his warmness. "I can't think of anywhere I would rather go to eat. Shall we say eight?" She smoothed herself back into her chair giving him a sidelong glance coupled with a grin. "Off with you Director or I will not be capable of doing anything for the rest of the day."

Polyakov meandered through the Directorate stopping and talking to the staff and visiting offices. He enjoyed this aspect of the job as it gave him the opportunity to find out what was going on at desk level and to get briefed on ongoing and arising situations. The staff reciprocated his interest. While as the director, his appointment demanded he played politics, his first love was the operational aspects of his KGB Directorate. In his time in the Directorate Polyakov had modernised the office, replaced the old facades and decorations had been upgraded into bright modern offices. Whilst the nature of the work didn't allow for open offices throughout Polyakov had brigaded task groups where possible into generous spaces. This was no small undertaking in the old building at Dzerzhinsky Square.

He moved on and into Tsygankov's office complex. Tsygankov's secretary welcomed him warmly and buzzed her boss. Tsygankov appeared at his door welcoming Polyakov, holding the door and waving his General into his office. "Katrina if you don't mind can I ask you to find us some coffee and cakes, lots please," Tsygankov requested continuing at the same time to usher the Director into his office and a comfortable chair. Tsygankov sat opposite him. Their relationship had grown warm over the years, they had no work secrets from each other and the philosophy of no surprises was religiously adhered too. Polyakov was even aware of Tsygankov's lost love another by the name of Galena. Galena was now in London heading an off the books criminal organisation using all the skills and deviousness taught her by the KGB.

"Well Carl, good to see you back and I want to know all about it. I am told you even went into battle I must say that was a bit more than we were expecting you to do." Polyakov studied him. "I haven't seen you looking so bright for a long time. But first you wanted to see me."

"I didn't expect you to come to me General but, you are a welcome diversion from the paperwork that seems to have built up into a mountain." He waved his long arms at a mountain of files on his desk. He grunted. "It serves me right for going away for a few days. And General, as you know I delegate just about everything I can so how this build-up has accumulated I can't think."

"I needed the exercise to clear my brain anyway and I had a less than a pleasant breakfast meeting with the chairman who was not going to let me reform us. In a way he is right, the world is changing and we need every asset we have."

"Ah well another time another place perhaps General."

"Could be right, anyway enough of my troubles what about yours?"

Tsygankov was at a loss for a moment as to where to begin. This was despite the fact he had been rehearsing this interview the last few weeks. "General what I need to talk to you about is both personal and work related." Tsygankov looked round his office with its heavy furniture and panelled walls, it had been where he had spent willingly countless hours working for the General and now it seemed to close in on him. He leant forward in his chair, resting his forearms on his legs clasping his hands together to steady them. "There are two matters; the first is succession. That is my succession. Together we have made my semi-retirement work; I will qualify that, in that it's really been full time with a few holidays taken these last two years. We both know in our hearts that the department needs a good man, I am the wrong side of seventy now for goodness sake. My mind is still as agile as it ever was thank goodness but physically I simply can't do what I used to." He sighed. "It was brought home to me starkly in Afghanistan where willingly I involved myself in an operation which I enjoyed immensely, but more of that latter." He nodded to himself and stated carefully, "In truth we both also know that Shabarshin is managing the shop and you would I am sure confide in me that he will one day head up the First Directorate when Mikhail Gorbachev promotes you out of this mad house." Tsygankov almost grinned. "So my suggestion is Shabarshin takes on full power of the deputy and learns the ropes; he is a good man and vastly outshines anything I have done in my time. He is a good man, General."

Polyakov was quiet for a moment and a natural break came as Katrina knocked and bought in the coffee and cakes. When Katrina had placed the refreshments on a table by their side she left them alone again.

Polyakov said. "Do you know Carl that is one of the longest speeches about yourself I have ever heard you make? Let's suppose we go along with your thoughts, does that mean we will still have your support and help as and when?"

"Oh course and I would be greatly saddened if you or the KGB ever felt you could not count on me. Not a problem, General, I assure you."

"Hmm, and you really think you can give all this up and not miss it?" Polyakov saw the hope in Tsygankov's skull-like face. "Okay, let's do it, when now?"

"Yes now. But General no matter whatever you may ask me to do in the future to support yourself and Shabarshin I would like to run one last mission 'off-line' but with support and funding."

"Okay but let's get Shabarshin in now. Please ask Katina for another cup and I think a bottle of best vodka. Also I need to call to let Galena know I am with you for the rest of the day. May I use your phone?"

Tsygankov went to find the new-to-be deputy and Polyakov sat at his desk and called Galena. He could see Carl's jotting from Afghanistan and the name Saied on the notepad arrested his attention.

**

The three generals were closeted for two hours working out the details of the handover and Tsygankov's another attempt at retirement with on-call access as and when the other two generals needed his assistance.

"Job done and my congratulations to you both, I am sure the Directorate will continue on its course without interruption to its performance although I expect General you will want to add some emphasis on the sub-continent where you cut your teeth on this business and I expect Iran is still a hunting ground of yours I think, that could be useful at this time." Turning to address Tsygankov he asked, "Carl can I ask, could you please get Katrina to draft a memo, something special, for me to send out to the troops about the changeover? At the last count I think someone said we were way over our 2500 manpower establishment figure."

"Quite so, and I can assure you Director you can't spare one of them," Shabarshin mocked.

They both laughed. "Let's get at the vodka Comrade General Shabarshin and toast you and Carl."

When Tsygankov re-joined them he drank the glass of vodka poured for him and refilled the glasses. "And now my Generals, I need to tell you about my trip to Afghanistan and my swansong mission that I am looking to you both to support me as," he thought for a moment before bending down to their height, "it will be my retirement present to keep me occupied and out of your hair for a month or two while the new deputy gets his feet under the table and the department fully underway with new management."

When they were all seated and the vodka bottle on the table between them Tsygankov began. "You are both aware I have a few loose ends to tidy up, not least Saied and Major Brown. You could argue that we have more important matters to work on and this is the reason I have waited until now so I will not distract the department from the current work load. Nevertheless there are good reasons to pursue my quest. Brown will succeed the Head of his section and is a clever and resourceful man who we could well do without hanging on our shirttails. No man is indispensable but he has no natural successor in place so we will disrupt them. It may even result in that section being closed down and their responsibilities being absorbed by the other two services.

"I propose we use Saied to execute the plan now he is back from the dead and then have him eliminated so there is no trail back to past operations. Always on the lookout for talent, I met two exceptional men out in Afghanistan who I thought may be of use to me on this mission but more importantly as recruits into this directorate for the future. They are Captain Vladimir Servo, Spetsnaz GRU, and Captain Vasily Vladimirov a KGB intelligence officer with the 4th Army." He paused. "And I was wondering if I could borrow Carla Kashmiri Tskhovbova from time to time. She would be a great distraction."

"She is a distraction wherever she is," Polyakov said dryly.

"You will not be popular Carl, Kashmiri is only the reason many of my now staff come to work every day rain or shine. You had better not lose her. Morale will plummet, including mine," General Shabarshin chided.

"Carl, this operation will have to be deniable. Where will you operate from?"

"I want to operate out of my dacha on the Volga. I have room for the players there and it's remote"

"Then you had better tell us the plan. Leave nothing out; we don't want any surprises Carl." Polyakov was in earnest now.

"No surprises General." Tsygankov went to his safe and brought out three copies of his operational plan. "A copy of the plan I want to enact, for you each, so you can track me on my progress. And now let me tell you about the operation, which incidentally I have called 'Vesuvius'." He smiled.

An hour later the plan was signed-off; there were a few changes suggested by the others but the plan was substantially unchanged from Tsygankov's original concept.

"I will have Saied, Servo, Vladimirov and Tskhovbova report to you for a four-month period at your dacha by within the fortnight. I am looking forward to my first battle with the GRU to get Servo released; they will want something in exchange. So Carl, I think you need to brief me on that horrible pile of files on your desk and then you can get down to your place to prepare for your first guests," General Shabarshin remarked.

"I will be on my way; Carl come and see me before you disappear, I still haven't heard the full story of the attack on the insurgent training camp, how would dinner tomorrow night suit you? Why not bring along Katina and I will ensure Galena comes too, my place eight o'clock."

"Thank you, that would be very generous of you General."

Chapter 11

BRIGADIER ROBINSON'S BRIEF

The team finished up their lunch while Rodney put the finishing touches to the draft plan. The conference room's normal dusty aroma had become diffused with the smell of fish and chips. Mould was collecting the empty cartons and plastic cutlery and Jane and Reid were resetting the tea and coffee cups for the final operational briefing of the day. Graham, true to form, was cleaning down the table and straightening up the papers.

Pat and Sharky sat either side of Rodney, helping him to complete the brief when he showed signs of flagging. It was not that he was disinterested or stuck, quite the contrary, Rodney was fully committed, just wrecked from the night before and the weight of work generally.

It was close to two o'clock when he felt he had a rough draft on paper. He read it through and could see a few gaps which he would fill in when he produced a final draft for the Brigadier.

Rodney called the team to order when he felt happy he could get the message over from the draft to them. "Ladies and Gentlemen, let's see what we have landed ourselves with. I am going to leave out the introduction, justification and the courses open and go straight to the execution.

"The concept is that each member of the team takes one of the actions we have identified. Graham you will co-ordinate, support and arrange resources to the rest of the field teams, as need be, supported by our Quartermaster, finance and the secretariat team. We agreed that with our limited numbers we could only concentrate on three areas. Area one is the money. Two is the communications between the IRA quartermaster, his suppliers and his clients or customers. Three is the FBI paramilitary department and any informers they have."

He looked round the group for confirmation that they were all with him. Without exception, all the parties at the table nodded their assent. "Good. Subject to approval, Mr Reid and I will go and see the FBI. Jane, Pat and Andrew you have to find the money; who has the money, who is supplying it and why and who is spending it and on what. In addition is there any trade in 'kind'. Or gift aid. It is a big job so three of you need to work together to make any headway. Lastly, Mould and Sharky your task is the communication traffic. I don't need to tell you that there are not just GCHQ and the Yanks to go at, but it could include physical surveillance too. Any questions?

"I know the overall concept is to suck dry other agencies and feed off of their knowledge but we will need to do some original work too and we are pitifully resourced with no back-up but ourselves if a team gets into trouble." Andrew was seriously worried on this count but only voiced what they were all thinking including Rodney.

"Good point Andrew and I been thinking about that too. I have an idea to put to the Brigadier for some muscle and expertise, we will see. Anything else you can think of?"

"What are we going to do with our current case load?" Jane wanted to know.

"Good question and I don't have the answer to that at the moment but I will come tomorrow. So stand by all of you. Give me an hour to type this up for the boss and then each in turn to my office give me a five-minute verbal and written brief on what you are doing and where you are with it. That way I should be able to give the boss his briefing and the state of nation of our department. Okay?" There was no dissent. "Let's go to it then." Rodney was pleased at the team's support for this out-of-way assignment. He had no doubt in his mind they would face many challenges and his main concern he'd found was the section's credibility. If they failed and failed embarrassingly it could undo all the good work the team had done in the past. Robinson's small but effective department was well regarded but it had it dissenters, no more so in London Centre where the Foreign Office thought the department should be under their control. Fortunately for them this Prime Minister and the head of the Security Council wanted an independent team with no political and other affiliations. As Rodney had told his team, "We carry no baggage. We serve the nation without fear or favour."

***

At half past three, Robinson called down to Major Brown to chase him for his brief. Rodney was still trying to get his papers in order but told his boss five minutes. Five minutes later Rodney, as good as his word, was sitting in front of his boss and had handed over a copy of the brief and other notes. He waited while the Brigadier scanned the papers.

"Thank you Rodney, good draft and I am going to the meeting with it as it is. Any issues taking on this task as far the team is concerned?"

"A couple of points to mention now, I thought you would like a complete picture." Rodney pointed out a sheet at the back of the pack. "If you look at the current liability sheet you will see there are a few jobs we will need to close out and that could take a week, maybe three weeks, no more for sure if we hit them as a team?" He paused for the Brigadier to find the paper and read through it. "The second point is resources. At this early stage we are feeling a little exposed and could do with some muscle to watch our backs especially the Mould and Sharky task. We need some boots on the ground in Ireland. Think they need to be part of the team, not some imports from the other agencies."

"Got anyone in mind?"

"Bit off the wall, but the two Welshmen downstairs on duty could be useful; I've got them to send in their details. They are young enough to run and old enough to have a steady head. I have spoken to them and I would ask you to appraise them on your way out. Bit off the wall I know but they are eager for more than a dead-end security post. If it's a go, we could indoctrinate them over the next few weeks?"

"Tell you what I will do. I will have a look at them and if I agree with your evaluation I will get them seconded for a trial and get Avery back to train them. He is only pushing paper over at 6 and I know wants back in with us. How is that? Anything else you might want?"

"If we are to go after the money we need some specialist help. A banker type, he needs to be someone who knows the banks at home and internationally, who can manoeuvre within that banking world without attracting attention. Previous experience with the security services and some knowledge of the IRA financial set-up would help. We may need a hacker from 5 at some stage too," Rodney concluded.

"Okay, see what I can do, anything else?"

"Don't think so. But I am sure as long as the budget is flexible we should be able to be flexible too as the situation demands."

"In that case I had better get moving or I will be late. We will talk later tonight or in the morning. Don't wait for me to return but just keep the mobile handy." Robinson gathered the papers and rammed them in his briefcase; grabbed his coat and hat and was gone before Rodney was out of the chair.

Chapter 12

THE TSYGANKOV DACHA

For his retirement dacha he had set himself up on one of the smaller islands in the Astrakhan area of southwest Russia. True it was an idyllic spot, few neighbours and several hectares of vines and orchard land abutting the river escarpment of the Volga on three sides. He should he knew simply retire completely but he thought again that he had one more chance to settle a score for all time before he lost the ability to call on the resources of the KGB.

Having flown into Astrakhan a week after the meeting with the two generals once he had fully handed over to his successor, his hands were free and he now sat on a floating restaurant in the harbour. The Akvotoria floating restaurant was one of his favourite watering holes and he was well known by the manager and staff and always drew a few glances, not just because he was a memorable figure but most locals knew his profession and could not fully understand why he was settling in the area. Men of his ilk tended to want to remain in striking distance of Moscow.

This time of day, early evening, was his favourite more so this early part of the year with its early transition from winter into summer. The area had little rainfall but it fell throughout the year and this stopped the area being classified as arid. Tsygankov actually liked the normally benign winters and the hot summers. It suited his broad-shouldered lean frame.

As he scanned the menu to choose one of the local specialities, his eye was caught by the fish section. On offer tonight was sazan, bershik, vobla, catfish or pike caviar. In this southern tip of Russia, Russia's last outpost, he felt at home. He ordered the catfish and a bottle of white wine. Exceptionally they had acquired somehow a few crates of white wine from Kosovo, which he knew was excellent and he thought much under-priced and appreciated.

He had chosen a riverside table with two seats and watched the ships big and small cross in front of him on the wide Volga River. The Volga basin many kilometres wide at this point stretched away into the distance to meet the Caspian Sea a little over 50 miles to the south. At less than 30 metres above sea level and emptying into the Caspian Sea, the river as it got wider slowed. Where Tsygankov had his dacha only an hour away, the river was narrower and Carl loved the roar of it when it was in spate. Its spray would cool his island for which he would be grateful in the hottest summer months and for any of the water drops and moisture that fell on his land.

The manager brought the wine and poured it for Tsygankov to taste. "How on earth did you manage to get this wine from Kosovo?" Tsygankov swirled the glass looking at the wine's clarity. "It's very good but I thought that they could only make enough for home consumption?"

"True." The manager sat on the spare seat. "But in the Tarter Bazaar there is a wine merchant that finds spare wine in the areas where there is low production, he specializes you see? So many bottles in his cellar are rather special, like this white. I think Kosovo benefits from its land-locked situation and the bowl in which it exists, bounded as it is with hills and mountains surrounding its centre. I like to try the unusual, a bit like our menu."

Tsygankov smiled, he was enjoying this simple company. "Tell me about the Tarter Market, I have been there a few times but I don't know much about it."

The restaurant was quiet and the manager was happy to talk and Tsygankov felt relaxed; he had handed over his duties and thought he remembered dimly the Chinese saying. "That when you are between the ages of 50 and 70 or was it 80? It was the best age period, you have put in your time and paid your dues and could now do what you wanted."

"You probably know something of our history as I seem to remember you saying you have recently settled in this area. In 1300 the Tartar Golden horde fought and won this land, and the local Tartars ruled until the Russians then conquered Astrakhan in 1558 and rebuilt the city and the Tartar Market itself had new life breathed into it. Traditionally it is known for its great stalls of watermelons and the like, but in the Bazaar and surrounding shops you can buy anything you could want."

"Well tomorrow I do need to shop. I am moving into my dacha for an extended period and there is a lot I need to buy to set the place up. I could do with a guide if you know one?" Tsygankov questioned.

"Not a problem, where are you staying?"

"Tonight? Just down the road at the Hotel Petr on the Gubernatorial prospect. I have a Land Cruiser so transport is no problem and I want to buy a large trailer, so for the immediate items I want I should be able to transport them with me. I assume most sellers can deliver the larger items."

"Good. My oldest son Petrov will be your guide, not only that he will arrange transport for you, goods that you can't carry tomorrow so they arrive all at the same time. Petrov will call on you; say nine in the morning, as few of the shops will be open before that." Tsygankov nodded.

"And now I must go and chase up your order and telephone Petrov to warn him he is working tomorrow."

"Thank you, first stop tell him will be to buy a largish trailer with 4 wheels I think."

"Not a problem," the manager called back. Tsygankov was left to his thoughts to plan his purchases on the morrow. The dacha had the space and enough rooms but more furniture and food stores needed to be bought in quantities. The dacha was well appointed, all the services connected and the kitchen was fully kitted as were the ensuite bathrooms. Tsygankov's own bedroom, study and living rooms were finished and fully furnished. He had had the local builders fully employed for the last year and it was fortunate the work was now finished as they had promised.

The Dacha had been a rundown farmhouse and apart from the roof, which had to be replaced, he had had it extended and the stables converted into guest accommodation, housing three apartments each with a bathroom and kitchenette. He had toyed with the idea of holiday lets but was still undecided. "It might be better to preserve my privacy and buy an apartment or three in Astrakhan City and rent them out, I need to do something with the money I made and a bank holds little charm." Tsygankov had thought having now seen the city, high-end rental for professionals was a distinct possibility. The city was a trading centre between Europe, Central Asia and the Caucasus so would tend to have a quantity of expats working for companies and at any one time looking for accommodation.

He knew Astrakhan had always been prosperous even if today its future depended on its disappearing sturgeon used for caviar production and its disputed access to the Caspian Sea for oil production. The sturgeon would come back with the imposition of farming and population control. With a population in the area of around half a million it was not crowded. Access to the oil, he was sure, would be sorted out; Azerbaijan and its Baku oil town would always need the hand of Russian friendship, her giant neighbour to protect her from her neighbours.

Tsygankov left the city early afternoon the following day, paying off Petrov, who had proved invaluable in satisfying the long list of purchases Tsygankov and Petrov had put together. The purchases were loaded in the trailer, vehicle boot and on the roof rack. Some larger items and fuel stores Petrov would arrange transport for and deliver the following day. The big 4-litre motor made light work of its load. Tsygankov crossed the bridge to the west bank of the Volga and travelled north on the M6 E40 motorway. After an hour he passed the sign for the town of Narimarov and began to look for his turning near the sign that advertised the town of Verpelebyazhye to the north.

The turning came up fast and Tsygankov had to break hard, and turn quicker than he intended onto the metalled road. Worried his loads had shifted; he checked them before the bridge to the island. His island had a link bridge spanning over a large farmed fishery which was taking advantage of the race between the island and mainland. As he bounced over the bridge he looked down at the concrete fish pens.

To the far side of the elongated teardrop, north-to-south shaped island the main flow of the Volga moved by, shaping the northern end of the three-kilometre long island into a wooded blunt point. The bottom half of the island, a little over half a kilometre wide at is widest point, was spotted with temporary and semi-permanent small dwellings used as mainly as holiday and weekend getaways. In the middle of the island the dwellings on its southern half petered out. To the north only the dacha of Tsygankov was to be found at the very apex of the island, where it commanded views of the river on all three sides. Tsygankov had bought out a campsite owner, the only other occupancy on his half of the island and cleared the area of human habitation. A two-and-a half metre high dry-stone wall now separated his land from the rest of the island. The right side of his part of the island shelved to the water from a beach. The left side of the island and front was protected by escarpments. The beach and escarpments were protected by the same two-metre stone wall enclosing the whole of his land from casual visitors.

Leaving the bridge, Tsygankov drove north on another metalled road that soon petered out leaving a rough earth single track road. After a kilometre the dust and scrub that formed the basis of most of the long deserted home plots gave way to scrub and a few trees with the winter grass showing. Another half kilometre and the last of the sparse deserted homesteads were left behind. The remainder of the land was Tsygankov's own property; gated and walled. Mostly this land before his enclosure had been left to nature and meant the olive trees, scrubs and grasslands were verdant.

For two hundred metres south of the house, the environment showed signs of cultivation. A large diverse orchard that had been overgrown was now tended. An olive grove, which he had admired from the start of his tenure, bode well for the future crops of oil. A few hundred or so mature grape vines had been brought back under control. A highly organised vegetable patch was supported by an all-weather greenhouse powered by solar panels to draw water and for heating. A deep pond, slightly elongated to follow the orientation of the island measuring some 50 metres by 80 and mostly around 8 metres deep, was full from the winter rains and water pumped from the Volga. He would stock the pond towards the end of the summer. Much of the rock to wall his land and extend the dacha had been quarried from the pond at the start of the project.

Tsygankov drove round the pond to the west, appreciating his estate and wondering why he was risking another mission instead of simply settling down here, managing and developing his estates for his remaining years left to him. He shrugged with the thought, "Plenty of time to enjoy this after Major Brown has been neutralised."

Tsygankov drew up to another car, a hard-top Russian version of their famous jeep. Switching off the engine he clambered down from his 4 by 4 and stood for a while breathing in the fresh air. He stomped off to the dacha to find his live-out housekeeper and her husband who was to maintain both the property and grounds for him between them. They had agreed to meet him at this time and help to unload the material he had brought with him. They both lived on the island at the southern tip and had been a great find as far as Tsygankov was concerned. The wife Tamara was in her middle to late fifties and still a dark-haired beauty and with a career as a nurse matron over, she was now a cook, homemaker, organiser par excellence and administrator all in one. Her husband Mac Szukaj was a retired VDV captain who had worked his way through the ranks and served as an airborne combat engineer, who fortunately could turn his hand to anything. Mac, although in his middle sixties, was as strong as an ox and standing a little less than six foot was still ramrod straight in his stance.

Before he got to the door Tamara and Mac appeared from the converted stables, smiling and waving in greeting.

Tsygankov was surprised how quickly they unloaded his stores and moved them to the areas they would be used in. Any construction or final placement could wait until the morning.

Tamara had the place heated and the evening meal on. She sent Tsygankov off to his rooms at the top of the house to bath and get ready for dinner. She and Mac as agreed would join the General tonight and use the opportunity to discuss what was still needed to be done or considered and any other issues they needed to address.

When Tsygankov entered the large kitchen/diner he found the couple ready for him. The house was warm and he was pleased for the thought he had put into the energy requirements of his complex. The principal power for the house came from a water turbine he had installed below his escarpment into the race. Backup power, if needed came from the fish farm supply and backed up again by a small gas turbine generator installed in one end of the stable block with the gas bullet located out of sight to the rear of the block. Solar power generated both heat for water and electrical charge for the bank of batteries for a gas turbine "black start" and other emergency lighting and backup circuits.

The kitchen was welcoming and the food smells inviting. Tsygankov opened a bottle of local red wine and poured while Tamara served up a meat stew with dumplings and fresh bread. "Next year," Mac said swirling his glass of wine, "You could be drinking your own vintage."

Heaven must be like this, Tsygankov thought. So they ate and talked long into night about Russia past and future. Mac and Tamara both had had life experiences that Tsygankov could relate to and them to his. Tsygankov talked about his hopes and plans for the cultivation and development of his land and Mac had many suggestions and advice about the land that the General found helpful and in line with his own philosophy, Tsygankov expected the future to auger well for them all.

Chapter 13

THE ROBINSON MEMORANDUM

Rodney pushed his way into his flat, picking up a pile of free magazines, leaflets and mail deposited that day. "I really don't know how these trash makers can justify the waste of the resources and energy they use to print this junk mail. Let alone where on earth do they source all this paper?" Junk mail annoyed him intensely because it was using resources and energy that could have been channelled into more useful purposes. He felt the same about polystyrene cups and other one-time use paraphernalia.

He walked into his kitchen/diner living area, throwing the junk mail in the bin and switching the kettle on in one smooth movement. He sat at the dining table and opened his mail. Apart from a few bills there was only one letter of interest that made him sit bolt upright.

He had to look twice, could it be real or was it a plant, a trap of some kind. He scrutinised the envelope sent from Moscow yesterday – it looked real and had not been tampered with. It was addressed to him simply as Brown followed by his address. "It is thin, only one piece of paper thick," he thought. His curiosity aroused, he carefully slit open the letter and carefully removed the single piece of paper, only holding it barely at one corner with his finger and thumb. In very feint black writing it simply read:

"Dear Major Rodney Brown
I will be in touch, but stay alert in the meantime.
A champion for Chekov."

Rodney could not believe what he was reading; he stared at the note and re-read. Nonplussed he blurted out loud, "How can this be? Who can this be? Chekhov and Gipsy were dead and my own beloved Valeria." As far as Rodney knew, that was the end of the dynasty. Certainly Valeria had never claimed to have a son or daughter for that matter, perhaps if it was true, was it a son, daughter of the original Chekhov, perhaps a friend or confidant? Maybe it was a sympathiser or someone out for revenge. He turned the envelope over. There was no return address or anything else on the envelope that gave him any clues. He decided to take the letter and envelope to the team's laboratory tomorrow. He would get in early before anyone arrived and see if he could lift any prints to give him a clue as to the sender's identity and have the envelope tested for DNA matching.

He found a plastic document sleeve and carefully placed the letter and envelope in it before locking it into his briefcase.

Switching off the kettle for his tea, he changed his mind and decided instead to have a drink. He opened a bottle of Bordeaux Claret and put a microwave meal in the oven to heat. The claret was light enough to drink deeply but not heavy enough to give him a hangover tomorrow. He poured nearly half the bottle into a microwave jug and gave it 30 seconds in the oven and then poured it back into the bottle. It was his own special process he used to stimulate the wine, in order to release its aromas and to warm it. He was thought a heathen by his peers but what did they know their loss he always thought. He poured himself a half glass, smelt in the aroma and then swirled it gently, smelt the wine again then drank deeply rolling the wine around his mouth alert to the alcohol rush flooding his body. He sat in his easy chair to mull over memories and tried to plan his next move, the note had really thrown him and he did not want it to cloud his current work programme.

He slept fitfully, conscious perhaps he had to get up early. Not able to sleep he got up at five AM and was in the small lab belonging to the section, before six AM next morning. He bought two breakfast baps on the way in, from a hole-in-the-wall café near the office. He bought a newspaper from a kiosk. When Rodney arrived at the office he made himself tea and carried his mug of tea, newspaper and baps with briefcase into the laboratory.

Searching the chemical cupboard for a ready-made-up solution of *"Ninhydrin"* Rodney found a bottle freshly made the day before. He pulled on plastic gloves to prevent getting purple stains on his hands and then carefully poured a quantity into a small clean sterile bottle.

Next he prepared the work area, putting down his newspaper to protect the surface from staining and then carefully laid out the letter and envelope. He got the other resources together and plugged in the lab iron. His aim was to develop any latent prints. If he failed he would get the team scientist to do a more destructive test using silver nitrate or iodine. He preferred to use ninhydrin which was a test that could be repeated; the other methods were one-time only tests.

He spread the paper and sprayed the solution evenly all over the letter and envelope. He would repeat the process for the back of the letter. Laying the letter to one side, he put down a cloth towel and then a dry paper towel and placed the letter on top. On top of the letter he put a damped paper towel and a dry one on top and covered it with another damp towel. He ironed the whole edifice for several minutes. A check by lifting up the top covers to reveal the letter showed the first appearance of purple outlined finger prints. This process never failed to enthral him. A few more minutes ironing and the prints on the paper were distinct.

He had suspected, more hoped, that the writer may have been nervous, sweating and sebaceous fluids would be transferred as the writer handled the letter.

The envelope itself was covered in prints which was to be expected but he may be able to get the department's contact in the FBI to make something of them.

He repeated the process on the front and back of the letter and got more prints.

He leant against the lab bench and drank his tea and finished off the baps; pleased with himself he stood guiltily, almost to attention as the team's scientist entered the room. He didn't get a chance to explain why he was there, the team scientist got in first.

"Playing detective I see, again, Rodney." The scientist, Dr Christian Jules Day was amused. Day could do just about anything or get anything done in the world of chemicals, autopsies, medical, software programs, gismos and electronics he swam in. "I do hope you are going to clear up."

"No issue, Christian. While I do, could you look at my efforts." Rodney indicated the fingerprints he had revealed.

While Rodney put the kit away and tidied up, Day studied the prints through a magnifying glass. "Good job Rodney." Day said at last. "Got some really clear prints, so it should be no problem matching them if they are on file anywhere at all?" Day beamed at him. How they had gotten Day was a mystery, he just appeared one day and set up his lab.

He claimed to be a side-moved scientist who had objected to some experiment or other in a government laboratory. He seemed perfectly happy in the department, lived just round the corner and was a valued team member. Rodney often wondered if his move was on ageism too as Day must be well into his seventies, maybe more. He supposed he was being paid by someone and was on the books for he was not on the team's organisational staff roll or in the team's budget.

"Well Doc, that's what I wanted to talk to you about." Rodney took a breath. "Can you separate the prints from the message and hike the prints around anonymously so to speak. Plus try our contact in the FBI with their files. I am just hoping that they have pulled in the Military Intelligence files by now as I suspect this message could be from a foreign possible intelligence or military source. I don't need to tell you this is 'need to know'. That is you and me and the boss."

Day nodded. "No problem Rodney, I am too old and wise to tell tales, plus telling tales takes energy, and is a distraction, don't you think?" He didn't expect an answer; he looked at the letter and envelope again. "I will compare these two and only the letter-matched fingerprints will go forward for analysis. I think I might also investigate the paper and its likely source of manufacture. Not too hopeful if it's foreign but you never know. Give me a day or two and we will see what we shall see." He paused. "Would you like me to test for DNA, may be able to get something if you haven't washed it all away? Long shot, but may be at least it is worth a try I am thinking."

"Yes, let's do that." Rodney thanked Day and shook his hand before picking up his cup and briefcase. "This really is sensitive and for me personal, an unwanted blast from the past."

"Leave this to me, my young centurion." Day opened the door and ushered Rodney out.

Rodney nodded to the team as he went to his office. Mould was at his elbow as he put his hand on the door handle. "Would you like a cup of tea, boss?"

"What are you after, Mouldy?" Rodney was curious.

"Not a lot, but I was going to ask for a few days off like. It's my other half; she is giving me earache about jobs I promised to do and, well… haven't."

"As long as your desk is clear of anything urgent currently or you can get someone to take responsibility for it, as the deal I am offering after your leave is not only a trip overseas and a fortnight's grace to help out the current stuff as we should expect actions coming our way from the meeting with the boss yesterday?" He grinned at Mould.

"When you come back make sure you come in ready for a trip to a hot country. You need have packed your big hunter outfit, as the day you get back we are off to Somalia."

"No sweat. Tea?"

"Yes strong and sweet, just like my old sergeant major made it, not Earl Grey."

"In your dreams, Major Brown, sir." The sir was slurred into an Irish brogue.

Rodney laughed. "Bugger off and get that tea and don't be long!"

"And one for me too, if you please, Mould." The Brigadier appeared round the corner next to Rodney's room. "But for me Earl Grey, weak in a pot please, no milk, if you don't mind." He indicated Rodney should lead him into his office.

Mould rolled his eyes. "Officers, they never change," then he added mentally, "Thank goodness."

Once they were settled, the Brigadier began to talk to Rodney. He normally had a deliberate way of speaking, low in tone and each word seemed to be weighed carefully. Even more so when he wanted to get information over as was the case now.

"I have put together a memorandum for the team from my discussions with the powers last night. It contains the actions you and the team put together and contact names from GCHQ, 5, 6 and Military Intelligence you can refer to for information and help." He passed his memorandum to Rodney. "Read it while we take our refreshments when they arrive, I am in no hurry." He settled himself and opened the daily paper he preferred and was rarely without.

"There is something I need to tell you." The Brigadier looked up from his paper. "Last night when I got home there was a letter waiting for me. It was posted from Moscow and it had a simple message and said it was from a supporter of Chekov and that they would be in touch." Rodney pushed his hand through his hair. He handed Robinson a copy of the letter. "I tested it for latent prints this morning and got a good set of prints off it. Doc is going to try to find a match on the databases including from our friend in the FBI." He sat back in his chair. "I am undecided if it's a plant or genuine. So I am going to treat it with circumspection."

Robinson put down his paper and started to read the note out loud: *"Dear Major Rodney Brown I will be in touch, but stay alert in the meantime. A champion for Chekov,"* he handed it back to Rodney. "Interesting, probable, does not express my feeling about this well. Of course I did, do know Chekov had children – two sons and a daughter and they would be in their early to late twenties possibly middle thirties by now, if they are still alive. If they are what they do and where they are we don't know. We were supposed to help them but they simply disappeared from view when Chekov was killed." He looked into the corner of the room before adding. "Think you should be careful, it could be a trap, but follow up the prints – you never know."

"I was thinking, if it is genuine, could it mean Tsygankov is out there somewhere and we are under attack?"

"If it is genuine, it's possible, but the man must be over 70 now." Robinson took a moment to rationalise what he had just said. "Come to that so am I. Makes you think. You have enough on your plate at the moment, leave Tsygankov to me, I will get the 6 London Centre to alert our resident man in Moscow and find out where he is and what he is doing. Our Moscow resident these days is a particularly effective individual. My oldest son."

Rodney smiled. It was the first time the Brigadier had ever mentioned his son to Rodney. He knew he had a son and daughter and lived in a big detached property and with a Victorian walled garden in Pimlico. A widower, the Brigadier lived for his children and the department. The few times Rodney had had to meet Robinson at his house he always thought how lucky he was, as most of the other senior men had their houses in the country and he knew the inconvenience many of his peers experienced when summoned to their man's residence deep in the English countryside. He got back to his work. "Doc is going to try for some DNA on the letter or envelope and I was wondering if you had anything from Chekov we could compare. It is a long shot I know."

"Let me think on that, there is the list of course but there may be other items in my box. I will get back to you on this. Ah the tea…" Mould kicked open the door with his foot and placed the two cups and the pot of Earl Grey on the desk. "Well done thank you. Now Mould, in about ten minutes," said Robinson, looking at his watch, "two potential recruits will be knocking on the door. Their task will be to support you and Sharky in the field and be extra muscle if it comes to that. I would like you with Sharky and Reid to interview them and test them out. Then bring them to Major Brown and myself in an hour and a half if they are any good for us."

Mould looked at Rodney who nodded to him. "As you wish, sir." Mould was grinning as he confirmed he would, closing the door behind him.

Robinson flapped out his paper after pouring his drink and continued to read the editorial. Rodney began to study the Robinson memorandum and take notes to help order his thoughts. The room settled into a sombre silence.

Robinson interrupted Rodney only once to confirm he had got agreement on the budget and the three weeks' grace to clear the workload. "The PM was not overly enthusiastic that key members of the team were involved in the Somalian hostage release. In fact the PM wanted to pass it over to 6 but 6 couldn't oblige. So it's still yours but she did say, don't get hurt," Robinson said seriously with a grimace playing on his lips.

Rodney shook his head in disbelief. "Should be fine, the hostage negotiator believes we should be good for the pickup early week after next, at the upcountry exchange as agreed. Personally I am looking forward to a bit of sun, no matter how brief." Head down, he got back to the memorandum and his note-taking and the silence between the two men returned.

Chapter 14

MOSCOW

While Rodney puzzled his way through the Brigadier's document the two Russian Captains, Vasily Vladimirov and Vladimir Servo who had been in Moscow now for a week, were preparing to travel to join Tsygankov. Saied had tethered himself to them like a dog. All three were still a little perplexed at their sudden move as Servo had not the slightest inkling that Saied and he would have a chance to work together after he had supported the doctor who had to get Saied fully fit. But none had any complaints at this sudden change of plan; it gave them a much needed opportunity to shake the dust of Afghanistan out of their hair.

Vasily was more circumspect after the Director General Polyakov had outlined the mission to the team. The briefing had been brief. Details were sketchy. They would work out of a dacha in Southern Russia and the target was in Western Europe, England to be exact, against a Major Brown and his men and only that it would involve other third parties.

For the week the team had been thrown together, various specialists had pumped them full of knowledge, ranging from tradecraft to survival in an alien environment. A large part of the week was devoted to the UK public transport systems, its geography, renting and setting up safe houses and the way to obtain vehicles the supplies they would need. The week was conducted all in English; no Russian was spoken at any time. When Servo asked early on in the week in Russian for clarification on something the instructor said, he was thrown a dictionary by the instructor. But the instructor to be fair went over the item again slowly and explained it using different English words. One item that mystified and intrigued the team was two sessions on the Irish problem and the IRA.

Major Carla Kashmiri Tskhovbova, the KGB officer who had joined them, was exceptionally attractive. A well-formed figure, she stood five foot eight in her stockinged feet. A Slavic rounded face with her full lips and hazel eyes, framed with medium-length auburn hair that shone with interesting streaks of many subtle shades. The bonus was she had a sense of humour and gave her three new partners as good as they gave, if not better.

The three men now all in casual civilian clothes, well lived-in leather bomber jackets, dark blue jeans and Algie ankle walker boots; Saied sensibly sported a black shemagh around his neck against the Moscow chill. Carrying their leather belt wallets the three men were standing in the entrance talking together on the steps of the Directorate as Carla approached.

Servo watched her confident stride as she smiled in greeting. "I could lose myself in that," he thought again, "at least get into serious trouble."

"Gentleman are all you ready to go?"

"All ready, our kit is in the bus," Vasily returned.

"Let's go then and get to it," Carla smiled.

"What are the arrangements, they don't seem to have told us anything meaningful except to get ready to travel to the dacha?" Saied was still feeling slight effects of the wounds, slight twinges from the tug of the stitches the doctor had insisted he had to put in to pull the skin together. And he wanted to scratch them. He was conscious it made him slightly irritable and he tried to hide it from the team. The only one he didn't fool was Servo who understood the irritating effects of seemingly minor flesh wounds as they healed.

Carla frowned. "Moscow airport and fly down and hire a car. It must have cross country capability and drive up to the Tsygankov dacha, which will be our base." The smile returned. "Quite a change from the norm don't you think?"

Saied forced a smile. "Sorry, just a bit miserable today; my wounds seem to be feeling the cold and damp of this city."

Servo gripped him round the shoulders. "No issue Saied, we understand. The sooner we get you out of here to a warmer climate the sooner they will mend for the better. Come on let's go, I heard Tsygankov likes to share his whisky and lays a good table, we should be so lucky. And the climate is drier and milder compared to here, what have we got to lose?"

"Knowing the General from the old days, quite a lot; it might have been safer to stay in Afghanistan," Saied replied wryly.

"Do tell," asked Carla.

"How long have you got?"

Chapter 15

THE QUARTERMASTER'S ENFORCER

The night was matt black, bible some would have said, no moon only the far lights of the race stadium gave a warm glow, its lights bouncing off the low-clouded night sky. The reflected light formed a canopy against the black sky. A sea mist dampened the air.

A man stood stock still, gazing up at the same patch of sky, listening to the gentle groans generated by the wind in the yew trees that grew strongly in the Dowdallahil Cemetery to the northeast of Dundalk. The wind from the west bought the smell of the Irish sea to him and he breathed it in deeply.

The cemetery covered three or more hectares and the man placed himself at the crossroad at the centre of the facility. He felt the ghosts of those he had known and those he had laid to rest. They didn't worry him. "There would be time enough to meet them properly in the other life, and spend an eternity discussing 'what ifs' with them." He grinned at the thought. He was not evil by nature, just hardened by the "cause", driven by the necessity to carry out tasks that in another life he would not have considered possible.

His mind was filled with the immediate job at hand and the actions he had to take over the next few days. He tried to clear his mind – he needed to ponder on yet another proposed ceasefire and how he felt about the whole idea. But this time it felt different. His initial reaction had been to think they had sold out like they did before in 1920. "It is an interesting comparison, so it is," he thought to himself. "As those that continued the struggle finally achieved full independence for the South a few years later." This final thought cemented the decision he had been toying with since the end of the previous year. "Not for me or those that think like me."

He confirmed his decision by mouthing, *"Oglaigh na h Eirean,"* he continued, "It is to be the RIRA, the Real IRA so it is." He shook his head slowly. "But not today, but it needs to be very soon, it is going to take a finite time to put all the pieces in play." The Quartermaster hung his head. "What a fucking mess. Why won't the Brits just fuck off and go away? Why won't the Prods just fuck off to the mainland?" He stepped off the road into the shelter of a large grave headstone. He had sensed more than heard people enter the cemetery.

Turning on his heels and away from the race course direction, he faced towards Dundalk town; he could just make out the town skyline. He chose the new location he had found earlier in the shadow of a large mausoleum to stand unseen where he could watch men approaching.

Still in a thoughtful mood he ruminated on his chosen residential location "Dundalk, County Louth, do I enjoy it over the North, I think so," he thought, "a great location, strategically located approximately midway between the two largest cities, Belfast and Dublin." It was, after all, the principal centre in the middle of the East Coast. Within a 30 mile radius there is a large population to disappear into. A 50 mile radius brings in Ireland's two main cities, Dublin and Belfast, increasing the catchment to in excess of 3 million. Good roads M1/N1 National Primary Route, actually equidistant between the two cities. The fast reliable inter-city rail network that he thought ran mostly on time, when it was not being disrupted by the boys. And a good position in relation to international airports, north of Dublin and south of Belfast. He considered his decision to base his new party here not just himself and it fitted in well with his thoughts. Satisfied he had put that to bed, he bent his attention to the group of men that approached his position.

He stepped out of the blackness, his outline suddenly stark and forbidding as the men got close to him, startling the lead man. "Jesus Q you scared the hell out of us," the man whispered.

In his quiet speech he asked the man, "Must be a guilty conscience, so it is?" He didn't wait for a reply. "Where is the man?"

The men pushed forward a figure tied and gagged in front of him. "You know why you are here." In the darkness the man shivered but the Quartermaster saw the nod of the head. "I just hope you think betraying us to the bastards is worth the punishment due." The man tried to speak through his gag but nothing intelligible could be made out.

The Quartermaster turned to the tallest of the group in front of him. "Take him to the grave." When the man heard these words he fell to his knees and then tried aggressively to stand up and bolt, knocking over one of the minders, head-butting another. The rest of the men fell on him, beating him to the ground. He had no chance.

He was gripped under the armpits and made to stand and then forced stumbling deeper into the cemetery; one of the two men dragging him took a handful of his hair, twisting forced him forward as the man tried to dig in his feet to stop the motion. He wriggled but to no avail – he was held fast. Breathing hard now, the men holding him forced the prisoner to kneel at the head of an over-deep open grave.

At a nod from the man, the Quartermaster's enforcer stepped quickly forward and pulled the man's head savagely back, so his nostrils were flared and facing upwards, wrenching his hair tight on the scalp to hold him in position. The enforcer reached into his coat pocket and brought out a phial flicking off the top. He carefully poured its contents down into both nostrils of the prisoner and stood back quickly.

The reaction was startling – the man immediately arched his back further seemingly to breaking point and writhed and convulsed on the ground. The other men stood back, some alarmed at the cruelty of the execution and others simply watched, listening to the gurgles and snorts of the doomed man. The man's movement stopped within a few minutes and he lay still on one side curled in an embryo position with his neck tendons and hands clawed in agony.

Several of the men crossed themselves.

"May God have pity on his soul for I have none? No reprieve! No last minute rights for a traitor! Put him in the grave, men and put a foot of soil on him." With that the Quartermaster turned his back to walk away.

"Q, I need to talk. Can I buy you a drink over at the race course?" Liam O'Neil, the enforcer and Quartermaster's link to the other IRA engineers was at his most serious. "Something's come up you need to decide on."

Dundalk Race Stadium was more than just a racecourse; it had state-of-the-art facilities open all year round situated on 147 acres of land and had good drinking and eating facilities.

"What's that troubling you?" The Quartermaster was still walking away with Liam from the others who were too busy attending to the grave to pay any attention to them.

"The Russians want to talk they have a proposition for us," Liam whispered.

The Quartermaster stopped and stared at O'Neil intently then relaxed. "Did you know Dundalk town's name, which was historically written as Dundalgan? It has associations with the mythical warrior Cú Chulainn. The town's crested charter from 1189 reads *Mé do rug Cú Chulainn Cróga*. Do you know what that means, Liam?"

Liam thought for a moment and then said, "I gave birth to brave Cú Chulainn."

"Seems appropriate somehow don't you think. Now buy me that drink and a bite to eat, I am suddenly hungry and tell me about our new friends, has to be said, you have my attention, so you have. The Russians you say? Well, well, well that's a turn-up for the books and no mistake."

Chapter 16

THE DACHA TEAM FORM

Servo drove from the airport serving Astrakhan in the hired Discovery Landover. He liked the machine's power and its firm suspension. "We could have done with a few of these in Afghanistan, eh Vasily?" Servo turned to look at his partner in the back with Carla, inadvertently pulling the wheel over so the vehicle moved over the centre reservation before correcting the steer.

"Yes and watch the road!" Grabbing Servo's seat headrest, shaking his head in despair, Vasily settled back in his seat. "God preserve us from giving toy soldiers things to play with." Servo and Saied both laughed.

Carla just smiled. "Now boys behave, we have not even started this adventure yet."

They were on the motorway going north and Saied was navigating. "Coming up to the hour, should be there soon. Yes got it, only one more kilometre to go and then we turn right. Looks a tight turn so be ready, I will count down for you." Saied was enjoying this. He was relaxed and felt at home with the people around him. He was unusually shy around Carla as she radiated the sort of confidence in any company he could never match. She seemed completely at ease with herself, she had no side to her and treated everyone the same. Calming angst among the team wherever and however it appeared.

"Turn in two hundred metres. We have one hundred to go, fifty now, twenty, okay Servo turn now." Servo went smoothly through the gears and swept round the tight turn.

"What's next?"

"Cross the bridge and turn left. Then drive north for about one and a half kilometres. We should be close if not there then. The dacha is gated and walled so we shouldn't miss it," he added. "When we get there if the gate's shut I will get out and open it."

"No problem."

Shortly after two in the afternoon they swept round the pond and parked next to Tsygankov's, Land Cruiser and Mac's Jeep.

They were all impressed with the dacha's size and the rest of the estate. "Just goes to prove what I have always advocated," remarked Carla. "If you want space and a place to live you need to get out of Moscow." She gazed round. "Just look at this pad."

"Come on let's announce ourselves to the General," Vasily ordered, climbing out of the vehicle.

Tsygankov appeared at the door and waved them in. "Welcome to my home. Food, drink and then I will show you your rooms so you can settle in." He led them through the hall past the sitting room on the left and the study on the right. The generously wide corridor opened into a very large square kitchen/diner.

The smell of a goulash soup heating on the stove was being stirred by the housekeeper and had the new arrivals' gastric juices running. Tsygankov introduced the team to Tamara and Mac Szukaj, explaining their supporting roles.

Mac waved to them from the table where he was placing baskets of warm freshly baked bread on it before coming over and shaking their hands. In Servo he recognised the soldier traits, he himself exhibited when he was younger; in Saied he recognised a warrior, a hardened man but who could be trusted and would be loyal. Vasily was a different matter, a young man by Mac's measure who was like liquid mercury who could adapt to any tilt of the plate. Vasily was a man to be circumspect of, if not wary of at the very least. Carla he took to and loved instantly, she reminded him of his own beloved Tamara when she was younger.

The team sat, the men discarding their jackets onto the back of their chairs. Carla's coat was taken by Mac and hung on a hook by the door.

Tamara brought the large heated cauldron of soup to the table with a ladle.

Tamara and Mac went to make their excuses, to leave the team and Tsygankov to their meal, but the General would have nothing of it and insisted they stay to eat with them and tell the team about the country environment and places of interest they had landed in.

Once they had all filled their plates and the glasses were charged with a blood-red wine Mac began to talk to them. "Let's start, with looking at what the dacha has to offer and island it stands on."

Chapter 17

SCOPE AND TRUST

Major Brown put the 'Brigadier's Memorandum' down on his desk and smoothed the document. He sat back in his chair with his hands behind his head and the chair tipped back on two legs; he rocked back and forth, waiting for his boss to finish another article in his newspaper.

Seeing Rodney still in his chair, Robinson collapsed his paper folding it carefully for his future interrogation. "Well Rodney are you happy with the document?" Robinson quizzed.

"Good stuff sir, follows the brief in all but not a lot." Rodney's attempt at humour did not go unnoticed. "I see it is signed off by the other chiefs, but not the PM or her secretary? I wonder if we trust her completely."

"That is very astute of you Rodney. How far do you think you could throw me? Seriously if there is one woman, never mind politician, I trust it is Mrs T. It was the chiefs and I that advised her not to sign. You should know that she wanted to, that's her all over, we will not see her likes again I fear." The Brigadier's eyebrows were up showing white under the brows and his light skin under the eyes seemed to Rodney particularly drawn and paper-like. Why he should notice this now was not sure but certainly the old man did perhaps show age at times of stress.

Rodney grinned. "In that case, in the case of Mrs Thatcher I would have to throw her a very long way sir."

"There's your answer then, in Thatcher's case I do give her the benefit of the doubt that she simply didn't sign because we told her not to and she thought our signatures would suffice. Rest assured Rodney, she would have signed it of her own volition without a second thought if we had let her," the Brigadier retorted in almost a whisper.

"I can live with that, it just seems to me there is more to this than meets the eye and I don't want to go in with one hand tied behind my back."

"Fair, if not very subtle. Let's just say that with the ceasefire and peace talks there are some in the IRA who are not with the flow. In fact to be blunt they are not playing at all and these especially harder members want it all now, not tomorrow and not limited."

"Ah so this might mean, to bring some of the hard members over to the peace side, unsavoury concessions might be offered?"

"Your words not mine Rodney, but I might add than in any negotiation, the very word indicates some give and take is almost guaranteed and required to meet at an acceptable way forward for both parties." Robinson watched Rodney wrestle with the situation which he knew himself was unacceptable. "Look at it this way, your brief is limited to looking for a potential seismic shift in the attitude of the IRA and consequential future escalation of the violence with even more deadly weapons and explosives." Robinson was not annoyed at this interchange but he did need to bring it to a conclusion. "Notwithstanding your gut reservations that we may be being used, how do you feel about the mission aims?"

"I have no issues about what we are going to try to achieve. I also have no reservations about the methodology. I am naturally cautious about the mission as it should be covering ground already being attacked by our sister agencies and Military Intelligence. Ergo my gut question is still: why us, why now? Accepting only this is a watershed period in the evolution of the fight. So sir, in conclusion, we want to help. If it turns out we find something to bring this dreadful conflict to a speedier end or save lives then we must give it of our best."

"That's quite a speech for you Rodney." The Brigadier was impressed.

"Okay then, let's recap sir. We are going to major on three areas. Mission creep is not to happen without referral. The three areas are: follow the money, watch the Quartermaster and his lieutenants and monitor communication traffic, electronic or otherwise, and go and find out what our FBI brothers have to tell us."

"Good. Now your extra resources you asked for." Robinson dug into his briefcase and fished out a copied list of names and contacts. He handed it to Rodney. "The banker specialist you asked for works for the Bank of England, he was previously an in international investment and merchant banker so knows the way through the morass of bank etiquette at home and overseas. He will be briefed today. He was chosen because he is security cleared and has been used successfully before by the SIS. Mr John Brown. Here are the names and numbers of staff at 5 and 6 and MIL as well as GCHQ who are tasked to help you. Avery is coming over today to sort out the two new recruits, subject to their approval by the team and us."

"Looks good sir, everything we asked for, thank you."

"Interestingly enough it was the two new recruits that gave me the most hassle, 5 and 6 wanted to drop in their men. I wonder why?" Robinson's rhetorical question raised a laugh from them both. "How about we stretch our legs and refill our cups before we have to interview the two men."

In the tea room they found the two new recruits and the team sharing banter. "Settled in then?" Rodney questioned.

Reid typically protective moved everyone out. "Give the Major and boss some room, move out while I make them a drink." He was really saying go away and I will brief the chiefs.

"Well what do you think?" Rodney asked the question for both himself and Robinson.

"They will definitely fit in and be very useful as back-up and on recce for Sharky and Mould. By the way Mould and Sharky know them from tours in the Province they each did five tours there so know the county and love it and its people. I think it's a Celtic thing. Did we get Avery to do the trade craft with them?"

"Yes be here today," Robinson said. "Doesn't seem much point in myself and Rodney vetting them but think we would like to acquaint ourselves with them, so wheel them in once we have our tea. Which, Mr Reid, I think you volunteered to make and bring us. As you know I am not one to stand on ceremony but my Earl Grey blend does need to be made and delivered in a pot." He added over his shoulder making his way out of the tea room and back to Rodney's office, "Only one spoon for a pot that size."

Reid gritted his teeth but not in anger it was his habit and it was an icon the team relied on to know all was well.

Reid pushed the two recruits in ahead of him and the tea tray. "Sirs, your teas. I am also delivering two breathing Welshmen." His Scots accent was noticeable.

"Sit down and tell us who you are and what you are," Robinson invited who now sat at the desk leaving Rodney to half perch on the windowsill.

The men sat facing the desk, alert and at what could be taken for sitting to attention. Both dark-haired and sharp-featured, around 2 metres high, well-built and fit looking. They could have been brothers with their coal black eyes and squared-off chins. They wore dark blue single-breasted suits, white shirts and Welsh guard's ties. Their black brogues were highly polished.

The man to the left of Robinson spoke first. "I am ex-company Sergeant Major Fred Jones late of the Welsh Guards, 38 years of age. My CV, sir," he said, handing over one page of script.

"And I am ex-company Sergeant Major Lewis Jones, 39 years of age. My CV sir." He passed his single page CV over to the Brigadier.

The Brigadier ran his eyes swiftly down the pages of the men's history and accomplishments and passed them to Rodney.

"My first question is what on earth were you doing downstairs on the door with CVs like yours?"

"Truth is told sir , my long-time friend Mr Mould out there said he reckoned it would not be long before the department would need some help, so we sort of wangled it to get the post here and to be on duty whenever the Major came in."

"You're hired," the Brigadier said brightly. "That is exactly the attitude, forward planning, anticipation of future events and bold initiative we look for from team members here." Looking over his shoulder looking at Rodney he commented. "I thought this was your idea Rodney."

"So did I!" He smiled. "Makes you think though, that the staff seem to know what I am going to think before I think it?"

"It is a principle of war that is sir, to anticipate the commander's future intentions." Lewis explained.

"Okay, so what am I thinking now?" Robinson teased them.

Fred Jones answered for them both. "Why are we out so young and why didn't we stay for more rank or a commission? It was the redundancy round we got caught up in. We would both have stayed longer if we could have. Both of us, along with others would say that redundancy is a blunt tool, causing the service to lose experience and the good along with I dare say some deadwood." He looked down at his shoes. "Bloody shame sir, begging your pardon. The Queen's men we are and will always be."

"Your feelings are not unknown and are shared by many a senior officer, including yours I might add, who I know and chatted to last night." Robinson took delight in seeing their faces light up. "The Colonel was very supportive of you both and very sorry to lose you.

But you have come to a good home, in from the cold you could say, as you will find out."

"Very grateful sir we are and will do our best to not let you or the Major down."

"Of that I am sure. Now, let's see what points in these CVs are going to be of most strength to us here. Both done the sniper's course; well, it does mean that you will be competent at covert observation. Patience is often a virtue in our line of work. Also the course in escape, evasion and resistance to interrogation specialists; good stuff this. Passed the demolitions and explosives course, both passed out on the parachute course and one tour with them. Regimental boxers etc. and can use the usual PC packages. Good report writing is also part of the game. Anything you would like to add, Major?"

"No I don't think so, apart from welcome to you both. Mr Avery will be here later today to teach you trade craft. In the meantime you need to get together with Mr Reid to take you to our admin and secretariat and get you kitted and on the payroll."

Both men rose and shook hands before leaving Robinson and Rodney.

"Well what do you think, Major?"

"I would say Mould and I have good talent-spotting ability. Don't you agree sir?"

"It does seem that way, Rodney. Time will tell as ever."

Chapter 18

TSYGANKOV'S DINNER NIGHT

At seven that night the team formed in the sitting room, entering together. Tsygankov welcomed them with warm drinks of hot wine and herbs. The day had been, by Moscow standards, mild but as night fell the temperature dropped and a mist developed.

The rooms they were lodged in were spacious and warm and the whole dacha appeared to be powered by an efficient heating system with a constant temperature in whatever part of it they were.

Three, three-seater dark-blue deep leather sofas were spaced around the wood burner, and on the wall to the right of the fireplace was a large wall-mounted television set into the wall at an angle of 45 degrees with stereo built in below it. The walls were wood-lined, red cedar, and lent an atmosphere of warmth and comfort. Tsygankov himself just cleared the beams in the ceiling and seemed to shrink what was the very large room. Triple double-glazed patio windows were set to the front of the house. A hatch on the opposite wall to the right of the television opened into the kitchen. On the hearth was an oblong carpet framing the sofas and covering the wooden floor. The wooden flooring with its under-floor heating, which was carried throughout the ground floor, was warm to the feet.

They had all taken a drink of the herbed red wine they had had at lunch, which they were surprised to find out was from the grapes grown around the dacha and it made for an interesting introductory conversation with their host. They complimented him on their accommodation and his house, he refilled their glasses and then Tsygankov bid them bring their drinks into the kitchen/diner.

The thick wooden plank kitchen dining table that could sit ten people in comfort was set for five. The room was spacious although square and ran along the whole of the rear of the house. Outside the dining area was a terrace accessed through double-glazed patio doors. The terrace ran to the cliff face that overlooked the Volga as the river split into two, one run feeding the race and the other the main river. A pergola framed the area and grapevines climbed the pillars and the crosspieces. At night the patio was lit up with spotlights partly for security and partly for aesthetics.

In the kitchen area the housekeeper Tamara and her husband Mac were putting the last touches to the dinner. Mac struggled to the table with a large terrine of "*Ukha*", a warm watery fish dish thickened with potatoes and olives, at the request of Tsygankov. He placed it in the middle of the table and bid the General and the guests to sit. His wife brought over baskets of freshly baked bread which was to be a signature item during their stay.

Tamara, wringing her hands dry on a towel, explained to the table "General, gentlemen and lady the rest of the meal is in the oven and on the hob. As you wished, General, there is "*Pelmeni*" and vegetables, on the hob, with meat to the traditional Ural recipe and a few made with fish for Mr Saied. In the slow oven keeping warm are the blinis, stuffed with apple and raisins. The wine is open, so if there is nothing else we will get off and leave you to your meal?" Tamara took off her apron. "Just leave the dishes piled up. We will be in early in the morning to get breakfast and can run them through the dishwasher in no time."

"If you are sure, what can I say Tamara but thank you and to Mac of course. I will see you in the morning." He waited and watched Tamara and Mac leave then turned to the table guests. "Servo, please be good enough to pour the wine for everyone. Saied, please would you be good enough to serve the soup."

Servo got up and came round to Tsygankov with the wine and poured a taster. Tsygankov sniffed the wine, swirled it and watched the tears of wine like oil curtain run down the glass, smelled the aroma once more and held his glass out to Servo. "Fine Servo, fill up my glass please then serve the others, even though this is our own wine I like it and hope you will too. Whoever the previous owner a hundred years ago was who planted those Corsican vines here did us all a favour. As Mac said at lunch with luck this year we may be able to have our own vintage with a bespoke label."

He stood and addressed the table switching from Russian to English. "From this moment on in the confines of the dacha we will speak English, we will need to be fluent and practice makes perfect, as they say?" He raised his eyebrows. There were no challenges; although a soft groan emanated from Servo whose spoken English was the weakest of the group but on the up.

When the glasses were full and the soup dispensed Tsygankov proposed a toast. "I want to give a toast from a famous Scottish Regiment the Queen's Own Cameron Highlanders (79th of foot) whose motto was 'for King and Country!' I think if we substitute our Chairman for their King we can empathise with the simplicity of the motto. I just need to explain that their regimental hat badge carries a deer's antlers emblem. Can I ask you to rise for their toast to that icon?" Tsygankov's deep serious voice respectfully recited the toast without notes with a restrained emotion that left the guests quiet for a moment after it was done, each considering their own immediate fate to come and past encounters.

"The land of hills, glens and horses;
Where the ptarmigan thrives, and where the red deer finds shelter
As long as the mist hangs o'er the mountains and water runs in the glens,
The deeds of the brave will be remembered. Health and success forever
To the lads of 'Cabar Féidh', the Deer's Horns forever!"

When the spell was at last broken by Servo applauding the Brigadier the room relaxed and meal began. The team was hungry, yet despite the volume of food for the main course followed by the dessert, little was left over before they were all fully sated.

The talk at table had been free, covering the world as they knew it; shared experiences and countries and cultures they had visited worked in and inhabited. Of the mission they knew they had to wait for Tsygankov he would brief them soon enough.

Carla and Vasily cleared the table from the first two courses, stacking the pots and dishes on the side draining board over the dishwasher. Together they took the blinis out of the slow oven and carried them to the table while Servo poured more wine for everyone. It seemed Saied drank alcohol when in the company of those who did.

Tsygankov went to his fridge and brought out a jug of cream. "For those who would like some cream, help yourselves." Tsygankov looked round the table at the relaxed guests. They melded well, he thought as he watched them power through the dessert, Tamara would be pleased. "Anyone have a closing Toast for us to celebrate this first meal together? After all, only problem drinkers don't toast before drinking."

Vasily moved his chair out and stood before them. "Not sure this is entirely appropriate but I have been waiting for a chance to use it ever since I too visited Scotland and heard it in a Scottish pub given by an old man to others of his ilk."

"Right, thank you Vasily, hang on a moment while we get the coffee pot and the vodka. Carla could you get the pot, I will fetch the vodka." Tsygankov grabbed a couple of bottles from his store and returned to the table and poured each of them a glassful. "Right let's have that toast. If a man cannot toast his comrades with his drink then I say again he has a drinking problem!" Tsygankov ordered, paraphrasing the old Russian toasting cry

Vasily bent to pick up his vodka and stood stock-still while he gave a toast:

"For every glass and every plateful
Lord makes us forever grateful
And while no one would be ever be sinful
Let us eat and drink until we have had a skin full
So here's to thee and thine,
So here's to me and mine,
So here's to everyone we know,
The rich and poor, and high and low,

And here's to those we ought to mind,
And here's the whole of humankind
And before we leave the table
Let us toast our absent comrades if we are able,
Comrades!"

Vasily raised his glass and drank it down in one and placed it firmly upside down on the table to show it was empty.

The rest of the table rose laughing and toasted him before settling back to their chatter.

"Well done indeed Vasily," chuckled Tsygankov, looking at the captain and once again experiencing the feeling he had known him in some past life. "A budding poet I think in the making and an excellent Scots accent, quite the mimic." Tsygankov's long arm reached out down the table, upturned Vasily's glass the right way and refilled it.

Vasily took his glass and stood again, throwing back his vodka taking the fiery spirit down in one. The others gave the Russian cry of "*Na zda-ró-vye!*" following Vasily's example.

"Yes very good toast Vasily, I will get you to write that one down for me. And appropriate, oh I think so." Tsygankov waved his hand to them to refill their glasses. "Now about tomorrow. I want Carla to take you three gentlemen into the city and get yourselves kitted out as far as possible to blend into the environments you will find yourself in from time to time. Carla, I want both smart and casual for them and you. All of you at one time or another will be in England and possibly all of you in Ireland, North and South. Saied, in addition you will need to go to Split and Libya to see a contact there so you will need a smart lightweight suit as well." He flipped from his pocket a gold credit card and a pin number attached to it in Carla's name as well as a fat envelope filled with roubles which he also passed to Carla.

He continued, "Breakfast is at eight in the morning, every day. I have some duties early so I will not be joining you but on your return from shopping we will get down to basics and I will brief you on the tasks ahead. Also each of you has a new identity with legend which you will need to learn." He stood and the table went silent and they all stood in respect.

He waved to them a goodbye enjoying the moment, "Please, amuse yourselves for the rest of the evening. I will be in the study if you need to see me. Otherwise, until tomorrow then." He bowed to them and left them.

Once he closed the door to the kitchen on them, he heard them start up talking over one another, and in English, the click of bottles on glasses and laughter. "Ah what it is to be young and enthusiastic, I am not sure I ever was. Another lifetime perhaps when existence itself was a daily struggle," he thought with regret, making his way silently to his study to work on his notes for the mission.

Chapter 19

MAJOR BROWN CLEARS HIS DESK

A week later Major Rodney Brown sat at the head of the table with his team around the sides. "Good morning to you all, time to put up. The purpose of this meeting is for you to confirm our ongoing work is closed out and or handed over so we can get on with the new task. The exception of course is a small task Mould, Sharky, Mr Reid and I will handle from this morning."

He paused, placing a list of current business flat on the desk in front of himself and scattering copies down the table for the team for them to scramble for a copy. Once they each had a copy and had resettled in their seats he began by taking up his pen and said, "From the top of the list, please report."

Rodney opened his notebook and said, looking at the table towards Andrew, "The champion of each task is named against each serial; Andrew you are first to report."

They worked through the list and within a couple of hours had cleared the list, identifying a few minor gaps that needed plugging.

"Well done you lot, good outcomes. Now all bar Mould, Sharky and Mr Reid, I want the rest of you to begin to plan in detail how you are going to accomplish your various tasks allocated to you in respect of the IRA operations. We will meet in five days' time, that's the Friday morning when I and the terrible three will be back, all things being equal. Should we not be back on time, the Brigadier will chair the meeting and hear your plans." He called for the list back and declared tea break.

***

Later Rodney sat with Mr Reid, Mould and Sharky. Sharky was the first to speak. "Look boss, this job is bollocks, it's not our bag at all; it should be done by the Special Ops Group in 6. Seems we are being lemoned or set up as scapegoats if it goes wrong." Reid and Mould shifted in their seats, a gesture that Rodney took as a silent agreement with Sharky.

"Happen your right; neither is the new task we are facing, after this holiday laid on courtesy of the tax payers. Look at it positively, it does expand our remit and influence. A good job means we are more employable, just think of your pension." He paused, he could see he wasn't convincing them. "Okay, I agree it's a little out of line, but the Special Ops Group is tied up elsewhere. Just think of the poor sods we are going to get out and their smiling families when you bring them back home. And anyway the Foreign Secretary asked for us especially as I am led to understand."

"This job is going to blow our anonymity if we have our faces plastered all over the papers?" Reid had a point.

"We will just have to manage that and I think we can. I thought about it a lot and as I see it there are not going to be many if any cameras at the exchange point or along the route and when we come back. The negotiators' handlers will take the people off our hands once we get them to Mogadishu. And once we are inside the aircraft bound for Dubai we can leave our vehicles later after the circus has gone home and get to our own air transport."

"Okay, I can see you have thought this through, boss. I withdraw any reservations so let's do it, not that we were ever not." Sharky was back on side and this meant Mould too.

"Okay, to confirm the arrangements. We leave in an hour for Northolt and the Crabs will fly us out."

"You mean the Royal Air Force!" Mould cut in, he objected to the nickname.

"Yes alright the Royal Air Force," conceded Rodney, "will fly us out to Cyprus and then we change to a Royal Air Force Hercules and they fly us into Somaliland. It is a bit of a one horse airfield for those that have been there before but normally safe. From there we have a local charter, think it's the last Dakota aeroplane in service but it is anonymous. The Dakota will fly us into Mogadishu. We are picked up by a friendly warlord who takes us to the exchange. We hand over the ransom, collect the punters and come back along the same route. At

Mogadishu on the way back we hand over kidnapped people to the handlers at the airport."

"Sounds too simple?" Mould said quietly. "Something is bound to go wrong – what is plan B?"

"What's getting your goat, young Mould?" Rodney was perplexed; he had not expected Mould to push back. "We are not going in without weapons and the UN is on the ground at the airport to witness the exchange."

"As you ask boss, I had a holiday week from hell." Mould looked suitably contrite.

"You daft sod, do tell." Reid slapped the back of Mould's head.

"My other half had a list of jobs. I cracked though them hoping to get some quality time and then she thought it would be good for me to do other jobs she had thought of. Talk about mission creep, you never saw anything like it. So I'm bloody knackered and not a little pissed off."

"Serves you right you silly sod. I told you to book a week away. The jobs were just a way of ensuring next leave you take her somewhere nice. I swear you have the longest pockets of any mate I have ever known when it comes to spending a bit on a holiday. Remember the caravan you hired for us all at the seaside? It was a mile from the sea and nearest pub and in the corner of a farmer's field. No amenities. No anything." Sharky burst out laughing and so did the rest.

Mould looked sheepish. "Alright, alright! You are right on all counts, guilty." He looked at Rodney and the rest. "Sorry mates, Sharky's right it was a home goal. Won't happen again. I'll get Sharky to book me and the wife a week away next time." From the look of delight on Sharky's face it was going to cost.

Reid was still puzzling over an issue that concerned him so raised it. "Rodney, it is a query really with reference to the ransom, it is just that our policy is never to give into kidnappers let alone murdering bully-boy warlords."

"Fine, now I understand what is getting up your noses and I can set your minds at rest. There will be no ransom payment per-say."

There was a silence in the room.

"But you mentioned ransom earlier, or did my ears deceive me." Reid persisted.

"I did, a slip of the tongue. It's repaying a favour, so I suppose you could argue the ransom was paid years ago."

Chapter 20

TSYGANKOV AND CARLA

On return from the shopping trip while the men went to their rooms to sort out their purchases Carla went to see Tsygankov. Carla Kazimira Tskhovbova knocked on the study door and heard Tsygankov call in English. "Enter."

Carla took her cue and went in and spoke in English as they had been instructed, with little difficulty and little accent. "General, I wanted to return your card and of course the remainder of the roubles." She placed the card and roubles on the desk along with the receipts from the purchases in front of him.

"Did you get everything you and they needed?" Tsygankov checked with her.

"Everything. I made somewhat of a dent in the finances but good quality Westernised clothing was so expensive." Carla glanced around the study. Like the sitting room on the other side of the entrance corridor it was panelled with bookcases on two sides and patio doors to the front. Behind the General's desk were three violins in glass cases. They gleamed in the warm light. Reflections generated by the polished wood of the walls and the large knee-hole dark teak desk with its glass top reflected back from glass cabinets.

Behind the desk the three glass display cabinets, each holding a violin, drew Carla's attention to them and Tsygankov turned round following her gaze. "Ah my violins interest you Carla?" Tsygankov swivelled back, looking into her eyes.

"I am just a little surprised, General. They do look particularly fine examples."

"Violins were a passion of mine and I played quite well. It was my release from the day-to-day attrition of the job, regrettable." He held up his gloved claw of his hand. "I am no longer able to play." His internal angst against Major Brown and his crew he kept in check. "I think that is why I keep my back to them most of the time as I sit at my desk; the memory of a lost time is painful." He sighed. "But you don't want to hear about that and I can still appreciate their beauty."

"I would be interested to know more of these three violins and why you kept them if the memory is so painful?"

He looked at her for a moment. "Huh, perhaps. Take a seat I will fetch each one in turn and you can tell me what you make of my three trophies."

Carla made herself comfortable in a leather club chair while Tsygankov swivelling in his chair, rose and unlocked each of the cabinets in turn. He bought each to her in turn and let Carla hold and inspect them and pluck the strings to hear their tone.

When the violins were back in their locations and secure he returned to his desk chair and settled himself in. "So Carla, tell me what you have discovered and what you think of them."

Carla hesitated. Was this a test? "I believed all three may be Stradivarius but now I think only two of them may be. That the one on the left is original, pre-nineteenth century when they had fingerboards and necks were lengthened to take the extra tension from increased pitch of the diapason. In the middle one of the three you can see where the neck is raked back so that's a post-nineteenth century one. What makes me think they were made by Stradivari?" She brushed back her short hair and re-crossed her legs before standing and perambulating slowly round the room. "It's the warm feel grain and colour of the wood. I am led to believe it's the sun and warmth in Northern Italy where Stradivari lived and worked that gives the violin its colour tone and timbre."

"Very good analysis Carla and you are right on every count, but what of the third one?"

"Difficult. I thought originally it was from where Stradivari lived but I was being egged on by the other two violins. Now I think it is probably something quite rare, late 17th century perhaps by Pietro Guarneri and as such worth a very great deal of money, if not a King's ransom?"

"My God Carla you astound me. How do you know so much about violins?"

"Ah, well General like you I am a violin player and when young I wanted to be a luthier, a maker of violins. There was a luthier in a village where we used to stay and he taught me much about the history and the differences between the famous luthier of the past. I never forgot what he told me. But life had other directions planned for me. I nevertheless studied the master luthier and their works intently and have never quite lost my passion for the instrument and the craftsmanship that created them. So I thank you for letting me see your collection, it was a rare treat for me."

"Play me something if you like."

"What would you like to hear?"

"I think something uplifting? Noisy perhaps? Do you know any work by Donald Francis Tovey?

"Oh yes, quite well, he is a favourite of mine. How about playing the Scherzo in the second movement of his Sonata Eroica, opus 29 for you?"

"Wonderful and it would please me if you used the Stradivarius." Tsygankov was smiling as he got up to retrieve the violin and bow.

"Are you sure?"

"Absolutely, his instruments were made for playing not gathering dust." He handed the violin to Carla who took it gently and then quickly tuned it and tensioned the bow.

With a quick deft tuning and a few preparatory draws of the bow and plucking of strings to make sure all was in tune, and with a small adjustment to the top string Carla launched into the Scherzo. Carla played it faultlessly and when she had finished a silence descended on the room as the vibrations of the last note faded away.

Tsygankov clapped, shattering the mood, "Excellent. Thank you Carla, your talents are wasted in the Directorate you must ensure you keep practising, you play like the violin was made for you. Would that I had been so good, in my time." He held out his good hand for the instrument and took it and the bow from the reluctant hands of Carla who would dearly have loved to exercise the instrument for longer.

"There will be other opportunities, another time perhaps Carla?" Tsygankov could well understand the younger woman's disappointment at not being able to play for longer.

"The pleasure was all mine. Just to have the opportunity to play one of the master violins has long been an ambition of mine. It just felt, well, so right."

"I have others, 20 or so by the masters eminently playable that would interest you. There are others as well, several in need of attention. My collection is smaller than it was; I did sell some of my collection to part fund this dacha but those I sold were of no consequence. You can look at the remaining collection and play any of them at any time. They are stored in an environmentally controlled part of the wine cellar. The door is to the left of the stairs as you descend into the basement. Visit when you can, I will show you around. But now it's time for work I am afraid. We will continue our discussion on violins and the luthier at some other time," Tsygankov said almost with regret but indicated the session was over. "Please go and round up the team, it is time to tell them why they are here. Tell them to be in this study in half an hour."

Chapter 21

TSYGANKOV OUTLINES THE MISSION TO THE TEAM

When they arrived in the study Tsygankov had put up a whiteboard on a trestle and maps adorned the walls. Each of the four chose a club chair and sat waiting expectantly.

Tsygankov handed out an operations order with the mission defined and the detail tasks of each of them defined.

In addition each had a pack of documents with their own individual "legends" which they would need to learn to convince anyone who had cause to question them about their identity. The legends were good enough to fool anyone who may want to know who they were and where they had spent their existence from childbirth to date. Passports, licences, money and credit cards were also contained in the package and matched the name from the legend.

"Read what you have and I will be back in an hour with coffee. No notes are to be taken and the documents don't leave this room yet, I will direct what you can take with you," Tsygankov warned before leaving them to their studies.

When the General returned, the room was buzzing; he frowned and the team subsided into silence. Behind him came Tamara with a tray of hot drinks and sandwiches.

When she left, the team looked to the General expectantly.

He smiled unexpectedly. "As you see you have kept your given names almost, but your background has been changed to suit your task, it's a twist but will prevent one of you or more inadvertently blurting out the wrong name. Jean, I am afraid your surname Saied was too risky so, lady and gentlemen, let me introduce Jean Salomon and so to the tasks for each of you. Mr Salomon, would you please do the honours and pour the tea and hand out the food.

"Curious choice of my name, General, you know of 'King Salomon II,' of course?" Jean said moving to the tea things.

"Funny that was why I chose the name Salomon. I was looking for a name for you Jean, and was reading a historical article at the time about King Salomon II. For the unenlightened of you, in 1811 King Salomon II of Eastern Georgia wrote to Napoleon offering to bring in Turkey and others onto Napoleon's side to help him defeat Russia. As you say, curious choice of name but I thought interesting and memorable."

He turned to them all. "During this phase and the build-up to the mission and its execution on the target, which may not be fully divulged until nearer the day in case of the unlikely event the target is compromised unknowingly?" He looked at the team seriously then smiled unexpectedly. "And so now let us address ourselves to the overview of the operation and immediate and individual tasks.

"The overview is simple. We want to deal a blow to our English cousins. A blow that will set them and their capability back several years and rid us of a special secret service team at the same time. This team has interfered with our operations over the years and caused untold damage including the ousting of our well-embedded KGB and GRU officers from the UK in 1971 and 1977, as well as the rolling up of our men and networks in the USA. They called it 'the year of the spies.' They should not be underestimated, and even captured me once. Thankfully as you can see I was rescued by no lesser person than our own General Polyakov." He was thoughtful for a moment. "We were young then, not as wise as we are now. On the other hand not sure the outcome would have been so successful if we had to think about it."

He paused for the mission's aim to sink in to the team. "Now to achieve this mission we need several things: first the product, odourless Semtex H. Semtex H contains PETN 40.9% RDX 41.2% a binder of styrene-butadiene 9%. It has a plasticizer n-octyl phthalate, tributyl citrate 7.9% less than the original mix but since it is easy to mould well, an antioxidant N-phenyl-2-naphthylamine 0.5, it should have a dye 0.5% Sudan I (red-orange to yellow) but the batch we are interested in is not dyed almost colourless."

He drew a breath. "Next we need the help of others who are committed to hurting the British. In this case I have got an agreement in principle from members of the real IRA, the RIRA to support us. They are committed to continue the struggle and will have no truck with the ongoing peace negotiations."

He smiled again, drawing circles with his index finger on the top of his desk almost coyly. "Of course by us I mean the real IRA think we are Russian nationalists who are terrorists ideologically driven to hurt any entity that threatens Mother Russia. Whatever or whoever they believe in private we are, they are happy enough to support us." He eyeballed them. "There is no connection to the KGB. The initial contact between them was by a deniable asset who has since been sent away for the duration." He looked directly at Servo and Carla. "They are expecting the next contact face-to-face to be made by us and it will be on their turf in Ireland."

"Now the other products we need are initiators and detonators, all the rest of the paraphernalia we will need can be bought in the country and will be put together by the IRA bomb makers."

He looked round the study at the faces of the team, they were stunned as they took in the enormity of the mission they had gotten themselves involved in. But he comforted himself with the thought that none had protested and none had avoided his gaze.

He did not feel he had to justify the mission but wanted to emphasise its importance. He talked to them for some time on the need to degrade the enemy and why, without telling them the target, he told them of the possible consequences and outcomes they would achieve if they were successful. He asked for questions.

"Leaving the mission to one side, what can we know about the opposition we may be trying to evade from time to time?" Vasily was interested and it showed as the others nodded agreeing with his question.

"How long do you have," said Tsygankov lightly.

"As long as you can afford to give us," was Jean Salomon né Saied's reply.

"So be it. Well principle. And briefly, we will want to fight shy of what they call their MI5, they are a secret intelligence service although we think of their sister service MI6 as the SIS. MI5 is quite old as an organisation. Nearing a hundred years old, they did well against the Germans and the others but did not quite have the same success against GRU and KGB. Their sister services the secret intelligence service or MI6 and GCHQ is really the enemy of the GRU and KGB."

Tsygankov warmed to his subject. "In MI5 until recently they operated both at home and were almost worldwide, but the SIS MI6 seems to be taking this over the overseas commitments, which makes sense as they are run or funded at least from the Foreign Office, so we believe. Notwithstanding, in 1971 the mass expulsion of GRU and KGB personnel from London in 1971 gave the British Secret Services their break to get on top of our spying efforts. MI5 still have a presence but there are strains between the two organisations over territory. Now MI5 as we speak are stretched not only with the Irish problem but all the other terrorist groups, not to mention Sikh extremists and a Chinese containment problem and others that have and continue to spring up." He paused. "We believe the paramilitaries are dramatically increasing their numbers on the UK mainland, not only that but adding soldiers to the core, skin-heads thugs etc. This is good and bad for us. We need to ensure we are only involved with the real IRA, so we can't be betrayed by some undisciplined loose-mouthed drunken thug. It will be up to them if they use them for muscle, but in that case we will not be present in person. I don't want you compromised or discovered."

He refilled his tea cup. "Two further or perhaps three of these organisations need to be understood. The first is Military Intelligence; they are good at what they do and a threat to the IRA in that context. 14 Intelligent Groups in Northern Island have a long reach. They have various black ops running in the province and Southern Ireland and run informers, some at quite high levels within the IRA. The next is the Metropolitan Police. They are being readied to take over the mantel of anti-terrorism within the sovereign borders of Great Britain in a few years' time perhaps, or so it is reported. There is a branch SO13 that is the anti-terrorist of the Met. Now bear in mind the Metropolitan Police Authority is the largest police force in the UK and is split into 4 branches with a Deputy Commissioner over each of them. The specialist branches cover the whole of the UK in support of the smaller forces. Any of the 4 can hurt us including the local police force. Lastly there is a small group that is like an octopus; its tentacles reach into all the other organisations. It is welcomed by them and trusted by the others. They see it as their safety valve and a sweeper-up of any mission that either does not sit well in one place or another or they don't want to touch for whatever reason."

He could see he had their attention. "This small group of professional dedicated individuals led by an old brigadier guards general, ably abetted by his deputy Major Rodney Brown ex-Special Forces and a handful of old soldiers, have over the years created many problems and havoc for many and for the KGB in particular. They seem to live a charmed life. They say old soldiers never die, they just go to hell." His voice was as ever soft and calm. "It would do us all a great favour if they ceased to exist. In my experience it is the people, either individuals or teams not the organisations that are important."

"I would be remiss if I didn't mention some of their technology and how that is important for us to understand. GCHQ is, as far as we are concerned, like an eavesdropper – that is to say they monitor communication traffic and have a computer with software that analyses messages, honing in on keywords. So we will need to be careful and will have to have some innocuous codes for our operational matters. More of this later. They do also have name and facial recognition at key entry points to the country and share this with Ireland. The special branches of both countries work together. But you are all fresh faces to Britain with the exception of Vasily who I am sure is sure-footed enough to escape being photographed."

"But if we are using our own names will not that be dangerous?" Servo queried.

"Good question, but as you are travelling on Australian passports the link between you and your name as you are not travelling on a Russian passport will be broken, but always bear in mind the danger of facial recognition if you are photographed, we simply at this stage don't know how good their system is. I also want to remind you, dangerous as the authorities are to your liberty, the RIRA are the greatest threat to your wellbeing. They will not hesitate to kill you if they think you are a threat to them. They are extremely dangerous people but let's hope, in this instant, to others, not us." He smiled to lighten the moment.

He then turned to each individual and gave them an overview of the task they would be involved in and needed to carry out.

Before turning to Jean he settled himself comfortably in his high-backed brown hide leather chair behind his desk. He put his arms on the chair arms, his head back and half closed his eyes. He concentrated on how he was going to pass a lot of information logically and quickly but above all with both enthusiasm and humour.

"Jean and all of you, we have around three months to D-Day. Now Jean, phase one of your involvement I think you are going to like. You leave the day after tomorrow. Your first stop is Bratislava. Hire a car and go to meet the contact in Split. I have allowed a day for the drive down. Once in Split, go to the hotel Jadran on Sustipanski facing the marina. The contact will meet you and take you a safe area and will show you the consignment of Semtex we pre-ordered. Once you confirm it is the right product by scrutinizing the lab report against the specification and testing a sample, the contact will arrange for a test firing from a piece of the Semtex you select. Once the test is successful, the contact will drive you and the product back to Split. At Split one of our own agents will help you load the Semtex on to a boat, if not preloaded, well wrapped and sealed in oilskin into a specially fashioned fuel tank on this boat. One-time seals will be used so you can check later the consignment has not been tampered with." Tsygankov opened the drawer to his desk and passed a picture of the boat to Jean. "The boat will be driven from Split into the Canal de Midi in France by the agent. A good boat and fit for both the Mediterranean and its vagaries; it can be pretty rough at times but the boat is fast enough to make landfall before mishap. Most importantly it draws only one and a half metres, a draft that will allow it to navigate the Canal du Midi, entering the canal at the Port of Setes, southern France. The boat will be moored at Setes Marina, plus four days from leaving Split."

Tsygankov consulted some notes he had before him. "During those four days the boat is in transit you have to get back to the airport in Croatia and fly to Libya to meet the Libyan contact, a colonel in their Secret Services and confirm with him that the list of items we asked for in early January have been dispatched and received by the Quartermaster of the IRA. The list of items is in the pack. Micro ATUs (automatic timing units) mini pulse switches and detonators, vehicle tracking equipment, initiators, detonators etc. You have to see the contact, sort out issues if the order has not been met in full and then travel to Port Setes to meet the agent at the marina. Jean, it is not absolutely essential, that you have to have two people to navigate the canal but it is strongly advised for a swift passage night and day." He paused, smiled. "You have about 130 miles to go with a maximum speed of 8kmh and you also have to slow passing other boats. Restful you might think, not quite. Before you get to your destination in Toulouse you will go through 50 lock gates taking you and the boat to a height of 190m before descending through though another 15 locks to Saint Saviour Toulouse at a height of only 50 odd metres. Quite a descent. I know you will research the canal but here is a statistic – it takes about half an hour to get through a lock gate. So allow an hour. And it is also important to know some if not most are only working dawn to dusk. Not the greatest time of year for daylight; on the other hand the traffic should be light. So I have a target time of two weeks for the trip in the canal with an additional week for what ifs." He smiled at Jean who was grinning.

Jean was very pleased with the trust and the opportunity he had been given. "Thank you, General, for a great adventure. I will see places and experience cultures I never thought was possible."

Tsygankov nodded, pleased. "Full details of your task later, when we shall have a one-to-one discussion of your mission in detail." He looked at the rest of the team. "Same applies to the rest of you."

"Vasily, your task is to find out where the regiment, I will discuss with you later, will be hiring their marquee for their annual summer ball. Find out all you can, as we intend to hijack the firm and its kit and set up the tent with the help of manpower from the IRA, but with an added surprise." He consulted his notes again. "And to hire various safe houses and procure cars and vans, separate from those that our liaison resident staff member at the embassy in London will have set up ahead of time. There is also a list of items to buy, including a camper van which we will need to modify. We will speak later, but in any case be ready to travel the day after tomorrow."

He turned to Carla and Servo. "Your task is to meet the IRA contact that has been set up in Ireland. They will need to supply the muscle to erect the marquee and sort the bomb kit to remotely detonate our surprise. You have three weeks to meet and negotiate with the IRA; after that you collect the camper van from Vasily and drive to the continent to meet Jean with the Semtex. A man and woman travelling together is a better combination than two men."

He let the effect of what he had just laid on them to sink in. "Okay, any questions?"

Carla asked, "What about Jean and the agent on the boat?"

"Jean will make his own way back to UK flying from Toulouse to London and make his way to Vasily wherever he is then. The agent will take the boat back to the Med."

Servo the soldier was troubled. "General are we going to bomb the officer corps of a complete regiment?"

Tsygankov was still. "Not just a regiment, a corps and their guests."

Vasily sensing Servo's reticence and to show he too had reservations asked, "Sir, there will be collateral damage: wives, friends etc."

Tsygankov was resolute. "Yes there is likely to be some, including the key members of a little known group from their secret services."

Saied looked down and shaking his head slowly added, "Major Brown I suppose."

Tsygankov was inwardly annoyed but didn't show it, he appreciated the team had been given a task that was unpalatable. He did understand that and they would need time to rationalise in their own minds that the mission was on balance important to Russia. "Indeed Jean, the Major. A fitting end to a troublesome competitor and we feel a way of degrading the effectiveness of the enemy. The IRA will take the blame as there will be no link to us by the time the event takes place."

Carla was the last to speak. "An audacious plan General, not as straightforward as it seems I think. I can see why we will need to work together if we are to achieve the mission in the time frame. It will be a great challenge for us as a team in a new environment."

Tsygankov took this remark from Carla as a positive sign, he had got through what had seemed to him to have been at worst a mini revolt or at least a push back. He decided to pass over the uncomfortable moment. He could see from the body language of the team that they were still with him and more importantly intrigued with the mission. He took the decision to keep up the momentum of the meeting and to give out the timings for the one-to-ones. "Servo and Carla we will meet in half an hour to go over your detailed tasks. Vasily, come to see me plus two hours and Jean if not after lunch first thing tomorrow for your one-to-one sessions. Let us see how we get on with the first two one-to-ones. I don't want to rush the meetings as once you're out in the field it may not be always convenient to talk," having said that, he pulled out of his desk four mobile phones, "We have satellite phones for you. They are encrypted devices so you can feel free when talking to the number set in the memories which are all of yours and mine too. I have a communication centre in the basement and satellite communication system there. To make un-encrypted calls you simply press this icon on the phones." He went round the team showing them the button to press. "Just in case, I've set the dacha landline in too, but that is not encrypted so be careful what you say if you have to use it over an open line. Last but not least," he brought out from the back of the desk four laptops. "These are iris activated. Again satellite machines and encrypted. So when we have our sessions I will show you how to set the iris security up with you, if you need help. They are otherwise all set up with the normal programmes you would expect loaded and email etc."

He smiled as the team gathered their belongings. "Now it's time to get your heads down and learn your legends and sort yourselves out. I will test you on them when we meet. Right away with you, thank you for your attention. You can take your papers with you and take your cups and plates back to the kitchen please."

Tsygankov collapsed into his chair at the desk after they had gone. He was not sure if he had expected Servo to push back and certainly not Vasily, or perhaps not? But positively he convinced himself they had accepted the task and would carry it out well he was sure.

After a minute he went to the patio doors and stepping through them to the grounds, he shivered even though the day was mild. He looked around at all he had created and felt at peace. He stepped round the lake taking in its tranquil surface. He saw his own reflection in the dark waters, it was gaunt and unlovable. He sighed cursing his vocation, great height and physic that had seemingly barred him from finding a lifelong companion and now his claw of a hand.

He smiled to himself thinking that on the other hand he had had a good life and was rich enough in retirement to do whatever he wanted. He broke his reverie and looked away from the lake surface at his developing garden and vines stretching into the distance. He could hear the Volga rushing by through the race and fancied he could smell the river and hear it murmur as it lapped by the island. He walked to a side gate on the west side of the garden and punched in the code on the gate security pad to release the lock. He went through it leaving it open. He wandered down to the long beach and amused himself by trying to find interesting shaped driftwood.

He spent some time picking up, and discarding specimens of driftwood until he found what he was looking for. A three-foot bleached, twisted and gnarled branch. He collected it and made his way back to the garden. Carla and Servo found him strolling round the plants looking intently at his grounds. They stood respectfully at a distance until they caught his eye.

Servo ever slightly in awe of the tall General was also conscious that Tsygankov was carrying the full responsibility for what he felt privately was a dangerous adventure as any situation he had ever found himself in. "Sir, it's time."

Tsygankov looked up, waving them forward towards the study as he strode purposefully after them. When he caught them up he said, "Sorry you had to come and find me but I must admit I get lost in this land and I was just thinking when this is over, my time with the KGB will be at an end, I may get a few sheep and a couple of pigs. Chickens are a must. And a dog I think."

"Definitely need to get a dog, General, and a few cats to keep the rodents at bay and birds off the fruit," Carla added supportively.

Both Carla and Servo were surprised Tsygankov had let them into to his domestic inner thoughts but they didn't show it.

Chapter 22

THE JOURNEY TO SOMALIA

The flight from North Holt to RAF Akrotiri for Rodney and his team was unremarkable. They were met when they landed and immediately transferred on emerging from the VC10 into the waiting hold of a Hercules. The Hercules load master was already on board and waved them into the body of the aircraft.

The rest of the Hercules' crew joined shortly afterwards and introduced themselves. The aircraft captain, a squadron leader, explained the route they would take to Somaliland and the duration of the flight and apologised for the lack of comfort. The aircraft was on heavy drop missions and cargo space was cleared of seating for the cargo lifts.

They made themselves as comfortable as they could in the rigging and anything else that they could find and got a few hours' sleep.

When they arrived after a bumpy flight and landing, Rodney and his team clambered down from the Hercules stiff and hungry. They thanked the crew and arranged to call them back when they had a time for pickup. Sitting among the cargo and net seats was not their idea of luxury travel, but they had been there before so nobody minded.

Mould did remark that, "He would like to see any other civil servant have to put up with what they did." He meant his comment it as a team thing, a joke.

Reid didn't see it that way. "You still got a mood on. Man up."

Mould laughed. "Got you." Rodney and Sharky laughed.

Reid could see he had missed the point. "Silly sod, I owe you one for that." And playfully he pushed Mould on the shoulder.

True the crew chief had offered tea during the flight just before they touched down hard at Somaliland airport in a cloud of dust and sand. All the team grabbed a few bottles of water without being told as they left the aircraft. Rodney noticed and was pleased to see them take the water as it meant they were already switching on to the mission. Small things like that would mean the difference between failure and success.

Early March and the heat was already oppressive and the smell of Africa was overwhelming. The airport seemed to consist of long runs of mounded earth bunds to divide the various aircraft parking pans, a 1960's terminal in the far distance that the passengers had to take a bus to be processed.

Waiting in a Land Rover to greet them was the British consul and an local airport immigration officer.

"Brown," Rodney introduced himself offering his passport.

The immigration officer took it and beckoned the other three of Rodney's team to hand over their documents. He said nothing but looked through the documents with little interest and then at the consul knowingly. "They are going on in the Dakota and will return later and fly back with the RAF, is that the situation?" The consul looked at Rodney who nodded.

The immigration officer handed back the documents, "In that case, happy hunting to you but don't be late on the day you return, the airport is closed at night." With that he handed back the passports saluted and left the group calling up a lift from a passing bus.

Rodney looked at the consul, a tall gangling man with white thinning hair. The consul introduced himself and Rodney was surprised to hear a Midlands' accent. "I'm John William Brown Consul, for the moment at least. Been doing some work here for HMG and as the regular consul is away today I was deputised to meet you. So if you need anything just ask, call me Bill."

"Think we are fine Bill, just need to find the Dakota in this jungle of mounds," remarked Rodney smiling as he looked carefully around the area, at tailplanes showing above some of the mounded bunds. A breeze stirred the dust making them all squint.

"Sorted, your plane is at the back of the airport area when you are ready I will drive you over. Do your know Alex your pilot?"

"Not yet, is he good?"

"Oh yes and as you will no doubt hear he looks after his plane like a pet. He is a Welshman despite his name, which is McGuiness. Been around Africa for 30 years with his plane and been in more trouble spots than he should. Don't know what you're doing but if it's trouble you could not have a better man to ferry you around," Bill Brown stated, not looking to know any more out of natural curiosity, most would have. Rodney analysed this lack of curiosity wondering if it was a product of Bill's HMG background or just good sense and was grateful not to have to elaborate.

"Mr Reid, would you and the other two collect the bags and we will be off." Rodney chatted to Bill for a while about the country before climbing into the Land Rover, grateful for its air-conditioning, to wait as the other arrived and climbed into the truck with the heavy bags.

They drove round the airport and Rodney looked at the scrubby land and stunted trees. Local people in their coloured clothing worked on the land here and there and could be seen carrying on their heads bundles of possessions as they arrived and left the airport. Brightly painted old and battered African buses trolled to and fro along with rusting taxis and bicycles. Despite the activity the airport had a deserted forgotten atmosphere to it.

The old Dakota loomed up high and proud being inspected carefully by a stocky built white-haired man around 60, burnt bronze by the sun. He was standing by the Dakota checking an engine cowl. When he saw the Land Rover pull up he broke off his inspection and strode towards them removing his sweat-stained bush hat grinning showing a row of strong white teeth. "You must be my party for Mogadishu." His voice was deep and strong with a hint of his Welsh accent noticeable. With a nod he acknowledged Bill Brown who waved back.

Rodney clambered down from the Land Rover followed by the rest of the crew. "That's us, Alex I take it."

"That's me, boy – jump on board, lads, and we can get going. You must be the boss man?" he enquired of Rodney.

"That's me."

"Right you can ride up front with me, the rest of the crew can spread out around the rest of the cabin. As agreed you are my sole charter there and back." He checked himself. "Bill, you coming for a ride?"

"Thanks Alex not this time, got responsibilities to attend to. Call me on the way back and I will meet you." With that he returned to his vehicle and waved as he drove away.

"Well Alex, we are in your hands now."

Rodney asked Alex if Bill often took trips with him. Alex tapped the side of his oft time broken nose, his eyes crinkling in amusement. "Well son if you don't know, it is not for me to speculate."

Rodney stared after Bill, clearly not the simple soul he appeared; he made a mental note to check him out when they got back.

Settled and door closed, Alex fired up the aircraft. Rodney stared out of the side cockpit window at the wing and its engine running up. Alex completed his checks. Been in one of these before, Rodney?"

"A few times, in another life with a parachute strapped to my back. How did you get her?"

"Long story but in brief she was flying in Burma 1945 with the Canadian Air Force RCAF 435 Squadron, my father was a crew chief with the RAF seconded to the Canadians and transferred to the Canadian Air Force after the war following his beloved aircraft to Canada and took the family with him. He retrained as a commercial pilot and when the time came to retire he took the plane along with him, we bought it and used it as a commercial venture. When he passed on he left a few bob and I had some money saved up, I brought it over here, all 64 feet of it, with its 95ft wingspan and twin 1200HP engines. Had some extra fuel pods added which extended its 1600-mile range to 3000 miles for the trip across the Atlantic. That was an epic trip. It was just me flying along with my earthly belongings. Did some chartered work in the UK and Europe for a short while. But what I really wanted was Africa. Africa has been in my blood since I was a kid in short trousers, don't know why. Travelled here, got in with your lot and the yanks and with other charters – been a good living for me. Not many parts of Africa I have not been to over the years" He puffed his cheeks out. "Here goes."

Alex flicked the switches and started the other engine. Once the engines were run up, Alex added a little power taxying until he brought the plane round to face the runway.

Getting clearance from the airfield control tower, he taxied a short way and then applied the brakes and pushed on the power. The old craft shook and Rodney glanced at Alex who smiled back. Alex eased the brakes off and the aircraft rumbled down the runway, gathering speed until the Dakota bellied off and into the air. "We made it again then, my beauty," he laughed, patting the control consul, looking at Rodney briefly as he brought the plane round to fly south to Mogadishu. "Do not worry, young sir, she is as good as new – only 30,000 hours on the engines and frame, or to put it another way around 5 million miles. She's good for three times that if she's looked after." He paused correcting the flight path before adding seriously. "And I do."

Rodney watched the land rush beneath them and the shadow of the plane bobble over the contours of the landscape. Small settlements came and went and the droning of the engines nudged him into sleep. After a while he felt Alex shake him awake, "Time to prepare yourself, son." Alex was out to sea coming round to the north in a wide sweep, and then rushing along the coast into the shoreline of Mogadishu airfield. "Sea looks inviting today but don't be fooled. It's full of sharks, just like the warlords of this benighted country." Alex pulled the undercarriage down and Rodney heard the satisfying clunk as the wheels locked into place. His first impression of the airfield was of a low airport abutting the sea, poorly maintained buildings and wide expanses around the airfield until the city edged up to it. A few broken and abandoned airframes littered the outer perimeter of the facility and other flights in that day were lined up near but not too near to the terminal.

Alex joined the cue and waited for the steps to appear. Rodney unstrapped himself and went back to see the team, by the looks of them they too had slept the journey, "Cannot blame them. It has been a protracted journey overall," he thought to himself.

"Ready."

"Ready as we will ever be," grunted Sharky. "Could eat a horse I am so hungry." Nobody disagreed.

Alex saw them off the aircraft and addressed them all before he waved them towards the terminal building.

He lifted his Welsh voice above the airport noise. "Remember, my gentlemen, this is Somalia and trust no-one but your minder and keep an eye on him too. I will be waiting for you, engines running, when you return." He waved them away.

Customs and immigration were as ever chaotic in a third world airport, even though the warlord's minder fast-tracked them through with much shouting and backhanders as they were passed from one official to another.

There was a crush of people around them at all times and it was claustrophobic in the extreme for the team. They were glad to emerge into the heat and hubbub of excited people who thronged the entrances and exits of the terminal, each one shouting to another for what Rodney had no idea. The heat although oppressive was bearable after the terminal.

The outside area of the terminal was ringed with a concrete high wall and guard posts with armed men who double or triple manned each post. A country at war with itself and the only quick exit to sanity was the airport. Rodney hoped that they would have no issue getting back in through the exit entrance rabbit run manned by local police.

The minder extracted them from airport and through a final check point fifty yards further on from the rabbit run. This check point was manned by Mogadishu local militia. The local militia started to give the team a hard time, pushing them around and making grabs for the bags which Rodney's men held on to, until the minder shouting pointed up the road at the heavily armed jeeps of his warlord. The militia fell back with something that sounded like an apology.

Reid expressed the thoughts that were running through all their minds. "Don't think this place is on the list of favourite tourist destinations these days," and then. "What a fucking shame, it had so much potential."

They found themselves thankfully outside the militia cauldron in a vacuum of calm. On the road just outside were five four-wheel vehicles lined up waiting for them. The front two had open truck backs with 50 calibre machine guns mounted and half a dozen men festooned with bandoleers of bullets for the replenishment of the curved magazines for their AK machine guns.

The other three four-by-fours were personnel carriers with tinted windows.

They were split into two parties, Rodney and Reid were allocated the middle vehicle and Sharky and Mould into the last one but two of the vehicle convoy. Before they entered the vehicles, after the experience with the militia, Reid opened the packs they had brought and handed out the weapons. A side pistol for each man and short Israeli Uzi machine pistol with six magazines apiece. Reid had decided on the Uzi. He rated the weapon highly after working with it as a very young soldier attached to the Israeli Special Forces, shortly after the Uzi had been introduced to them in 1954.

Rodney could feel the eyes of the warlord's minder on them and was seen to disapprove and showed some unexpected nervousness. It didn't seem the minder had expected the team to be armed and tried to protest. Reid gave him the death stare and he backed down. "Weapons tight gentlemen," Reid hissed through his teeth. The minder shrugged, slapping Reid on the shoulder accepting the inevitable. The four men loaded magazines into their hand guns and Uzis and cocked before entering the vehicles.

Rodney's vehicle was not empty. The warlord sat quietly smoking in the corner of the passenger seat. The air-conditioned vehicle was a relief as ever after the heat and Rodney and Reid scrambled alongside the Somali. "Welcome to Somalia." The warlord's English was good and without accent, his voice had a deep baritone quality to it. "Major Brown, let me introduce myself, please call me Simon. Our African names are generally incomprehensible to the European ear." He held out his hand which Rodney and Reid shook.

They could both feel the strength of the handshake and his brown intelligent eyes read them quickly. He relaxed, liking what he saw; like any good soldier he had to sum up men quickly, 3 seconds to determine friend or foe was all it took. He could, he had decided, he could trust these two whites, which was important for the exchange ahead.

"The day is getting late so we are going to my secure compound about a mile up the road, there we will eat and drink and get an early night as we will be leaving at dawn in the morning."

"Thank you for your offer of hospitality, I was rather hoping to get the transfer done today," Rodney said.

Simon could see the disappointment of the faces of the two men. "Rodney, it will be dark in an hour or so. The exchange point could be three hours at least away up country depending on the road conditions. Trust me, we don't want to bumble around the bush in Somalia after dark."

"Good point Simon," said Reid agreeing, "and good sense, and I for one am ready for a shower and a proper meal."

"Don't worry, Rodney, if we leave at dawn around 5 AM we can do the whole exchange thing tomorrow. I have stood up the hostage handlers who will take the hostages off our hands and their air transport to meet us tomorrow afternoon. I will also ensure your plane is ready and gets away quickly. You need to be back at your staging airport before dark," Simon explained seriously. "Although we all know Alex, your pilot, and don't think the normal rules apply to him, well not very often. He will get you back and landed even if it's pitch black when you get there." Simon chuckled.

Rodney and Reid only had a few moments to take in the environment and the road and people around them before they turned a corner into a narrow road and into a five-metre high walled compound. They entered the compound through a well-spaced and guarded double external and internal solid gate arrangement. The area between the gates was big enough to take the five vehicles comfortably. The inside gates remained closed until the outer gates were shut and secured. Inside the compound some 500 metres square where guard towers were seen every 250 metres and at the corners, all of which were manned with armed guards overlooking the 5-metre reinforced concrete walls."

Reid whistled. "This is some secure compound, Simon?"

"Indeed, it was an old army transport depot amongst other things. It does very well for me. The barrack block's over there for my men, although some as you can see prefer to fabricate their own shelter-type houses against the compound's central dividing wall. The wall separates the working area from the administrative and logistics stores area. This means the shelters enable their wives and women to be with them. I don't mind, it gives the men something more to fight for when we are attacked. Oh we are frequently before you ask." He paused. "But not I think tonight, they know we have guests and will be extra alert."

"How many men do you have, Simon, in this place?" Reid asked as Mould and Sharky joined them carrying the bags.

"At any one time around 120 fighters, another 50 or so domestic staff of course and my business staff." He pointed out two large warehouses and parked oil road tankers. Old dismounted road tanker barrels and some fabric oil tanks "I have an import export business for general stores, machinery oil etc., plus fuel reserves for the airport. It is profitable. Yes, before you ask, arms too." He swung round. "But we need to be more interested in my house, what was the old army headquarters building where you will stay tonight. Come get your showers over quickly, the food's almost ready and I bet you could do with a cool local beer. You will probably want several beers by the looks of you?" The team were sweating freely and the dark patches under their arms gave evidence of being hot and bothered.

The house was protected by sandbag Sanger's to the front which would give protection to the fighters if the house was attacked. The first 2 metres of the house wall were similarly protected by sandbags. Rodney and the team noticed this and looked to one another. The preparations of the defences meant the warlord took the threats to himself and his men seriously.

They were shown up to the top floor and distributed two to a room. The beds were made up and toiletries and towels were laid out on the bed. At the windows, blast minimising net curtains were hung to prevent flying glass in the event of a bomb attack.

In the distance they could hear intermittent automatic fire from time to time. But nothing that was near enough to worry them.

After Rodney and the others had showered and cleaned themselves up, the team met on the open veranda area just outside the house entrance. A few chairs, benches and tables made a recreation area under the spreading branches of the trees which gave cover from the African sun which was now beginning to set. It would soon be dark and quickly at this latitude.

The sounds of Mogadishu were all around them, echoing off the compound walls. In the stillness of the compound a human hubbub reached them at times from the fifty thousand or so souls in a refugee camp reaching from the shore to the eastern wall of the compound. The spicy smell of African food cooking, whether coming from the house or from outside, reminded them they were hungry.

The four men sat quietly waiting for their host and their dinner, each lost in the thought of how many times they had waited for the action to begin in this place or that. Mentally they prepared themselves for the mission tomorrow.

As the dark descended they could see mobile-armed guards strolling around the compound. The team looked at each other. "Think we might be safer here than in our own back garden back home," Sharky remarked.

Reid grunted. "Do you think so, I don't," he leaned forward, elbows on the table. "Look all of you, not accounting for a wavering man who has been bought by another warlord for money, and this is Somalia where anything could happen at any time. Just make sure you are ready and that Uzi I gave you doesn't leave your side." He sat back.

The other three looked at him and Sharkey nodded. "Happen you're right Mr R. Time to switch on."

"Good lad. From now on we watch each other's back, get in the role, from now on. I want us to move as though we could come under fire at any time, so think about field's fire and crossing each other fields of fire at all time, it's only for 24 hours and even you lot of old boots as you are should be able to manage that." Reid was relentlessly firm with his orders to them, they knew he would not countenance any dead men on his watch if he could help it.

"Got the message," confirmed Rodney, and Mould and Sharky nodded.

The lights in the seating area went on and Simon appeared with a tray of beer. "I thought we might eat out here, as it is another fine night in Somalia."

Chapter 23

TSYGANKOV TALKS TO SERVO AND CARLA

They were sat together in the General's study around the desk. On the desk were maps of Ireland, England and France from large ones showing the main arterial routes to two halves to maps at town and street level. He also passed them the latest edition book of road maps for the three countries in large format.

"Just so I am clear. Let me fully understand this General," quizzed Servo, his voice deep and serious. "We are to go to Lanesborough in southern Ireland, rent a cruiser on the river and fish." He swivelled one of the maps round and stuck his finger on the town. "And wait to be contacted by the IRA."

"In one, Servo! IRA linkman, Liam O'Neil is the man who should be contacting you amongst others; his boss is known as the Quartermaster and addressed as Q. Once you are contacted, the task is to persuade him of our credentials and commitment and that we have a credible plan which we need their help to execute."

Tsygankov added slowly, "Once O'Neil is happy with your credentials it is likely he will take you to meet the Quartermaster, but if he hesitates you need to play the resources card. In this context Jean is our ace in the hole. By the time you meet O'Neil, Saied will have carried out his first task and the load manifest of Semtex. There is enough for both of us and for them for a couple of year's mayhem. That's entry fee into the IRA plus the items we had landed with the last shipment they received from Libya. A copy of that manifest is included in your papers and should help with the proof of who you are."

Tsygankov paused and then continued. "What we don't want to do is give O'Neil the target that needs to be held back for whoever the IRA nominates as the task commander."

Carla was thoughtful. "What are these particular men like? From everything I know of them they are very cautious; you did say they were dangerous people, why do you think they will want to work with us willingly."

"Good point." Tsygankov leaned back in his chair and half closed his eyes. "A few years ago the IRA had a turbulent time. Gaddafi was in a bind he had allowed, even encouraged the IRA, who were already experienced, technically and competent in murder and mayhem, to train further in Libya and they are still there. The CIA got to him and he had the IRA men interned. Not long after that in the scheme of things in this topsy-turvy world, Gaddafi had a change of mind and the IRA men were freed and returned to the training facility. Later some of these men were released back into the fray and others replaced them. Gaddafi expected some spectacular attacks that would justify his support to the IRA." He paused, "Are you following me so far?"

"Yes sir, and was he rewarded?" Servo wanted to know.

"There were one or two spectacular attacks, for example the attack on the British Conservative Conference in 1983 where they narrowly missed killing the Prime Minister Thatcher. There were waves of bombings in Northern Ireland so on and so forth. But not all the teams returned to the struggle and have yet to perform."

"The mission planned would certainly meet Gaddafi's vision," Carla remarked with sadly some reticence, not knowing how Tsygankov would react. "Personally I think he is unstable, unlike Thatcher who I had a sneaking regard for, both for her handling of the Falklands and the miners not to forget her poll tax idea which was poorly handled by her team, in the same way the grey suits snipe at her." She grinned, disarming any comeback from the other two. "Not sure why I bought her up. Maybe the new Labour Party man in favour it seems with the British public, is completely the opposite and a threat to us in that he and the Yanks seems hell-bent on getting peace at any price, from the briefing papers I read in Moscow before we left to come here."

"You constantly surprise me Carla with your knowledge and views. But I don't think even the Labour man, as he only has influence and not yet the power at least, or the Americans, may get the peace process sorted out before we strike. But they will certainly settle not with the real IRA with whom we will be dealing. Now you asked me what they were like. Take your average terrorist's antisocial demeanour and double it. They are tough and ruthless. No quarter asked and no quarter given, so be careful and stay alert. Of one thing you can be sure, they work in the shadows and are cautious and untrusting," he put his head to one side. "But you are both up to it or you would not be sitting here in my study. Don't you think?"

Now Tsygankov continued. "To answer your specific point about the IRA cells, Gaddafi spent so much money on them and security so they will be in deep cover known to only a few but you can bet on it the Quartermaster will know where they are as he is probably supplying them on the mainland of England. I expect he will activate a cell plus others to support you, if he agrees."

Carla and Servo looked at each other, neither man had any doubt of the dangers they would face in a foreign country.

"Back to work! To enable you both to blend in and acclimatise yourselves to the Irish, you two are going on holiday. It has been decided you will travel as tourists and I sincerely hope you like fishing. I have planned a one-week itinerary for you which will start in Dublin, go south-west to Cork round the Island to end up hooking round north-east to end up in Lanesborough." He laughed at their delighted expression. "I think even you two will spot a tail in that time and will have blended in with the locals by then." He added, "Carla, you are the one if anyone will draw a tail as you can play the flamboyant rich tourist with ease. I am now corrected by you and thank you for that you too made a brief trip to England. So as with Vasily, your legend and name is one thing but their face recognition system could pick you up. But let's assume not, it was some time ago you visited and so they may not have you on file." He had almost finished. "Jean will have your itinerary to give to the Libyan contact man who will pass it through to the IRA. They will pass it to the Quartermaster for O'Neil so he can join you as and when it suits the IRA."

"Interesting idea that we give the IRA control to manage the pace during this part of the mission," Servo thought out loud. "But what exactly does that achieve?" he looked at the General.

"Quite a lot I think. Servo, you are to be Carla's minder for all intents and purposes as far as the world at large are concerned. Hopefully they will not contact you until Vasily has sorted the target marquee company and it has been identified and what manpower trucks and resources it has etc. And Jean has the product shipment sorted and in play and on its way. Your task as a team is to ensure the IRA is up for the mission without any prevarication. You support them as necessary and see every aspect of the plan goes like clockwork." He drew a breath. "My intelligence indicates we have around eleven weeks maximum to have every piece of the jigsaw ready to go, with two weeks in hand."

"Wow that's tight," commented Carla.

"Not really I have been planning this for over a year, longer if the truth be told, and it just needs a nudge to get the whole thing ready for the execution," Tsygankov remarked in a throwaway answer.

Servo thought about it, "Thinking about what you and Carla have said, even so sir, if we are fishing for maybe two weeks, could be. Something I have always wanted to do, don't get me wrong and a week setting up the IRA, a week to get to the mainland and link up with Vasily and get the camper sorted out. Say worst case, two weeks in France. Then close target recognisance of both the target and the marquee firm, it looks I think a tight timeline." Servo ran his hand through his hair, it was beginning to feel long to him. "But General, on balance I believe do-able. Carla and I will just have to motor once the IRA is on board."

"Good, we are set then. I need to give you another envelope with your travel, car hire, hotels and fishing permits etc. At your first hotel your fishing gear and everything you could conceivably want will be delivered on the day you book in. Any further questions at this time?" Tsygankov demanded. "Let what we have discussed sink in for a moment, read yourself in and if you have any other questions come back to me before you leave, OK?"

Servo shook himself. "Sorry, two quick questions. If Vasily's brief is to set up some safe houses for us, will there be a bolt-hole too if needs be, and will the kit contain any self-defence measures?" He didn't want to go into the lion's den without some form of protection.

"I was waiting for you to ask, Servo. Not all bad news to both your questions. Because of the situation, carrying guns through customs is not advised. We came up with a solution, with the kit at the hotel will be delivered two shotguns and ammunition, some will be doctored for long range and narrow spread. And Servo, your Spetsnaz special spring-load wrist knife will also be in the stash." Tsygankov saw Servo smile. "One of your trips will be a fishing and shooting trip, so having guns in your possession with the appropriate international end-user licence clearance will not raise any suspicion if you are stopped and asked for any documents that give you the authority to carry guns. So you will have some defence if needed. And while you are in Dublin take the opportunity to visit a hunting and fishing shop and top up your equipment as you think fit." He rustled some papers on his desk and put on his frameless glasses for the first time. "Vasily has, as one of his tasks, to check out the three safe houses and stock as needs be, but they should have been well supplied by the London men including more arms. They have been rented by our London team and are doted around. One old farmhouse although remote very near the Target, a first floor flat in London near London City Airport and a house near the Channel Ports. They should suffice, but I am going to instruct Vasily to rent one other property near the Port of Harwich that only this team will know about." He handed over the papers. "You need to learn these other three addresses and take notes as necessary; I need them back within the hour to brief Vasily. Now in the context of contact you use the usual Embassy number and code words. Just ask for Vasily or me. It is not my intention to travel to England unless there is an extreme situation that arises that needs my presence. I am simply too well known to authorities there and it is not as though I could disguise myself," he let out a full roar of laughter.

Servo and Carla could not help joining in the merriment.

"Go and get yourselves sorted, you leave tomorrow with the others, so this evening's dinner will be special. Please ask Vasily to come and see me next in about half an hour. I need some more air to clear my mind, tell him I will be on the beach if not in the garden."

Chapter 24

THE EX

The warlord's convoy bounced through the grey of the failed city of Mogadishu, even the people wore seemingly colourless clothing. Any colours there were made grey or dulled with dust and clothes washed in grey water.

All Rodney could see was misery and poverty everywhere. Rusty battered and mud-covered vehicles were the norm. Detritus of abandoned twentieth century artefacts littered the roadside. Buildings were shot up and war damaged. Old cars stripped and burnt-out; cardboard, plastic, and old machinery added to the dusty environment and were strewn around or stacked in some places around and against the high mud walls of houses. Other walls and roofs of wriggly tin, bent bullet-holed, grey and rusting added to the feeling of poverty everywhere.

Even the vehicle's air-conditioning couldn't disguise the smell of sewage and sweet smell of sweat from the outside overlaid with that distinctive smell of Africa.

They used a road out of Mogadishu running to the north, which was wide and made of beaten earth and stone, occasionally metalled but mostly potted and rutted. The five, four-by-fours raised clouds of choking dust that billowed behind them, covering the walking populace and abandoned rubbish in yet another layer of grey dust. Occasionally children appeared from nowhere and danced laughing and smiling as they chased the convoy until they, like the city, were outdistanced and left behind.

Above all, the day before Rodney had been taken aback by the heat of the day when they had deplaned so the morning cool was welcome as it was deceptive before the furnace of the African sun rising in the east caught up with them.

Reid who had been studying the passing vista shifted in the seat beside him and leant forward so he could see Simon. "Tell me, Simon, how this exchange is going to go down," queried Reid.

"Well of course!" Simon's deep-throated laugh. "You need not worry; all is set with my fellow clan chief."

"A fellow clan chief – not sure what a clan chief is?" queried Rodney perplexed. "Forgive me but the organisations and politics of Somalia completely defeat me."

"Let me help you out Rodney on that. We probably have another two hours and a half to the meeting point and that's more than time enough to give you the main points." Simon settled in the corner of his seat, twisting to look at them with one hand on the passenger grip handle to help steady him in the bucking vehicle. The road was now little more than a double track. "Okay, five minutes to look at life in Somalia – here we go. The first thing you need to understand is that we are on the brink of a civil war, you might ask what's new, but this time it is different, don't ask it just is."

"I had read something whereby the leader Siyaad Barra and his regime were not cutting it," Rodney commented.

"It is a tragedy for all the country, yet again. The first order of things is the need to know that in Somalia there are six main clans each with its own warlord. Some of these clans traditionally treat with each other more than others. There are also sub-clans; fortunately my sub-clan is part of the Abgal and the Haba. The Abgal and Haba are joined at the hip so to speak. I am married to the one of the Haba's warlord's daughters. Lucky for the captives don't you think?"

"So it appears." Rodney was intrigued. "And what of the other clans, tell us about those Simon?"

"Well for that I just need to go back, just, say to 1980. There have been wars before that of course but 1980 was the point where matters took a turn for the worse. Traditionally the clans worked together on a basis of compromise and negotiation in order to do business on a civilised basis. Didn't always work of course but generally it made for a peaceful co-existence. The really strong and stable element of the clan is actually the sub-clans called Diya. They are tied together, inexorably bound by commerce and by the tradition of blood. If blood is taken then blood is owned and has to be returned."

"So what went wrong?" Reid asked, caught up in the story.

"In a word Bara, Siyaad Bara came to power and his style was to deliberately, criminally in a way, to disrupt the balance of the clan interactions by pushing aside their traditional tendencies to compromise and accommodate in all things in order to try to avoid conflict." He frowned and his strong face showed concern and sadness. After a moment he resumed. "Bara forced us to politicise and take up arms to become, as you might say, militarised. Plus we now have other problems like the emergence of Al Quaeda and look-alikes and others who would make mischief and add to our troubles." He fell silent.

"You said there were six clans."

"Well yes, it's complicated as the names don't always match up as you might think. The clan you are meeting today are under the leadership and protection of Ali Mahdi's. Mahdi's means 'deliverer' or 'saviour'. His name does not feature in the names but is part of a block. Here goes, we have the Hawiye, Darod, Isaaq, Diri. Then there is the group that forms the Rahaweyn block and another grouping forming the Gadabursi block." He hurried on before Rodney could ask which block they belonged to and he was not sure in any case he would get a straight answer or even understand it. "Matters are coming to a head and in competition with our Ali Mahdi; there is another war-like power-hungry general so matters are fraught."

He paused to light a cigar, offering the packet to Rodney and Reid. Rodney declined but Reid, to Rodney's surprise, accepted. "Thanks Simon it has been a while since I smoked a cigar." Reid looked particularly smug to Rodney as he rolled the cigar round accepting a light from Simon.

"Great," thought Rodney, "Just what I need, stuck in a metal can with two smoke generators."

Simon took up the story again. "We are a northern-based clan and the two opposition parties now in existence are the SDF and the SNM. That is the Somali Democratic Front and the National Movement. In the south we also have the USC, United Somali Congress. So it all makes for a monumental problem for this small country. We all, in our own way love our country for all its problems and poverty." Simon waved his hand at the scene around them. "If you are now confused, think how the average private individual with little schooling feels. It is just so fragmented and confusing for the citizens to be able to cope with."

Rodney, looking out the window of the vehicle as they passed through a small farming village, was thinking about the way of things. "You know, Simon; it seems to me that you and the other leaders have an awesome responsibility to the people. How you can discharge that with all this trouble brewing I could not even imagine. I remember one of my instructors telling me once that Nietzsche famously said: 'Those who set out to destroy monsters must be wary they don't become monsters themselves.'"

Simon and Reid looked at Rodney whose face was grim.

Simon countered by saying, "A very deep philosophical point Rodney for so early in the day. Unfortunately there is an old Swahili Bantu saying 'you fight fire with fire', fortunately it's an old saying, but more simple than Nietzsche." He laughed bringing Rodney out of his momentary fug.

The land was changing they were now going through rough wooded country which undulated and twisted with obstacles of both dry and water-filled banked streams and gullies. The four-by-fours groaned, waddled and shuddered as they forged ahead. The men in the open truck gun platforms hung on tightly, swinging and riding the sway and bounce of their vehicle; they seemed perfectly at home and joked and laughed with each other. The land closed in on them with increasingly dense forestry turning to jungle before it suddenly opened and onto a plain with trees dotted around throwing dark shadows on the ground in the stark sunlight.

Noting the interest of the Englishmen in their surroundings Simon explained. "This is the main road to a township called Balcad. Before we reach it we will strike the north-east off road to aim for the Ballen National Game Reserve, close to the Webi Shabelle River. With luck you may see a few large game animals, there are still a few left but terrorists, poachers and local people have devastated the larger herds for food, most in order to simply survive. We used to have tourists but now all we get is terrorists." He laughed bitterly.

"Regrettably so do we and in our case the IRA is particularly a problem to us," Rodney commented bitterly. "And like some of your terrorists they seem to be funded by Libya?"

Simon was thoughtful for a minute before answering. "It's true what you say. A few of my warriors were in the past terrorists themselves. The story they tell of the links to Libya are certainly concerning, especially they tell me of the many other terrorist groups they rubbed shoulders with. A couple of my men, it will be a great surprise to you, were trained by your IRA specialist trainers in Libya who the president's secret services employed. They talked to me all about it."

Reid was on to the link with the IRA immediately. "Any chances these men still have contacts, in particular with the IRA trainers in Libya?"

"Almost certainly, we could open communications if we needed to, there are Somalis in Tripoli mostly working for better wages from my own clan. Yes it would be possible." Simon's response was cautious. "The men are from my clan who returned and simply took a wrong turn, as the young men tend to do but they soon saw the error of their ways. They were quickly disillusioned with the terrorist way of life and asked to be reinstated. They had to prove themselves again to all the clan and have managed to do that over the last few years, so now the men and I would trust them with our lives."

Reid was thinking for a minute or so and then gave voice to his thoughts. "We would give our right arm, not literally, but to know about shipments from Libya to the IRA and who was paying for the arms. Is it just Gaddafi-driven or are others involved somehow?"

Simon looked at Reid. "There may be a way, but it would cost, not a great deal but money would have to change hands."

Rodney took up the conversation. "Do you have any idea what that price would be?"

"Let me think about it for an hour or so," Simon replied.

"Thank you for even considering it. It has particular relevance to my team at this time." Rodney changed the subject. "Before the troubles here, or at least when there was some normality, what game did you have? You mentioned it has been badly affected?" He wanted to know.

"Thankfully there is still some game I am pleased to say, not nearly as much as before when we had a good ranger set up to manage the national parks. We then had a balanced ecology with all the big game. There were lions, elephants, hippo, kudu and gazelles. The grey Hamadryas baboons thrive of course and you will no doubt see some, don't get close they take no prisoners and the bite is awesome. Snakes, we have loads of them, most good to eat. We have a great variety of shrews that seem to thrive, from the tree shrew to the one we call the elephant shrew. Giraffe and of course the buffalo are still with us. The buffalo is another animal to avoid. It is the great herds of zebra and the like that have suffered the most. With the loss of the great herds the predators, the big cats, find food hard to find so their numbers are well down. Surprisingly our black-backed jackal and the wildcat have survived the predation and of course the crocodile are also good to eat particularly, the tail tastes a bit like pork."

In the far distance, a triangular stand of three trees a dozen yards apart with broad flat canopies growing into each other's branches formed a large shaded area. Beneath the spreading limbs were a group of people with several trucks and four-by-fours lined up in a way to add to the shaded area.

"Ah see there, Rodney, my esteemed father-in-law and your hostages. Now listen to me carefully, whatever you do, hear or see, stay neutral in your manner. Show no aggression and only speak if you are asked a direct question. That goes for you too, Reid, and please tell your men to do the same. Keep your weapons strapped to your back and dangling so they pose no threat. I can assure you will get plenty of notice if matters don't go as planned." He added grinning, "It is our way to talk loudly and shout at each other with much stamping and arm waving. Do not be alarmed at that."

In another five minutes they drew up on the other side of the trees to where the warlords' vehicles were parked.

Simon's minder was the first out of the vehicle, followed immediately by Simon, who signalled for Rodney and Reid to stay where they were for a moment. The remainder of Simon's group stayed in the vehicles, even the men who had the responsibility of manning the vehicle mounted machine guns sat quietly on the sides of the open cabs, their hands away from the guns.

There were a few waves between the groups and a few shouted greetings.

Rodney and Reid watched Simon go to and greet a tall well-built older man. The man was dark even for a Somali. He wrapped powerful hands around Simon and lifted Simon's slim frame off the ground. Both men were laughing. He set Simon on the ground and indicated waving to all Simon's men to join them. Simon too waved to Rodney reinforcing the invitation.

To one side of the clearing, which now held some fifty men, was a fire with a large animal turning on a spit. A closer inspection by Rodney determined it was a big antelope. There were a few women who tended to the men, bringing native beer, tea and other drinks in battered tin mugs.

Rodney was invited with Reid to sit with the two warlords while Sharky and Mould were talking with their vehicle crew and men from the other warlords' group. It seemed that everyone was getting on, to Rodney's relief. Rodney looked around but could see no sign of the hostages they had come to collect. A stab of apprehension assailed him but he kept his expression unreadable.

The elder man had introduced himself gracefully as Salin Bay and it was soon apparent he was interested in Rodney's party and what was happening in the UK. Rodney patiently talked to Salin and he could see Simon was nodding and pleased with Rodney that he had the sense not to raise the main purpose of their visit.

The morning wore on and the women began to strip the antelope carcass and feed the men with strips of meat. By now the two groups had completely intermingled and sat in a rough circle around the principals.

Simon thanked his father-in-law for the feast and his hospitality. Salin waved his thanks away and stood and called to two of his men. Rodney strained to understand what they were saying but could not understand a word of the quick-fire exchange. The two men ran to the trucks. Salin returned to Rodney and beckoned him to follow him and Simon and Reid followed at a discreet distance. He led Rodney out of the circle to the back of a covered truck. Salin's English was halting but articulated clearly. "Major, before I give you these people you need to understand I do so with joy." He dug in his pocket and brought out a carefully folded letter which he handed over to Rodney to read.

Rodney opened the letter; it was from Her Majesty's Office and it was signed. The gist of it was that it was hoped that Salin would remember her young officer that had freed Salin's father when his father was captured along with German soldiers in the Second World War and helped him back to his clan. It would seem to them that Salin's life was a gift from a British officer or he would not have had a father. Any onus it would it seem would not be forgotten if Salin would hand over the hostages to her men so they could be returned to their families. Rodney was nonplussed and his startled expression brought a throaty laugh from Salin. "All is well," he said. "I am sure Simon explained blood for blood. A debt is paid I think."

Rodney thought for a moment, "Let us not look on this as a debt repaid but a friendship forged," Rodney said, shaking his hand. "The hostages – are they here?"

"Oh yes," Salin wrapped on the canvas and his two men pushed the canvas back to show the dark interior. Three white people were sitting on canvas chairs manacled to the truck structure. Salin ordered the manacles to be taken off the two men and a woman hastened to obey the warlord. When they were free they shook the stiffness out of their limbs and were helped down out of the vehicle.

It was a moment before they realised there was another European standing looking at them. Rodney saw the hope leap into their eyes for a moment and then fade. "No it's okay, you are going home. Stay as calm as you can, keep your eyes down. Now you walk out with me?"

Despite Rodney's instructions they were all over him in a second thanking him for rescuing them. Rodney had to push them away and was said firmly, "Don't thank me yet we have a way to go and if you want to thank anyone at this time please thank Salin Bay." He indicated the tall proud warlord.

Rather hesitantly they each in turn shook the warlord's hand. He for his part seemed embarrassed but pleased nonetheless and retained his proud stance.

Rodney looked over at Reid; they read each other's thoughts perfectly. All they had to do now was get away from the warlord and back to Mogadishu without mishap. The tension and as the leaders they felt it more than the others, was high; so close, but so far from safety. Reid gave a rare smile to the Major. "Well, boss, shall we go, the sooner we start the sooner we get home?" Reid clasped Rodney's shoulder, spinning round, pointing him at the warlord.

Chapter 25

TSYGANKOV TALKS TO VASILY

Vasily entered the General's study quietly and, as was his manner, closed the door softly behind him. Vasily found Tsygankov was turned away leaning against the door jamb of the patio doors, apparently appreciating the view. Vasily stood in the study awaiting the General to acknowledge he was there.

"Vasily," Tsygankov said without turning, "let us walk a bit. We can talk as we wander."

As they walked round the estate Tsygankov gave the younger officer the outline of his task, adding layer upon layer of detail until he led them back to the study.

"Vasily," Tsygankov entered first and turned to welcome him in, "Please pull up a chair to the desk; let's get this over with and I can go back to walking round the estates before lunch. Incidentally what do you think of Jean – I would appreciate your thoughts?" Tsygankov's remarks were offhand.

Before answering, Vasily as he had been asked, moved his chair to the desk, so he was face to face with the General. "Clearly I see Jean as a soldier more than an assassin. I judge he has in his own way a sense of honour and would be slow to anger and revenge he would take at the appropriate time. Servo thinks a lot of him, rating him highly and trusts him implicitly for his own reasons. Lastly and not least he is highly intelligent and, considering the little I know of him, has pleasant enough manners. I don't think I have heard him raise his voice once or swear. How do you rate him sir?"

"Much like you I acknowledge, even respect, his abilities and knowledge," Tsygankov responded in kind. "And now let's put Saied to bed and get on with your task. Think you will enjoy England again and the people. First I want to give you the opportunity to put questions to me about your task, before I get down to my instructions for you in detail."

"Well I have looked at the mission and the documents you gave me, and one item was not clear to me and that is how to find the right marquee supplier. I am sure I can find out one way or another but it's an unknown."

"Sorted that early on but it will need checking," Tsygankov replied. "We have the name of last year's supplier but you will need to check they are using the same company this year." He paused for moment thinking. "If not, you will have to use your wiles to find the company. Time is not yet an issue but we will need to move quickly when the time does come."

"That's it?" Tsygankov asked and Vasily nodded. "Well let's get on then." Tsygankov went through the contact protocols for him and the team and centre to ensure Vasily felt he would not be simply adrift in a foreign company and unsupported. Tsygankov spent time on the safe houses set up and gaining access and how Vasily needed to behave with the immediate neighbours so their suspicions would not be raised. He counselled him on the local people he would meet and the reasons he should avoid non-UK nationals, especially those from eastern bloc counties who might break his cover. He talked about the banking system and drawing money. He explained that the services and utility bills for the safe houses would be handled by others and where he should redirect and post any bills arriving at the properties. He reminded him how to drive on the left side of the road and that the cars would already be garaged with each safe house. He described the rationale for choosing the houses, for each safe house could be needed in support of the team. Whilst he had confidence in the London contact that had set up the houses stores and cars, he wanted Vasily to hire another safe house. He emphasized the need to report in every other day so that he could monitor progress and support or tweak the plan. He saw Vasily's role as key and central to the scheme and told him so. He checked and confirmed that Vasily was ready for tomorrow and his departure to the UK. Lastly he told Vasily why he wanted him to rent a bolt-hole and where and why; that only he and the other three would know about. He explained it was extra insurance in case there was a leak.

"Think that should give you a good start so any last questions?"

"No I don't think so. If I get stuck I will refer. However, think I would like to walk the estates before lunch with you to clear my mind which is now full of everything from cars to I don't know what?"

"Come on then, let's get some air, let me show you my beach and then have a look at what's growing out there on the ground."

Chapter 26

THE HOSTAGES

Reid leaned across to Salin and Simon who were in conversation. "Excuse the interruption, can I make the people ready to depart? I think the sooner I can get them to the plane and they can sort themselves out the better for them."

Salin agreed readily, he didn't want them hanging about.

The hostages were in poor shape physically. Rodney soon learned they had not been physically abused but they had been kept in a tin hut for several weeks after they were captured on the border working on a National Geological survey.

After capture they were marched for days on meagre rations and it seems handed over or sold to the warlord Salin. Although Salin fed them slightly better, he had not allowed them any freedom for a moment until today.

Simon and Reid helped the hostages to the vehicles and sorted them out as best they could with some new clothes and a wash down.

Rodney went back to the warlord to thank him again and for his hospitality. Salin bade him good luck as he took his leave of Salin and collected Sharky and Mould.

Mould pulled Rodney and Reid to one side. "Got a bad feeling, boss. It seems this area is not strictly speaking the warlord's territory, his is further north. This area is a haven for all sorts of villains and terrorists hiding out, so we had better look out on the way back." Sharky showed his agreement by suggesting they take a different route back.

"Good work, let's hope for the best and plan for the worst. I had better have a word with Simon. Although I am sure Simon knows what's in front of us, I will get his take on the return journey, whatever, the sooner we are out of here the better and get those three poor sods to their plane."

Simon listened to Rodney's concern and request to vary the route back. "Hmm, you are right to be worried. I was surprised we made it here with no issues. As for changing the route it is a problem, there are some choke points we have no control over and have to go through them, we have no option in the time frame. On the other hand there are parts of the route we could vary. In some ways Rodney, as you will have now worked out, it's a negative exercise as any ambush will be at a choke point – for example the waddy crossings as they are the only way out?"

"I can see it's an issue and moving off the trail adds to the time any hostile has to get ready for us. Perhaps we had better get going as fast as we can safely." Rodney agreed.

Rodney relayed his conversation with Simon to the team and looked at Mould who was still not settled.

"Look boss. Sharky and I will join the front truck to give more room for the National Geographic lads in the vehicle. And add to the fire power on view." Mould hooked his head for Sharky to follow.

Reid turned to follow Rodney but at the last moment decided to beef up the rear vehicle with his presence. Rodney did not object; it saved him asking Reid to do just that.

Simon gestured for the men to mount up and waved to his father-in-law as the convoy moved off. Salin had his party packing up and gazed at the departing vehicles' dust cloud and called his lieutenants forward for a conference.

The first two hours of the journey went well and with only another hour to go they approached another gulley with a fast flowing stream at its bottom, yet another choke point of most danger.

They saw the lead vehicle pull over to the right to form a cover party for the crossing. Mould and Sharky dismounted and called the rear gun truck forward seeing Reid on board Mould clambered aboard with him. They would now form a weapon platform covering the convoy from the other side of the waddy once they themselves had crossed.

Mould and Reid with their crew drove their vehicle down the steep sides through the stone and bounder-strewn stream and were making their way up the gulley to the other side. As they reached the lip of the waddy a single shot rang out from their left. A bullet thudded into the vehicle bonnet. The vehicle driver pressed his foot to the floor and swung the vehicle over the lip and to the right. Allowing the gun crew to come into action and let rip at some cover where they thought the shot had come from some 200 metres away.

There was a flash from the area and an RPG streaked towards them but passed harmlessly overhead exploding some hundred metres further on.

"Come on, Mould, let's get a fire platform set up and some eyes and ears on the ground." Mould was off the vehicle and followed by half of Simon's went to ground and rolled away to find a location to work from against the attackers.

Back on the other side of the gulley, another gun truck with Sharky on board got ready to support the other truck on the far side of the gulley. The other jeeps had pulled back 50 metres, taking cover behind some dense foliage and dead ground. Simon and his men with Rodney made their way forward, weapons made ready. The hostages were made to stay in the vehicles. Simon gave his second-in-command orders to stay with the hostages and left him two further men to guard them.

The rest along with Rodney made their way forward and into the gulley.

Reid shouted to Sharky and Mould. "Location and numbers?"

Mould replied "Two hundred metres to the left. We countered ten light weapons and they have an RPG launcher," Mould shouted.

"Right, listen in. Keep their heads down. Suppression fire, from me now," Reid ordered them. "Sharky get your gun vehicle abreast the enemy and rake them, move!"

Rodney sized the initiative. "Look Simon, Reid has been doing this stuff for near forty years. Here is my plan, let him sort it." Simon looked at him dubious but interested.

Reid, seeing no objection from Simon, went on doing what was second nature to him.

His vehicles team put down 50 calibre shells on the enemy steadily keeping their heads down.

Sharky got his vehicle moving along the gulley at speed, firing onto the enemy position along with Reid's team. When they drew level with the enemy they drove down the gulley and out the other side as quickly as possible "Okay, here we go." Sharky shouted as they came over the lip of the gulley.

The enemy switched its fire to Sharky's vehicle but it was mostly ineffective. A stray bullet seared Sharky's right cheek taking out a lump of ear. Sharky swore and wiped the blood off his face; the pain would come later, for the moment he felt nothing.

The enemy was now caught in crossfire from two directions. The remaining enemy swung again, knelt up and tried to put some fire onto Reid's team. Reid ordered his gun vehicle to close with the enemy, and with other men poured suppression fire into them and they soon put their heads down again.

All the fire power from Simon's side was now concentrated on the enemy and they crumbled under the punishment they were soaking up. It was not long before the enemy fell silent.

"Simon, Rodney, rest of you, off you go up the waddy and take charge of the other fire team." Reid hopped back on the gun truck. "We go in one minute to clear the area. Let's just get it done."

The battle now stilled, Reid got his team to swing the 50 calibre over to cab and drove the rest of the way towards the enemy. Reid saw two men rise up, one was blown backwards ripped apart by the 50 calibre and the other simply flopped down.

Simon and Rodney advancing with the rest of the men and the other gun truck racked the area.

In seconds it seemed to Simon and his attacking force that the three enemies left alive were throwing down their weapons in surrender. One last desperate enemy of the three tried to run and was cut down by a well-aimed shot from Simon himself.

All the enemy were accounted for, and apart from a few scratches and bullet holes in the vehicles it was all the evidence they had, that they had been in a scrap. Sharky's flesh wound was much admired by Simon's men. Reid added his comment. "Silly sod, what is your wife going to say?"

Simon's men collected the enemy weapons and any information they could off the bodies. All the evidence pointed to them being irregulars without clan affiliations, probably terrorists. For Simon it was a good result and one he thanked Reid in particular for. "Very impressive Mr Reid, any chance you and the team could stay a while and train my soldiers in this sort of defensive counter attack? It was a great demonstration for my soldiers and one they will talk about tonight with their friends."

"If I was twenty years younger I would be tempted. Plus there is a job we have to do back home, but when it's done I will have some leave coming. If you are still of a like mind when I am off I'll come and give you a week of my time – in exchange for being wined and dined like we were last night, and a club flight ticket via Dubai or

Nairobi whichever is cheaper." Reid, now back in the vehicle with Rodney and Simon, sat back in the seat smiling to himself. It was good to know you still had the skills and they were appreciated.

Quick as a flash, "Deal," said Simon, offering Reid his hand and another cigar.

Rodney groaned, he could only imagine what Robinson would say when Rodney told him one of his men was going back to Somalia on a paid holiday. In his corner smoking contentedly, Reid again read his mind. "Don't panic Rodney, I will speak to the Brigadier as and when, if it happens."

"How the hell did you know what I was thinking?" Rodney was amazed.

"Simple my Major, everyone knows officers have simple minds and are always thinking how they can cover their rear end when they need to tell the boss something they think will upset them. I guarantee you the boss will be delighted. Don't you think Simon?"

"Knowing the Brigadier as I do, I would be surprised if he didn't want to come as well."

"You know Robinson?" Rodney was surprised at this new turn of events.

"Oh yes, we go back a long way." Before Rodney could dig deeper Simon changed the subject. "You will want to know if I have come to a decision about what it might cost to get the intelligence you wanted out of Libya. I think a working budget of £20K in sterling or $30K in dollars, whichever you prefer. That would be in the ball park. I don't see it costing anywhere near that but better to have a comfortable budget than be scraping for pennies at a crucial moment. It will cost no more than that, what's not spent after my costs will be returned," Simon confirmed.

"I am interested. More than that, I am very interested. Let me get back to the UK and talk to my clan boss." The reference to the clan boss made Simon smile. "What I will do is send you an email with our list of priority intelligence items that we need to know about. If you confirm you can supply within, say a six-week timeframe, send me your bank details when you confirm and we will arrange for the funds to be transferred? How does that sound?" Rodney asked.

"That arrangement would be fine for me. Six weeks should be ample. If possible we will improve on that."

They reformed the convoy and made their way steadily back to Mogadishu entering the town as before on the same road. In Mogadishu they first pulled into the compound. Rodney and his men collected their bags and the team and hostages had time to get a much needed shower and change into new clothes. A quick lunch and the team were on its way within the hour.

They then drove directly to the airport. The gun vehicles peeled off and parked as twenty-four hours before. The three people-carrying vehicles – one with Simon and his minder, one with the hostages and the other with Rodney's team, after they had picked up an immigration official were escorted onto the airport pan driving up to the hostage handlers at the steps of a waiting aircraft.

There were press cameras and officials there crowding around the vehicles holding the hostages. Before they got to the airport Rodney's men and their baggage had been transferred to the rear vehicle. As the excitement around the hostages continued, the rear vehicle slipped quietly away to the far end of the airfield where Alex waited with his Dakota engines running.

Chapter 27

TSYGANKOV AND SAIED

At the dinner the day before the team was to leave, Saied and Tsygankov broke after the main course and left the rest to fight over the dessert.

In the library, Tsygankov and Saied quickly reviewed the mission and the General ensured Saied fully understood his task and how he was to accomplish it.

The mechanical details covered both men and ensured that Saied had the right documentation and travel documents to enable him to complete his first tasks.

Tsygankov spent ten minutes talking to Saied on the actual targets and what he saw as the final hours before the bomb was activated. Saied for his part had little doubt that the General's orders would be carried out by the other to the letter. But for himself the mission had overtures of Tsygankov's cruel solution to removing witnesses as he had done with Saied's men after the attack on the South African Centre outside Cape Town where Saied had stolen the decryption device for him.

Saied wanted to know, "What about the team and I after the mission is complete?"

Tsygankov was pensive. "I must say that I imagined that Carla, Servo and Vasily would return to their Directorates, and probably they would retire me. For yourself, you have many choices. You can return here and spend some time deciding what you want to do about your future. Or you could consider becoming an agent for the KGB, or return to your mercenary role. It's up to you."

"Really?" Saied was cautious.

"Really, with this fee and what you have slated away you don't really need to work very hard. An agent appointment may suit you."

"Hmm, one last question, just so I am in concert with the others – is it now confirmed that any IRA personnel involved in this mission are to be silenced where it is possible?"

"Oh I think it would be best Jean, don't you? We don't want any third party witnesses to our workings. Yes they are to be eliminated but I leave it to the team to organise it so it looks like it had nothing to do with us." He watched Saied nod. "Good that's that. Now let's join the others before they devour all the dessert and drink all my vodka."

Chapter 28

RODNEY GETS THE GO

"Welcome back Rodney. I hear your trip to get the hostages out was more than a success."

"Thank you Brigadier but how did you hear about it?" Rodney was nonplussed, he had only just arrived back.

"Simon phoned me from Somalia. You probably didn't know but he was attached to my regiment as a very young man, when he was a Military Intelligence officer with the then Somalia Foreign Office and when I was the then Commanding Officer."

"My God he never said a word about knowing you in that way, only that you and he went back a long way."

"That's my Simon, a man of amazing talent even then, they put him with me to learn about how the British Army went about its business."

"Talking of talent. He is a talent spotter too. He wanted to employ Reid to train his men."

Robinson was amused. "I trust Mr Reid said no."

"Not quite, he sort of indicated that he would go back on a leave for a week and give Simon's men the benefit of his experience."

"Not sure that's actually allowed, could be illegal and not a tacitly sanctioned black OP?" Robinson was thinking. "It might be possibly palatable if Simon was, say, working for us in some way."

"Well actually now you mention it, for a sum Simon may be able to do us a good turn in the context of the IRA." Rodney saw he had Robinson's attention. "He seems to have some staff that have been with and seen the IRA men in Libya. It is not too much of a stretch to imagine that they may have seen both the IRA and any Libyan contact that was involved with them."

"What are you proposing?"

"I was going to suggest we put a shopping list together, an intelligence wish list and with priorities."

"What will it cost?"

"Simon suggested a budget of £20K to 30K, what's not spent we get back."

"Done and knowing you have the list already in mind. So spill the beans." Robinson, sitting behind the desk, opened his notebook. "I need to make a few notes if that's okay with you Rodney, for the boys' club tomorrow morning. Great initiative, just what they wanted us to do. Think outside the box!"

"To be fair to Mr Reid he was the one who spotted the opportunity. I am thinking of asking Simon to backtrack six months. Where possible to get details of shipments to all third party groups not just the IRA and say six months going forward. Secondly to photograph any current IRA men in Libya and any Libyan official or other third party they have contact with, and again over the same time period going forward. As an ex-intelligence officer Simon will appreciate the importance of timely reporting in, which I will emphasise to him."

"How are you going to communicate back and forth with him, we might need some secure way of doing this." Robinson was thinking out loud.

Rodney rummaged through his briefcase and bought out a 1-inch thick book 6 inches by 6 inches, "Before I left Simon he gave me this one-time code book; he has its sister. I was surprised at the time but now it makes sense."

"It is sorted then, Rodney, at least for the time being. If we need to beef-up the message exchange at a later stage so be it." The Brigadier was beaming. "Do you have anything else for me? What about Simon, anything from him on communications from the Middle East?"

"Simon and I exchanged emails and phone numbers. We have another arrangement too. Simon has a cousin in the UK if Simon needs to distance himself from us, but to get information to us the cousin will contact me. Photographs will be sent without comment followed by a separate coded message with information as needs be."

"Certainly sounds as though you have this matter covered." Robinson continued to scribble in his notebook and asked without looking up, "What's your next move?"

"I am going to shut my office door, get the Simon situation set up so he can be in action this day." He paused. "And then going to get all the team together this afternoon and find out what's going on. I need to check they have cleared their desk or delegated anything outstanding. Then I am going to get the IRA mission you gave us on the road."

"Good, that's what I wanted to hear."

"Is there anything else for me or on your mind sir?"

"Don't think so. But can you look in tomorrow night before you go. I would like to get up to speed myself on the IRA mission. You never know I may be able to contribute."

"Good idea, look forward to it." Rodney gathered his things and left the Brigadier to work his way through the hostage operation report Rodney had compiled during the journey home.

Chapter 29A

TSYGANKOV SEES HIS TEAM OFF

"Time to go," Carla said reluctantly as she finished her breakfast. Although Carla had only been at the dacha for a few days she was enthralled with it. She felt at home and at peace for the first time in many years. The opportunity to play some of the world's most well-crafted and expensive of Tsygankov's violins was something she could only have dreamed of the previous week. The sooner the mission was achieved the sooner she would be able to return. The dacha and its environment were so different from anything she had had the opportunity to stay in for a long time and she was reluctant to leave.

Saied, when he woke, thought of the blanket of security the dacha offered and forced himself to switch on to the task ahead. He had no illusions that his various actions were critical to the success of the mission which would at times need his special skills honed over years of learning to survive in diverse environments and situations.

On the surface, both Servo and Vasily seemed calm and accepting of the part they had to play. Neither in their hearts looked on this as just another job. Servo for his part was still uneasy with the mission's aim. It was not in his nature to punish the innocent along with the enemies of the state. Vasily too was torn in his loyalties to Tsygankov.

The team were finishing their breakfasts and were of like minds in one aspect at least, they wanted to get at the mission and get it done and move on.

Tsygankov appeared in the room. "We leave all together in one hour so gather your things together. Saied and I will be flying with you as far as Moscow. I need to see the Director, but will be back here tomorrow night, and Jean you need to get your connection to

Bratislava. We go together in my car. Vasily, Carla and Servo go in the hired Land Rover and hand it in; we are on the same flight to Moscow and then the onward connections to London and Dublin as fits your task. Do you have any questions? No. Well then good luck to you all." He paused. "Once this task has run its course you will need to come back for a debrief; you are all quite welcome to stay on afterwards for some R&R."

Saied smiled to himself as he thought of Tsygankov's previous track record and the mantra that repeated itself to him was: "Dead men tell no lies." The offer of R&R was attractive but did he want to spend his time watching his back?

Tsygankov had spoken to General Polyakov the night before on the mission's progress. Tsygankov had picked up the feeling in Moscow that the enthusiasm for the mission was cooling and the upper echelons were getting cold feet. So Tsygankov and General Polyakov had agreed Tsygankov should return and stiffen the backbones of the stakeholders.

Tsygankov himself had always anticipated that there would be opposition from the weaker members of the committee who were party to the mission and would be worried about any backlash that would come back to them if anything went wrong or they were exposed. He had prepared a brief and in it emphasised that the cut out was him and that no other party could possibly be implicated. It was just one example of this philosophy why the mission was mounted from his dacha and not from Moscow itself.

Any trace to the Russians would look like a rough operation mounted by terrorists determined to undermine Russian relations with the West. He was under no illusion that he could expect a difficult time when he spoke to the committee, but he had been there before and his reputation as a master spymaster he felt would carry the day.

He was just thankful that Gorbachev, the General Secretary of the Communist Party of the Soviet Union since 1985, was not yet president.

Before the appointed time to leave, Tsygankov's team had formed outside with their luggage and were waiting for him to appear. Mac bought out the General's bags and loaded them into the vehicle. Mac would drive the General and see to his needs before the flight.

When Tsygankov arrived he called them together. "Before we leave I almost forgot to show you the underground communication centre. Think it is worth a five-minute tour so you know what's available to you when you need to get in touch. Follow me please."

He led them back into the dacha and to the stairwell next to the study. He led the way down a flight of stairs with the steel door on the right that housed the violin collection and down another flight of stairs to another steel door.

He punched the code into the door lock and pushed open the door and a large underground cavernous room was immediately brightly lit by wall and overhead lighting. The room was dry and warm. "Right in front of you the satellite and internet stations, fax etc. To the left, a video conference facility with Moscow, unfortunately they want me in person, hence my trip. We can use the facility to communicate and it will be useful from time to time to use this method when we talk depending on and subject to security constraints perhaps from your laptops. To the right the operations centre with the usual paraphernalia for command and control. As you can see there are ample opportunities available to you to keep in touch with me and each other."

"Impressive. Who will man the centre?" Vasily asked, intrigued with the magnitude of the centre for a private individual.

"Not an issue unless you intend to keep me up infinitum. Any contact will set an alert off on my satellite phone. I will be able to get to this facility in seconds. So don't worry about being out on a limb. Rest assured I will respond to your calls."

"Think we need to move, General, or we will miss our flights." Saied nudged the General.

"Okay, let's go to it." Tsygankov waited till all the team had left the communication and command centre before locking it and following them out to the waiting vehicles.

Servo, out of respect for the General's rank, followed his vehicle out of the dacha as far as the airport, although he wanted to put his foot down and overtake Mac's steady progress many times. At the airport he dropped the other off at departure and drove his Land Rover to the rental return. Paperwork done, he joined the rest in the departure lounge for a second breakfast. "Eat when you can and rest or sleep when you can." It was the universal soldier code.

Chapter 29 B

RODNEY GETS HIS TEAM ON THE ROAD

As Tsygankov's team were landing in Moscow, the London team was waiting in the conference room for Rodney.

Rodney arrived, as he always tried to do fully prepared, for a meeting. "Good morning Jane and gentlemen, and the Jones, welcome to the fray. Mr Avery how nice to see you are you staying for the duration."

"Certainly looks like it, if you have a part for me to play then it would be my pleasure to support the team?"

"Good enough and yes need you to support us. You are in command of the Welsh Jones team." The room laughed.

"Right let's get to it." Rodney opened his file. "Point one, has anybody not yet cleared their desk of any task that would divert their full attention from this mission?" He looked round the room. "Graham, anything outstanding?"

"I am clear."

"Jane?"

"Clear."

"Pat?"

"Clear."

"Mould?"

"I will be clear by tonight."

"Why?"

"I just need to type up my report ex-Somalia."

"Fair enough, Sharky?"

"Clear."

"How is the ear?" Rodney could see the wound plaster protecting the right cheek and ear.

"It only hurts when you make me laugh," said Sharky

"I will try to minimise that eventuality," Rodney retorted. "Take it the wife is okay with the duelling scar?"

"She just said what Mr Reid said, 'Silly sod,' but she did suggest I was getting a little old to be still playing soldiers."

"Thank you Sharky for that insight." Rodney pressed on.

"Andrew?"

"Clear."

"I take it Jones one and two and Mr Avery you are available and ready to go?" He received a nod from the three men.

"Mr Reid."

"I am at your service, let's get it done."

"Wonderful, now has anybody managed to progress this mission while we were away sunning ourselves?"

Graham was the first to report. "I have converted the old upstairs conference room. The room for those who don't know directly above this one is a fully-kitted operations room dedicated to this mission alone. It is fully kitted out now with communications, boards, white boards etc, etc. Had the temporary room partitions removed so we have the full length of the room."

"Well done, good choice, it's bigger than this room and plenty big enough to house the whole team working at once, without getting stir crazy or getting in each other's way. I will centre myself on that room from tomorrow morning when not out on task. But in those instances Graham will be able to contact me within minutes." He paused, "Graham come and see me after the meeting, I need to speak to you about another player we have in play in Libya." The meeting stirred.

Andrew spoke after looking at Jane and Pat. "We have met with the Banker John Brown and have been in touch with all the other branches' contacts of his that he trusts, that could possibly have any information on IRA funds."

"Good, have you spoken to the FBI?"

"Ah we make an assumption that as you and Mr Reid had bagged the FBI that it would not look professional if we approached them too."

"Good call. As the FBI has been raised as an item, Mr Reid would you make an appointment for you and I to see the FBI London liaison officer tomorrow afternoon, any time after lunch or for lunch if she prefers; first check out with the Brigadier he may want in."

"Mr Avery, Mould and Sharky are tasked with working with GCHQ and Military Intelligence reference communication to and from the IRA Quartermaster and his immediate team. With our two new additions we are now able to mount a targeted surveillance on the IRA Quartermaster's team in the country. Your task Mr Avery is to support the surveillance team reporting directly to Mr Reid, who needs to be kept abreast of developments every minute of every day, and at the same time you need to communicate with Mould and Sharky re. intelligence and developments. Mr Reid with Graham, would you see that everything Mr Avery and Lewis and Fred need for their trip is sorted. Yes Graham, before you ask, I want them armed. I wish the team in place observing within the next 36 hours. The game, as my favourite hero would say, is afoot. Yes and again before you ask?" Rodney opened his file and withdrew a sheaf of documents, "Here are the faces of the Quartermaster and his immediate team and the last two documents show firstly a map to his residence, the second is addresses of his accomplices and their current vehicles and their known registrations. Graham will get the background on each and what is known about them to you before you leave." Rodney paused for a few minutes to allow the team to organise their notebooks and think of any points.

"Do you have any questions? If not, get your brain around this and we meet tomorrow at 1700hrs in the operations room. Now before you are free to run to your tasks, a moment please. Jane, Pat and Andrew, I would like to meet the Banker before I meet the FBI so could you have him here for 0830hrs tomorrow, my office; Mr Reid and I need to have a briefing on how the money can be moved without being traced, laundered and in any other way manipulated or hidden."

Avery wanted to clarify. "Just so there is no mistake, we are talking about a covert observation only at this time no close target recce?" Avery needed to know, as to carry out a CTR or close target recce was a major undertaking and could involve specialist and surveillance equipment inserted into the target's house and surrounding environment. CTR was a specialist task for trained men and he was unsure in his mind if the two Welshmen could carry this out unaided.

"Good question. At this time we are talking covet op for which your team is more than qualified. Bear in mind for the future that we may need a CTR but that will be done by the regiment or 5. Good question why, because I would appreciate it if you would gather as much intelligence on the residence and surrounding environment. Ground, security, possible approaches, people, animals' pictures and more pictures etc, etc. All the endless lists of the usual and unusual stuff which Mr Avery I know from past experience you can cobble together well. Gathering this Intel will not be wasted, as even if we don't use it Military Intelligence may well. Okay with that?"

Avery and the two Welshmen nodded, a little relieved they were not going to have to carry out the task just get the data to help whoever would.

"Anything else? No?"

Rodney folded his file. "Let's go to it. Graham with me, I now only need five minutes and then you focus on the needs of the surveillance team until their needs are satisfied."

Rodney strode from the room, his limp hardly showing. The rest of the team were about to break off when Reid held them back. "Stay. Right let's get whatever we have on your appropriate board in the operations room sorted by tonight when I will bring the boss and the Brigadier to view our progress, let's say 1800hrs. No excuses, professional job as I know you are all capable of. Mould re your report, get it done in your own time tonight. We have all got a lot invested in this task and we will achieve." Reid was deadly serious. "Graham you had better get off to the boss.

Graham made his way to Rodney's office. He found Rodney at his desk head down. "Graham, good I have story to tell you." Rodney explained about the deal with Simon and the one-time use code book. Rodney wanted Graham to send Simon the new phone numbers he had had installed and to run the code book. "And Graham, we will need these telephone numbers routed to your control room."

"No problem."

"Think we need a safe in the room."

"For the moment I've got three steel combination cabinets. One for each of the sub teams."

"Well thought out and the room, let's live with that unless the situation changes. I had taken it for granted the operations room would be manned 24/7. Any ideas?"

"Well Rodney, I thought the first week to fortnight would be as ever chaotic. So I have planned to eat and sleep in the ops room. Don't think it will be all that onerous by the very nature of the mission and if it is I will shout for help. After that I judged that Andrew, Pat and Jane will be spending a lot of time in the room on research and reports. So they could rotate a night shift between them for a while until other resources become available or I need to revert to 24/7 for a period."

"That works for me, thank you very much for that; it was an item on my bucket list to sort. Let Mr Reid know your plans, he will make it happen." Rodney put both hands flat on his desk and rose slightly, indicating the session was over.

"I thought I would mention that Mr Reid wants the teams to set up their desks and paraphernalia for you and the Brigadier to inspect at 1800hrs tonight." Graham, head down, was scribbling in his notebook.

"Thanks for the tip, I will show suitable surprise when Mr R summons me." Rodney grinned.

Graham rose and as was his nature shook the Major's hand. "Good luck with this one sir, it is going to be a bitch."

"Thank you for that Graham, but with you at the helm I am sure it will go better than if you were not." Rodney opened the door of his office and watched the gangling figure of his operations room controller walk purposefully down the corridor. "A man on a mission," Rodney thought. He wondered if Graham had a family for he never spoke of one. "A strange cove, but for all that an effective operator?"

As Graham went to his tasks if he was surprised didn't show it, he was never surprised with what was thrown at him in this most interesting of the secret services.

Rodney, thrown back on his work, found he couldn't settle to the files that needed his attention, and as way of a diversion turned his attention instead to refocus his mind to his list of tasks to do. He ran down his list of things to check where he was with them and what was left to do. Near the top of the list was the scientist's name, reference fingerprints and DNA. Time to check it out if anything had been found of use. The files could wait.

When he entered the lab, Christian was engaged with a slide under the microscope. "What you got, Doc. Anything interesting?"

"Be with you in a minute Rodney."

The scientist finished off his study and wrote up a note on the slide and waved the slide at Rodney. "A sideline of mine is cataloguing the footprints of different crude and refined petroleum products. I am preparing a database and paper for the environmental agency. It should one day enable them to identify quickly what product is polluting where," he added, "and concurrent in concert with the bomb squad and brother military I am helping to footprint some lesser known explosive compositions."

"You never fail to amaze me with your breadth of interests. No explosives stored here I hope." Rodney commented and he meant it. "Any results on the fingerprints etc?"

"Yes and no. I do have some small samples of explosives here, and no they are not going to blow the place up." He laughed then grew serious. "Your letter and its prints. The FBI came up with a name and was about to mail me the details but then half an hour later I get a call from the Brigadier, who told me to stand down for the moment and that he would explain when he could. It may be interference from the CIA, perhaps or the NSA. The individual it would compute to me is probably in deep cover and whoever is running him doesn't want him disturbed."

"Oh bloody hell. Don't the Americans know we are on the same side?"

"Fortunately for us Rodney, and I have shared this with the Brigadier, this individual has been to the UK a few times." Rodney went still and watched Christian intently seeing a smile creep onto the face, crinkling the wrinkles around the eyes and slight upturn of the lips. He could not dare to think the doc had found something, despite the Americans. He waited patiently for Christian to tell all. "For some reason it would appear this individual was spotted around five years ago going in and out the Russian embassy and was followed out of interest. Very enterprising of our sister services don't you think? Photographs were taken and fingerprints lifted from a beer glass in some London pub. Followed to Scotland and his meetings recorded and photographed. So we have him. Not only that, the SIS shared the finding with MI our Military Intelligence people who started a file on him at that time. As you will be only too well aware, while the Russians have a file on all our service officers we are not far behind, especially when it comes to the commissioned ranking officers, including the KGB and GRU." The scientist fell silent.

"Okay, I give in, who is it?" Rodney final lost his battle to let the scientist unfold his findings in his own time.

"Well we are not sure who he is."

Rodney was nonplussed. "I don't understand?"

Christian reached behind him and pulled a file from a pile of work in his pending tray. He passed the file to Rodney who flipped open the cover. Staring up at him was a young man in his middle-to-late twenties. The name typed on the photograph read Captain Vasily Vladimirov KGB Intelligence Officer. He looked at the MI file notes which gave a chronology albeit incomplete of the officer's career. He noted the Afghanistan tours where he was supposed to be now. Had he got someone else to post the letter or was he back early?

"You can see the dilemma, on the face of it the man is who we see. But the real Vasily Vladimirov is not the man who is now a KGB officer. The real Vasily and his family, he only had a mother in fact, disappeared from their village at the same time this young man entered the KGB academy. The real Vasily was an invalid, needing specialist surgery to correct a genetic defect."

"Are we saying there was a switch? How come the KGB security vetting services don't pick this anomaly up on a routine check?"

"I confess I am a bit out of my depth, but when I took my findings to the Brigadier about us having Vasily on file, instead of being annoyed that I had not let things lie as instructed he was delighted and offered me a rise, not that he could, as I am funded elsewhere, but appreciated nevertheless." Christian ran his fingers through his mop of grey hair. "I think it was the thought that we had something the Americans didn't. I left the file with him and he came to see me two days later. If you leaf to the back of the file you will see a Russian death certificate for the mother, a few weeks before our man entered the academy, who died it would appear whilst she and her son were on holiday in East Germany."

"Nice one, they were obviously lifted out through a Berlin pipeline," thought Rodney. "Are you hanging on to this file for the time being?" he said.

"Brigadier Robinson thought that it would be wise. Who would think of looking for a file like this in my lab in open view?" Add to that he is following up on some other intelligence to try to get the file completed to date and to find out exactly where the mother and son went."

"Did the boss tell you about Chekov?"

"Yes. The whole story, we had quite a session. I am not normally a whisky drinker but I think we had bottle between us." Christian laughed. "It seemed to us when we had put the world to rights that this young man could well be one of the sons of Chekov."

"We shall see. But I admit I am intrigued. Why would a son of Chekov take someone else's identity and deliberately go into the bear's den. And why has he come to me now, if it is him, is it serendipity? A fortunate happenstance or is there something more sinister going on." Rodney was thinking out loud. He paced the lab floor back and forth.

Christian watched him closely. His younger colleague was clearly worried.

"Can I suggest, Rodney, you see the Brigadier? From what he told me of the Chekov affair two other key characters need consideration, General Polyakov and Tsygankov, there seems to me a link."

Rodney handed the file over. "Hang onto that, Doc." He turned to leave then remembered the DNA issue. "Did anything work out on the DNA route?"

"Nothing yet. Go careful Rodney and as the note said, stay alert. I am sure the Captain would not have broken cover on a whim, so treat the words on the note seriously."

Chapter 30

TRAIL IN SPLIT

Saied landed in Bratislava late afternoon. He had a day to get to the Hotel in Split the following night. He had decided on the flight in to drive through the night as far as he could get before taking a break. He would drive all the way, if he felt up to it. His documents were as good as the originals and on arrival he had no difficulty with immigration or the car hire firm.

A long drive equalled comfort in his mind and he opted for a big ford, a Mondeo, with satellite navigation. He spent a little time familiarising himself with the controls and the satnav set up. With his large-scale book of maps and the satnav he worked out what he determined was hopefully the fastest and quickest route to Split; there did seem several options.

The car was full of fuel but he pulled into the airport fuel shop to stock up on travelling rations as he liked to call his food and drink haul.

He cut through the top of Hungary and aimed for Zagreb. He took a break in a late-night petrol station with café that was open and refuelled. He studied the route again before heading for Split. From the map it now looked a nightmare of a journey and he wondered if he should have gone due west from the airport into Austria and then hooked south. Too late for that now, he shrugged to himself. He could always come back that way to prove one or the other.

By the time he was approaching Split it was dawn and he need to find a place to refuel. Finding a 24-hour service station in Croatia's second largest city was not a problem and he hit one as he came off the route into the city centre.

He refuelled and had a large strong sweet coffee to brighten his day. He headed to the garage bathroom where he splashed cold water over his face and thus refreshed, if only temporarily, he drove the last few miles to his hotel.

The hotel was quiet at this time of year, well before the tourists swamped the place, so it was no trouble to get a room technically a day earlier. After he had showered he took four hours' deep untroubled sleep which took him to lunchtime. He didn't expect to be contacted until the evening and he didn't want to go to the boat to draw attention to both him and the boat crewman.

After his marathon drive he felt he needed to get some air and stretch his legs. "Time to be a tourist," he thought. At the hotel reception he asked for a map of the area and any guidebooks they had. The reception had a surprisingly good section of material and he took what was offered and wandered off to study them.

The day at just after noon was just mild enough to sit on the terrace for a while. He decided to eat lunch there. It was his way, his unwritten law, not to drink once an operation was underway, so he took a coffee on the terrace of the hotel which overlooked a beach and the smaller of Split's many marines.

After his wake-up drink, his start-of-day fix as he thought of it, he called for the lunch menu. While he was waiting he fancied he could see his boat and the two crewmen, one young one older and a woman working around the vessel making ready for sea. The menu when it arrived was uninspiring for his mood, another time he would have welcomed what was on offer but he decided to eat out a little later, perhaps in town.

Finishing his coffee he casted the lunch menu lazily aside, an action that suited his mood. He placed the hotel tourist literature on the menu but kept the tourist map of the town. Jean stood and stretched and then wandered down the steps to the deserted winter beach. A cool wind unexpectedly sprang up as he got down to sea level and whipped up sharp shards of sand around him stinging his face and exposed hands. Jean put his hands deep into his coat pocket after pulling up his scarf around his face. The wind dropped as quickly as it had arisen. Stepping onto the marine, he turned left and walked past the tongues of berths stretching away into the Adriatic. At this time of year this marine was barely a quarter full and he was able to make out the gentle rise and fall of the *Harlequin 11* cruiser that he hoped to become crew on in around a week's time. The *Harlequin 11* was clear of other boats, moored half way down and on the inside of the outer berth.

The sleek craft looked fast and comfortable from the corner of his eye and as he walked by he could see the glass patio like doors of the boat's diving and captain's control platform. The doors he knew would lead into the saloon of the boat and that there would be a step down into the cabins at the far end of the saloon. High captain and mates chairs with the wheel and control consul were affixed to the diving deck giving a good view of the bow and sea ahead. The vessel was a faded Mediterranean blue which would make her difficult to spot at sea.

He walked on, leaving the marina behind to the eastern headland marking the start of the city harbour and perambulated around the historic monastery that guarded the approaches to the inner harbour and city of Split.

Consulting his map he began to walk into town, determined to find a place to eat for lunch. On the outskirts was a café that took his fancy. It was a drop-in, advertising Dalmatian home cooking.

Entering, he found a table towards the back and placed his back against the wall. The other customers were a mixed crowd of sailors, seemingly artists and misfits. A taciturn owner, slow to show hospitality especially to a stranger, served the clients as though he was doing them a favour. Jean chose the house speciality for the day and was rewarded eventually with pasticada stuffed olives and overcooked chips. He took water and a glass of tea.

Fortified, Jean headed into town, he had read about the Diocletian palace and he wanted to see it. It took an hour to find the palace which was set back from the centre of town. It intrigued him that Split had first achieved fame when Roman emperor Diocletian (AD 245–313), he had read, who was noted for his persecution of the early Christians, had his retirement palace built here from 295 to 305. After his death the great stone palace continued to be used as a retreat by Roman rulers. When the neighbouring colony of Salona was abandoned in the 7th century, many of the Romanised inhabitants fled to Split and barricaded themselves behind the high palace walls, where their descendants, his literature said, continue to live to this day. He fancied he could see the antecedence in some of the faces of the people around him.

He had read the history of Split over coffee with its over-flowingly rich history, it was too complex to fit into just a couple of sentences, he thought, but attempted in his mind to precise it. Split was an area which was earlier inhabited by the Greek colonies; Emperor Diocletian should be, he noted, considered its first citizen of Split and its founder, starting his lavish villa of around 300 square metres near the great city of Salona in AD 293, only to retire from the Roman throne to live within its walls after building it for ten years before his death.

Jean was fascinated and tried to parallel his native Palestine to this environment. He found similarities; what Palestine lacked he reasoned was an Emperor like Diocletian to bring his home state alive. He read of the turbulent centuries that followed the emperor turning the villa into a city, conceived by the fugitive inhabitants of Salona who fled from the Avars and the Slavs. Many authorities changed hands in the city, and in the years that followed the city grew beyond the Palace walls. It had Croatian Kings in the 10th century, followed by Hungarian and Venetian administrations. The French ruler for a while giving way to the Austro-Hungarian monarchy. In the 20th century, Split went from the Kingdom of Yugoslavia, through some tragic, yet heroic times of the Italian and German occupation during the Second World War. Split was one of the centres of anti-fascist resistance. After the war it became the socialist Yugoslavian republic.

Jean could clearly see its history had left its trace in the everyday life of the city that seemed in many ways to be moving steadily forward despite its older buildings. He now understood why Split was the centre in every way of this part of the coast. On his way to the palace he noticed again the echoes of history and its numerous layers; clumsiness was inevitable, even so, the rashness in development was all a part of this city's originality he thought to himself. What he liked about this location, apart from the architecture, was the blue of the Mediterranean that seemed so welcoming. He put it on his list of favourite places and one that one day he might consider living in, at least revisiting.

His visit to the palace was not disappointing and halls below the palace hosted a couple of exhibitions by local artists. One was by an impressionist artist with some curious sculptures the artist had carved out of marble. The other exhibition was very modern almost cubism which Jean thought clever, but contrived.

He wandered back to the hotel getting there around six o'clock, and had a word with Reception who handed him a message in a sealed envelope. The message was simple; it was for him to meet on the boat, the *Harlequin*, at 1930hrs that night.

With an hour and half to kill after his walk, he was hungry and whiled away the time in the Hotel Jarden's restaurant. The food and the service were excellent, it helped, he thought that he appeared to be the only one eating this early.

Wrapping himself up against the chill of the evening he left via the terrace and beach to the marina. The berth pontoons were floating and he made his way cautiously down the one leading to the boat, which heaved gently under him. Although it was getting dark there was a fisherman fishing off the beginning of the pontoon and another he could just make out on the far end of the berth.

A man tall and rangy, in worn jeans and a yellow waterproof, windcheater stood silently waiting for him, one foot on the boat and the other on the pontoon. As Jean got close enough to shake the man's hand the man turned and beckoned Jean to follow him into the cabin.

The cabin was well appointed to the point of luxury that Jean was unaccustomed to. Brightly lit, it revealed two further men who were talking and seated together in leather easy chairs to one side of the cabin. They were drinking beer and smoking. What they didn't do was introduce themselves but stood instead to shake Jean's hand.

The man who had led Jean into the cabin did however introduce himself as the Captain.

Jean, used to fencing with suspicious people and those wanting to live in the shadows, took the lead. "Gentlemen, let us get down to business shall we?"

The taller of the two men, smartly dressed in a dark suit and white shirt, brought out from his jacket a paper envelope. "Please, this is the specification and batch numbers of the product." The man's accent was strongly Russian not unlike Servo's. Unlike Servo, this man was in his fifties and wasp thin with wispy greying hair. His companion, Jean deduced, must be the muscle – the bulge he had noticed in the man's jacket confirmed Jean's first thoughts.

Jean accepted the envelope, took out the specification and brought out his own list from his inside coat pocket to compare the batch number and specification. He read the lists carefully and after a while was satisfied that both lists tallied. He looked at the men and nodded, "It looks good to me, and the product is where?"

The Captain thumbed to the forward cabins. "It is in there awaiting you inspection."

The older man indicated Jean should follow him. In the first of the cabins on the two twin beds the explosive was laid out for inspection on black plastic sheeting. 250 kilograms, in 50 packs 5 kilograms each, spread out equally on both of the beds. Saied, after counting the packs selected five and cut from each a small sample, "We will test these five; if all is well the deal is done." He smelt the samples, they were for all intents and purposes odourless.

"Once we have tested them we will need to speak to your principal about the payment."

Jean smiled, pulling his satellite phone from his pocket. "Once the test is successful you can speak to him and do what you have to do."

They joined the others in the main cabin. "Captain, the agent and I will go and test the samples he has chosen. We should be about an hour; we will then return and if all is well we will be away. In the meantime, if you don't mind, my companion will remain on board to guard the product and keep you company."

"That will be fine; we can chew over the way of things." The Captain smiled, a slight French lilt to his speech and Jean noticed him for the first time. Hair bleached almost white by the sun, with skin bronzed and lined by the sun and time in the open air. Fit certainly, around forty, and cords for muscles but enough to be useful. What intrigued Jean more was the old French Foreign Legion motto tattooed on the back of his right hand, "*Valeur et discipline*". And the current one, "*Legio Patria Nostra*", The Legion is our Fatherland, on his left hand.

"*Jusqu'à ce quel'heure, mon Legionnaire Capitaine*," Jean said and the Captain laughed a deep rumble and wagged his finger at him.

The Russians missed the joke and the main man was keen to get off, "Shall we go? We will use my car as we will need the initiators to test the samples and they are in the boot." The older of the two men ushered Jean off the boat. "We are going to need to drive for about fifteen minutes to a small cove at the end of this peninsular of land. It's deserted and half a mile plus away from the northern marina and as much again from any other habitation. The location should be fine and we will not be disturbed."

They got to the cove down the road marked, "*Taliste Marina Ta*", just after eight. The night was now fully set and it was as black as the ace of spades under the trees where they parked to one side of the road. There was no traffic or walkers to trouble them. As they emerged from the trees onto the lip of the cove, the moon was coming up and it reflected light on the oily surface of a still sea. The weak moonlight reflecting off the sea gave them ample light to make a shaky but safe descent to the tiny stone and shingle-strewn beach with the sea lapping quietly over the pebbles.

"You have been here before I think?" Jean whispered to the man.

"Yes I have been here more than once, at least. See the large man-sized rock against the cliff? There is a small cave behind it. More an indentation really, but it will satisfy our needs. I will set the charges; do you want to witness the setting of the charge?"

"Yes. Wait, let us now choose between the samples. One test will be enough; as you were prepared to test all I can now assume all is well," Jean directed. Jean held out the samples on the palm of his hands and the man chose one of them at random.

Together they set the sample and the electrical initiator and covered the charge in sand and small stones and then fed wires to the other side of the large rock. The man attached one wire to the battery he produced from his pocket and touched the wire to the terminal. The explosion was muffled but its blast moved the air around them and moved the rock slightly off its, base causing it to rock backwards and forwards a few times. A shower of small stones and rock chips was blasted into the air around them and into the sea.

Jean was impressed with the explosive power of such a small sample. "Good enough let's get back, you can make your call." Jean told the man. When they were in the car Jean dialled up Tsygankov who answered after the third ring.

"Jean?" Tsygankov read Jean on the dial.

"Yes. We tested the product. It is odourless and almost clear, just a little translucent. The specifications match. The agent would now like to talk to you to conclude the deal."

The business was concluded quickly between the agent and Tsygankov. The agent handed Jean the phone and started the car. Back on board the Russians shook everyone's hands, declining the offer of a drink.

Jean and the Captain were alone on the boat. "Time I think to introduce myself properly, Captain, as we are going to be spending some time together. My name is Jean Salomon."

"My name is Jean Paul better just call me Paul, and my two crew who you are about to meet and who have been keeping watch are Juliette and Dmitri."

"Ah yes the fishermen."

"Indeed. Now let's get the product shipped away shall we."

Jean helped the Captain stash the now double-wrapped explosive into twenty-five bundles carefully into the specially adapted petrol tank. The wrapping was impervious to water and fuel, and the Captain back-filled and topped up the tank with fuel. The fuel opening was sealed with a one-time use seal as a check against the explosives being tampered with.

Jean Paul called his crew in and introduced them to Jean. "They will help me with the crossing; we will travel without stopping excepting for weather and refuelling. Once we get to the Canal du Midi, the crew will leave the boat and you will replace them. I will pick them up on the return leg. I am quite happy to run the boat by myself the return leg of the channel, looking forward to a little peace actually." He smiled. "You need to leave now as we will cast off shortly; I would rather be at sea as soon as possible just in case those two return if they decide they can sell the product twice, if you understand what I mean."

Jean shook hands with them all and wished them a fair wind. "I look forward to seeing you in a few days then, quite an adventure I think."

Jean Paul grinned adding. "Hope you can cook." It was a throw-away remark but Jean nodded, indicating it would not be a problem.

As he left the crew he said to Jean Paul, "It would be helpful if you had plenty of spices, I like to cook with them." He exchanged his mobile phone number with the captain and was passed the captain's business card with his number and email details.

The Captain bunched his hands and showed Saied the backs of his hands. "By the way, as you can see I have been around and spicy food is a favourite of mine; there will be plenty of spices and food for you to cook with."

"*Jusqu'à l'heure*, until the hour." Saied waved a farewell.

Chapter 31

THE BANKER

Jane, Andrew and Pat had the Banker Mr John Brown in the offices by eight o'clock in the morning to prepare him for meeting Rodney at eight-thirty.

Rodney had no idea what to expect and the Dickensian figure in an old shiny dark suit that the team wheeled in to his office, was a surprise. He had expected a dapper city gent, this man was almost scruffy. Topping six foot four but now stooped with age, his overlong white wispy hair framed with bushy sideburns, a long face with a sad countenance was highlighted startlingly by bright coal-black eyes.

Rodney advanced to shake his hand. The man's hands were dry and liver-spotted but the grip was firm and strong. "Mr Brown, welcome to our little group I hope you are being looked after by the team?"

"No complaints so far. I gather we share the same name but I don't think we are related." The Banker's voice was pure Oxford and loud, but a hint of southern Irish brogue could be detected. Rodney thought he might be a bit deaf. "My understanding from your colleagues is that you would like to have an insight into the world of IRA money and the chances of tracing it."

Rodney nodded; indicting the Banker should take a seat in the easy chair. "Could we get you anything, tea, coffee?"

"No I don't think so, perhaps later."

Mr Reid sat behind Rodney who resumed his desk chair and the other three found a seat where they could.

The Banker started slowly, "In the context of money and where does it come from and from whom and how do they get it to another without a trace is one question to be answered. In principle it is quite easy to do really if others cooperate. By others I mean banks, bankers, Inland Revenue, IRS in the case of America etc, Company House, authorities in general etc, etc. So we need to concentrate on the 'who' and the 'how' to begin with," the stated without preamble. "In your difficult quest, my suggestion would be to begin with the 'who'. You or others will have some intelligence already as I do, let us gather everything we have from whatever source." He put his head to one side and smiled. "I often find in cases of this sort it pays to talk to the target's opposition, the competitors, as they are usually only too happy to shop the competition. You can make the mental leap in this case to the Protestants' organisations. They are still spitting blood about the 1995 Anglo Irish agreement, where they saw their favoured status disappear and they see themselves treated no better than the IRA. Further they don't feel they are being listened to. Clever propaganda has tended to cast them in the role of thugs and loud-mouthed empty vessels. Perception is reality. And don't discount disaffected IRA organisations and staff, defectors etc. I understand the FBI is an excellent source in relation to the disaffected and the defectors."

Rodney interrupted. "Mr Reid and I will be talking to the FBI and will feed back any information relevant to you and the money team."

The Banker fumbled in his jacket for a handkerchief. "Hmm, need to ask the right questions of course. I will let you have some pointers this morning which may be helpful. The name of the game is to picture this task a giant jigsaw puzzle in which we shall gather increments of data and patch them into the picture until it makes some sense or until way forward has been completed. Rather like a snakes and ladders game within the puzzle." The Banker looked directly at Rodney and Reid, grinning. "Got to say I am very excited at having the opportunity to partake in this adventure. The exercise is long overdue in the way you are tackling it. I have been banging on about this for years and here we are at last. It has been a hobby of mine. So you will be pleased to hear I have quite a bit of the jigsaw already to get us started, may even have a ladder or two to climb. Now that tea I think." He beamed round the room and Rodney, who had on first impression thought the team had been given an old duffer, now realised beneath the dull exterior they had been given a champion for the cause. Rodney sent Andrew to get them all tea. He sensed the room was captivated by the Banker as in a few sentences he had reverted their attention.

"Do you really think you will be able to trace the money and the routes and who gets it?" Reid asked and the Banker waited for his refreshment to arrive.

"Yes and no." The Banker smiled. "But fear not, we shall most certainly make a greater dent into their *modus operandi* than anybody else has done to date or I will retire or something." He had an infectious laugh and it spread round the room. "I do want to tell you something about the state of the nation as far as money movement and laundering is concerned. It is not a great picture as far as dirty money is concerned."

"Dirty money?" Jane queried.

"Let us define it as any money that funds terrorism and its corruption or simple corruption. Unfortunately there is no global force that is in existence to fight it. Would be a great step forward for everyone concerned if it was formed from a spin-off from this exercise, if all goes well. Job for life I think for your team if you want it." The tea arrived and he continued, "Not enough is being done to tackle the backers, the originators of the money and I hope this will change and be one outcome of this investigation. Now more than ever we need to stop the flow of funds and destroy the pipelines it travels through. This dirty money runs world-wide into not millions but trillions. Think on that. Think on lost tax for one matter and the help this money could otherwise be put to alleviate poverty and just about any other malaise in this troubled world of ours. We will need to operate at two, possibly three levels. The large and small backers, the legitimate businesses bought by dirty business or inherited and the revenues generated from drugs, prostitution, protection and the like." He drained his tea. "Another please, Andrew, if you don't mind? To get some traction on this problem we need real teeth and the political will of our masters. Whereas I see Rodney you would be interested in the hardware pipeline for the arms, the Quartermaster, Chief of Staff and his active service units, we want the Accountant. We want to look into his books. If we cannot get his books we need to create a fair copy of them. Let there be no misunderstanding about this funding for the IRA, part of your task could get ugly. You can bet your bottom dollar that some powerful people will have their fingers in the pie. We are talking about politicians, bankers and backers to name but three. There are also vested interests in this country and others. The American Irish vote lobby for one. The Irish government for another and despite all indication to the contrary, the very last thing Dublin wants is annexation of Ulster and to have to cope with not only its Protestant majority but the economy too as well as a section of the community that would be uncontrollable. It would be a security, cultural and financial disaster for them. As for our quest, there will be howls of indignation and rage from some seemingly holier than holy perpetrators. So we had better have our eggs in a row and our facts watertight before we spring the traps I have in mind. My question to you is, are you up for it? I am of an age where whatever I do is not going to be career limiting and this investigation could be physically dangerous to your team. So I want your commitment now or I walk." The gravity of what he was saying was dawning on the team members present and a silence settled on the room.

Rodney looked round the room at his staff. Each in turn nodded they were in. "Looks to me John that you have your team. Mr Reid, clearly the team-work needs to be protected and their findings as time go on. Would you please appraise Graham that the data room is now exclusively our project team's eyes only, only the Brigadier may countermand that order and through me only. I want Graham to get the team its own safe put in the operations room and a wall dedicated to their 'jigsaw' with a metal security blind. Got it?"

"Good as done, boss."

"Will those arrangements suffice, John?"

"Good start Rodney. I can see we are on the same page. Now with your leave I want to get started with Jane, Andrew and Pat. The first order of business will be to plot all the data I have gathered over the years that focus on the IRA and its funds, its backers and laundering pipelines. Once we start I need to remind you there is no going back." He stood and shook Rodney and Reid's hands, maintaining direct eye contact, before gathering the finance tracking team to him, "Come on Jane and you two gentlemen, let us to it, not a minute to lose." He turned to Rodney as he went through the door and tapped the side of his nose. "Time is money."

After he left, Rodney and Reid looked at each other. "Well boss, I think we got a winner there. We could not have asked for better help I judge. Our lot are going to have to run to keep up, did you see the look on Pat's face?"

Rodney laughed; he too had been struck by the look on the faces of his money-finding team which was a mixture of bewilderment, excitement and expectation. "I just wished the Brigadier had been here to meet and hear the Banker. I don't know where he dug him up from but I suspect they are old sparing partners."

"You could be right Rodney, don't suppose we have heard from Simon yet?"

"Not yet but early days."

"I had a call from Avery this morning about our surveillance team. They are dug in across the valley from the Quartermaster's house. They have some footage of people in and out and we should get that tonight with Avery's first report."

"Have you heard anything from Sharky and Mould about their task?"

"Silence; but they will surface if they get anything."

"We may have another friend in court. Do you remember me mentioning an Inspector Coveney who was with the South African special branch when we were involved with Tsygankov out over the decoder?"

"Yeah I remember him vaguely, something about he and his lads getting the break on the mercenary team that stole the device."

"That's right, well shortly after he did an exchange with our police and liked the Scotland Yard ethos so much he transferred and rocketed up the ranks. He is now either the superintendent or may even be assistant commissioner now of the SO 14 antiterrorist branch."

"Interesting, so do you and I see him before or after the FBI London liaison officer?"

"Well I was thinking we see them together, how about lunch and take it from there."

"Don't tell me, fix it for today. Sherlock Holmes pub, upstairs table?"

"Great idea. I am going to see the Brigadier about the Banker and he may want to come to lunch himself; hope he does, his expenses account seems limitless as far as our secretariat is concerned, it's a rare month they don't knock mine back first time I put them in."

"Fair enough, in which case I will stand the two guests up but wait till you come back to me about the venue. Just a thought, the old man might want to host them in the Wellington Barracks officers' mess for appearance and security sake."

"No problem. I will confirm with you one way or the other in the next half hour." Rodney collected his notebook and left Reid reaching for the phone.

"Rodney."

Rodney was exiting the door. "Forgot something did I?" he asked Reid.

"No, it is just that the ladies in the secretariat have the hots for you or so they told me. No wonder you have to make extra visits to get your expenses through." Reid had a superior look on his face as he punched numbers into the phone, not even looking at Rodney as he spoke. Rodney for his part gave Reid the finger.

Chapter 32

CARLA AND SERVO

After they left the others at Moscow Airport, Carla and Servo waited for their flight to Dublin. Of all the airports in the world Carla thought Moscow was the one airport she felt comfortable in. True a new terminal was planned but she liked the proximity of the people. At this time of year the weather was still cold enough for the ladies to be sporting long fur coats and fur hats. They looked great, she thought, unlike the outlander who could be picked out in their synthetic padded coats and jackets. The smell of acrid cigarettes reminded her of her home. The men on the other hand were a little drab in dress but the splendid Russian fur hats, the Ushanka, made up for that. Bored for a moment with people-watching, Carla looked over to her relaxed companion.

Servo was gazing around like Carla taking in the environment. She studied him for a while. He was no doubt a fighter but his demeanour and deportment set him aside from the normal thugs Carla was familiar with. "I could have a worse assignment than to be closeted with this man for the duration." She smiled to herself. If she wanted to progress a relationship she would have to make the running. Initially in the beginning at least.

Servo for his part just felt relaxed if not a little bewildered. Only a few weeks ago he had been fighting in Afghanistan where every day was a step into the unknown and possible life-threatening danger. He thought to himself, "Here I am sitting with a beautiful woman. Been wined and dined by a General in his dacha. I am about to fly to Ireland for a few days' fishing and a chat with an unknown organisation, unknown to me at least." He chuckled.

Carla looked at him surprised. "Do you want to share the joke?"

"Oh nothing really, I was just thinking over the whole situation, it is so completely off the wall. One minute I am fighting the Mujahedin in the mountains of Afghanistan and the next here I am sitting next to you in Moscow like an old married couple." He laughed again.

She smiled at him. "Well in that case darling, you had better pick up your case and mine because they have just posted our flight." She stood up with him and then handed him her flight bag. Putting her arm through his she added joyously, "Come Servo, take me to Dublin!"

They enjoyed the flight together and chatted, swapping histories, reinforcing their legend as friends and lovers. They watched together as the plane circled and glided into Dublin. At immigration they passed through unchallenged but the customs officer, noticing their Eastern European accents against the presented Australian passports, signalled security and they were tagged by security as 'persons of interest' and photographed by a security ceiling-mounted camera before they left the terminal.

Their details reached Irish Special Branch later that day and were shared with the mainland sister organisations as was regular custom and practice.

Others were waiting for them too, but unlike the security services they had a personal interest in how the pair would act and who if anyone they contacted or met.

At the car hire Servo upgraded the car to a Land Rover, thinking it would be more suitable for the country roads. It was just an excuse, he liked the vehicle as he thought it was as near as he would get to his Russian Jeep, which he admitted to himself he missed.

They drove into Dublin and as the day was moving into the late afternoon they decided to stay in the city before moving out to the country the following day. The car hire staff had given them directions and recommended the Clontarf Castle Hotel in Castle Avenue, Dublin, if they wanted something special and different.

Carla punched the address into the on-board satnav. It took just over half an hour to get to the hotel. Servo for his part had been watching a grey Ford following at a distance for some time and as it followed them off the R107. The Ford continued to follow them as they swung into the last quarter of a mile of road leading to the hotel.

Servo watched in the rear view mirror, the Ford go past as they turned into the hotel entrance.

"Wow look at this place, it really is a castle." She put her hand on Servo's leg. "You really know how to show a girl a good time," she teased him.

Servo's face coloured up, which Carla noticed and thought to herself as charming. "Carla I have to admit it does look like we have fallen on our feet. We were followed by the way."

Carla surprised him. "Grey Ford probably a Probe, nice sports car when new. The car was scruffy – unwashed exterior, dirty windscreen, probably a ten-year-old banger. Two men, one about thirty and the other slightly older but I think sharp-featured. A bit rough looking, both of them. Black bomber jackets and rolled-up balaclavas on their heads. Think they are the scouts for our man rather than the authorities. How did I do?"

"Better than me!" He pulled up near the reception. Carla got out and went ahead of him to check on the reservation and the room. Servo unloaded the bags and followed her in.

"Great reception area," was his initial thought. The next thought was that, "It was going to be expensive just glad it is not my money."

Carla noted they had booked a deluxe room and they were soon shown up to the room on the first floor. Servo set the bags down and looked around. A big television to go with the large room, easy chairs, dressing table, desk and a mini bar, tea-making facilities and en suite bathroom were the main points he noted. It was slightly old-fashioned but in keeping with the castle itself. The high king-size four poster bed was certainly going to be more comfortable than his steel-framed field bed back in Afghanistan with its stretched springs.

When the hotel porter left, Servo turned to Carla. "Carla, has it escaped your notice there is only one bed. Even if the bed is a massive one, it's still only one."

She looked at him, shaking her head in mock disappointment. "Oh really, well we are supposed to be a couple. And couples sleep together. So we can sleep together but it doesn't mean we have to actually sleep together?" She turned away so she could not see his embarrassment. He would get used to it in time.

"Let's freshen up and sort out our kit and then go and have a drink and some food."

"Okay, good idea."

They walked into the hotel's Knights bar with its dark furniture, knights in armour and a grand piano with the lid up. Carla walked over to it and struck a few cords. "Nice instrument and in tune."

"Do you play?" Servo was interested.

"A little, but my passion is the violin." She ran her fingers down the keyboard. "Did you see the violins in the case at the dacha?"

"They looked expensive and old."

"Both and worth a fortune, I hope very much to get a chance to play them when we get back."

Servo naturally cautious thought to himself, "If we are lucky enough to get back?" He dismissed the euphemism and smiled at Carla. "I for one look forward to hearing you play."

They settled themselves into the seat in the corner of the room, their backs to the wall so they could watch the whole of the room and who entered and left. The waiter came over and took their order. Servo wanted to try the Guinness and Carla followed suit. The waiter wanted to know if they were eating in, and when they readily agreed he brought over menus for them to study while he went to pour the drinks.

The restaurant was called The Fahrenheit and it claimed to be one of the finest restaurants in Dublin. The restaurant menu was certainly promising

Carla chose the local cooked fish and Servo the air-dried beef flambé, a speciality of the restaurant. When the drinks were brought Servo ordered and added a bottle of Chardonnay Pays d'Oc for Carla and Merlot for himself to be waiting on the table when they were called. The waiter wanted to know if they wanted a starter and they dived back into the menu. Carla chose the oysters and Servo the whitebait.

The Guinness was new to them and the initial bitter iron taste brought them up sharp. Once they were over the initial shock they sipped it, carefully adjusted to the taste, and enjoyed the creamy textured experience.

When they were eventually invited to the restaurant by the restaurant manager with an old-world charm they were shown to a table where the waiter held the chairs and settled the couple in. Another waiter brought the starters and the wine waiter poured the drinks.

While the starters were a treat, nothing prepared them for Carla's large pan-fried fish and Servo's beef that was brought in flaming on a sword and carved at the table. It was a great night and the two Russians enjoyed every minute of the experience and each other's company.

To finish they went back to the bar and both had vodka-based cocktails and coffee, neither despite the quantity they had consumed showed the sign of drink. There were few other guests in the hotel at this time of year and no-one stood out to them as a threat, so they enjoyed themselves.

Servo at last escorted Carla to the room. "It's still early here but I think time to sleep; we will need our wits about us tomorrow." Carla was talking as she took a chair and jammed it under the door handle. Servo raised his eyebrows. "Force of habit, and don't want you escaping now I have you in my room." She laughed and he echoed the delight. "I am going to shower before bed."

"Good idea I feel grubby after all the travelling, so after you. Slight problem Carla, I don't wear generally anything in bed, I didn't bring anything." Servo was slightly embarrassed.

Carla's voice was husky. "Oh Servo, that is not a problem it is an opportunity, for neither do I."

When Servo finally slid into bed he thought Carla was asleep and with a sigh lay on his back looked up at the ceiling. He felt Carla stir and move to him sliding one leg over him and tucking herself into him. He was aroused. It had been months and months since he had lain with a woman and this one was special in every way. He was conscious of an awakening arousal in him. He was fully turned on, enjoying the feeling but chiding himself to behave. In one movement Carla slid her body over his and took him slowly into herself, closing her thighs on him so there was no escape. A bond between them now existed and both knew it was special.

"How clever of Tsygankov," was Carla's thought as she wrecked herself on Servo and he on her.

In the morning at breakfast Servo had picked up the *Irish Times* and scanned the paper for items of interest. Carla would concentrate on her haddock and poached eggs. She was thinking that as they had not yet had a call from the other members of the team or contact with the IRA they should stay put at least for another day instead of charging around Ireland.

"Hey Servo, listen I have got an idea." Carla leaned over and pushed Servo's paper down so he would look at her.

"Let's hear it."

"I think we should stay in Dublin for another day. The logic is that we haven't heard from the team yet and no message from the IRA when clearly they know we are here."

Servo chewed the idea over. He had had a similar thought when he had checked the reception on the way to breakfast and nothing was in their pigeon hole. "I would not push back on that idea. I would certainly like to hear from Vasily where our bolt-holes are in England.

Not only that, I would like to take a look round Dublin. Remember on one of the briefings in Moscow they indicated some of the bars owned by the IRA to us, well let us show our faces in a few that might just get a reaction."

"Servo that's exactly what I was thinking. Well close at least."

"It would also give us a little time, we are supposed to study the road and waterways before we head up country. Besides I want to have a look at a sports gun and angling shop. I would like, if nothing else, a bit more of an arsenal."

"Love it, shopping expedition. You find your designer hardware and then you can then come with me to find a designer number for dinner tonight. Deal?"

"Deal, now can I finish this paper?"

Chapter 33

VASILY

As he had been briefed, Vasily went through immigration head down. At immigration a smiling officer and guardian of the British shores swiped his passport and asked a few seemingly innocent questions. Vasily's slight Eastern European accent coupled with his Australian passport caused the alert customs officer to flag Vasily and placed him in the "persons of interest file". The file would be shared with security that day and his photograph from his passport enlarged and tagged with the pictures from the other security cameras that track passengers from the aircraft to the exit doors of the airport. The camera security system at the airport was state-of-the-art and there is no place to hide from all of them. Tsygankov would not have been aware of the recent upgrades even if someone was in some clumsy bureaucracy dungeon of the KGB building in Moscow. In this context his man was now a follow-up statistic for the security services.

It would be a matter time before Vasily came to the attention of the top security echelons the IG (Intelligence Group.) Within this circus, information would be shared automatically with Robinson's team.

He stood in a tight group waiting for his hold bag and strolled calmly through the "nothing to declare" lane at the custom and excise station.

Emerging from the exit onto the concourse he mingled with other welcoming parties, placing his black briefcase carefully against his right leg so he could feel the pressure of the case. He bent down removing the Aeroflot cabin luggage label. As the crowd milled around he felt the case pressed against his leg ease away. From the corner of his eye he saw a man stop next to him put his case down and swop his briefcase for an identical one of his own.

Vasily waited another few minutes bent and attached his cabin tag and hefted the briefcase. The briefcase was distinctly heavier.

He went in search of a café and bought himself a pot of tea and a BLT sandwich. Before long he spotted himself as private an area at the back of the airport café as he could find. Settling himself, he opened the briefcase away from prying eyes. Principally it contained as far as he was concerned the core elements to satisfy his immediate needs. There were three envelopes containing keys, with the safe house addresses on the covers. A large-scale soft-covered book atlas of the UK had been slid into the lid inside pocket and several pages had flags attached. There was also a UK pay-as-you-go mobile which he decided to exchange as soon as he could for one of his own. He fired it up and saw it was fully charged. He scrolled the menu for numbers. They had logged in the three safe houses and the embassy liaison officer contact numbers. "This is a very useful start for me, someone has thought this through," he was impressed. A slim rectangular box filled the entire bottom of the case. He opened the lid and saw three of the small PPS silent pistols with nine loaded magazines of 6 rounds. There was a note which advised him that heavier weapons were stashed in the safe house in Wallop. "That," he thought, "will please Servo. Goodness knows what he is he thinking without his personal arsenal that he has not been separated from for years I just cannot imagine."

His next thought was, "Knowing Servo he will be tooling up somehow." He searched the case lid pocket again and found three vehicle car fobs with their registration and safe house address on a tag for each bunch.

He had to make a decision. Which house to go to? His gut feeling was to go to the safe house at Nether Wallop. It was the only one of the three houses that made sense as it was close to the target and the weapons were there.

He broke open the envelope for the house. There were clear directions to follow to find the house, he read:

"M4 from the airport to M3 going west. After Basingstoke junction 7 look for the A303 travel down the A303 to the junction for the A343 and head south towards Salisbury. At the George Inn Junction turn right for Nether Wallop along Farley Street, find Church Hill road to your right and after about a mile there is a large complex with a B&B called Halcon. It will be signposted. Half a mile further into the country there is a large wood, which is fenced and gated. At the gated track entrance go through and follow the track into the wood for a quarter of a mile and there is the property. Keys to the gate are on the bunch. The landlord is away overseas and the agent in London so you will not be disturbed. The legend is that you are a writer and need isolation."

He decided on car rental rather than public transport or a taxi. He could do some shopping on the way, even though he felt sure the house would be provisioned. Renting the car was not a problem but it took time and the longer he spent in the airport the more uneasy he became. It only needed a policeman with a sniffer dog to pass him who would pick up the smell of the gun oil or ammunition. He was relieved when he got to the front of the rental queue and they had several car options available for him to choose from. The transaction done he moved quickly to the rental park to find his car. Once secure in his own space he spent some time in the car familiarising himself with his route on the map provided against the instructions. "Probably it was a two hour drive." He noticed the large town of Basingstoke at Junction 6 on the M3, an ideal location to come off the motorway get what he thought he might want and then get to the house.

The car he chose was a diesel seven-seater people carrier, automatic with built-in satnav. The last thing he wanted to think about was gears on the right side of the drive and direction. It would be enough to think about keeping to the left side of the road, which was all very confusing and unnatural for him. He set a satnav waypoint for Basingstoke and the main destination for the Middle Wallop safe house. He would delete both on arrival.

Arriving in Basingstoke he parked in the Anvil car park and shopped. Blacks for outdoor gear and working boots, Marks and Spencer's he knew of and got some really good quality British casual outfits, and from there he found Sainsbury's food outlet where he purchased enough wine, whisky and food and cooking provisions to keep him going for the few days he needed or until he got himself orientated. He bought a cheap pay-as-you-go mobile and a charger from one of the many phone stores.

On the way out of Basingstoke he stopped at Curry's and PC World for a printer and a few packs of stationery. He wasn't sure if the safe houses had a radio or TV. He bought a modest Ghetto blaster with wide radio band range including short wave. He chose a selection of music CDs he felt would suit the team. He prevaricated about a TV but eventually settled on a 32-inch flat screen TV with an indoor aerial with separate signal booster unit, just in case.

Ready at last, the time was approaching lunchtime. He could see the small shopping outlet site had a McDonald's and a Pizza Express. He chose Pizza to take away and ordered a large one to take with him. He could reheat it later.

Less than an hour later he was at the Middle Wallop crossroad and turned right to Nether Wallop. The name made him smile. It took another ten minutes to find the house location. Despite the clear evidence of military around Middle Wallop he noticed, with blue berets, the village of Nether was an idyllic old-fashioned and traditional village set in the Hampshire countryside.

As he approached the safe house he was pleased to see that the village houses and population were left behind. The Halcon complex was the last of it. After Halcon there were no other dwellings and the wooded area that hid the house came up on the left as expected.

Pulling in, he quickly left the car and opened the gate. He swung the gate open just enough to allow him to drive in. Once in, he reversed the process, making sure the padlock was secured in place

The house was set back in the dense wood completely out of sight of the road. Quickly he went into the house to check it out. Entry was carefully made, he wanted no surprises, this was after all now enemy territory. Upstairs there were three bedrooms, a double and three singles with twin single beds in each room. All with bedding resting on the beds so they just had to be made. A large bathroom serviced the floor, with a smaller en suite for the master bedroom.

He checked out the water and heating. The water was on and the heating on frost stat. He turned up the heating and heard the satisfactory click of the thermostat.

Downstairs there was a dining room, large country kitchen with a large double oven, gas range hobs and fridge freezer, cutlery and china. The place seemed well appointed; the liaison officer had left enough provisions to service the team's needs for a few weeks. The sitting room, in addition to the radiators, had a wood burner and patio doors leading to the south west onto a sitting area. From here the army airfield could be seen. There was a utility room leading off the kitchen with downstairs shower and separate toilet room.

From the front entrance door the stairs faced him, with the sitting room on the left, and to the right the dining room which led into the kitchen and service areas. A back door exited from the utility room. Under the stairs he noticed the locked double-sized metal gun cabinet, something he would explore later.

Before he unpacked the car he scouted the area around the house and circled the wood. From the height of the location to the south, the house could oversee some of Nether village and had an uninterrupted view of the Middle Wallop Army Air Corps airfield and its hanger and accommodation buildings stretching off into the horizon. On the other three sides it was open country.

The airfield was busy with helicopters taking off and landing. The army airbase in size, small compared to the Russian air training centre at Torzhok in the region of Tver, but he thought more compact.

He looked at his watch and the darkening sky which threatened rain. "It is time to get sorted out and the car unpacked; after that eat and then get a plan together," he prompted himself. He needed to get the camper purchased and sorted before Servo and Carla joined him in a week or so. He would make that his priority tomorrow; after that the safe house on the east coast that only the team would know off.

As he turned back for the house he almost missed the overlarge double garage tucked away in a dense yew thicket of the wood that was growing tightly on three sides of the garage and its branches threatened to enclose the front as they grew untended. He pulled the doors open and revealed an almost new black BMW 3 Series. The theory was a new vehicle would be less likely to be pulled by the police if it was driven within the law. "Nice," he thought. "I will look forward to burning some rubber with that!"

After heating up his meal he sorted himself out and fixed up the television, which had surprisingly good reception, he suspected because of the house elevation. He watched the news programmes and he transferred the numbers from the supplied cell phone to his satellite phone and his pay-as-you-go. He took out the battery from the supplied cell phone. He could not take the chance that the London Russian Embassy KGB staff, or others for that matter, could track him through it. He made a mental note to search for tracking devices on the BMW and in particular for listening and camera devices secreted in the house by his fellow London-based KGB. It was after all what he would do in the case of strangers on his turf.

Chapter 34

SAIED'S LIBYAN MINI ADVENTURE

Saied's body clock was shot to pieces by the time he arrived in Cairo and got a cheap charter flight to Tripoli. This was not so much from the loss and gain of a few hours but the two massive drives to and from Split from Bratislava mostly overnight. He tried to work out how long it had been since he left the dacha but failed.

He scrambled along with the crowd off the plane when they landed at Tripoli and into the baggage hall and customs. He was soon through and on the arrivals concourse looking for the contact that was to meet him.

If he had not been slightly out of sorts and jet-lagged he might have picked up the fact that interest was being shown in him by two Somalis. The two men had been initially tracing the movement of the Libyan IRA liaison intelligence officer, LIO for short, for the last two days since Simon had given them the dual tasks of reporting and photographing contacts with the IRA LIO and copying manifests destined for the UK if they could.

Simon's men had picked Saied out at the airport as a possible, by, at first, chance alone. It was the second trip they had made to the airport that day. He was the only one on the flight that was not a Libyan and had no relatives or friends meeting him. A quick check on the airline's computer by a Somali brother working at the airport showed him arriving from Cairo previously ex Moscow. They had watched him with one eye on the LIO who was on his phone with his back to Saied. Saied lingered on the arrivals concourse for a while trying to orientate himself on the airport layout. The LIO finished his call, turned and scanned the arrivals area. He picked up Saied in seconds. The government intelligent officer that Simon's men knew handled the IRA team strode over to Saied and made himself known to Saied before taking him to one side, clearly giving the passenger directions to a meet and apologising for not being able to host Saied that day. The older of Simon's men moved in close enough in time to catch the end of the conversation. "Until tomorrow then, eight okay, at the Al Khums port main entrance, once again so sorry that I cannot host you till then." Saied waved the excuse away claiming he was fatigued anyway and a good day's rest would suit him anyway. The two men shook hands. The other of Simon's men took Saied's picture with the LIO and had it emailed it to Simon in Mogadishu before they left the airport.

Saied's first action after the short meeting with the LIO was to get hold of a hire car that he could use to drive to Al Khums for the meeting contact tomorrow. The port of Al Khums being 60 miles east of Tripoli on a reasonable road. He hustled round the car hire firms in the airport until he found one that could hire him a four-by-four with air-conditioning and a plug-in satnav. A cancelation gave him his break, a newish Toyota jeep, even so already showing a few bumps and scratches and was incredible dusty both inside and out.

It was lunchtime by the time Saied had the car handed over to him and chose to drive off to Al Khums along the coast road and stop on the way to eat once clear of Tripoli. He hoped that food stalls or eating houses would be plentiful and possibly a hotel for the night. He almost stopped several times on the road, but truth be told he was not yet hungry and nothing at the side of the road or the eating shop and stalls in the villages tempted him. Semi-consciously he wanted to get to his destination and flop and chill out. Where that would be he didn't know. It slightly niggled him that the LIO bus man maybe had not even fixed accommodation or recommended a hotel.

In the end he ended up going past the town centre of Al Khums before he found a resort hotel to stay at.

By the time Saied had had his car on the road, Simon's men were waiting for him in a battered Toyota. They followed him and it was soon obvious he was heading in the direction signed for the port of Al Khums. The meeting at the port in the morning made sense to them as often arms consignments, it was known, left from there.

They were puzzled when he slowed at the port signs and then drove on. A mile on he pulled into a resort hotel on the beach of the port road. They watched him take his bag into the hotel.

Satisfied he would be staying there overnight, they turned their car around and returned to Tripoli to make a call to Simon and agree and sort a surveillance operation for later in the day once they had his agreement. They had little doubt he would agree, as the IRA training camp was south-east of Al Khums and likely this man would be going there after the port meeting.

A complicated affair for the Somalis to arrange at short notice, as they would first want identify a Somali brother they could trust and who would have to be someone who was legitimate in the port to keep track of Saied and the LIO once they were inside. Not difficult, as there were Somalis working in various capacities and the brotherhood would ensure their co-operation, but they still needed to be careful. They would also want to mount surveillance and kit for tomorrow in a hillside overlooking the IRA and Libyan training camp some twenty miles south east of Al Khums. These men and the spotter would need to go in tonight, under cover of dark and bury themselves in the high ground away from and above the camp so they had God's eyes on. The driver and leader of the Somali effort on behalf of Simon took a hand off the wheel and rubbed his thumb and forefinger together and looking over at his companion said, "I can feel those dollars now."

His older companion grunted. "Let's just wait and see, this all seems too easy and too quick for my liking."

"Think positive my friend, we as Somalis are invisible here no-one takes any notice of us poor folks, thank Allah."

Saied's hotel was almost on the beach, pretty new by the looks of it and a family friendly atmosphere. He was welcomed warmly by the owner who called a porter for Saied's bags to be taken up to his room before sitting Saied down in the reception area and pouring Saied a much needed ice-cold mint julep.

"I am sorry. Am I too late for lunch, I have just flown in you see?" enquired Saied, sipping his drink.

"By no means, why not take a table on the veranda overlooking our beautiful blue sea and I will send a waiter to you with a menu." The manager led the way. "Although this is a Muslim country, our president is an enlightened man and we are permitted to serve alcohol in moderation. This is a favour to our tourist minister who is progressive in these matters. In fact we have an excellent local rosé and or white wine if you wish?"

"Perhaps, let's see what you have in the way of food before I choose."

"Some would say our food is uncomplicated and some refer to it as tent food, but what do they know. However we have a speciality today that I urge you to try. It is lamb Shorba, an authentic Libyan home stew with garbanzos. I guarantee it, or it's free to you. Just the sort of meal for a day like this to set a man up, as it is neither too hot nor too cold."

"I can't really go wrong with that recommendation. I will go with that and a half bottle of rose," Saied confirmed, breaking his rule of no alcohol, but hell he wanted to relax a bit. The alcohol would be out of his system by the morning anyway.

As the manager turned to go, Saied stalled him. "Am I right in thinking I am on the doorstep of Leptis?"

The manager put his hand on Saied's shoulder and called over the waiter passing on the order. "Only about a kilometre up the beach to the west are many Roman buildings of antiquity." He pulled up a chair and sat with Saied. "The monuments were built by Septimus Severus who later became the emperor of Rome. Leptis was thought to be the most beautiful of all the Roman cities. The monuments that remain include; a coliseum, amphitheatre, public buildings, a market storehouses and dwellings. We have the Leptis museum and Leptis Magna. It is a most pleasant walk along the beach from the hotel and I recommend it after your meal. Not for the faint-hearted but as you walk through Leptis from the beach and inland for a quarter of an hour you will come to Hadrian's Arch that was the monument that stood in front of the Roman city." The manager looked up as the waiter arrived with Saied's food. The manager stood and bade Saied enjoy his lunch and added, "Enjoy. The hotel has some leaflets and literatures on Leptis if you want to look at it or you may just like to explore for yourself. Until later then, my friend."

Saied unwound over the meal and wine. He signed for the fare and strolled down to the beach, undecided if he would visit Leptis.

The blue clear water of the Mediterranean beckoned. Saied sighed, took off his shoes, tied the laces together and slung them round his neck. He bent and rolled up his jeans to his calves and paddled in the sea cooling his feet. As he splashed on he noticed the small fish in the shallows and the odd larger shadow deeper out. His mind was in freefall rerunning the visit to the dacha and Split. What tomorrow held for him he didn't know but he knew he needed to be alert. He walked on slowly to the west toward Leptis, still undecided if he would visit the monuments. He was enjoying the water running through his toes and felt a sense of freedom. Before he knew it he was opposite Leptis.

He stood looking at the old city for some time. The magnitude of the place surprised him, it was truly massive.

He dried his feet as best he could and replaced his shoes and rolled down his jeans and went towards the city. Leptis was almost deserted of humans, just a few who appeared to be archaeologists scratching in the ruins and studying the structures. Goats wandered about looking for food, doing much the same as their human counterparts; he supposed it was too early in the year for the throngs of tourists that would swarm the ruins and it was also midweek. He strolled the dusty avenues between the monuments and decided he would after all walk to Hadrian's Gate. Later on his return to the main site he spent time at the museum and the Magna before retracing his steps along the beach to the hotel. He realised he had needed the mindless exercise after the last few days of constant travel to clear his mind. "And a mini adventure into the past," he thought to himself.

At the hotel he collected the tourist leaflets from the reception and went again and sat on the veranda and ordered a long cool drink. He flicked through the literature to confirm in his mind the sites he had seen and what they represented. He had an early dinner and called it a day.

Back in his room he sent a long text message to the General confirming he was in Libya, who he had met and what he had done so far and that he would meet the LIO in the morning and hoped to be able to travel back tomorrow for his next phase.

Chapter 35

THE Q SURVEILLANCE TEAM

The two retired guardsmen came to the same conclusion within seconds of each other as they lay watching the IRA Quartermaster's house from across the fields.

"You know this is bollocks," Lewis commented slowly. "There is a better way."

"I had been thinking just that now. We have his pattern sorted and need to take advantage of its weakness."

"Think we need a meet with Avery."

"Agreed. Just so you know what I was thinking. You will agree he only seems to have one regular contact come to his house. Who we now know is Liam O'Neil, nasty bit of work that one." Fred eased his position. Lying hidden up for hours takes its toll. No matter how insulated you were from the ground, the cold and damp eventually found its way through to the core. "He meets the callers at the door and then moves out from the doorway and stands in the middle of the long driveway to talk to them. His house has good PIR and camera surveillance, but there are two blind stops – front left and front right. My idea would be to put a couple of directional microphones in his hedge aimed at the drive where he normally meets callers."

"Good idea. I like it. I was thinking that never mind GCHQ and their Irish Telecom people are supposed to be tapping his line, I think a local tap is always best as we have a vested interest."

"Let's add that to the list."

"A little off the wall I know but O'Neil leaves his car on the road as he makes his visits. Bit risky but we need a tracker on it. To my mind he seems to be the runner and minder as Q always seems to have him with him if he ever travels."

"I agree it would be good to track where the bastard goes but it is dodgy."

"I was thinking Avery might do that for us."

"It's a thought. Right let's get out of here and find Avery."

They carefully backed out of the hide, careful to leave no sign of their presence. They would have preferred to have found a house or old building where they could have set up the observation post in the roof and use a loose tile as the window on the target. It was just not an option in the environment they had found themselves in. So they had dug a hide in a hedgerow. It was well camouflaged and even the farmer who had walked his field with his dog the night before had missed them, true the dog had wandered over out of curiosity but had run off when Fred loosed a little pepper spray at the him as the dog nuzzled the camouflaged net and branches to the hide front.

Avery was staying at the hotel some ten miles away but when he got the call agreed to meet the team half way at the location they had all agreed. A public house, that never seemed to close, even though it didn't seem to have many customers.

The two ex-soldiers had sorted themselves out and tidied up, remarkable feat when you considered they had lain in a field for two days and nights. Avery was waiting with three pints of Guinness on the table towards the back of the pub. The owner barman if he thought anything as the three men greeted each other did not even look up from his behind the counter television.

"What's up?" asked Avery.

"We had a few ideas to put to you." Lewis took the lead. He explained what they had seen and how they thought they could improve the surveillance at this particular target. And how important they thought it was to track O'Neil.

Avery thought it over before responding, asking several questions to ensure he could answer the same questions if they were asked of him. "I have got a few directional microphones good for a hundred metres or more and with them transmitters. I can have the satellite-tracking bug flown in today, not an issue. GCHQ can put Mould or Sharky on it 24/7 and do have direct communication with them. That way we can lie back from any vehicle and follow on task. I am thinking if the microphones work, which I am sure will, we put a rebroadcast station in your hide, that way we free ourselves up to follow who we like when we like. We need to scramble the transmission. Not an issue and we can pick up any traffic on my sat phone if I set it to monitor the frequency. Don't want our friendly Garda stumbling over our operation."

"Sounds good to me. How about you Fred, does it do the job?"

"As my first sergeant major used to say, it sounds like the dog's bollocks." Avery laughed. He had not heard that expression since he left the army.

"Okay, let me have half an hour to sort this out. Then come with me to Dundalk and wait to hear if they are going to fly in the stuff at Dublin or Belfast. They will need a courier as we don't want the stuff sent freight. We set the kit up tonight. One last thing, I will get them to send over all intelligence on O'Neil's home and watering holes. I fancy we bug his car there not outside Q's house, too risky. If we are bumped there, the whole show is off."

Avery left them to make his call. Fred went up to the bar and asked for food. Hot if possible. By the time Avery came back the two men were tucking into what looked like a double all-day breakfast supported by large bowl of chips each. Avery, not one to miss out, ordered the same.

While he waited and enviously looked on he told them, "The changes you asked for are approved. The kit arrives at Belfast Aldergrove with a courier in about six hours. That should be plenty of time to collect it and set the stuff up tonight."

Chapter 36

THE FBI AND SO14 MEETING WITH BRIGADIER ROBINSON

At around eleven niggled, Rodney and Reid climbed up the steps into the foyer of the old Guards Chelsea Officers' Mess where they were warmly welcomed by Brigadier Robinson. He led them into the large anteroom with it dark polished furniture and big leather easy chairs.

Portraits of long past officers and battle scenes ringed the walls. A steward in whites arrived to take their orders for pre-luncheon drinks.

The three men chatted about the operation so far and what they had learned. Just before lunch they rose to meet their guests.

The FBI London Liaison Officer Carol Winsor and Deputy Assistant Commissioner Robert Coveney SO13 Anti-Terrorist Branch arrived together at 1300hrs and were ushered into lunch by their hosts.

There were half a dozen officers dressed in greens who were scattered around the dining room tables and were hurrying to finish up their meals; only the field officer in full scarlet uniform seemed languidly lingering over his dessert. He looked up as the party of five entered and a look from Robinson that said it all, smiling, He received a nod from the duty officer and the Field Officer quickly finished his dessert and disappeared along with the last of the others.

"Welcome to my mess, for a long time now my second home so to speak," said Robinson indicating where each should sit.

The silent stewards served the meal courses with wine, and the five exchanged pleasantries and the Brigadier explained the portraits of the great and good that oversaw the room with its highly polished mahogany tables and chairs. The tables were adorned with silverware, silver statutes and cutlery. The guests were impressed as they were meant to be.

Carol remarked that, "Being in a room like this was a calming experience, even if removed from normal life and surreal." Robinson grunted, not quite sure how to respond.

When the coffee pots arrived with the brandy, Robinson dismissed the stewards. "And so let us get down to business. Please help yourself to coffee and brandy as you see fit."

Carol was very direct. "Business, what business is that Brigadier?"

"After I have explained why we have started a side investigation into the IRA at this time, I will get Rodney explain it to you Carol and Robert and what we want to achieve, where we are and how you might help us."

"Fine as long as this meeting never happened," Carol warned.

"Quite so." Robinson smiled. "Let me tell you about this mission."

It took almost an hour for the two men to brief the guests and at the end of it Robert was the first to respond. "Well, novel and long overdue to have a focus team like this on the case. Bloody big ask though all the same." His South African accent had smoothed and he sounded more like a man from Bristol.

"I agree," Carol concurred. "What do you need?" Carol was around forty, a fiery redhead, hair shoulder-length, shaped so the wings of the hair floated evenly on either side of her face hiding a thin long white scar from her left temple to chin. Carol was a typically American business woman, smart, and well dressed in a dark suit, with a bounce jacket and pencil skirt that accentuated her trim figure and a high-necked silk white blouse. Although only average height, her black patent stilettos made sure she had eyeball contact with most of the men with her."

"Carol, what I and Mr Reid would like from you are two main things, anything else you can throw into the pot would be a bonus for the team."

"Shoot!"

"First can we meet the IRA defector you have in safe custody?"

"May be possible, why him in particular?"

"He is reportedly senior enough to have details of IRA funding and the way it operates. He may be able more than likely to tell us about arms shipments. We realise that the FBI will have been over this ground when he was debriefed but we would like to talk to him."

"I will see what I can do. We already know they diverted some of the money gifted from Libya and other sources into real estate.

Including and not limited to several pubs in Dublin, houses, office blocks, business and the like. When Ireland as it will becomes part of the EU eventually, the IRA investments will increase in value of that we have no doubt, so they are well funded and at some stage they will realise some of the capital assets to fund fighters and weapons. Our man may have some other details on the IRA financiers that we have overlooked. And I take it you want the bookkeeper. When would you like to visit him? You realise it is a trip to the States and a travel when you get there, so it's two days there and two days back. What was the other matter you think I can help with?"

"As for visiting as soon as possible, our people in the field and at base are getting dug in and I don't want to be away as I expect results will begin to filter in within the week and I want to be on hand when it does."

"If you want to take a chance and get on a flight tonight, I am pretty sure I can get you clearance. Whatever way it goes you will be met and looked after and I will make sure our files on the IRA are opened to you. And you get a briefing on our ongoing efforts against them. How's that for an offer?"

"Good enough for me thank you." Rodney looked at Reid who nodded his agreement.

"Just a thought for you it may pay you to split up to save time as you are both going, one to see our man and the other to the FBI headquarters?" Robinson put in helpfully.

"Better idea," Reid said, "If we forget the visit, I'll take the files and briefing and you take the man."

Rodney acknowledged his agreement. "Other stuff, think we should wait until the visit and files so we don't waste your time by duplicating our efforts. Carol, if I could see you after the visit that might be helpful."

Carol thought about Rodney's reply for a moment before replying and then said, "You know what, Rodney, I am due a visit back to headquarters. Goodness knows the director has been trying to get me to go and see him for the last month so I think I will come with you. He thinks if I don't visit HQ at 935 Pennsylvania Avenue Washington every so often I will go native. He is probably right. Book three flights, has to be American Airlines, it's our thing – is that okay with you Brits?" then Carol added, "Book Club Class, will see if I can get us upgraded."

Rodney was curious. "Is the man I need to see nearby or out of town?"

"Definitely out of town but you and Mr Reid in your service days would have at least made a visit to Quantico, he's near there and does the occasional tutorial for our special IRA unit."

Reid smiled and thought, "So she knows our history, what a clever lady."

Carol had not finished. "Rumours are dangerous things but you will know we think we have a mole in our team who does, we know, feed intelligence to the IRA. We will get him but you need to be aware of that as we are of the rumour that Mrs Thatcher has approved a back channel to the IRA and Tom King her secretary is not all that happy about it, if I know about it so does our mole."

"That is news to me, that one about the PM. For the pot what is taxing my people is the rumour of differences of opinion in the IRA high command," commented Robert.

Carol fed more information into the people round the table. "It is said that, perhaps that is too strong, that they will split into the real IRA and the continuity IRA. The former wants to move on and the latter wants to continue with its traditional shoot and bomb itself to the table. Therefore if the split does come, the continuity arm will want to step up the pressure and the frequency of incidents to ensure its street credibility is perceived as massive." She put her head down and slowly shook it from side to side twice. The hair swept round her face revealing her scar which the men noticed. The men's thoughts, if they had any were this was one tough lady. "Now if we are done let's get to work!"

Robinson was delighted. "Could not be better, thank you Carol for sharing your information with us. Just so you know we Brits will fly on anything that has seats, wings and an engine – and I think American Airlines qualifies." The meeting laughed. "Mr Reid would you put in a call to Graham and get him to pull the strings of the secretariat, let's aim for an overnight flight so you can all have time to pack and get some sleep on the way."

Robert Coveney joined the conversation. "I take it you will share as needs be, the findings with me as it applies." His South African accent was softened over the years and he could easily have been taken for a Bristolian, but not the way he emphasised the word "applies", which was pure Africana.

Robinson addressed him, "Have no fears on that count. SO13 will be fully involved as we unearth intelligence against the IRA. And now your role in this mission is one I hope of support if we stumble over something where we need you to send in your team to support us." He added gravely, "I have feeling something of particular importance is being planned and sooner rather than later. If I didn't and this was simply a fishing trip, I don't think I would be putting all my resources into this exercise." Concern showed on his face, which was intuitively picked up by the FBI liaison officer.

"Do you want to share your concern with us?" Carol probed.

"I am not sure I can clearly explain my thoughts to you at this time. It is all out there floating in the ether. Call it a gut feeling with the justification of current IRA trends, the possible changes to its organisation you explained so eloquently, coupled with a recent reminder from the past that the Russians are possibly active."

"Do you want to expand on that?" Carol was gently insistent.

"To be honest with you I am not sure I can at this time. I need to ask you to trust me a little longer."

"Fair enough, I know you well enough to drop the matter at this time." Carol smiled at the Brigadier. "We will wait out for your call to arms." With that Carol slowly stood, raised her right arm and swept it round the room at the portraits of the past. Her wave action seemed to indicate the close of the meeting. The men rose smiling and followed her out of the room chatting with each other about the twists and turns of life in general.

Chapter 37

SAIED'S DAY OUT WITH THE LIBYAN SECRET SERVICE AND THE IRA

Saied was up early and breakfasted well with the hotel owner. The owner, a rotund man in his sixties with sparse wispy hair, told Saied about his country and the president and his followers. He spoke quite openly and Saied was surprised at his candour, especially open hostility to the police state and the many informers that were a curse on the innocent. He explained the ethnic and tribal divisions that one day he felt would be troublesome along with the incomers from the desert that did not all simply want shelter from despotic regimes in the south.

Leaving the hotel in good time after the owner had elicited from him a promise to return in better times, Saied drove to the docks to await his contact. It was not that he was uneasy about the meeting, but he felt he was in the position of the poor relation. He knew that Russia had a low profile here, although after the recent attack by the Americans on Tripoli in particular he had heard from the hotel owner that the Russians under Air Marshal Koldunov was awaiting the call from Libya to find out why the Russian supplied air defensives failed so spectacularly.

The owner was surprised at the unhappiness of many of his friends with the president. He had explained to Saied that Libya, by reminding him that the country was an artificial creation of three regions – Cyrenaica, Tripolitania and Fezzan – was pulled together by the United Nations after the defeat of the Italian colonial territories. So while he would have expected the current unrest to be seen in Benghazi in the east but not here in this area so near to Tripoli. Saied smiled at the thought that only the Americans could call a mission against Gaddafi, "Operation El Dorado Canyon."

His smile broadened into a grin as he pulled up and parked his car to the side of the dock main entrance when he remembered the hotel owner's wry remarks that, "Do you know what he did our president? After the bombing he declared a victory. My God what a man he is!" And then, said the hotel owner spluttering, "He renamed my country the Great Socialist People of Libya Arab Jamahiriya." He was laughing so much his eyes were watering.

Saied clambered down from the four-by-four and stood looking round. The gate area was busy and a hundred or more people milled about and traversed the area. Some of the people both women and men were no doubt looking for work, others a hand-out and the rest legitimate workers of some sort. As ever the area was brightened by a few store holders selling wares and food. A mobile ship's chandlery was in operation and two men were working on an engine. Next to the chandlery were a welder's tent and a metal bench with a brazier stuffed with irons. A blacksmith hammered at a small boat's propeller. Saied breathed in the mixture of the salt air and old oil. The noise of the blacksmith's hammer was almost drowned out by the hubbub of the people and the noises from the working of a small but busy port.

Simon's men had followed Saied from the hotel and parked up at the farthest point in the car park from the dock gates so they could make a quick getaway if they needed to and would not be boxed in by others. They mingled with the crowd near the gate and saw Saied's contact with his bodyguards emerge from the dock entrance. Their approach was well advanced before Saied had picked out the LIO out from the crowd.

Saied stood alone just watching the blacksmith, but suddenly spun on his heel as he sensed the approach of his contact into his comfort zone. The man he noted was not dissimilar to himself in height and looks; they could at a pinch be taken for family members. Saied took all this in with a single glance, and accepting this man's eyes were Mediterranean and his hair whilst dark like Saied's was silver streaked at the sides. Saied thought him a few years older than himself, perhaps more. The man was dressed in a dark well-cut suit with a matching tie and starched white shirt.

"Mr Salomon." The man reached for Saied's hand to shake it. "Let me reintroduce myself properly this time, Colonel Khalid Bareli, and again apologise for not hosting you yesterday but we are flat out after the American attack with this and that, as you can imagine." His

English was flawless, without accent. The Colonel's countenance was serious and the eyes cold. Not a man to cross, was Saied's quick summation of this particular individual. He looked from the colonel to the two bodyguards and back to the colonel and took the offered hand.

Saied was gracious as was expected of him as he was after all an invited guest, "No apology is necessary Colonel, I had a most memorable afternoon and evening and good company at the hotel with the owner." Saied gave the name of the hotel and the Colonel's face cracked from a stone to delight.

"That old ruffian. I should have shot him years ago, but," the colonel shrugged, "he is my father's younger brother. I trust he was as irreverent as ever, if he were not I would be disappointed."

Saied smiled despite himself. "He was the perfect host, Colonel."

"Good to hear it. Now let's see if we can't help you with your quest. Come follow me." He took Saied by the arm for a moment to orientate him and then led the way into the dock entrance. Simon's spies photographed the meet and followed up after the Colonel's party.

Inside the port the colonel's party went to what appeared to be part of the harbourmaster's quarters. Crossing the entrance hallway they climbed the stairs to the second floor. The room across from the stairs they entered was guarded. Inside the room Saied noted it had a picture window overlooking the docks. There was a desk and old wooden leather-topped meeting table with a man sitting at it drinking coffee from a small cup. He rose as they entered the room.

"Mr Salomon, let me introduce Captain Hopkins the captain of the ship that is carrying our arms to the IRA in Ireland."

Hopkins was by his nature a good judge of men and shook Saied's hand heartily. "Welcome, perhaps there will be time to look over my ship later." He looked from Saied to the Colonel. When they didn't respond to him, he shrugged without showing offence and pointed out the window. "That's her over on the left astern of the pilot boat." He smiled, his weather-beaten face crinkling around the eyes, clearly proud of his ship.

"Perhaps," the Colonel offered at last. "But now, let us get the business out of the way." He went to a safe in the corner of the room. He withdrew a fat buff file and went and sat at the head of the table. He beckoned one of his men to him and sent him for refreshments from his favourite food stall, mainly for himself but also the meeting and dismissed the other bodyguard.

He gathered Saied and Hopkins to the table and bade them sit. "Now Mr Salomon, tell me what is the state of play from your side?"

"As my masters promised, the special consignment of Semtex I saw personally onto our boat in Split. I will re-join the boat in a few days, before handing it over to our team members who will see it safely to the location planned in England."

"Good, now our good Captain Hopkins here has been putting shipments into Ireland since mid-1985 in his Vessel the MV *Casamara*. A small cargo ship as you can see it is in true, but, sufficient to get more tonnes of arms to the IRA. So far it has done so without a hitch"

"Where do you drop the stores, to the north or south of the island?" Saied showed interest in the Captain to get him onside.

"It is not without reason we offload in the south of the island, to the south east and not the north. The south is three times the size of the north and the Irish Army and the Garda, the Irish police, are sparse on the ground where the IRA army of small boats visit me to discharge my cargos. Very different for the north, which is swarming with British army and police," Captain Hopkins explained. "But I still need to be careful and we have just renamed our ship the MV *Kula* in the hope to confuse the authorities."

"Thank you Captain, you must have a charmed life, I think certainly not one without adventure." Saied cocked his head on one side, studying the Captain for a moment before addressing the colonel, "And now to the point of my visit – did the list of items from my General make safe landfall?"

The Colonel pulled out of the file a copy of the ship's last manifest. "As you can see from this, the goods arrived and were taken into care. You can keep this for your old spymaster's file, oh yes I know him, we have worked together over the years as necessary."

Saied reached out and took the papers. He studied them in silence. "That looks to be all in order. Well done, Captain Hopkins. I was wondering if you would let me and the Colonel have some time alone."

"I need to be away now anyway, we are victualing another new ship for the future; mine has limited cargo space as the Colonel said and I need to see to my next cargo and the men. I wish you well in your venture. Until we meet again." He threw up a half salute and as he left the room a Somali entered the room with the tray of refreshments, followed by the bodyguard.

Saied opened his briefcase and took out his phone and a mini scanner. With the colonel looking on, Saied powered up the scanner and phone. He rolled his scanner over the delivered manifest and loaded it onto his phone. He typed one word "LEAD" (Libyan end arms delivered). He hit send to Tsygankov, Servo and Vasily. "There Colonel, Tsygankov now has confirmation and I know he will be most grateful to you."

The Somali served the two men, taking in the room and the fat file in front of the colonel and his open safe. His Somali team members he knew would be back tonight to copy the file and anything else of interest for Simon. As he bowed out of the room, the colonel called him back and gave him a tip. Saied thought this an odd gesture from the man, it was not in keeping with Saied's opinion of him as a cold ruthless individual; perhaps it was to impress him.

The Colonel and Saied ate hot breads stuffed with lamb and drank the black bitter coffee in companionable silence until Saied broke it. "I surmise you must be ESO?"

"That's correct the 'ESO', The External Security Organisation of the Libyan secret service. My remit is wide, not only the IRA but other terrorist organisations my president wishes to support."

"The IRA must nevertheless be in the premier league for him."

"True."

"You referred to my Spymaster do you know him?"

"Never met personally but General Tsygankov is one of my heroes in a sense and our contacts have always been profitable for both of us. For a start he is a survivor, which we all must be." The colonel was quite open. "Not least he doesn't tolerate wastrels."

Saied recalled the General mentioning Libya. "Do you know, on a sea voyage several years ago he once told me that he learned a great deal by studying your organisation? He was particularly impressed at the way the ESO had set up the communications between the IRA and yourselves."

"You mean our in country student organisation."

"I suppose I do."

"We found that the best way for a terrorist group to communicate with us was for us to place students in the country's universities. In the particular case of the IRA in Ireland, Trinity College amongst others, we have sent our people to study there. All communications for the time being between ourselves and the IRA are through the Libyan students' union. It is a very effective organisation and a way of bringing on our younger talent."

"He mentioned recently to me that you have an IRA training camp where they pass on their knowledge to you and vice versa, actually here in Libya."

"It is not far from here and an ideal location too for both of us to practise many skills. As you will be working with them on this project, whatever it is, how would you like to visit the training camp? I am due there this morning anyway and lunch is always good and served around midday. It would, I think, make up for the meal I should have hosted for you last night."

"My flight is not until nine tonight, so yes I would like to visit and see these IRA men, to get the feel for them. It will be the first time I have worked with them, so it would be useful to get their measure."

"So be it. They are a tough lot, even I would not like to get on the wrong side of them. But let's keep that to ourselves shall we…" he paused. "You can travel with me, one of my men will drive your car and afterwards he will drive you back to Tripoli and the airport. You will have seen the airport, it's a bit of a mess since the Americans hit it but I have little doubt your flight will take off without delay."

Leaving the port they drove south-west deep into the desert for a good hour or more. The flat coastal landscape had soon given way to increasingly deep valleys and hills sharply defined by stark shadows. As they descended into yet another valley, a fenced enclosure was in front of them. It took up the whole of the valley five hundred yards wide and double that, stretching along the narrow valley with its mainly deep dry waddy dividing the site along its length. Saied could imagine that at some times in the year the waddy would be watered and flooded by the infrequent seasonal rainfall.

A dozen or more compact single-storey buildings formed around a central hub and took up a quarter of the far half of the enclosure.

"Quite a site," Saied complimented the Colonel.

"More to see than meets the eye, for part of the complex is underground. The underground part of the complex matters most of all, to me and the IRA at least." The colonel came back. "There are laboratories and workshops and an underground range. All this is necessary. We like to think of this as a campus for the modern terrorist to get his skills honed to perfection." His smile was cold and did not invite of a response from Saied.

Entering the compound Saied noted the security, it was everywhere. They parked in the centre of the complex and were met by three Europeans.

While Saied hung back, the Colonel shook hands before introducing Saied to them, "Mr Salomon please meet Ian, Joe and Thomas. They are keen to talk to you, come." He led the way into the centre building which was the refectory and central meeting place. "I have a bit of work to do so I will pick you up for lunch." With that the colonel left the group to themselves.

Saied chose a table and sat as the three Irishmen took their places around him.

Joe, a stocky man in his middle thirties, with dark brown short curly hair was dressed like the others in desert camouflage fatigues with a utility belt holding a knife and pistol and was the one who offered Saied a bottle of cold water. "Need to keep the liquid level up in this climate but I expect you know that? So you have something going with us back home, is that right?" Saied was not unfamiliar with the Irish accent and this man's accent was soft not harsh like he had expected.

"What do you know about it Joe, if there were a job on?" Saied asked cautiously.

"Not a lot, I confess, except that the Russians have a proposal and we will be considering it," Joe replied for them.

"I am surprised you know we are the Russians," Saied said lightly. "I heard the IRA security was second to none, perhaps the Colonel mentioned it?"

Joe understood Saied's caution and sought to reassure him. "Not the Colonel, our boss back in the old country, we had a message from him a few weeks ago. Communications are, shall we say, limited when it comes to sensitive issues so you will understand our curiosity. By the way, your two people are there now." Joe bent his head to the table for extra privacy so the security cameras around the room could not pick up his lip movements. "Listen, we are being watched so be careful what you say. Now we belong to the man who is going to make this whatever it is for you Russians happen back home. We are due back in a few weeks so get a good look at us because we will be showing up when the time is right and if the scheme is approved."

"Hmm, even so I am afraid there is not a lot I can tell you. Except my part was to come and meet the Colonel to ensure the arms you will need are in place." Saied looked round the group. "And I can report they are, that's it. Tonight I travel back. And then back to a boring desk job."

"I don't believe you. You must know more than that for fuck's sake, we want to know what the job is." The third member of the group, Thomas, scowled at Saied. Saied studied him; his face, it was rough-hewn unshaven scared and nose broken to flat. Saied judged him to be a thug, certainly not the brains. He could not be sure but the man was on something drink or drugs. His voice harsh, gravelly like a long-time smoker. With Thomas's intervention the atmosphere changed. Unnecessarily Thomas added, "What a waste of space. Wanker!"

"Thomas is it? Let's understand each other." Saied was taken aback by the man's aggressive attitude and he needed to understand what was behind the outburst so Saied said quietly and reasonably, "You don't know me and I don't know you or your companions." Saied bunched himself sitting forward on his chair ready to react. "I would like to think as a guest here you might extend me the traditional courtesy expected in an Arab country. So choose and do it quickly, are you friend or foe?" He smiled with his hands open in a gesture of contrition.

Thomas stood hands bunched. "Challenge is it?" He pointed a thick-fingered hand at Saied. "Don't know who the fuck you are, but you will bleed like any other rag head." Joe stood, and put his arm round Thomas, pressing Thomas back into his seat.

Joe sat back down, angry with Thomas. "Thomas, cool off or you're out, this is your last chance." Joe turned to Saied, "My apology for Thomas, his outburst was unforgivable. I regret he is not good in company and has few social graces, do you see."

Thomas coloured, furious and out of control stood and threw his chair over. "Fuck you, Joe. I knew you bastards had it in for me from the start." He was looking hard at Joe and Ian. "And as for you, Sunshine…" He was shaking with fury and didn't finish his rant but stomped out the building.

Joe sighed and nodded to Ian who stood up and shook Saied's hand and wished him well. "See you around, Mr Salomon, so I will." Ian followed Thomas out of the building.

Joe shook his head from side to side. "It's nothing to do with you, Thomas was a mistake from the start, a born bully, but a brave man for all that and I am afraid he finally shot his bolt yesterday when he beat one of the Colonel's men half to death and not for the first time. That incident was the last in a long line of bad-tempered tantrums and misbehaviour. He should never have been sent out here, he is completely out of his environment and simply can't cope with the regime here, so he can't. We can't always choose the men who want to be soldiers and fight alongside us but we can test them, and those that fail to come up to the mark, well they just get discarded. Thomas is now such a man."

Saied noted the past tense but showed no emotion. Joe continued, "I persuaded the Colonel to give him one more chance. The Colonel knows he has blown his last chance; he will have been told about

Thomas by now and will expect us to deal with it, he is after all one of our own." He fell silent for a while. "We are ambassadors here for our cause, as you are, here to be helped and to help our hosts. It's important, so those that fail as spectacularly as Thomas or cannot be trusted have to be taken out. They cannot be allowed to go back home and talk. Nor can they sour our relations with our backers, especially not the Libyans."

Saied said nothing, his only thought was Joe he had now clearly identified as the leader here and that Joe had just decided on an summary execution order, was it meant to impress him or was he also being tested?

Joe reached into his utility belt and withdrew a hunting knife, and pulled from the back of his trouser belt a Webley .445 pistol. He laid them on the table and looked from them to Saied.

Saied picked up the pistol and felt the weight of the gun, it was not one he had used often. Good balance and stopping power. A close quarter weapon, even with his experience 20 maybe 30 metres to place a shot where intended was all he would have guaranteed. "They say revolvers never jam. Is this the IRA weapon of choice?" he laid the weapon carefully on the table.

Joe picked up the subtlety of Saied's remark. "Yes it was and yes it is." Saied just knew it was the weapon Joe wanted him to use. "We like it."

Saied stirred in his chair; he looked at Joe and hoisted the Webley. He spun the bullet barrel. When it stopped, he broke open the gun taking out the bullets and checked each of them in turn. They were in good shape and live rounds. Not blanks. With the gun unloaded he snapped the gun back together with a flick of the wrist and checked the mechanism and firing pin. Reloading the pistol he checked it out nodded. "Now?" Saied looked up at Joe.

Joe looked at his watch. "About now I should think." One look at Joe told Saied this was the moment, and he could not back out.

Saied followed Joe out into the bright sunlight. The midday sun was all but overhead and Saied felt the sun's heat warm his face and shoulders and it felt good and he was just happy to be alive.

Joe led him away and down into the deep dry waddy. They carefully made their way down the full length of the dry bed until they were close to the fence line. Ian was standing over Thomas who knelt on his knees, hands cuffed behind his back.

His face was bruised, one eye closed, and lips cut and bleeding. He waited head in his chest resigned to his execution. Thomas twisted his head and saw Saied and Joe approaching. Thomas spat a piece of broken tooth along with some blood and snot. Saied held the gun down swinging loosely in his right hand.

As they approached Thomas, Saied gazed up at the top of the high bank of the waddy. Looking down at the scene before him was the Colonel with his bodyguards flanking him to the left and right. Each of the bodyguards held an AK 47 at the ready, butts in the shoulder. Saied did not acknowledge him or them.

He walked forward at a normal pace with Joe now behind him and Saied noticed Ian move to, one side of the kneeling man.

Hardly stopping as he reached Thomas, he brought the gun up in a blur; put the gun between the man's eyes, pressing it for a fraction of a second hard into the brows to raise his head. Thomas' eyes blazed defiance, for his part Thomas in that last second of life saw only regret in Saied. Saied pulled the trigger. The gun bucked in his hand but he held it rigid. He felt, more than sense the man spin away from him. Saied turned, not waiting for the man to fall, in an effort to outpace the smell of death before it reached him. Saied walked back with Joe leading the way back up the waddy.

Anyone looking at Saied would have thought the man was on an afternoon stroll without a care in the world, but inside Saied was seething, he was reaching a point where being the instrument of death for others was becoming an anathema for him.

The Colonel joined them as they reached the refectory. "Lunch I think. It was well done Mr Salomon, you're clearly a professional. Joe, ask Ian to join us we have much to discuss." The Colonel put his hand on Saied's shoulder in a gesture of friendship. "After lunch let me take you on a tour of the facility and its secrets underground. I want you to be able to tell General Tsygankov about all we have to offer, should it come to pass that he has need of our services."

He slapped Joe on the shoulder. "Joe's explosive electronics and electrical lab will be of special interest I think. That's something we benefited from as we made a clone of the IRA electronic workshop in Ireland.

Joe added, "We have no doubt about the British's ability to eavesdrop so we had to counter that and find ways to nullify or mitigate their intrusion into our business. So half the lab here, as in Ireland, is taken up with counter surveillance electronics and anti this and that."

Saied's mind was elsewhere although he outwardly showed interest. He wondered if he would be lying in the sand now like Thomas if he had not taken the shot. "Probably."

High above them on the lip of ravine half a mile away, Simon's Somali men had seen all and recorded the events on film. They moved back carefully and hiked the two miles to their waiting vehicle.

The record would be transmitted as soon as they got back to base later this afternoon. Apart from breaking into the dock tonight, when one of their team a skilled locksmith would unlock into the Colonel's safe and photograph the file, the job was done. By tomorrow night they expected to receive their bonuses and would be out in Tripoli celebrating.

In London that night before he left for the flight to America, Rodney would receive the first of Simon's intelligence and the shock that Saied was alive and involved.

Chapter 38

VASILY

Vasily woke to the sun streaming into the bedroom. Not quite up to the standard of the General's splendid dacha but the cottage, if that is what it was, was comfortable and warm.

After breakfast he again took a walk round the property. The garage interested him. It was big enough for four cars and space to spare. It would make an excellent bomb factory. Finding a place to put together the bombs had been a question mark for the team but now the garage on the property, away from prying eyes, had resolved it.

He got his kit together and got the BMW out of the garage. He thought better of it and decided to take the hire car instead. He might just be able to drop it off somewhere.

His trawling threw the Yellow pages had pinpointed a site he fancied that sold the sort of motor home he wanted. Maybe 40 miles away he judged, near Newbury and an easy run. The name of the establishment amused him, as did the road Chieveley running into Worlds End Lane.

He could swing back into to Middle Wallop up the A343 and onto the A303 towards Basingstoke until the A34 crossed it. He would then go north and take the first turn-off to the left once he crossed the M4.

Within the hour he was at the gate of the motor home place. Parking, he had a quick look round the lot; there seemed to be plenty of choice and one in particular caught his fancy.

The office, a long single-storey modular building with a camping shop to one side that sold the necessities of life for motor home owners, was on the left. In the centre he noted was a sale room and he assumed the right end of the building was the back office.

In the sale room there was a seated man. He was tall, around fifty, and fit-looking with receding black hair and of a cheery disposition; the man rose moving to meet Vasily at the door.

"Good morning what can we do for you?"

Vasily shook the man's hand. "Fairly simple, I need to buy a 4-berth motor home. And the vehicle needs to be reliable and ready for the continent. I would like to buy it today and have it ready to roll say by tomorrow night, how does that sound?"

"Would new or used be your preference?"

"I am not sure. This is a new market for me and I have a budget which I would like to stay within." He turned and half pointed at the motor home that had taken his fancy when he arrived. "That motor home looks about the sort of thing I had in mind."

The man laughed. "Great choice, come and have a look at it." He collected a set of keys from his drawer and led Vasily to the van. Standing back he gave a quick rundown on the vehicle. "The Geist Phantom! 2 years old, 7.5 metres by 2.3 metres wide. 4 berth and up rated 3litre Mercedes engine instead of the normal 2.2litre engine. Got everything, even television and satnav built in and with 16k on the clock just run in. Taxed and ready for the road." He paused. "We could get it ready for tomorrow? We like to give our motor homes a final check over before we release them to ensure there are no surprises for you or us."

"Has it been on the park for long?"

"No, we exchanged it for a new model about a month ago. Some interest but nothing serious as yet. The larger than normal engine puts some people off, I think. But the reality is that the MPG is not too dissimilar to the smaller engine. The larger engine doesn't have to work so hard. But there you are, people are people."

After a moments hesitation Vasily said "Okay, let's talk price."

"Well first have a look inside at least, it is immaculate and it's been valeted and all water and gas pipes renewed and certified. Apart from the engine with a few miles on it, it's like a brand new motor home."

"Fine let's have a look inside then."

"Call me Jim," the man offered his hand.

"Vasily."

"Okay, Vasily come on up."

The interior had been customised; it was state-of-the-art. "Wow, this is some home, leather and wood finish everywhere. I am sure my friends will love this machine. Let's see if it is in my budget shall we." Vasily eased into the driver's seat. Jim passed him the keys and Vasily started up the engine. It sounded quiet and sweet even when he revved it. He looked at the various controls and dials. Unusually for its time it had a custom built-in satnav. "Air-con too I see. What do you want for it?"

"Well we have marked it up at £34,000." Jim sucked his teeth. "There may be a bit of room to play with the price."

"I would like to pay cash today. How about I give you £30,000."

"Try again," Jim was smiling.

"£31,000?"

"You are getting there."

£31,500?"

"Okay, deal. "Jim offered his hand.

"Thank you that's great." Vasily was genuinely pleased with himself at the purchase and the price. "I need to find a bank and get the cash. I saw a sign for Newbury; would they have a few banks?"

"Plenty and you can park in the town centre; there are several places to choose from near the centre. If that is a hire car they have most of the rental people represented there. I could run you down tomorrow if it helps?"

"That would be very helpful and save me a problem. What about paperwork; tax and insurance etc.?"

"If you have proof of ID and your licence we can do the insurance here as you will need that to drive off. We have a special insurance for motor homes that covers not just the vehicle but body shell and its contents etc. Think about it."

Vasily had a concern and he voiced it. "I need my two companions to be on the insurance, but they are in Ireland fishing at the present time."

Jim thought about it. "We can sort that. Have them fax over copies of their licences and proof of identities to me." He handed Vasily a business card. "To that number, before we sit down tomorrow."

"I can do that. I will see you later with the money, so until then…"

"Do you want a drink of coffee or something?"

"Later I think when I return." Vasily looked at his watch. "I had better get going and I'll have lunch before I return, let's say I should be back around 3 this afternoon. How is that?"

"That will be fine, the kettle will be on." He waved to Vasily as Vasily climbed into his car.

Newbury old town was a revelation for Vasily of what not to do to a historic town. The old and quaint squashed and butted up to the new and brash. Vasily thought the town planning people, who ever they were over the years and the councils past and present should all be shot or worse.

On the plus side he found a Barclays bank and was quickly able to secure an interview with the customer service staff.

At first it proved difficult as they had £5,000 limit for unannounced withdrawals. But it was a race day and deposits of cash had been steadily arriving throughout the day to be brigaded up for a security van collection at the end of the afternoon.

With a good story under his belt, after the request got escalated by the customer focus staff, to the under manager, Vasily got his funds. After all, he was supporting local business. It helped also not being local; everyone seemed to have a soft spot for the Australians and New Zealanders. It seemed everyone he had met had a relative or acquaintance down under.

Given the standard warning about carrying so much cash on him by the manager, Vasily was allowed to leave happy.

He searched for a pub to have lunch and found the Wagon and Horses on his way back to the car park he had chosen earlier to park in Pelican Lane. The old worldliness of the Wagon and Horse suited his mood. He ordered a beer-battered fish, mushy peas and chips, something he had been looking forward to and was not disappointed. With a pint of cream flow John Smiths, which he savoured like nectar, he was replete. At the end of the meal he took out his phone and called Servo to update him and to ask him to fax over his and Carla's documents to the number he read out.

At Pelican Lane, a police officer was checking the cars. Vasily watched him. Vasily believed in the need for detail and gathering intelligence if only the appearance size and shape of the enemy was another part of the data-gathering process. Two youths entered the car park fooling about so they didn't notice the police officer at the far end. One of the youths picked up a stone and threw it at a windscreen of an up-market car and the other jumped on the bonnet. The stone bounced off the windscreen. The officer alert raced to grab one of the youths. The one on the car bonnet was too slow and slipped off as the officer pounced on him. His partner ran towards Vasily. Vasily easily tripped him and stamped on his knee cap before grabbing an arm into an arrest hold. The officer had the other handcuffed and marched him up towards Vasily and his captive.

"Well done sir, here let me cuff them together, don't think they are going anywhere." He cuffed them through the bars of the railing and called on his radio for a police wagon to pick them up.

Vasily stood and waited, "If you are okay with this, I will be on my way."

The officer towered over Vasily and smiled, "Well sir, we will need a short statement from you at the very least."

"Oh I didn't think. Look Officer, I have an appointment at three up the road – can I come back afterwards and give the statement then?"

The officer was dubious but relented. "Okay, let me have a few details, contact number address etc. Just in case."

Vasily really didn't want to get involved but he knew instinctively if he didn't play the part he was in trouble. "Sure my passport," he handed it over. "I am on holiday from down under staying at a holiday home," he fished for the address before handing it over. "And," he flicked the phone to display his number, "I am available to you Officer at any time."

The officer finished putting the details in his notebook and handed the passport back to Vasily. "Thank you sir, that's great. Hope you will not be too late for your meeting and once again thank you for your support. Not looking for a change of career are you?"

"Not today at least. You're welcome." Vasily smiled and shook the policeman's hand.

Back at the campervan sale lot, Vasily handed over the money for the campervan. The man laughed as Vasily counted out the money. "I didn't realise you were bringing cash; it is normal to present a banker's cheque. This is fun, not seen this much cash for a while in one place."

"Well I hope you have somewhere safe to keep it."

Jim called out for Beryl. A lady appeared from the back office, about Jim's age, a cheerful fair-haired woman with an hour-glass figure. "What now?" She eyed Vasily up and down noting his new clothes and deciding Vasily was honest at least.

"This young man has brought cash, as in cash, and I would really appreciate it if you would take it back to the bank and bank it in our name.

"Foolish man," she chided Vasily. "Okay, hand it over. I will see you back home Jim and don't be late." Jim crossed himself.

Chapter 39

THE FBI MAN

"Well SAS man, fancy seeing you here. Spells trouble I dare say." The FBI IRA informer got up from his easy chair and, with the remote in hand, pressed the button and shut down the television news programme he had been watching.

The man's opening remarks and demeanour seemed open and without angst. Rodney had been driven to a leafy suburb on the US base. The bungalows in this part of the camp with the gravel drives and grassed areas were typical of quarters for officers and their families to be found on any American camp across the continent. Fly screen to the door and air conditioners were signature icons as was the red-tiled roof and white walls in and out with double glazed windows set in to help keep the glare of the sun out. It was cool inside and tidy. The front door had opened into a family room that had a couple of three-seater settees and a large coffee table to serve the needs of the two settees, set at right angles to each other, to form the frame for a very large American television that could be seen with ease from either seated area. The TV had one of the biggest screens Rodney had ever seen, and the man noted with amusement Rodney's interest. The room was devoid of any other furniture, not even a picture.

"Trouble, no I don't think so. You seem to have landed on your feet." Rodney kept his voice neutral and studied the man. Sixty he was, maybe more, with a mop of ginger hair and freckled face. The man was in relatively good shape if a little fat around the gut area, and, he concluded, very Irish.

"No trouble you say, in that case follow me to my study. Jim be a pal and make myself and the Major a pot of tea would you." The FBI man who had driven Rodney from the airport to the house grunted and was soon heard clattering in the kitchen/diner.

The study was as chaotic as the lounge had been utilitarian. Bookcases lined three walls, full of books and research magazines. So full were the shelves that magazines threatened to cascade from them at any moment. The desk, with its PC and telephones was littered with papers. A paper basket overflowed with trashed and unwanted papers. The man sat in his leather desk high-back chair and waved to Rodney to pull up one of the two spare chairs in the room closer to the desk.

"Let's get to it then, SAS man, call me Kiernan for want of a name."

"Kiernan is a good Celtic name. You obviously know about me – how would that be?" Rodney was curious.

"I followed all you young heroes on all sides in days past. And in your later careers, some fell by the wayside unable to cope and adjust to life outside the military but many did well for themselves. Knowledge, as you well know, Major, is power. I was particularly impressed with you Major when I found out you gave the Russians a bloody nose and threw that traitor Lawson out of the window. You may not know it but you are something of a legend with our Yank friends."

Rodney was startled and couldn't hide it.

"Don't be so surprised, there are few stars in this world of ours that stand out."

Rodney could not help grinning; this man was good, he wielded flattery like a weapon. "Is that good Irish blarney or are you going to interview me?"

Kiernan laughed. "Tumbled me have you. Well now, come on Rodney we can do business, I like a man with a sense of humour, I don't get much of that from my minders."

"Still, not a bad cage, eh. Do you get much freedom to go outside the wire?"

"Yes and no. But to tell you the truth so it is. This camp and its military town is as big as London. It has everything a man could want. At some times of the year it's as green as home, and the American ladies – well they fall for the blarney like skittles in a bowling alley." He paused. "Truth is I do get enough freedom as I want. There are some restrictions but I can live with that. Plus I've a good pension and everything I need. I write now, novels, not under my name. I write mostly fiction with little fact thrown in for good measure. I will give you a signed copy to read on the way home."

He could see Rodney had another question. He sighed, "Let's get your next question out the way shall we. Why did I defect? Easy Rodney, I got sick of the blood spilled by both sides and the poor British Tommy. It got more and more like a power struggle and pensions for the boys than the cause. And they did not care a fig from where the money came or what thugs joined the ranks. Oh I would love to see a united Ireland but it's a pipe dream. Let's live and let live."

"Thank you for that explanation Kiernan, it was on my mind."

"Tell you what Rodney, you ask me the most important thing to you right now, that you want me to tell you, and I will if I can."

Rodney noted the qualification. "If I can." But he let it go as the FBI man brought in a tray of tea for them both.

"Darling man you are Jim. Do you want anything to eat, Rodney?"

"No I am fine for now but the tea is welcome."

When Jim left and closed the door Rodney took a scrap of paper from his inside pocket and passed it to Kiernan. It had one question on it. *I need the name and location of the IRA accountant and his books?*

Kiernan studied the paper for a long time and gazed out of the window. Rodney waited patiently drinking his tea. Kiernan bent his head and scribbled on the note, *£25,000*, before passing it back to Rodney. "It would go to the widows and orphans of all the fallen." Kiernan's eyes were bright with moisture.

"Agreed." Rodney let out a sigh.

Kiernan got up from the desk and motioned to Rodney to follow him. Jim was waiting in the lounge with the same news programme playing softly. "Jim, Rodney and I are going out for a smoke, join us if you will."

"No thanks, go ahead. I will just wait here for you."

When they were outside and Kiernan had lit up. He showed Rodney round the house and gardens talking while he pointed out his efforts and a vegetable and mini fruit orchard of which he was justly proud, and then he began. "What you will already have understood is that the IRA has a lot of money. It comes in from all sorts of people, organisations and countries that would do us harm." Rodney again noted the, 'who would do us harm.' He had to think that the man's phrase was genuine or he was a very good actor and no doubt on the debit side he had had lots of practice.

Kiernan continued. "They invest and turn the money into clean businesses, mostly. Now for you to get to the Accountant, and the books is going to be complex. To start with there is a board of senior members and they deal with money and cash strategy. One man, the Accountant or more correctly the company secretary, executes the agreed strategy and arranges for the targeted business and premises to be acquired through a myriad of offshore companies." He looked at Rodney. "To prosecute the buy and sell, they use half a dozen solicitor companies at home and abroad. The records, well now, you are into a maze but you can be pretty sure the Accountant has a record of the complete business and its breadth of operations at any one time. I can give you the Accountant's name and his addresses in the Channel Islands and in Dublin. I can give you the names of all the solicitor companies as of a few months ago. Lastly I will give you the account numbers of the three main banks they use. All these three have an account manager, each true to the cause. I will give you their names too but only, -- if you don't share them with the FBI. This is for your team only and that lovely fella Robinson. Oh yes Rodney, he and I go back many years. He was a major like you in Belfast in the early days almost before the troubles. His men caught me a rag-arsed Finnian of a youth trying to make a Molotov cocktail to throw at the 'Pigs,' the old armoured personnel carriers. Do you know what he did? He was with his sergeant major when they brought me to him in his armoured car. He sat me down and got the sergeant major to pour me a whisky. Then he talked to me about what I was doing and the consequences of actions like mine and the harm it was going to do to the province. Finally he gave me the look you will be familiar with when he searches your very soul.

Scared me to death, so he did. He nodded at the sergeant major who took me out and fetched me such a clip round the ear I was deaf for a week, then told me to get home to my mar and the gipsy warning if I crossed their path again. I can tell you I stayed away from activities, till I learned Robinson's company had left the province. Such events as that scare us Rodney, and we never forget them. A bit like Lawson's unwanted flight out the window, to his death, by you?" He said with a grin.

"Allegedly." Rodney smiled. He could see Robinson sorting this man in his youth. A story he could tell the Brigadier and was sure he would see a smile at the phrase. "Allegedly," he repeated at him. He chuckled.

"So SAS man, will that do you?"

"Oh yes Kiernan that will do me just fine, just fine." He spun on his heel. "Did you want the money sent here or do you want me to distribute it through some third party?"

"Send it here; it will be safer for you, and me."

Rodney bent to the vegetable patch and took some dark soil in his hand and let it trickle through his fingers. "Good soil."

"Sadly the soil is not native to the camp. I have to buy it in and mix it but it's improving year on year."

"I was in Africa recently. The soil there was red. They told me it was washed in blood by all the people who had gone before. A good story but one I can relate to. I want to stop as much as you do I think with the soil of Ireland from going red with the blood of the innocents."

"Believe you do. Come on back to the house I have some copied and do some scribbling to do, while you keep the FBI happy swapping stories. There will be a large envelope with stuff they already know inside and another smaller one you can slip into your pocket. That should satisfy them you are not taking anything they don't already know and you can look at your data at your leisure. Just curious Rodney, you didn't ask me about the IRA infiltration within the British establishment?"

"No I didn't. Might have done, if you had not been so generous with your answers to my question, thought you had done enough. And I do expect that from the information my team get as they unravel the money and the pipelines it travels through. The individuals that would do us both harm will be uncovered." He said, as a throwaway comment, "You need to allow me to do some of the work or I am going to feel superfluous."

"So it is, Rodney. And as you find them Rodney, make them fly like Lawson, for the people of my beloved land." He was quite serious and Rodney suddenly felt the heavy burden of responsibility he had just accepted. Kiernan slapped Rodney on the shoulder. "Come on back to the house or the FBI minder will think we are scheming."

It was late that night that Rodney was reunited with the FBI and Reid in the FBI headquarters. The room he found himself in was high up in the building. High enough to overlook part of another American city that rarely sleeps. The city was lit up and the traffic seemed relentlessly on the move as the lights of the vehicles streamed to form a solid blur of light on roads before him.

Jim his minder opened the door for Rodney to join a meeting in an adjoining room. The meeting was chaired by an Assistant Director of operations who headed the FBI IRA Division. Introductions were made and Reid gave Rodney the thumbs-up. Clearly it had been a good day for him. Carol the London FBI Liaison Officer was not there but two other men were, they were shuffling papers getting ready to leave.

The AD OPS was keen to learn if Rodney had got anything out of the man that would be of use to them too. Rodney handed him the large envelope. "Regrets. I don't think there will be anything in there you are not aware of but it is good background stuff for us and a name or two. Would you like to copy the contents of the envelope just in case?"

"Jim please make a couple of copies." The long-suffering agent simply nodded and collected the envelope from Rodney.

Rodney was invited to sit by the AD OPS, and soon only Reid and Rodney and AD OPS remained.

Rodney opened the dialogue. "I want to thank you and your team for hosting us today. It was very useful to us and to know we are not fighting this organisation alone."

"No need to thank us Rodney. Has it been a nugatory exercise? Not at all. It has been for us also an eye-opener. Mr Reid has been able to close some gaps we had been puzzling over for a while and put some real colour on our efforts. Don't suppose you could leave him for a week or so, he seems to be a hit with our team."

Not again, Rodney thought. "Love to, but we have a task to sort first. It may be Mr Reid would like a trip back to you afterwards." Rodney looked at Reid who was grinning, thumb raised. "Take it from me he would appear to want to."

"Good, settled. Now you two are booked out tonight, so I need to get you to your plane. Carol is staying for a day or two. You realise she is a lawyer – it is a necessary qualification for all our head liaison officers in London – a good one too, specialising in international security laws and there are some legal matters relating to her duties that need her presence here."

"Nothing to do with the recent rendition issues by any chance matters between the US and UK?" Rodney probed, half serious and half in fun.

"Even the best of friends don't always agree and or embarrass each other at times." The AD OPS was grinning.

"I'll take it that's a yes then?" Reid put in.

"Now I couldn't comment, above our pay grades I would think." The AD OPS closed out the conversation. "Now let's get you out of here and back to the UK. Carol has confirmed she got you upgraded so it's a first class flight back." The AD OPS collected his papers and stuffed them into his briefcase and the UK men stood and prepared themselves to exit the room.

The AD OPS shook hands and gave Reid a thumbs-up, adding, "Look forward to seeing you soon." He gave them his card and turning to Rodney, "Just bell when Mr R is ready for a few weeks here. I have never seen the staff more motivated, he had them running for material today. I need to study the technique as the best I can ever get out of them is a trot at best."

Jim appeared unheralded so Rodney deduced he was either psychic or the AD OPS had summoned him somehow. Jim gave Rodney his papers and copies to his boss and then took them through security and into the street. A FBI black people-wagon was waiting for them to drive them to the airport. Reid took one last look at the FBI Headquarters and looked at Rodney. "You should see the place, boss, it's got everything we have not." Shaking his head he bent to get into the vehicle followed by Rodney.

"Yeah but how effective are they?" Rodney teased.

"Very," was Reid's response, a short and slightly curt reply.

"We will see," Rodney unconsciously patted his coat pocket to check the envelope, with he hoped the crown jewels of intelligence, was safe therein.

***

Ensconced in their first class facing sleeping seats, Rodney and Reid drank a brandy and dry as the plane took off shortly after midnight. The seats were at the front of the cabin and they had as much private space to themselves as they could have wished for.

"Don't know about you boss, but I am hungry as hell. I had something in their canteen, a late lunch, but that was that. Here," Reid passed Rodney a sheaf of papers. "Take a look at that lot, could be useful for us and I think scanning through the stuff you brought there is a lot more that will be of use to the team."

"Ah yes. Thank you. By the way he gave me other data for our eyes only, want to see?" Rodney reached into his jacket and pulled out an envelope. He waved the envelope at Reid. "If he kept his word, which is contained in here, it is the mother lode."

Reid reached over and snatched the envelope and broke it open. He read the contents quickly and lowered the papers to his thighs. "For God's sake Rodney, this is. If it's accurate and current, it's dynamite."

"Thought you would be pleased. Goodness knows what the Banker is going to do with it, but I suspect it will be ugly."

Reid leant over and held out his hand to shake Rodney's. "Well done boss, it is not often you leave me speechless but this is one of those times."

"Thanks mate. I have had some time to absorb the idea of holding this intelligence. I am thinking along the lines, for example, we may lift the Accountant and his books and PCs for an in-depth interrogation. Even thinking we might lift the crooked solicitors and bankers? What do you think?"

"Nothing at the moment. I want to digest the stuff first and get some sort of understanding from the Banker as to what we might do that's intelligent. Don't think that raiding is the only way to skin this cat."

"You may be right. But I am thinking we will almost certainly need resources no matter what. We could, for example, split the responsibilities for the different phases and tasks I think will develop, between SO13 and the Regiment."

"I like the idea of using the SAS, the regiment, if nothing else for security, they don't leak unlike civilians. And to use them for what they are best at – covert ops, observation and close target recces. But where we have the likes of solicitors and bankers to sort out it may be better to use SO13 and the Fraud Squad for the UK and Channel Islands. I also don't see why we can't use the FBI for the targets he has identified that are US residents. We don't have to tell them where the intelligence came from niggled, just the part we have discovered they play in the IRA order of battle."

"Agreed. So let's see what the Banker and his three acolytes put to us once they have had time to absorb the Intel and get a plan together. As ever it's good to talk to you Mr Reid, helps to clarify my thoughts."

"My pleasure, cheers," Reid drained his glass and called over the steward. "Can we have refills and any chance of something hot to eat?"

"Not a problem, sir we will be serving dinner in about five minutes. While I get your drinks please take a look at the menu and make a choice. If you are really hungry go for the steak and all the trimmings. I have got a great red wine to go with it. A Bordeaux Merlot with attitude, as they say."

Reid could see Rodney brooding, nursing his empty glass. "Is there something on your mind?"

"There is, in the excitement of the trip I forgot to tell you we have had a first communication from Simon and there is a lot to follow apparently. It should be there when we get back. But what has really got me puzzled is that Simon has sent me a picture of Jean Saied meeting the colonel of the section that runs the IRA training camp. We were assured Saied was assassinated. It seems not."

"This is not good news Rodney. What else?"

"Worse news, I think Tsygankov is out there planning something."

"What makes you say that?" Reid was serious now, personally the news appalled him but he kept his voice low and studied Rodney who was clearly wrestling with how much to share with him at this time.

"It's like this Mr Reid," Rodney related the events so far from the morning he received the Chekov letter to the discovery of the sender, a KGB Officer, who wasn't who he was purported to be and probably a deep cover CIA operative. And the photograph of Saied sent by Simon. His six senses telling him that he knew Saied was inexorably linked to Tsygankov.

When he finished, Reid sat back and looked at his boss. The Steward was back with the drinks and took the orders for dinner before Reid let his feelings go. "For fuck's sake boss, what the hell is going on? We seem to be sleepwalking into potentially a nightmare. The situation needs gripping now." He was angry that Rodney was only now sharing his fears and carrying the burden alone. He acknowledged to himself that the Brigadier was in the loop but he was their political figurehead and not the one on the frontline who would take the bullets.

"I can see you're pissed off, but I wanted to wait till we got back and had a look at the intelligence from Simon. To see if somehow we could make sense of the situation and by now the Brigadier may have some news on Tsygankov and the KGB Vasily Vladimirov."

Chapter 40

SERVO, CARLA AND THE IRA

Servo and Carla had a great day in Dublin shopping for the stores and clothes they wanted. They made themselves known in many of the pubs and eating houses around the shopping centre and picked up the surveillance team that they assumed the IRA had put on their tail. Carla and Servo picked up three different people on their trail. They were good but the KGB officers prolonged period crisscrossing the town, skill and alertness enabled them to mark the followers out. There were two men, who they thought were the two they had seen in the car the night before and a woman who they had not seen before. Half way through the afternoon the surveillance team seemed to disappear and Servo and Carla relaxed. They put it down to the facts that they had been made the followers and the IRA saw no reason to prolong the agony and were now satisfied they were who they were supposed to be.

When Carla and Servo got back to the hotel and stored their purchases there was a knock on the hotel room door. They looked at each other and went into alert mode. Servo stood to the inside of the door with his knife held by his side. Carla opened the door. One of the bell boys stood with a note in his hand and passed it to Carla quickly and disappeared down the hallway in haste.

Servo stood over Carla and together they read the instructions for them. They were to travel to Lanesborough on the River Shannon where a hired boat was waiting for them.

The route they were to take, the note read, was from Dublin and from there they were to take the road to Kinnegrad. From Kinnegrad they were to drive to Mullingar and onto Longford. At Longford they were to swing west to Lanesborough. At Lanesborough they were to drive through the town to the west and the bridge and then immediately past the bridge follow the signs on the right to Flagship Harbour marine and complex.

A description of the boat was given, as a Carlow Class 4-berth cruiser, and where they would find it; they were to pick up the keys from the admin building on the quay. The keys had been left in the name of Cornwall. They needed to provision the boat for at least four days, (p.s. it was suggested they get the provisions in Longford and eat in Lanesborough Keenan's just over the bridge on the left). They were to take the boat south out onto Lough Ree and fish and wait around the second set of three islands just east of Agharanagh.

"Specific are they not? I would guess they are going to track us, it is to be expected? Regardless of the restrictions Carla, I think I am looking forward to being rocked to eat, sleep, fish and relax on a boat with you for a few days. Don't think it is going to be as comfortable as this room though. But there will be compensations. Nobody will be able to hear us." Servo was smiling at her.

"Servo what do you mean? Let's make the most of our last night. I am going to play that piano downstairs later and have a great dinner with you by my side."

"I just hope Tsygankov's budget is enough to cover this luxury living. When I think of the last year or so I am astounded at how fast I have become a converted profligate capitalist."

Carla punched him playfully. "Think it's time we got our kit together and packed for tomorrow. Let's do it now before we go down for the evening so we don't have to worry about it later tonight or in morning."

Servo spun a large map of Ireland open and studied it carefully before answering Carla, "Okay. I am not sure how long it will take to get to Lanesborough, but a couple of hours at least, and a half hour at least to shop for food and anything else we think we might need. I would think we should allow three hours to be sure for the whole trip. We should aim to be there middle to late morning so we can find the boat and get it sorted and we can have lunch as they suggested before we ship out. That will give us three or four hours to find a place to layup for the night, in or around the islands." He showed Carla the map and the scatter of small islands on the Lough. "I think these large loughs can get quite rough in poor weather so I we should find somewhere that's at least sheltered from the prevailing winds."

Their last night in the hotel was not a disappointment; they ate again in the restaurant a truly memorable meal as they shared a flamed venison haunch infused with herbs and berries. After the meal they went in to the bar and Carla played the grand piano expertly. Servo sat close by, watching her over his pint of Guinness. He was under no illusion that after this mission Carla would move back into her old role as the KGB ice goddess and he would be as a passing wave dispersed on a distant shore. He was there and then he would be no more. His mouth curled into a slight smile. "He could dare to hope, why not?" he thought.

Later in the room when they curled into each other, Carla again took the lead and wasted them both in a measured and deep pleasure. Servo woke in the middle of the night from a deep untroubled sleep. There was a figure in the room bent over rifling the cases. The room's ambient light from the standby TV LED and a little moonlight filtering into the room was all Servo needed to zero in on the figure.

Servo was out of the bed in an instant and onto the figure; he landed a fisted blow to the neck, not enough force to kill but enough to put the person out of it for a moment. The figure went down in a heap with a sigh.

Without stopping, Servo ripped the cloth belts from the bathrobes hanging on the door and lifted the limp figure into a chair and tied a slight man, which Servo now discerned, arms behind him and legs to the chair legs. The man's head lolled but he was coming to slowly.

Servo woke Carla who slept on and in Russian quickly told her to get some clothes on while he pulled on his jeans and trainers. With Carla on the move he switched on the light.

To their surprise the man turned out to be the bell boy who had delivered the message. The bell boy was now awake and looking fearfully at Servo.

"And what do we have here?" Servo asked the man.

The man said nothing and hung his head.

Servo lizard fast slapped him hard across the face. Tears sprang into the man's eyes and a whimper escaped his lips.

"What did you say?" Servo was whispering.

The man still refused to answer so Servo slapped him again bringing out a red welt on the man's face and a grunt of pain. "I can keep this up all night so you need to start talking or it is a police cell for you."

The man raised his head, hope in his eyes that he might get away unscathed. He was only young; maybe twenty at a push, with a scraggy brush of hair above the upper lip struggling to be a symbol of manhood and Servo anyway had no intention of involving the authorities.

"I was just looking for cash. That's all. I saw the parcels and assumed you had money."

"Why should I believe you?" But in his heart Servo already did.

"It's the God's truth. They pay me pennies here for what I do and it is difficult to live in Dublin without the means to do so. Let me go and I will never do this again."

"If I do, what have you to offer me for such a large favour. How about you start with the name of the man who gave you the note to pass on to us?"

"I don't know his name but he is one of the boys. You know the IRA. You don't ask questions if they ask you to do something for them or you end up in trouble or dead."

"Okay then, what did he look like? Was he young or old? Was he tall short, long hair or short, colour of eyes, clothes?" Servo prompted him.

The bell boy looked at Servo who had now straightened up and stood over him just out of reach of any flying limb the man might get free. The man saw a six foot stocky man in his early thirties with the muscle build and stance of a soldier. Scars from battles stood out in white on the torso. "An iron man," was the bell boy's conclusion, "and not one to mess with. Around forty years of age, craggy face pockmarked, dark jeans and black bomber padded jacket. Good footwear, clean and polished black leather walking boots. Shortish, curly, dark brown hair and brown hazel eyes. His complexion was red to ruddy with a veined nose." He seemed to think for a moment. "He handed me the letter with his left hand, there was a small scar on the thumb knuckle."

Servo looked at Carla to make sure she had understood all the man had said. He got most of what the man had said but the meanings of some words were still difficult to decipher for him. He got a nod back to Carla.

"You are very observant, was there a car?"

The man hesitated again and Servo moved his stance which was enough. "I was at the front when they drove up. There was a lady in the back but I only glimpsed them as they swung round in the drive. The car was a dark blue Ford."

"A Mondeo by any chance?" Carla asked.

The man swung his head round to her. "Yes Miss, so it was for sure. Old mind and a bit dirty."

"Why do you risk entering rooms that are occupied, its crazy?"

"Less risky actually, especially when the people have had a lot of drinks like you two put away tonight, they sleep sound, normally, plus it's a greater risk of me getting caught by a maid or manager going in and out of an empty room, if the room is occupied I can always claim I took something to them. This is the first time I have been caught."

"Well that would seem to be that. Now what are we going to do with you eh?" Servo looked at Carla, they both felt he had begun lying but it was late and they let it go.

"I think he needs a souvenir to remind him every time he is tempted to be light-fingered, don't you love?" Carla handed Servo his Spetsnaz knife raising her eyebrows to emphasise the question.

"Bring me a towel," he turned to the bell boy. "Some parts of the world we know would chop off your right hand." The bell boy started to tremble. "But that's not my way." Servo held the man's jaw in a vice like grip and quickly razored off half of his whispery hair on his top lip. "Think that's enough?" He looked at Carla seriously who burst out laughing.

"Yes that's enough." She continued to giggle.

Servo released the man's chin and looked down on him. "Do we have an understanding or do we call the manager?"

The bell boy was ecstatic with hope. "Oh yes sir most certainly."

"Good." Servo untied him. "Now off with you my man, and not a word."

They watched him flee the room. When he had gone Carla hugged Servo. "That's was well done, my brave Captain. Now come back to bed and put the chair under the door knob so we can have the rest of the night without any more interruptions."

The next morning they had an early breakfast and were on the road by eight. The journey was straightforward and they found a supermarket in Longford which had a good selection of everything they wanted.

Servo put the bags in the back of the Land Rover and had a good look round for the Ford in the car park but could not spot it. He was sure it would be close by.

The country was varied and the old stone houses in the villages they passed through reminded Servo of home in some way. Carla loved the country and people she had met. She had remarked to him that it was a lush land prone to mists which gave it an almost spiritual feel. The people they had met were open and mostly friendly and welcoming to them as tourists. They had been regaled by a few Irish men and women they encountered of the problem the Polish and Eastern Europeans posed to jobs and housing for them and particularly the young. As they drove deeper into the country, some of the newer pebble-dashed bungalows seemed out of context in their settings.

Lanesborough, when they finally arrived, with its old world high street, was interesting and Carla wanted to explore some of the shops and Irish bars. Servo on the other hand wanted to get to the destination first and sort out the kit and the boat. He gently reminded Carla that they were on a job, which she took with good grace.

The town was perched on the entrance of Lough Ree and they glanced at the Lough as they left the town and crossed the river.

Carla was intrigued. "I read its original name in Irish was 'mouth of the river'. I will try to pronounce that in Gallic, *Beal Atha Liag.*"

"Not bad. Look, lunch on the left coming up. Don't know about you but I am hungry again."

They pulled into the hotel restaurant just after noon and were pleased to see other cars there and to find the dining room already serving the midday meal for a few early diners and they had no trouble getting a table that overlooked the Lough.

After ordering the set lunchtime menu and while they waited for their soup, Servo was talking about how much he was going to enjoy a few days' fishing as he had read the hot water stretch was no doubt aided by the power station outfall water from the processes of burning the peat. "Apparently Lanesborough and the Lough are a prime angling spot. Maybe we can eat the fresh fish I catch."

"I think you need to get a permit to fish, I remember Tsygankov saying something about it. I expect the hotel can supply or tell us where to get one."

"Us?"

"Oh yeah I am going to have a go and we will see who can finesse the largest fish."

Servo groaned but cheered as the bowl of soup arrived along with his pint of Guinness.

They spent the meal mostly in a companionable silence and at its conclusion paid for it and were able to collect fishing permits for a week from the hotel reception along with directions to the harbour.

They drove out of the car park crossing the road and headed north for a mile. Flagship Harbour was gated and fenced but at this time of day the gate was fully open and unattended. They drove through it and along a short earth road to the harbour that held the marina with its double storey admin building.

A car park to the left had a dozen cars in it but the marine was full of boats at this early time of the season.

In the admin building, which doubled as a chandlery and café/restaurant, a lady member of staff met them at the door.

"Hi, we are here for the keys for Cornwall." Carla kept her voice light.

"No problem, you are expected. I'll get the keys for you and point out the boat and show you over it. It is fully fuelled, new gas bottles for heating and cooking and ready to go. You are not going out tonight are you as there is a bit of a blow coming up overnight but after that the forecast is fine for the week?"

"We were, but happy to take your advice as it is the first time we have been here." Carla felt Servo stiffen and put her left foot on his right and gently pressed. She felt him relax to the inevitable. "And we can go and have a look round the town. Anywhere you would recommend?" Carla asked the woman as she handed over the keys.

"Rathcline Castle is popular, a traditional Irish tower house, but not much to see – Cromwell saw to that. The town has got some great pubs and eating houses, depends what you're after? Or we are open tonight and a good bar and food menu. Might be to your advantage as it's your first time on the Lough, could get some good tips on what to avoid and where to go for the biggest fish."

"While the town sounds fine, your hospitality so close to the boat is tempting," Servo put in.

"Fine, the shop and bar open all the time we are here, and for food tonight we will be serving between 6 and 9. Now let me show you the boat and its workings." The woman in her late twenties was, as Servo's soldiers would have said, "A pocket battleship with great warm brown eyes and with her long auburn hair had a welcoming package and a great place to lay your head on a cold night." It was the first time since he had left Afghanistan he had thought about his men and he wondered what they would say if they saw him now. He suddenly missed his crew and, despite Carla's company, felt alone.

The woman took them to the harbour and to the first of the pontoon berths. She jumped on board their boat, which was moored almost directly across from the admin building. She unlocked the door to the cabin. Inside she showed them the facilities and where the spare gas bottle was. Then she took Servo back to the bridge and showed him the controls and front and rear anchor lockers. The front anchor was already out and ready to slip when needed. When she had exhausted the briefing they thanked her for her help and waved her a goodbye as she climbed out of the boat and onto the pontoon.

"Let's get our kit on board, sorted, stored and the heating on, then coffee and a planning conference. We need to be alert and ready for the visitors as this is their home territory and we are the interlopers." Carla wanted to get on and Servo readily agreed as he was ready for some exercise after a few days of inactivity. He also wanted to make sure he was ready to fight if necessary, when, where and in whatever capacity that may entail. He was already working out how to defend themselves while on the boat and the options open to him.

Two hours later they were sitting down with a coffee in a warm cabin. Carla put her hand over her mouth and pointed to her ears. Servo picked this up as a sign to be careful in case they were bugged by the IRA.

There was a TV on the boat so Carla switched it on and turned up the volume. Back around the table, heads bent to each other so they could talk privately, from a large map of the Lough they planned their trip to the first set of islands to the south and west. Servo thought they may be able to anchor and shelter between the two and it could be possible if necessary to scramble ashore if things went wrong on board. The islands were supposedly sparsely populated with vegetation so they would see any approach and it meant that there were only two ways the IRA could arrive, from the east or west. If they anchored across a "cut" between two of the three islands then the person in the open back platform of the boat could see both approaches. They agreed once they were on the Lough they would take shift during the hours of daylight darkness so they could not be surprised in their cabin or bed. Servo commented, "I always fancied a bit of night fishing myself and with couple of lanterns swung outboard and if they are low enough it will give us the advantage of being behind the lights and it will illuminate the immediate area. I want to make sure we are behind the ships' lights at all times because it will make it difficult for the IRA to pick us out." He added on the weapons at their disposal that, "Tomorrow I am going to shorten the barrels of the two shotguns we bought in Dublin; we will keep one in the boat and the other on deck. My knife I will fit into my Spetsnaz spring-loaded arm holster device so it can be fired if needs be. Other than that it's head, fist, legs and teeth. But we are after all supposed to be friendlies so hopefully we will not need anything but our charm, or rather yours." Servo grinned.

"You think these men will not come as partners in a mission but potential enemies?"

"I am hoping for the best but we must plan for the worst case scenario. These are dangerous hunted men and will be suspicious of anyone not in their immediate trust circle. I don't intend for them to have any reason to attack us but that also means we may have to demonstrate strength and be as ruthless as they are."

"I would have thought they would have a lot of support and some space in the Republic and therefore be relaxed here." Carla was trying to understand just what threat they were under apart from the obvious.

Servo brooded for a moment, "As a simple soldier I try to keep abreast of the conflicts in the world, no matter how small or big, that have anything remotely to do with Russia's survival as a nation state. The IRA is the enemy of the British that we may one day have to fight. We all know the British historically and how they punch above their weight. I read some reports when I was in KGB Moscow headquarters when we were being briefed, that the British have a couple of thousand agents in the field in the north and south of Ireland. These agents are a mixed bunch and range from informers, some just for intelligence gathering, and infiltrators all the way through to a group of specialists that are systematically eliminating the opposition. My concern is that this group we are meeting may have an embedded agent who could alert the British to our mission here. We simply have got to be aware of that very real possibility. And we need to bear in mind that in 1981 the IRA council ordered their members to cease tit-for-tat killing of people that are known as the disappeared. I don't believe this faction of the IRA we are dealing with pays too much notice to council, or Tsygankov would not have chosen them."

"I can see that you have been thinking about this very deeply Servo. I will do my best to ensure I don't let you down and will give the people we meet my full attention. I would like to think I am a good judge of others so I have my antenna on full alert," Carla ended lightly.

Servo smiled. "I am sure you will."

"If we have finished up here, how about we go and try the marina restaurant? Last meal cooked for me by someone else for a few days."

They secured the boat and put "tell tales" around the boat which if disturbed would alert them to a break-in while they were out. Servo thought it unlikely as the restaurant overlooked the boat and one way or another they could keep an eye on it.

The Marina bar and restaurant was warm cheerful and busy and a couple were just leaving a corner table in the picture window that looked across the marina and Carla made a beeline for it towing Servo behind her.

The waitress called Maria they learned was over to clear the table and Servo asked her, "If the shop and ships' chandler's shop was open or could be?"

Maria looked at Servo as if he was joking. Seeing he was serious, she said, "Well Tom's still in the bar, I'll ask him if he will open up, could cost you a pint though I would think."

Her accent was heavily Irish and Servo had difficulty understanding her at first but got the gist of it. They needed to give the man a drink for his trouble. "No problem, tell him to order his pint or whatever he wants and come and get me when he is ready."

As it was, Tom came straight over once he knew he was wanted. "Welcome, you're the Cornwalls, how can I help you?"

Servo explained in his much improved English that they were going to ship out first light and need two poles and lanterns for night fishing and asked if the man could supply them on hire or purchase, and that they may want some extra fishing tackle too.

"Let's get it done now then and we can both go back to enjoying our evening. They call me Tom. Jack of all trades and master of none, but enough to help you out I am sure." Tom was a whippet of a man in his late forties, long-haired like a hippy and a head short of Servo. His wiry frame clad in the uniform of the marina staff a size too big for him that dripped off him, he was happy to help. It was the corded muscles on the man's forearms Servo noticed which he knew could only have been developed through hard physical work.

"Servo." Servo offered his hand standing to follow.

"Come along then Servo, let's get you kitted out." Tom asked which part of the Lough they were going to fish in. Servo told him he fancied the "cut", between the some small islands to the south-east.

Tom unlocked the shop door and flicked on the light. "As you can see it is an Aladdin's cave." The shop was stacked with everything a ship owner could want. "As for your choice of fishing area, it is not a bad choice and you should get a few big ones swimming through at night. Although it's a Lough, there can be an occasional small current out there but nothing to trouble you. It is a large body of water that can be whipped up if there is a storm, although the forecast is fair and the weather day temperature could reach 18 degrees but nights may be chillier. Now let's see." He pulled two hurricane lamps down from the shelf with movable side shields to direct the light. He added two 2-litre cans of kerosene and a bottle of meths to start them off, adding a small funnel as an afterthought. Tom went to the back of the shop and brought out two 10-foot boat poles and a hand of nylon rope. "Now what about the fishing kit, what don't you have?"

"Got rods and tackle line, a few hooks and floats but not the necessarily the hooks or lours that will catch your loughs fish."

"No problem at all; here is what I recommend." Tom went behind his counter and pulled out a few drawers and selected a few sets of floats hooks and lures with half a dozen packets of dried bait "winning kit," as he put it. He then added a few "flies and leaders" with a 'you never know,' look. "Might be a few trout out there and flies is what you want. Great when they are fresh out of the water."

"Wow that looks like everything we will ever need."

"Away back to your lady, I'll list the items and add up the damage and Maria can add it to your bill."

"Good enough and please have a drink or two on me."

"Don't worry about that, I will. I will put the kit on the boat deck for you in a moment, so don't fall over it when you get back to the boat."

"Are you sure, I can help?"

"No need, I can manage and I need to earn that extra pint don't you think."

"Thanks Tom, you are a star." Servo offered his hand which Tom took.

Tom took the strong hand Servo offered and shook it, noting its strength and hardness. "Soldier or hard worker?" Tom enquired genuinely.

"Was a soldier, a long time ago now, now I'm just a civilian at the moment. Not as much fun."

Tom laughed. "So true, I did my time in the Irish Infantry 3rd Regiment formed in 1923. Takes one to know one eh fella?"

Back at the table Servo told Carla what he had bought and told her to flex the card when the bill arrived and to smile.

They ordered fillet steak and chips with side salads on the premise they may be eating a lot of fish sooner than latter or so they hoped, and tonight to be washed down with pints of the draught Guinness they now had a taste for.

Servo was silent for a long time during the meal and Carla asked him what he was thinking about. "I was just wondering if this openness to the world was the right tactic and if we should not have been more secretive with our movements. We do seem to have left a trail a kilometre wide."

"It's what the General wanted. He thought that we were more likely to be trusted if we acted more like tourists than infiltrators."

Servo grunted, a characteristic that Carla had now come to recognise as an acceptance gesture. "I suppose so." Servo put his head down and attacked his steak, grinning at Carla.

"Bet Tsygankov didn't foresee our relationship could be so close. Or we would spend so much of his money." Servo laughed out loud.

"Oh I don't know, I think he knew exactly what he was doing and expected." Carla looked at him grinning.

"Allegedly." Servo whispered to himself and looked up at Carla for a second, taking a sip of his drink and then dove back into his steak.

As they went to pay their bill and return to the boat Tom surrounded by others waved them over from the bar. "Come and have a glass with me. You cannot drink Guinness without an Irish whiskey to finish. So what will it be Jameson or a Bushmills?"

Carla ordered for both of them. "One of each please, that way we can try them."

Tom ordered them adding. "*Uisga breatha*, is what we call our whiskey and that means water of life." He smiled and passed the glasses to them both.

Servo and Carla sipped the fiery liquid and then tasted each other's glass. Servo preferred the Jameson and Carla the Bushmills. They then toasted good health to Tom.

Tom turned to Carla and replied with an Irish toast to women.

"Here's to women of the Irish shore; I love but one, I love not more. But since she's not here to drink her part, I'll drink her share with all my heart."

Then Tom turning to Servo toasted him,

"May the Irish hills caress you; May her lakes and rivers bless you. May the luck of the Irish enfold you? May the blessings of Saint Patrick behold you? And may the best day in your past be the worst day in the future."

He raised his glass to them before drinking his whiskey down in one. And he got a round of applause from the room. He bowed and ordered Carla, Servo and himself another round.

Tom regaled them with stories of the Lough Ree fed by the River Shannon and the history of Lanesborough. "The town," he began, "On the western side of the river the town lies in County Roscommon. The eastern side of the river became known as Lanesborough following the granting of Rathcline Castle and lands, to Lord Lane on 24 August 1664 by King Charles II, in recognition of his loyalty to the crown. Lord Lane was grandson of Captain George Lane who came to Ireland during Elizabeth I reign and married the daughter of Cormac O'Farrell. Good man Cormac, and in 1664, Charles II granted Lord Lane a Royal Borough and this is how the Longford side of 'Beal Atha Liag' became known as Lanesborough. The town has seen many battles and invasions over the centuries from the time the Vikings first started invading Ireland from the 9th century to the 11th century. The churches and monasteries were plundered and robbed several times during this period by those heathens." With that last phrase Tom became very Irish. "These raids prompted the first bridge to be built in the town's defence against these raids. On the morning of the fair day in Lanesborough in February 1702, the ferry carrying 46 people and their fair day goods, capsized. Thirty-five of those on board drowned. A stone bridge was then built in 1706 as a result of this tragedy. The Lane coat of arms was carved in the bridge after the Right Hon. Lord Viscount Lanesborough who gave one hundred pounds towards the bridge."

"Enough of the town's history Tom, you'll put the guests to sleep," shouted one of the ladies in the bar party now gathering and growing around the bar to hear Tom. "You'll be taking the tourist guide's job to yourself next, along with everything else you do. Tell us instead about Irish whiskey?" A glass was pressed into Tom's hand and Servo and Carla looked on bemused.

"Well now there's a thing. You have to start by gazing at it like a beautiful woman before you sip." He took a sip and set the glass down on the bar. "Many of you will not know or appreciate the difference between our whiskey and the Scot's. You may take notes if you wish." He moved to a chair and stood on it as he gave forth addressing the room. "In the beginning you have barley. It is soaked and a little water left to enable it to germinate. This malted barley is then dried with smoke. After a few weeks drying it is crushed and mixed with water, now the mash, and yeast added to ferment. The result is?" He looked round the room. "God you're an ignorant lot. The result is beer!" He had them now and they were enthralled. "Now you distil the beer into whiskey. The difference between us and the Scots' and the Irish whiskey is that we dry our barley with coal and distil our beer three times. The Scots dry their barley with peat and only distil twice. Why we don't dry ours with peat I don't know, it would be easier to dig out than coal, anyway," he paused before finishing, "This gives our 'breath of life whiskey' a lighter texture, with a less fleshy and aromatic taste than Scotch, but like all the Irish it develops a nice finesse all of its own." Tom bowed, almost falling of the chair but Servo caught him and steadied him helping him down and to another whiskey as the bar clapped the old soldier.

Back on the boat they checked the telltales they had left and found them undisturbed. They then stowed the new kit left by Tom earlier and secured the boat for the night.

Servo was in a great mood and told Carla as she drew the curtains just how much he had enjoyed the evening. Carla added, "What nice people, how can there be so much angst amongst them on this amazing island, I will never understand it but I agree a memorable night."

They were soon hidden from the night. The double bunk in the forward cabin was made up and after a shower they slid into bed and engulfed each other.

Servo was up with the dawn leaving Carla sleeping on and checked the boat out. When he was completely satisfied all was well and they truly were fuelled up and had full water tanks he went on deck and loosened the ropes. Starting the engine he cast off, manoeuvred out of the marina and motored into the main river running south to the Lough. The traffic on the river was light, a few fishermen coming back from the Lough or going out for the day. As he motored under the Lanesbough town bridge Servo glanced up at the coat of arms. Carla appeared on the bridge at that moment with two steaming cups of coffee. Showered and dressed ready for the day, she took over from Servo who sat on the side of the boat drinking his brew and looking at the passing town. To his left was the hotel they had had lunch in yesterday and a small marina tucked behind it. To the left the commercial quays and docks with the Lough ferry tied up for the night and making ready for its first pass to the south of the day. The Lough opened up into a broad expanse of water. The surface of the Lough was glassily smooth. To the south the morning mist was still evident as it hung over the water limiting the visibility to under a mile. Servo waved to a man in a small craft who was fishing close to the shore.

Carla steered SSE cutting towards the east bank at a steady 8 knots. "I'll steer on this course but stay a hundred metres or so off the bank until we sight the first of the islands, sometime in the next hour or so.

So why don't you go and get washed up and ready for the day and then come and take over from me and I will cook up some breakfast. Looks like it will be a nice day once the mist burns off." Carla was enjoying the experience of steering the craft on an all but deserted Lough. It was quiet, only the sound now of their engine quietly throbbing and the sound reverberating around them. They drove a small bow wave and the shush of the water on the hull was a comforting sound lulling them into silence. The occasional negligible wash from some distant disturbance gently rocked the boat.

Servo finished his coffee and reluctantly made his way to the cabin to wash and dress for the day.

They had breakfast on deck; juice and had barely finished the egg and bacon sandwich washed down with black tea when the first of the small islands to the west began to appear out of the mist. These two were unsuitable as the ferry used them to cut through the deep water cut; what they wanted were the smaller islands off of the northern tip of a large island called Inchenagh. Inchenagh was shaped like a hanging bulbous ended exotic fruit with a slim panhandle neck to the north. The island was farmed from Agharanagu but not normally occupied. To the west of Inchenagh, on the main land was Anaghmore and to the east Agharanagu. It would be another hour before they got near to them.

They wanted to carry out a full survey of the two small islands off the large one, as they had they realised they had not one but two options; one was to anchor between them or to anchor off the southern one between it and Inchenagh. "Two cuts to explore for the price of one," Servo said to Carla. Servo was at peace and enjoying this part of the journey. And it would be a good chance anyway to practise his boat-handling skills when they arrived at their destination.

As they approached the northern most islands, Servo at the helm slowed to a few knots while he let the boat idle just underway and went to attend to the anchors and prepare them for release fore and aft. The islands separated now and he could just make out the main cut and pressed forward towards it. As he came closer, he picked his approach and called to Carla to go and stand on the prow and be prepared to drop the forward anchor when he told her to. The water was clear as the Lough began to shallow as the land raised itself to form the islands. He slowed again, checking the depth by looking over the side. He judged there were a good still several metres under the keel as he entered the cut. He aimed for a spot in the middle of the right-hand island nudging forward slowly. He brought the boat to a stop a few metres from the middle of the island and again checked he had metres under the keel. It all looked good as an option. He gently made his way through the cut and then steering round to the right around the southern smaller of the islands, he crept into the second cut with Inchenagh on his left. This cut was smaller and much shallower and the rocks below the surface could be clearly seen. The spot was idyllic and Servo thought better defendable, offering an escape and evasion option onto the larger Inchenagh Island. Carla called out the depth and warned Servo of rocks as they appeared. Servo managed to reach the middle of the cut without mishap. He called Carla to let go her anchor and head the splash. He let the boat drift out aft toward the larger island and let go his aft anchor, paying out until the boat was broadside to the two islands forming a tee bar. The distance between the islands was now only three times the length of the boatniggled, so in the event it was shallow enough to wade or a short swim to either land mass in moments.

They waited a while for the anchors to bite and made a few minor adjustments until they were happy the boat was fast. Satisfied they took a look round. A heron fishing in the shallow waters around the panhandle suddenly rose into the air. Servo took this as a good sign that there were fish about. The water between the two islands was very clear and they could see how the Lough bed rose to form the islands. There did not appear to be a current but the water moved and gently lapped around where it met the solid ground. They could see how the top of the Inchenagh panhandle curved away from them to the wide lands that formed the bulk of the island. Trees and hedges split the larger islands' land into regular fields. They could see no dwellings in their immediate vicinity on the low-lying island, but suspected if the land was farmed that there would be some shelter of sorts further in, if only for farming equipment. Servo was determined to recce the island later in the day just before dusk, judging any workers on the land would have returned home and if the IRA were to come that night they would not do so until dark. The smaller islands had vegetation and the odd tree and bush but were untended.

They spent an hour searching the boat again to check as best they could but found nothing.

"Time for lunch, I'll get it while you sort the fishing tackle. Let's make the most of our time here," Carla called, disappearing into the saloon. Servo followed and fetched out the fishing equipment and sorted them out on deck.

They fished all afternoon with Servo fly-fishing for lake trout. By late afternoon they had caught enough for a substantial meal and were very happy with their first day's effort.

At half four Servo stripped off to his jeans and put on a black fleece top and slung his trainers over his neck while Carla watched him expectantly. "I will be back in two hours," Servo told her as he slipped of the transom at the back of the boat into the cool waters of the Lough. The water came up to the top of his thighs and he waded the forty feet or so to the start of the panhandle. The river bed beneath him swallowed quickly to knee and then ankle height. On land he ran his hands down his legs to get rid of excess water and put on jeans and his trainers before jogging off into the island's interior. Carla watched him go as far she could, run and jump hedges until he was quickly swallowed up in the distance. Carla packed up her fishing kit and went below to prepare the fish for dinner.

True to his word Servo was back within two hours. "As we thought, the island is not occupied, although there is a small lodge at the bottom of the island and a short metalled road leading to a staging area and jetty, which is obviously the way the land owner arrives and leaves the island. All the activity takes place below the panhandle so I can't see any reason why anyone would come here by choice. It looks like our location is well chosen."

"Sounds good, now go and change, you're dripping water everywhere and dinner is in ten."

Servo spent the bulk of the night watch fishing successfully, aided by his lamps which brought a shoal of large fish into his fishing area and he hooked a three pounder which he cleaned and stashed in the cool box to be grilled for breakfast.

The IRA didn't come that night, the following day or the next night and Carla and Servo began to wonder if they had got their instructions correct. In the meantime they communicated with Tsygankov and Vasily to get the latest updates and feed in their own situation report. Tsygankov wasn't worried and told them simply wait.

Servo was sleeping after his night watch on day three when Carla woke him around midday. "There is a boat approaching and it is steering directly for us. Get up, Servo." Servo pulled on his jeans and a sweatshirt and before he arrived on deck watched the cabin cruiser as it stood off 30 metres away in deeper water. He could see three people, a woman and two men, on deck. Servo checked the shotguns were handy and strapped on his knife arm spring holster and slide in the knife handle compressing it against the spring till it locked. He checked the sweatshirt arm cover. He then joined Carla on deck.

"Is that the Cornwalls?" an Irish man called. Two others were with him; the woman and a young man stood behind and to the side.

"Who wants to know?" Servo called back.

"Now that's not very friendly, you have come a long way to see us and us to see you."

"Just checking." Servo shrugged the Barbour coat on with the loaded shotgun safe inside the coat's poacher's pocket. "Come on over and welcome."

"Now that's better, so it is," called the man. He started the boat engine and made his approach. While they waited for the strangers to approach, Servo returned to the cabin and quickly strapped the spring loaded holster holding his Spetsnaz hunting knife securely ready for release.

Servo watched them approach and took the line when the young man threw it to him. Servo lashed their boat alongside theirs. The older man leapt aboard and the other helped the woman over.

"I am Liam and my younger companion is Shaun but you will have met and this is Sheena."

Servo smiled at the younger man. "Oh yes, our thieving bellhop." It brought a grin from Shaun who rubbed his chin.

"It is. And I owe you one but as a guest you are forgiven so you are." The young man laughed and held out his hand which Servo took.

"Let me introduce ourselves – this is Carla and I am called Servo."

Liam nodded. He was late thirties early forties, as tall as Servo and looked fit and quick. Servo decided to treat this man with respect. The woman was a dark Irish woman in her forties. She was short and already spreading in middle-age but not unattractive.

Carla waved them to seats around the bridge deck and asked them if they would like to share lunch and have refreshments. "That would be very welcome Carla," Liam replied, appraising Carla. Servo noticed but kept his thoughts to himself. "Who would not?" he thought.

Liam took the lead, asking Servo while they waited for Carla to get the lunch and drinks, what they thought of Ireland and other small talk, touching briefly on the co-operation they had been asked for. Servo kept the conversation light and amusing.

Shaun was not so diplomatic and asked Servo if he was a KGB spy and got a look from Sheena and Liam. Servo held up his hand showing no offence. "Well Shaun, sorry to disappoint you I am a simple soldier that's been drafted in to support the task and will return to my unit once my part is over."

"Interestingly your English is quite good for a soldier, presumably you're Special Forces."

Servo could see no reason to be secretive about his origins. "Captain of Spetsnaz, fresh out of Afghanistan, and you could say from that point of view I find your homeland a joy and the people I have met great fun to be with."

Liam looked at him seriously. "Unfortunately Servo, it is a split and troubled land and you will see that for yourself when you scratch the surface of our skin."

Carla arrived with plates of grilled fish and mashed potatoes and greens along with a bottle of whiskey and cans of Guinness. They ate lunch and with small talk, and jokes about the bell hop incident, Sheena's interest in Russia and Carla, any reserve between the two parties was left at a low level. Only Liam and Servo remained ever watchful.

After lunch Liam asked Sheena and Shaun to clear away while he spoke to Carla and Servo. When Sheena and Shaun had left them Liam bent his head to them. "Okay, tell me what this is all about. On spec we have a small team in Libya, who will be returning shortly and who have met your man out there. They said he was a cool customer and professional."

"In principle we want the IRA to carry out in support of us an attack on the mainland."

"I thought so. Now at this meeting I don't want specific details just enough for me and my commander to have a meaningful discussion together. On the face of it we want to do this for our own reasons so that's the positive on the negative; we don't want to risk or use resources on a low-profile target. So what's the task and what's the risk?"

Servo and Carla were a little taken back that the IRA knew so much but they pressed on; Carla first. "Liam, the targets who will all be in one place at the same time are the key members of a small but effective section of the British Secret Service. As a double win they will be attending the Air Corps summer ball where many senior officers of many parts of the British Army will be attending. The outline of how it's done is the IRA with our support substitute the marquee team who will put up the tent for the ball. The odourless and colourless explosive, which is on its way, will be used to salt the tent." Carla paused.

Liam sat back. "Wow that's a big one."

Servo added. "Safe houses, cars and weapons etc., are already in place. It is the IRA's knowledge of the UK and its ability to man up that is the reason we are here."

Liam held up his hands. "Enough for now." He stroked his chin. "It is one hell of a plot and it's attractive. Imagine the aftermath and fallout." He ran his fingers through his mop of ginger hair. "I'll get back to you with an answer; if it helps I will be pressing for a yes to the task. Stay here and enjoy the fishing. Great dish of fish Carla, much appreciated I am sure so it was." He called Shaun and Sheena from the cabin knocking on the hatch. "Time to go home."

After they had left, Carla got onto Tsygankov to brief him on the meeting.

Chapter 41

MOULD AND SHARKY AND THE AVERY'S TEAM

Sharky and Mould sat in one of the small operations rooms they had been allocated, chatting to the Royal Signals Officer who had been attached to them for the mission to help them through the labyrinth that was GCHQ. The transcripts of conversations between the IRA Q and callers to date had been analysed by other specialists in the GCHQ Cheltenham party to the aims of the task. The specialists' comments and recommendations were written in the margins of the transcripts.

Sharky was speculating if they could get a bug and satellite transmitter into Liam's car. The Royal Signal Officer was not keen for many reasons, not the least that if it was found the IRA would have the latest technology and would reverse engineer and then have the technology to turn against us.

The phone rang and one of the attached GCHQ analysts answered it. "It is that Mr Avery for you Sharky."

Sharky waved the analyst to transfer it to his desk. "Sharky." He announced himself.

"Hi mate, comfortable are we, in the warmth and safety of GCHQ?"

"Just fine mate, what can we do for you?"

"We followed Liam to Lanesborough. He had a young lad with him and a woman. We got pictures and are firing them over to you. They took a fast cruiser out of a marina and we lost them, obviously as we didn't have our flippers with us." Avery heard the room laughter. "Till they returned to the marina six hours later. Think they have been to a meet. They are on their way back heading in the direction they came from. Our guess is Liam will drop the two passengers off and then go to see Q. So you need to be aware and listen in if you can when they link up at Q's."

"Got it, anything else?"

"Can you speak to the boss? I want to put my two best friends on a hired cruiser boat for a day or two and send them out into the Lough. Let's say two to three hours south on the water and see if they see any other craft that could have been involved in the contact my water tells me it may be worth it. I will stay on shore in contact with them via sat phone."

"Wait out back in ten, but in the meantime start the process."

Sharky got hold of Mr Reid who was with Rodney sorting the data from Simon. Reid covered the mouthpiece and talked it through quickly with Rodney as he felt sceptical, but he found Rodney was up for it. "Okay Sharky, get it sorted, make sure they look and act like fishermen and don't forget to tell them to get fishing licences, the last thing we want is them arrested and fined by the water bailiffs or whatever they have in the south." He put the phone down and saw a beam on Rodney's face. "Something amusing you?" Reid's face was set.

"No Mr Reid, just thinking how pleasant it would be to go on a fishing trip for a few days away from the office. Best case our boys catch something and we hear about the ones that got away."

Reid was not sure if Rodney was making fun, so grunted and got back to work shifting the data sent in by Simon from Somalia.

Sharky called Avery back and gave the go-ahead and the warning from Mr Reid. He added, "Think it would be sensible if there is a second marina in Lanesborough or nearby if you hired your rig from there, not the one used by Liam."

"Already on it, mate. Call you later." Avery was gone. Sharky and Mould shook their heads, they were concerned that Avery was, like them, getting too old to be out in the field battling.

"Old soldiers Sharky, they never die just regroup and go to the hell." Mould was in a reflective mood. It was something he put down to being in GCHQ, where unusually he felt completely out of his depth with the stuff he was handling and the clever people around him. He wished he was out there with Avery or at least back at the London base. Sharky on the other hand seemed perfectly at ease with the surroundings and the people shifting through and sorting out the communications as they arrived in the task operations room were analysed and dispatched on.

Next morning in the operations room Mould was still wishing he was elsewhere. "Anywhere but here," and gave in grudgingly to his fate, perhaps it was the act of relaxing into his situation that sparked something in the back of his mind and felt suddenly empowered. "There have been some interesting conversations between Q and Liam," Mould muttered to himself.

"Sharky," Mould stirred.

"That's me."

"Can you find a copy of that last transcript between Q and Liam yesterday afternoon?"

"Sure." Sharky wandered off to the growing set of arch lever files. Grabbing the right one he went back to his partner. "You really should make an effort to understand their filing system. It is quite simple."

"For you maybe but I like my own filing system and these ones baffle me. Whatever it is it's filed in one file in date order."

"Hmm, always thought you were underemployed. Here there is so much stuff it has to be broken down into subjects. So man-up my old friend and get with the programme." Sharky was not unaware his friend was out of his depth here and just hoped this phase would be over soon before Mould started to become disruptive as he knew he could be.

"Yeah, yeah, yeah, okay just for you." Mould was grinning and Sharky was grateful for that. Mould opened the file and leafed through it till he got to the transcript. He read it carefully. It read:

Preamble.

Sound of car drawing up and parking engine off. One car door opening and closing and steps on the gravel drive. Door bell rung. Silence. Door opens and more steps on the gravel drive. Sounds of two men greeting each other.

Conversation

Liam's voice. "The two Russians, the man and woman have left in the boat and on the lough and been on the water for a couple of days now, had Shaun on the shore watching them through my binos. Shaun reports they have just spent the time fishing day and night, so they are alert and Shaun says armed. There has been no physical contact with them but they have been seen on deck using a phone."

Q's voice. "What your plan?"

Liam. "I am going to get the boat out tomorrow morning and RV with them around Inchenagh. I think they have waited long enough for a contact."

Mould made a note of the location.

"I will pick up Shaun and clean him up and take Sheena with me. I think taking them with me will not be as threatening as if I were to take some of the boys, especially if the Russians are armed. I will make sure neither Shaun nor Sheena is in earshot of my discussion with the Russians."

Q. "OK do what you have to. I want to know the outline of their proposed involvement with us and a few details of their task so we can make a decision on how much help we give them. I am keen to make this work for if we break away we need all the money and friends we can get. Know what I mean?" (Note the accent and rasp of Q's voice according to our speech specialists is from the Dundalk area.)

"I understand. I will report back here tomorrow, late afternoon but as soon as I get back."

Men say goodbye and footsteps on the gravel drive, the door opens and closes shortly afterwards the car drives off.

Transcript ends.

The transcript was signed and dated as actioned. Mould sat back, musing over the implications. Picked up the phone and called Avery to give him the intended meeting area around the island of Inchenagh. Avery thanked him and cut the call. A few minutes later Mould grabbed Sharky's arm and told him they were going for a coffee. Sharky at first resisted, he was busy, head in one of the files. A look from Mould was enough.

"What's up mate?" They were in the staff canteen.

"Have you read the transcript you gave me?"

"Can't say I paid it that much attention. Not really in our scope but yeah the mention of the Russians did make me think. I assumed the intelligence agencies would be alerted and it would be handled by others." Sharky sipped his tea.

"So did I and the danger of assuming as ever is sloppy work. My gut feeling tells me this is important and so we should, that's you and me. We must be plugged in to hear the next conversation between Liam and Q." Sharky had not seen Mould so animated since they had got here and was relieved and determined to support him if it would get Mould out of his mood.

"Okay mate, just for you. It is nearly lunchtime, let's eat early and then get hold of our tame Royal Signals Captain and get ourselves set to hear the conversation."

"Thank you; I really have a bad feeling for this one."

"I hope you are wrong, mate. Come on, I'm buying."

The Royal Signals Captain arrived in the canteen for lunch, collected her tray and joined them. "What are you two up to, down a bit early for lunch? I have been studying you two and you are trouble. Mr Mould is like a caged animal and you, Mr Sharky, intense to the point of detail overkill." The Captain was in her middle to late twenties, tall for a girl, fit and took no prisoners with the staff they had been given.

"We want a favour and the answer has got to be yes." Mould was teasing but the Captain could see deadly serious.

"Ask away, we are here to serve you in case you forgot, not the other way around." The Captain filled her mouth with canteen mash.

"Good," Sharky took over. "This afternoon, probably late on, there will be another meet between our two triggers and we both want to listen in."

"And," Mould added, "My gut tells me the conversation is going to be one that we need to limit the number of people party to it. So you Captain, Sharky and me and of course the transcribers operator. That's all, so no loudspeaker stuff, headphones only. We will decide on the distribution once we hear it and if we need to refer it up."

"Spies after all, I was thinking you two might be a couple of has been admin clerks from London. I see what I can do Mr Bond." The Captain teased Mould but felt guilty as he was at this time an easy target.

Mould coloured. "I take it that's a yes."

"That's a definite yes. Sorry to tease you but this is the first time you have come alive."

Mould looked at her, head to one side with a smile. "Tell you the truth this place is not my environment and I did not feel I was achieving anything. Well now, young lady, I've got my teeth into something I understand."

At three o'clock in the afternoon the Captain called them over to the radio and gave them each a headset to put on. They three of them sat round the operator transcribers and listened in. The Captain called one of her staff over and ordered tea for them all. "And go into my desk top drawer and bring the pack of biscuits for us please."

They listened to the location's background noise for nearly three hours. They heard birds and the odd car, a farmer working the fields and someone leave the house go to a car to fetch something, they decided, and return to the house slamming the door.

Six o'clock in the evening on the dot a car drew up. The operator told them it sounded like the one from yesterday and switched on the digital tape recorder. The car door opened and slammed and they heard the individual walking quickly up the gravel path and knock at the door. As before, Q left the house so they could talk on the drive.

"You are a bit late Liam, I was wondering if you had defected, so I was." ("That's Q," whispered the operator.)

"No not defected but had to drop off Shaun and Sheena. Sorry I am a bit late but I've got what you wanted. It is dynamite Q." Liam told Q about the meeting leaving nothing out, emphasising the target, the summer ball and the attendance of a group from the secret services as well as other senior officers from other corps and regiments. He told him that the odourless and colourless Semtex was on its way and what the Russians wanted from them.

Mould, Sharky and the Captain were astounded and leant forward as if to hear more clearly what was being said.

"Bloody hell Liam, it's the big one. Let me think for a minute." They could hear Q pace the drive and almost hear him thinking. "When are our engineers back from Libya?"

"Ian and Joe should be back on the mainland in about two weeks, maybe less, remember Thomas didn't make it and lies in the desert six foot under."

"We should never have sent him, he was an embarrassment." Q was again silent, pacing. "Liam what I am thinking is that this opportunity is the catalyst to split off the IRA. I know you may have reservations but I need to take this to the Army Council. I am going to do this for two reasons. The first is to test the resolve of the Council to give up the struggle for a deal. The second is for me to see who is on our side and wants to continue the struggle until we get what we have been fighting and dying for."

"I was hoping to go back tomorrow with an answer for the Russians, so I was Q."

"No reason why not, we are going for this no matter what the council says my boy. Fuck 'em eh."

"Right enough Q. It will be one hell of a blow to the Brits." Liam's response was not victorious but grave, he was thinking ahead of the task before them and it would be dangerous and risky of that he was certain.

"Good Liam, get those Russians out of Ireland as soon as they can leave. We don't want to risk them being made by the authorities and jeopardising this opportunity." They fancied they heard Liam turn on the drive to leave. "Wait Liam, tell them it's a go and that we need the means to contact them securely twenty-four hours a day."

"No problem and good luck with the Council. I'll be back tomorrow night, call me if you want me round."

"Might leave it a day or two as I don't think I can get the Council together before the next meeting later this week. Good night Liam, well done you."

They listened to the car drive off, and the evening country sounds return to normal.

They sat in silence for space and took off their headphones. "Mould turned to the Captain and the operator. "Not a word of what you heard leaves this room do you understand. I need to talk to our boss. Can you make a copy of the transmission for me now? Sharky and I are going to London immediately so we need to take it with us. Captain, make two further copies double envelopes and mark it top secret SIS and military eyes only. Lock one copy in your security safe which you only have access to and get the other locked away in the buildings' secure archive keep. Don't care if you have to get the duty officer out of his bed to lock it away. Take the transcript out of the office file, add to it the recording of yesterday's exchange too so we have the whole story." He smiled. "And you young man, get today's tape transcribed so the transcriptions can be sealed with the recording copies." He got the attention of the Captain and the operator. "Any questions?"

"What do we do with the original recordings?"

"Password protect them to top secret eyes only for SIS and MIL INT. Can you get those passwords?"

"Yes but you are truly out of date, that is not what we do here today, we have an encryption system that changes the access code thousands of times a second." The Captain was bright-eyed. What a coup, she was thinking and gave Mould a high five. "We will get it done. Will you be back tomorrow?"

"Rest assured," Sharky promised. "You guys, sure you are okay with all of this?"

"Bread and butter stuff, sir. Give us half an hour to get your stuff ready. You will need to sign it out or you will not get through security."

"No problem. Come on Mr Mould, canteen and supper. It may be the only meal we get tonight." He picked up the phone and got Graham in the London ops room. "Graham can you please alert Mr Reid and the Major. Tell them that we have something for them to look at and it must be seen by them tonight. We will be in London by say," he looked at his watch, "nine-thirty in the ops room. Food and a drink would be appreciated." He put down the phone. "Let us eat – your turn. Do you want us to bring you two anything from the canteen?" The Captain and the Operator both declined saying they would eat when the job was done.

Chapter 42

RODNEY DIRECTS

Sharky and Mould were in the operations room shortly after nine and set up the play-back machine and copied the transcripts for Rodney and Mr Reid. They were chatting to Graham on the progress of the others at their various tasks and enjoying a late supper of fish and chips and steaming mugs of tea. It seemed that the others were making headway, especially the Banker's team. They had given Graham the transcripts to copy and read and he was as stunned as they had been.

Rodney and Reid arrived together shortly before nine-thirty.

"I hope you two reprobates have something worth me giving up a dinner night at Mr and Mrs Reid's. I was just about to tuck into the dessert," Rodney started. "Okay, out with it."

Mould took the lead. "Major, Mr Reid, what we have is the recordings and transcripts of yesterday's and today's exchanges between Q and Liam, his number two." Sharky handed out the transcripts and Mould played the recordings one after the other.

The four men listened in silence until the recording had finished, you could have heard a pin drop.

"I see." Rodney was shocked but razor sharp. "Graham, get me Avery on the secure phone and put it on the speakers."

"Avery."

"Good evening, you are on speaker. I have Mr Reid, Mould, Sharky and Graham with me. You okay with that?"

"No problem."

"Orders."

"Go ahead, Major." Rodney gave Avery the general outline and double checked that Avery had the full story about the transmission and the location of the Russian boat, before starting his orders.

"Orders: your two Welshmen are to make one pass, take a picture at long range of the two occupants in the boat with the contact as soon as they are on deck together. Okay so far?"

"Roger."

"They are then to make best speed back to the marina and dump the boat. One of your pair to go to Dublin Airport and the other to Belfast and wait out for the two triggers, who I can confirm are Russians, by the way, to appear at an airport. You are to try to follow the two Russians, as best you can in case they divert to another means of getting to the mainland. Do you have your portable printer with you?" Avery confirmed he had." Good print three copies of the picture of the party, one each for you over there and mail a copy over to Graham," he paused, "Okay so far?"

"Roger."

"Once the Russians have committed to a route and destination identified, phone in the details. I will have teams of watchers to pick them up and follow them to their next destination," he paused, "Okay so far?"

"Roger."

"Thank you, now I am going to get a specialist team to do a full close quarter recce of the Q environment and lay-in equipment and dig in. Once the specialist team arrives, which will be in the next twenty-four hours, get yourselves back here ASAP. Any questions?"

"No got it all."

"For good order repeat the orders back please."

Avery went through his notes satisfying Rodney he had all the points and added he would update his report on the current arrangements with sketches of where their hide was and pinpoint the location of the directional listening devices for the specialist team.

"Thank you Avery, I will let you go as you will no doubt have lots to do. You will need to pick up a couple more hire cars fuelled and ready in place for the team and to brief them etc."

"I'm already in planning mode Major." Avery cut the call.

"Mr Reid, please set up teams of watchers and a manager for the watchers for the immediate future until we get Avery back at least." Rodney was not expecting any resistance from MI5 in getting a team of their specialists who watched and followed targets. "I will speak to the Brigadier later tonight and get him to work his magic to get a specialist team from the Regiment to do the recce and surveillance." He looked at Mould and Sharky. "A good day's work I think. Well done to you both and Avery and his men. Now," he looked at Mr Reid who had been silent to this point, "we need to decide what we do with this bombshell."

The men in the room looked at Mr Reid to give his view.

"I would like to make three points." Reid began gritting his teeth, his Scots accent strong. "Point one: the interruption to Mrs Reid's dinner will cost me the price of a new dress for her. Point two: I will make a point of her taking Mrs Mould and Sharky with her with the instructions they are to buy a new dress each and I will pay. Boys this find is the dog's bollocks well done!" He paused, stood and went to shake each man's hand before continuing. "Third point: we should assume this has been set up by General Tsygankov, with or without the sanction of his masters. I suspect if it is sanctioned, as the enormity of what is planned dawns on them, they will pull back but we must not count on that. I think we need to let their plan develop but we need to have identified each player and where they are and what they are responsible for before we roll them up. They have some six weeks left to make it happen and that's a short timeframe for such a complex mission. So we must assume a lot of the infrastructure and planning is already in place." He paused. "A post script. We need to keep this knowledge tight. What's the situation at GCHQ, Sharky?"

"Only two people know about it; the Royal Signals the Captain and the Home Office operator who transcribed the transmission." He then explained about the two sealed copies.

"Rodney, if I may, I suggest we pull Sharky and Mould get the transmissions routed to here, we are going to have to make some changes anyway when the specialist team goes in. And until this is over we get the Captain and her operator attached here to run the communications and get the updates from the specialist team's signallers. Help Graham whatever. No doubt they have signed the official secrets act but they can do it again and I will give them the gypsy's warning. Also we pull the two copies and our Brigadier takes charge of them for the central intelligence meeting." He drew a breath. "We will need to put the two of them up somewhere close by."

Graham sparked up. "They can stay with me. I have plenty of room and it will make a change from me rattling around alone in that mausoleum of a pile in Pimlico. And it will give me chance to try out some of my culinary skills on people that might appreciate it." It was a dig at Mould and Sharky who soaked up Graham's food and never showed their appreciation.

"Thank you Graham, that is generous of you." Reid meant it and glowered at his two ingrates Mould and Sharky. They stared into space in all innocence. They knew Graham had marked them but they had early on formed a pact not to give praise to his food, which was outstanding, lest he stop trying to impress them.

"Let's do it. Mould, Sharky – get it sorted tomorrow please, up and running the following morning. Refer the operator and Captain's line chiefs to me if needs be." Rodney opened his notebook and scribbled notes on his actions and orders. "Could do with a pot of tea? I am going to stay here in the ops room for an hour or two to get my report and request done for the Brigadier. I want to be on his doorstep at 0600hrs with the shopping list and the plan. The rest of you get your heads down and that includes you Graham, I will wake you when I leave."

Rodney worked on through the night something was niggling him and it came to him as he was finishing up his dossier for the Brigadier.

He woke Graham with a cup of coffee. When Graham had got himself together he sat opposite Rodney. "I seem to be getting used to the night shift, but it can be quiet at times." Graham sipped his coffee quietly.

"That does seem to be the life of a bachelor, I do think sometimes we may be putting on you because you are single." Rodney was flicking through his report and his notes.

"I am sure that I would not have it any other way." Graham looked at Rodney. "God only knows what I am going to do when I retire."

"I would have thought a discrete B&B for the rich might be an option in that great house of yours. They would certainly appreciate its location and your food."

"Oh it's not that, I do have friends even some relatives somewhere. It's the job I love and its challenges." Graham was enthusiastic and it showed.

"Good. Challenges, well here is another." Rodney explained to Graham on a need-to-know basis about the note he received and the link of it to Vasily. "What I need to know is if he entered the country and when. I am sure he is here and unless he is in deep cover he will have left a footprint somewhere."

"What's his full name?" Graham was taking notes.

"Captain Vasily Vladimirov, a KGB Intelligence Officer, you can look at my database – there is a photograph of him from around five years ago, maybe less and a MI5 report on him when he was here on a look-see mission, so we know quite a lot about him. As the letter to me was posted it doesn't mean he was in the country at that time, I suggest you go back in two or three week trances from today."

"Likely he will be using his first name; it seems to be the norm these days for all sides. I will begin with the Border Force persons of interest file and then financial transactions. Vasily is not a common first name in the UK so I may find something. With the current high level of security status it is likely he may have been tagged by our Border Force. They seem to be tagging every other person because of the security threat at the moment, so it possible Vasily will be in the pot. Leave it with me overnight."

"Hmm, you have just given me an idea. When you are in the PII file see what Dublin's shared and sent over to us in say, in the last three weeks. You never know our two Russian friends may have been tagged. Long shot, but then that's our game is it not?"

Chapter 43

VASILY

Vasily woke in the safe house in Middle Wallop early. He had made an appointment with Monks, the estate agent, to visit a property in Norwich at two o'clock that afternoon. He thought it would be a four-hour flog and a further hour on that for traffic so he planned to leave by eight that morning giving himself plenty of time. He stretched and found his watch and switched on the bedside lamp. It was 6am. Swinging himself of the bed he tidied the covers back and puffed up the pillows. He could sleep anywhere when needs must, but he enjoyed a well-made bed when he could.

After a shower and dressing he sat in the kitchen enjoying a hot breakfast and pot of strong coffee. He cleared up and made his preparations to leave ahead of time and was surprised when his phone began to ring.

It was Tsygankov and the call unplanned, as they had spoken the night before. "General? Good morning."

"Vasily, listen I have been asked to attend a meeting in Moscow with the Chairman of the KGB and First Directive and General Polyakov. I am not expecting any issues but just in case I am delayed please let the others know where I am. I will take the mobile with me so we should be able to communicate, but just in case…" He let the sentence hang. "On another subject I have had a call from Carl, Mr Salomon, and he is well into the Canal du Midi. So all is going to plan. Talking to Carla last night it may be they will be heading your way after they meet the IRA again today. So stay in touch and keep me up to date, so far so good." Tsygankov was gone.

Vasily sat for a while trying to work out why Tsygankov would be called to the Chairman with Polyakov. "Was it good news, bad or nothing to do with this mission?" The KGB Chairman was a cold man and specialist in disinformation. Vasily knew Mikhail Sergeyevich Gorbachev's favourite and it was rumoured such was the atmosphere that existed between the two men that he was a block to the Gorbachev plans for reform.

Vasily had his own issues and worries that were taxing and testing him fully. How could he continue with this brutal mission? When he knew it was wrong and he would be seen as a traitor to his Russian friends if he now broke cover and went to Major Brown and his people. His inclusion in Tsygankov's plans had been at first pure chance. He was with Servo when he heard from him about the task to go in and capture Saied in a house in Kabul. Playing his cards carefully he made himself available to the Afghanistan KGB Colonel as counter weight to Servo and his GRU boss. He inveigled himself into the mission to capture and look after Saied and the task of picking Tsygankov up from Kabul airbase with Servo and his men.

He blamed Tsygankov for the death of Chekov and others and wanted to even the score. The inclusion of Servo and himself into Tsygankov's scheme was if not pure serendipity close to it.

Vasily was torn in the way to handle the situation he now found himself. As a deep cover CIA plant, his primary objective was to find his way up the ranks of the KGB until he was in a position to deliver material of value. As a servant of the West he could not allow the mission to go ahead and the havoc it would cause. True he had a conduit through Major Brown. He would ponder on the conundrum during his drive to Norwich and make his decision on the way back. Swearing softly to himself he picked up his day sack and his pistol.

He locked the house and set the alarm and went to the garage to get the mobile home. He had decided not to take the BMW for fear it was bugged and transmitting his position.

Checking the address he had been given by the estate agent he punched the address into the satnav and glanced at an overview of the route. Up to the A303 join the M3 turn onto M25 and drive north round the M25 to the M11 on to the A11, passing Thetford and on to Norwich. Where the A47 cut the A11 he needed to come off on the old Newmarket road, cross the bridge and hook back to find Hill Farm Close on his left and look for the third house in.

He had decided on Norwich as it was a place to nowhere, big enough to get lost in and routes to the four points of the compass including a route to Harwich if they were forced to use that route out of the UK.

The journey was pleasant enough and he appreciated the power of the three-litre engine. Much as he wanted to push down on the throttle he needed to remain invisible and could not afford to be stopped for speeding. Still the acceleration he had used from time to time left puzzled drivers in his wake.

He got to Hill Farm Close in good time and sat outside the house to wait for the agent to arrive. He had chosen well from the ads he had viewed. The house was detached and stood in its own grounds with a seven-foot fence and plenty of tree cover.

The Monk's agent, middle-aged and grey before his time, turned up in a bright red Vauxhall Cavalier. The estate agent, Vasily quickly decided, was fussy and serious with little sense of humour. Vasily was not sure the agent approved of the motor home or Vasily's comparative youth. So Vasily put him at ease by walking over to him and offering his hand, "Vasily – how do you do?" Vasily saw the man do a double take at his name and he had to repeat it. Vasily had often wondered about his name as a child and why it was given to him until he was given to read the account of Vasily Grigoryevich Zaytsev a world war sniper and hero of the Soviet Union. It had been hinted when he was in his early teens that he was related by some family member.

"Jim Monk." The agent took the firm handshake from Vasily and visible relaxed.

"Shall we?" Vasily waved towards the gate, indicating that Monk should lead the way. It was cooler but damper in Norwich, Vasily had noticed, but not unpleasant and summer was round the corner.

Monk unlocked the gate and led the way to the house, pointing out the outbuildings and garage. The house was Georgian and the big casement windows in every downstairs room gave uninterrupted views of the garden. It was fully furnished, centrally heated with good services and utilities and comfortable. It didn't take Vasily long to decide it was acceptable. Vasily was careful not to touch anything and leave his prints for the authorities to find.

Vasily told Monk the house was exactly what the family wanted and he would take it. Monk was pleased and showed it. The house had been on their books for a few months and the owners were getting impatient. "Okay Vasily, but we do need to go to the office and clear the paperwork. You could leave the motor home here and I could drive you in and out, it is on my way home so it is no trouble. I am not sure you will find parking easy around our office.

"That's very good of you Jim, thank you. Shall we go? I really need to get back south before it gets too late."

As it was Vasily didn't get back to his motor home until half four in the afternoon but he had the house for a three-month let and it was extendable for a further year and a half. The owners were in the USA on an exchange posting and not expected back soon, if ever.

Just past Thetford, at the five ways junction, there was a garage and restaurant of sorts. Vasily pulled in and refuelled and decided to eat a late lunch. The stress of being someone you are not had drained him, talking to Jim Monk on and off for a couple of hours spilling out his story and never deviating from his legend, he decided was one of the most difficult things he had ever done and he needed calories to boost his sugar and wellbeing level.

He sat in the restaurant finishing his day breakfast and second mug of tea when he remembered he had promised himself this was decision time. He took out his local UK pay-as-you-go phone he had purchased and looked at it, still torn about his decision. He sighed and heart thumping phoned then the number he knew was Major Brown's section.

Graham answered it promptly. He didn't recognise the number, why should he. "Good afternoon can I help you?"

"Could I speak to Major Rodney Brown please?"

"Can I say who is calling?" Graham noted the intonation of the voice and was making notes. Graham wrote "foreign, possible Eastern Europe, not young, not old" he added and noted the number.

"It is a friend of a friend from the past, tell him please."

"One moment, I am transferring you." Graham said, patching the call to Rodney in his office, While Graham started a trace on the caller's phone and location.

"Rodney a call for you I think it is a stranger, but friend of a friend."

Rodney opened his notebook noting the time. "Hello, this is Major Brown."

Vasily almost cut the call, his hands were shaking but he steadied his voice and calmly spoke to Rodney. "Major, did you get my note I sent a few weeks ago?"

"Indeed Vasily I did."

Vasily was shocked.

Rodney went on before Vasily could think, "Do you want to meet?"

"Yes I think I do. Today please, must be today. Do you know the service station where the M1 crosses the M25?"

"Sure what time?"

"I could be there around, I would think, eight if that's OK?"

"Agreed, you can't miss me, late forties longish unruly hair and I have a slight limp. I will be standing outside the main entrance reading a newspaper."

"Fine, till eight." Vasily without thinking thumbed off the red button to cancel the call. Vasily looked at his hands realising he was still trembling; he put them on his thighs to stop the tremors and took deep breaths until he had quietened his nerves. They had told him during his training about the time he would make a contact and the toll it might set off nervous release and rush of adrenaline. He felt a sudden release of freedom. The giddy happy feeling didn't last and faded quickly. He knew it was not the end and he had more to do in the shadows. But strangely the feeling of release did not desert him completely; he reasoned it was the bounce of sharing his secret with Major Rodney Brown. He had done his research on Rodney and Brigadier Robinson, despite the fact that it had been drilled into him by Chekov that he could trust them above all others.

***

In the evening Vasily arrived with his motor home at the motorway service located on the M25 and M1 interchange, shortly before 7PM. He chose a place to park at the back of the site among the long term lorries and trailers parked there, as best he could but made sure he was on the front grid for an easy escape route but screened from the side by trucks and trailers. He took out and put on his black bomber jacket and baseball cap, with the peak pulled well down and made his way to the service shops and restaurants. He found the main entrance and as he entered took off his coat and cap. To his left were the food halls. What he wanted was a seat in one of them from where he could cover the main entrance. He ordered a meal – fish and chips and a coke – and found a table that would do, but not brilliant. He waited for a couple to finish off who were sat at another table at the window next to the entrance. As they left, he picked up his meal and moved into their place, piling their meals remains together and pushing them to one side to make room for his plate. He had just under an hour to watch and wait.

Rodney sat at the back corner of the restaurant head down and studied Vasily while he watched for any telltale of other watchers. Mr Reid would take no part in the exchange between the two men when it happened but was there to watch their backs. Reid had been on post outside and had pinged Vasily as he pulled into the services and had noted his parking slot.

Reid, having declared the outside area clear of any suspicious third parties, sauntered into the food hall at half past seven, newspaper under his arm. Reid spent time selecting his meal and took it to an empty table at the entrance to the restaurant which gave him a view of the food hall and both Rodney and Vasily. He pinged a smartly dressed man who showed interest looking towards Vasily from a table near Reid from time to time. "Perhaps he was looking at the entrance waiting for someone," he thought. At ten to eight Reid folded his newspaper and placed it on his tray with the remains of his meal. He left the service customer area and disappeared though the main entrance doors and into the night.

At five to eight Rodney stood and stretched, he could see Vasily was getting anxious by the way his head was constantly on the move looking for him. Casually exaggerating his limp slightly, Rodney threaded his way through the tables passing Vasily where his trailing foot gently tapped Vasily chair as he said, so quietly that Vasily needed a second or two to understand what Rodney had said. "Follow me, Vasily." Rodney limped on and out of the facility.

From the darkness of an area to the side of the facility Reid saw the contact made and Vasily wait for a minute before following Rodney. His focus was then transferred to the man he had pinged. The man moved from his table quickly to take up Vasily's empty table with its view of the entrance. It was obvious now to Reid he had been waiting for someone. Reid refocused his attention on his two charges. Rodney led the way back towards the parking. He let Vasily overtake him. Vasily strode towards his mobile home. Vasily unlocked the side door and went inside to draw the curtains between the cab and the salon and then the side curtains. He switched off the light and opened the door to beckon Rodney from the shadows.

"You travel in style I will give you that." Rodney broke the ice looking round at the luxury vehicles interior. "Impressive."

"It is a gift, funded by a mutual acquaintance of ours," Vasily said lightly, studying the standing man opposite him. Rodney, he thought, had the stance and make-up of his friend Servo, slightly older but in good shape for all that. "Please sit." Vasily waved Rodney to a chair, as he took the chair opposite so they could have face-to-face eye contact.

Rodney took two nondescript pay-as-you-go telephones from his pocket. "These phones are just what they seem, ordinary pay-as-you-go and each loaded with fifty pounds of calls. Your phone is now comprised. We have the number and can trace it. Let me have it so we destroy it."

"If this was a confidence building measure," thought Vasily, it was a pretty good start; he reached into his bomber jacket and fished out his phone. He watched Rodney break open the phone and take out and destroy the SIM cards. Rodney then broke the phone in half.

"If you have occasion to call me again use this number. It is my mobile," he handed a number to Vasily on a novelette. "I don't need to tell you, to memorise the number, and then to get rid of the novelette?" Vasily nodded.

"Vasily, I think I can imagine the courage you needed to call me and I want to make it easy for you to go back deep undercover to do whatever you have been asked to do. The last thing I want to do is disrupt an ongoing mission. We have quite a few bits of the jigsaw so I probably don't need too much from you. This one meeting may be all we need." Vasily looked relieved. "By the way, I traced you through your fingerprints on the note and a little research which ruffled feathers elicited your history and when you were planted into the KGB. It was cleverly done." Rodney shifted getting his damaged leg comfortable. It seemed in times of stress his old wound throbbed for some reason he had never been able to understand.

Vasily wanted to talk and Rodney let him without interruption. Vasily covered Afghanistan and how he was able to gain Tsygankov's confidence. The training week they all attended in Moscow and the team members and build-up and briefing in the dacha for the mission. Vasily went into detail about the mission and the event to date and where they were to the best of his knowledge. When he had finished he saw Rodney was smiling.

"Tsygankov, he once told me our destinies were to collide again and he had not finished with me. Well he has certainly cooked up a meal to create maximum havoc. I now have enough, Vasily, to do what I need to do; we do not need to meet again." Rodney rubbed his chin. "Are there any questions you want me to answer, I will if I can."

"I have only one question and a request." Vasily's dark eyes bore into Rodney's seeking the truth and at the same time searching for deception.

"Go ahead."

"When will you roll the mission up?"

"A very astute question and an important one from your point of view, as we need to ensure you are out of harm's way. Above all we want to remove the IRA cells supporting you; they are the most ruthless of the organisation killers and will not lose a moment of sleep over the innocents they murder alone with the legitimate targets. Legitimate targets as they see it, at least in their twisted minds. Now we know the target and date we can close the loop once we have the IRA men brigaded in one spot. It would seem the mounting base and base where they will prepare the explosives will be the Middle Wallop safe house just before the hit on the marquee company. So you need to be away latest last light, the night before."

"How will you know?"

"We will know."

"How will we know when you are coming for sure?"

"The day you have to clear out I will send a text with the code word Chekov."

"What if it is imperative to meet again? A change of plan for example."

"I hope not but send me a text just with the time and instead of 'HRS' after it 'CHS' if it is to be in a location other than here you will need to risk adding the location."

"Fine, I am okay with that."

"You had a request?" Rodney prompted.

"This is a big ask. First the safe house in Norwich remains between you and I, agreed?"

"I can agree to that."

"And last but not least, I want my team members to be allowed to escape." He saw Rodney stiffen. "Hear me out please. Servo is a soldier just like you, not a thug or terrorist. He was drafted into the nightmare and I know he is not happy about the mission, but as a soldier he has to do what he is told. It is not his sort of war. If you knew him you would like him. He is very much like you. He is fierce and fearless in battle, but honest and loyal and doesn't have a vindictive hair on his body. Servo and Carla are an item now and I don't see Servo going anywhere without her. Saied is an enigma; he too is a soldier at heart and has his own code of honour and he saved Servo's life in Afghanistan so they have a blood bond."

"What about General Tsygankov?"

"That, Major, is a difficult one. He is over seventy now and has handed over his post in the KGB, this is his swan song." Vasily frowned, thinking Rodney's question on Tsygankov through in his mind. "I had heard of the old spymaster before I met him and he was known to me as a killer: cold, amoral, task focussed, ruthless and a most dangerous individual. He is single, wedded to the KGB and the Soviet Union his only mistress. In Afghanistan and at the dacha we saw another side of him. He has a clever brilliant brain and whether you believe it or not a good sense of humour. In another life he would probably be a great family man. Whatever happens he is going to be marooned in his dacha for the rest of his life after this mission and will no longer be a player."

"I will think on that."

"And your thoughts on the team escaping your net when it falls?"

"It's a big ask. What we, that's you and I, need to do is ensure no suspicion falls on you.

"How the hell do we do that?"

"Here's how. You tell me that your last task apart from collecting your mates from the airport is to call up the Army Air Corps mess and pretend to be an officer from another unit trying to find a marquee company as your normal one is booked up on the date you wanted them. Make the call to the officers' mess tomorrow night between 1600 and 1700hrs and ask for a Major Collins. Collins will take your call and give you the telephone number and address of a marquee company in your area. Within a week it will be a proper company with manpower and kit, marquees, trucks, the lot."

"But how does that take us forward with getting the team out?"

"When you come to take the company over there, there will be too many people on site to simply do nothing about it. So you take the lead and demand Servo, Carla and Saied stay to guard the staff for the 48 hours or so until the intended hit. You take what you want with the IRA men and return to the safe house. It will be up to you to keep the IRA men together and not to question your people being left to handle the marquee company and to keep them happy as they finalise the explosives and marquee." He paused for a breath. "I will text you the code word, let's say exactly four hours before we plan to roll the operation up. It will be up to you to make some excuse that you have had a call from your boss and need to go and pick him up as he wants to be in on the kill. You need to call your people and tell them to get the hell out of it and up to the Norwich safe house and you will explain when you get there. What I will do for you is ensure you are not stopped at the Harwich Ferry Port but use the camper for your exit from this country and to travel on the ferry. What you do after that is up to you."

"What do I tell them was the reason for the panicked escape? They will want to know."

"Say whatever you feel comfortable with. How about you had a feeling the house was under observation and you saw a movement out in the field? By the time you are together we will have been in and, being the country we are, it will be on the news by the time you get to Norwich so your action will have been justified. How's that?"

"Sound simple enough. There are a number of what ifs but I will work on them until I can cover them as best I can."

"Good, are we done?"

"We are done, thank you Major."

"Call me Rodney, all my friends do," Rodney said disarmingly.

"So be it, good luck Rodney." Vasily gave a full smile for the first time since they had met.

"Good luck to you Vasily, in whatever you do. My country and I will forever be in your debt. If ever you need help, ask. My team has a long reach." Rodney waited for Vasily to switch off the lights and exited into the night and to link up with Reid.

In the car home, Reid confirmed that there was no tail and he had been able to record the meeting through the walls of the motor home. He thought the recoding may need to be cleaned up a bit because of the traffic noise of the cars and trucks but otherwise it should suffice.

"I quite liked him," Rodney said. "Reminded me of us in our younger days when we thought anything was possible."

"Vasily?"

"Yes, he is under a lot of stress, of course with this on top of his deep cover mission; it must be difficult as hell. Glad it's not me. So I cut him some slack."

"Want to expand on that statement?"

"It's on the tape," was all Rodney would say. "What we need to focus on is how on earth do I get a marquee company set up legitimately and manned and kitted within a week?"

Reid was straight in. "We get Andrew to set up a company, he has done it before and can get hold of the kit. He is good at procurement from sources I don't want to know. We get Avery and his two men to man it, plus by then say Andrew, Mould and Sharky with Carol in the office. We need Andrew as he will have the manifest and some ideas about how the marquee goes together. He can train the others."

"Should work, but I don't like pulling Andrew out of the finance team as their work is important too, if for the longer term. Still once he's done and the company is set up and the kit sorted Avery can move it forward until the kit arrives and can set up the business and train the men. After that we just need him on site before the enemy arrives to take over."

"Let's go with that then as the plan. You will no doubt need to spend some time with the Brigadier so let me get the show on the road. Okay?"

"As ever, Mr Reid, you are on the button."

"Cost you," Reid said.

"Oh yeah, how much would that be?" Rodney looked over at Reid who was driving, with a grin playing on his mouth.

"Let's say once this is over, gratis, ten days' leave for me to go back to Somalia and work with Simon on his private army. Followed by and to be counted as work, a week for me and the wife on the department to help out the FBI. The FBI did say we could back-charge them for my flight and time."

"What will the missus do while you are working during the day at FBI Headquarters?"

"Spend the money Simon will pay me, down town in the shops and malls."

Rodney simply smiled to himself, "It's a deal."

Charter 44

ROBINSON AND RODNEY

Next morning at Rodney's request, while the team was busy on all fronts, the Brigadier was in his office by eight-thirty waiting for his deputy to arrive. He looked at his watch and saw the hour and minute hand tick over to eight-thirty. He looked up as a knock came on his door.

Rodney arrived with a bag full of papers and a small portable tape recorder.

"Cutting it close Rodney," the Brigadier was being at his most ex-guards and with a raised eyebrow questioned the reason why.

Rodney read the mood and knew the Brigadier was going to leave it unsaid, "that a good soldier is always five minutes early on parade." Rodney resisted the urge to respond, instead smiled through gritted teeth. "Apologies. No excuses and in mitigation only, it's been a hell of a long night – in fact two."

"Don't worry, you are probably feeling your age, my dear chap. I forget you are no longer that young bright-eyed captain that used to leap tall buildings in a one mighty leap." The Brigadier was relentless in his teasing, but seeing Rodney's darkening face relented. "Would you like cup of tea perhaps, Rodney?"

"That, sir, would be very welcome. I seem to have missed out on a cup this morning, never mind breakfast."

The Brigadier called for his part-time PA, buzzing the outer office, "Pot of tea for two and could you send out for a plate of breakfast sandwiches, eggs and bacon with brown sauce please. As quickly as possible please, got a soldier here with desperately low sugar levels."

"Thank you, just the job." Rodney took the papers and laid them out on the Brigadier's desk in order and set up the recorder to one side. "The reason I asked for this early meeting is that we have a lot of balls in the air and I needed you to be up to speed, just in case."

"Take your time, Rodney, I have all morning free and more time if necessary."

"Don't think that will be necessary but I do want to take you through the game to date. First, I would like to just confirm back to myself and Mr Reid that you managed to get a close-quarter recce onto Q's place."

"Just so you don't feel too sorry for yourself, it took me into the small hours to get it agreed. Fortunately for us there was a team of four from B squadron twiddling their thumbs in Derry. They have been told to link up with Avery to get briefed and go in today. It was agreed they would use the same communication routes linked back to GCHQ and relayed to us here from today. Oh yes Rodney, I came in early and got an excellent briefing from Graham on everything he was party to."

"That's just what we wanted and thank you for getting it sorted. On the subject of the transcripts between Liam and Q, which we listened to together early yesterday, are we still of a like mind to let them develop their mission so we can roll up the all IRA cells in on this attack when they are together?"

"Yes and no, Rodney. As long as we can control the game it's a yes, but once we lose that edge it has to be no – the risk is simply too much for us to carry. We will have to hand it over, are we agreed on that?"

"With reservations, yes we are."

"It is going to be a fine balance this one. But I do want to see it through to the end, you have my assurance on that."

"Just for my peace of mind how many know outside our team what is going on?"

"Much as I hate to share intelligence, in complex situations such as this, we are under a remit to keep our sister intelligence services in the loop, but it is classified as 'need to know' in case resources are needed from them. So it has been limited by the Central Intelligence Committee to the heads and deputies of MI5 and 6, Military Intelligence. The Metropolitan Police Head of Counter Terrorism and his deputy in SO13. The Chairman of the Committee and I have briefed the Minister and the PM. That's really as tight as we can get it for a planned attack on the mainland."

"It's facile of me to ask you if we can trust them as it's a *fait accompli*."

"Fortune favours the brave, my dear Rodney. Did I ever tell you my favourite war story from the Second World War of a brave aircrew that overcame adversity?"

"I am not sure you did."

"Does the name Lt Bragg USAF ring a bell?"

"No don't think so."

"Well, a diversion while we wait for our breakfast." Robinson leaned back in his chair and closed his eyes. "The pilot of a B-17 414 SQN 97BG was Ken Bragg and his co-pilot Boyd with their navigator Nuessle and bomb aimer Burbridge and the five crew of radio op and three gunners were in mid-air collision with a German fighter over Tunis dock on the 1st of February 1943. One of the German fighters attacking a 97th bomb group formation went out of control, probably with a wounded pilot, and then continued its crashing descent into the rear of the fuselage of a fortress named 'All American', piloted by our hero Lt. Kendrick R. Bragg, of the 414th Bomb Squadron. When it struck, the fighter broke apart, but left some pieces in the B-17. The left horizontal stabilizer of the fortress and left elevator were completely torn away. The two right engines were out and one on the left had a serious oil pump leak. The vertical fin and the rudder had been damaged, the fuselage had been cut almost completely through, connected only at two small parts of the frame, and the radios, electrical and oxygen systems were damaged. There was also a hole in the top that was over 16 feet long and 4 feet wide at its widest." Robinson paused in wonder shaking his head. "Imagine if you will, the split in the fuselage went all the way to the top gunner's turret.

"The aircraft tail actually bounced and swayed in the wind and twisted when the plane turned and all the control cables were severed, excepting one single elevator cable that still worked, and the aircraft miraculously still flew!" Robinson again paused to gather the detail. "The tail gunner was trapped in the tail. There was no floor connecting the tail to the rest of the plane. The waist and tail gunners used parts of the German fighter and their own parachute harnesses in an attempt to keep the tail from ripping off and the two sides of the fuselage from splitting apart. Even if they were motivated which I am sure they were it was a feat in itself.

"While the crew was trying to keep the bomber from coming apart, the pilot continued on his bomb run and released his bombs over the target. That's dedication for you. When the bomb bay doors were opened, the wind turbulence was so great that it blew one of the waist gunners into the broken tail section. It took several minutes and four crew members to pass him ropes from parachutes and haul him back into the forward part of the plane. When they tried to do the same for the tail gunner, the tail began flapping so hard that it began to break off. Imagine this; the weight of the gunner was actually adding some stability to the tail section, so he had to stay in his position. The turn back toward England had to be very slow to keep the tail from twisting off. They actually covered almost 70 miles to make the turn home. The bomber was so badly damaged that it was losing altitude and speed and was soon alone in the sky." Robinson opened his eyes and leant forward on the desk, arms folded.

"For a brief time, two more ME-109 German fighters attacked the All American. Despite the extensive damage, all of the machine gunners were able to respond to these attacks and soon drove off the fighters. The two waist gunners stood up with their heads sticking out through the hole in the top of the fuselage to aim and fire their machine guns. The tail gunner had to shoot in short bursts because the recoil was actually causing the plane to turn.

"On the way home, Allied P-51 fighters intercepted the All American as it crossed over the Channel and took pictures of the stricken plane. They also radioed to the base describing that the appendage was waving like a fish tail and that the plane would not make it and to send out boats to rescue the crew when they bailed out. It didn't happen, the fighters stayed with the fortress, taking hand signals from Lt. Bragg and relaying them to the base. Lt. Bragg signalled that 5 parachutes and the spare had been used so 5 of the crew could not bail out. He had made the decision that if they could not bail out safely, then he would stay with the plane to land it. Two and a half hours after being hit, the aircraft made its final turn to line up with the runway while it was still over 40 miles away. It descended into an emergency landing and a normal roll-out on its landing gear. When the ambulance pulled alongside, it was waved off because not a single member of the crew had been injured. No-one could believe that the aircraft could still fly in such a condition. The fortress sat placidly until the crew all exited through the door in the fuselage and the tail gunner had climbed down a ladder, at which time the entire rear section of the aircraft collapsed. This old bird had done its job and Bragg brought the entire crew home uninjured. There has got to be, Rodney, many amazing stories of luck and fortitude from the war but I like that one."

"Certainly seems the crew had a lucky escape from near disaster, a great story, told well sir. I am wondering why you chose that tale to tell to me at this particular time."

"Thank you Rodney. Well I see a parallel in a sort of way with your current activities. It is a frantic time for you keeping all the balls in the air at the same time. Your team are all equally busy trying to keep the ship on the course set them. You can move some from their stations to help others but not some of them for fear of rocking the boat. And above all it will need all your courage and determination demonstrated repeatedly to complete this task we have been set. Parallels like that with the story can be drawn I think so at least especially as it's a master lesson in staying at the helm and controlling events." Robinson saw Rodney's spirits lift and he got a smile. "Job done. We all need a bit of encouragement from time to time from the boss," Robinson thought to himself before adding. "Think I hear the tinkle of tea cups and smell the aroma of bacon and eggs even through my door. Shall we let them in?"

Breakfast over and the plates and cups cleared away the men got down to work.

Rodney quickly ran over the situation as he saw it on what Graham would have told the boss about and spent some time clarifying questions raised by the mind in Robinson.

The next item on the agenda was the intelligence they had had in from Simon in Afghanistan. The important items were first the meeting Saied had had with the Libyan Colonel and with the IRA men at the training camp, all of which had been photographed and the definition had been good enough to get a match on the two IRA men. Rodney got up from his chair and shuffled the papers on Robinson's desk to show the picture of the men and the details that the intelligent services had on file.

"Two top men, one in electronics and the other a bomb maker. We must assume until we know different that these two will be part of the gang." Rodney explained. "We have an all-point out on them with the border forces but, as you know, these people are devious and who knows what sort of entry route they may use. We just need to hope we get lucky but I am not holding my breath." He turned up Saied's photograph. "A man back from the dead. He was reported assassinated in Lebanon and confirmed by Mossad so he is a remarkable man."

"Are we sure it is not a double?"

"Absolutely sure, confirmed by a third party and more on him later this morning. Now I have given you copies of the ship's manifest showing arms shipments going not only to the IRA but other customers for the last two years. That was as far as the file went back but the intelligence is substantial and we have shared it with the other sister services and Military Intelligence. MI6 were particularly pleased as it seems they can make capital out of it with their Foreign Office mates."

Robinson leafed through the manifest file, his eyebrows getting higher and higher. "Bloody good work, we should be able to translate this lot into a profit of some sort if not concessions and favours for a favour." Robinson looked at his deputy. "You know, Rodney, you and the team never cease to surprise me or, I might add, the central intelligence committee."

Rodney grinned. "Well here is another one."

"Go on beat that." Robinson held up the manifest sheets in his left hand and waved the photographs in his right. His long neck fully extended and a challenge on his face.

"I think I can." He watched Robinson put down his documents tidy his desk, sit back in his chair and waited for Rodney to keep his promise.

"I met with Vasily last night."

"Did you? By God, you had better tell all?" Robinson was alert and expectant.

"First sir, the tape of the meeting, and then we can discuss the ramifications." Rodney leant over and pressed the play button. "It has been cleaned up a bit and if you listen carefully you can hear everything that was said, word for word."

Robinson scribbled notes while he listened from which to put his questions to Rodney afterwards. When the tape finished he looked up. "Goodness me Rodney we have it all."

"That doesn't mean we have won yet. There is a long way to go and tons to sort out." Rodney pointed to neatly typed sheets explaining his plan.

Robinson scratched his forehead, a sign that he was still gathering his thoughts, "I can see that. What about this replica marquee company and its manning for starters?"

"I have side-shifted Andrew for a few days to use his specialist skills he acquired in the commercial world after he left the army. He will set up the company, procure the premises, the kit, trucks, office etc." It is all in the plan and report on your desk here." Rodney pulled out his plan and actually handed it to Robinson.

"Talking of Andrew, how is the finance team doing? Graham tells me they are cracking on and producing a lot of paper and the Banker is furiously scribbling and shouting orders."

"I confess I am not up to speed as of the moment, it is a job to do today to get me back on track."

"Hmm, perhaps I could help, the Banker and I go back a long way we were at the same prep school and stayed in touch as you do. If you are using Andrew perhaps I could lend a hand with the team when Andrew is otherwise engaged. What do you think?"

"I am sure they would be delighted to have you work alongside them." Rodney meant it.

"That's settled then." Robinson started to read Rodney's report and looked up. "Think better with a drink, but tea will have to do for now, do us a favour and sort a pot for us, this could take some time to unravel." Robinson got back down to studying Rodney's paper with a sigh and the shake of his head.

Chapter 45

THE RUSSIANS

As Rodney was sorting out a drink for them, Carla and Servo were packing up the boat. They spent a last night after Liam had left them on the lough. It was a half-moon but enough light to see by without the lights of civilization to interfere. The lough reflecting was still and black as coal even in the shallows. Servo and Carla fished for a last time as the light faded, and caught enough for a large supper. They sat on the stern seats and drank down the last of Servo's bottles of Guinness, drinking in the light of the moon and the shimmering water.

Carla finished her meal first and wanted to know if Servo had thought much about after the mission was over. Servo was silent for quite some time. "It's complicated. But yes I have, and so far nothing thrills me."

"Like me you mean."

"Yes like you. But it's the other things that are confusing me. I am, I suppose, to go back to the war and forget this ever happened. My question to myself is will I be allowed to?"

"What do you mean?"

"I am a Spetsnaz that's GRU. This is a KGB operation. Put simply, will the KGB let me go, will they let me live knowing what I do? Putting myself in their shoes it is a risk."

"You could eliminate the risk if you transferred to the KGB?"

Servo laughed a bitter laugh. "And do what? Push paper, become a KGB thug or minder to the powerful."

"Not necessarily any of those things. There are lots of amazing posts that would suit your talents."

"Not sure I want any of it at this moment in time. I need to think it through. What about yourself?"

"I never thought about doing anything else than what I am doing till now. I expect I will just go back to my section and carry on." Carla was staring out at the water. "Pity we can't stay here though."

"Think they would not be too pleased at that. What would we do when the General cuts off our funds?" Servo laughed.

"Fish of course for our supper." Carla hugged Servo. "Whatever, though we might still be an item when we get back."

"Tempting, and you and me an item is the only thing right now that makes any sense." Servo was flattered but needed reassurance. "Do you mean it?"

"Oh yes Servo I do. I very much do."

They stood and came close. "That's settled then." Servo wrapped his arms round Carla and pulled her close."

Carla smiled putting her hands to his chest and gently pulling away. "Later Servo, work first and then play. You clear away and I will call General Tsygankov."

The satellite phone was on charge in the berth. Carla collected it and went on deck and dialled the General. He took some time to answer it and when at last he did, Carla could hear others in the background. "General it's Carla, you obviously are in company would you like to call you later?"

"Give me two hours, I will call you back and then we can talk privately." Tsygankov rang off.

Carla put her head into the galley, "Servo the General's got company. So he is unavailable to talk to us for two hours. So work delayed we can either sit up here and wait in the dark, and it's getting chilly, for two hours or how do you feel about crashing in the bunk and warming each other up?"

"I thought I would fish." Servo had a grin on his face.

"No chance, come and take me to bed, right now!"

"Race you."

Later they lay still, comfortable in each other's company and were lulled in the bed by the boat's movements. When the phone rang it surprised them even though they were expecting it. Carla reached for it and took the call while pulling on a coat. "Carla."

"Yes Carla, you called me."

"Well they confirmed today they are going to support the mission. We are finished here now so we are going to make our way back to the mainland as everybody calls it here and get Vasily to pick us up and take us to the safe house."

"How have you left it with them?"

"They have two specialists coming back from Libya within the week. These men will find their way to us at the safe house and begin to set up and then disappear until the explosives arrive. The men needed for the task will be drafted in over the next few weeks to familiarise themselves with the ground and the task."

"Sounds appropriate. Now listen, Saied is making good progress along the Canal du Midi so I see you and Servo meeting up in Toulouse with them in around ten days' time. In which case Vasily will need to host the IRA men himself as they appear at the safe house. You will need to begin to plan and get yourselves onto the continent in plenty of time for the RV with Saied and engineer the secret compartment for the explosive on the motor home. I understand from Vasily it is a substantial vehicle. Anything else?"

"Our contact out here has been a man called Liam. He has left his commander's number and the commander, apparently known as Q, wants to talk to you. What he wants to talk about, we don't know. The number is…" Carla struggled to read the number and had to go into the cabin for more light to read it. "Got it, or do you want me to repeat it?"

"No that's fine. I will call him later."

"Are you at home or it sounded as though you were in company?"

"I am in Moscow and was having dinner with General Polyakov and we have more meetings tomorrow and then I hope to be travelling back."

"Then good luck, General, we will call when we are met up with Vasily."

"Goodnight Carla."

"How did it go?" Servo handed Carla a coffee.

"Fine but he sounded tired. He probably worries about us." Servo shook his head he wasn't sure Tsygankov worried about them as long as his mission was achieved.

***

The truth was Tsygankov was not worried about his team or the IRA but he was put out that the Chairman of the KGB wanted to see him and with Polyakov at the same time. These trips back and forth to Moscow achieved nothing, but wasted his time. The Chairman and he had known each other for years without any problems between them, although Tsygankov did not completely like the man or count him a friend. But on the other hand they were old soldiers and fought in the Second World War in sister units so they had that in common at least.

"But!" Tsygankov had confided to himself. "He is as tough as old boots with unbending beliefs in the power of the cannon and will never change." Tsygankov thought Gorbachev was right to worry about the Chairman Viktor Mikhailovich Chebrikov, but not as much as he should if he gets rid of Chebrikov and appoints Vladimir Alexandrovich Kryuchkov in his place and that was on the cards.

Tsygankov poured himself vodka and sipped it thoughtfully before activating his satellite phone. He changed the SIM card for another and dialled up the IRA leader.

Q for his part was startled when the secure phone that had been sent him rang. "Q," he answered as he got up from his chair and walked out of the house.

"Tsygankov speaking. Apologies for calling late but thought you would want to talk."

Q asked, "Are we secure?"

"Oh yes, these secure phones are as good as it gets."

"Very well. I want to discuss this operation and how we interface with your people. There needs to be a few ground rules, don't you agree?"

"Of course, what do you have in mind?"

Q was surprised at Tsygankov's excellent English almost without accent. "For a start I see us as the executors of the mission and yourselves in the background as the facilitators. How does that concept sit with you?"

Tsygankov noticed the Irishness of the emphasis on the word 'you', it was he thought a red line statement and it suited him. "I don't have any issue with that and would prefer my people were out of harm's way when the action starts. How does that proposition sit with you?"

"That's just grand so it is. I don't want my people tangled up with yours. It is just not going to happen and I am glad we agree."

"Very well, I will brief my people and if you tell yours the stage is set. Do you want to discuss anything else or are we done?"

"We are done."

"In that case I wish you well."

"*Oíche mhaith agus codladh sámh.*"

"Translate please."

"It means goodnight and sleep well."

"In that case, *Spokojnoj Nochi* – goodnight." Tsygankov heard a quick harsh chuckle of the Irishman as he hit the off button. Tsygankov put his phone into his briefcase and gazed round the room. It was small and cramped with its dark furniture and nicotine-stained flowered wallpaper. With a grimace he looked at the bed, far too small for him and he would as expected have to sleep with his legs half hanging out.

General Polyakov arrived early at Tsygankov's hotel and joined him for breakfast. Tsygankov was grateful for Polyakov's company, he enjoyed the General's humour and his unconventional view of the KGB and of the reforms the General championed to make it fit for the future.

They arrived at the KGB Chairman's office for ten o'clock and entered the reception area. Apart from the KGB Chairman's PA the reception area was empty. Tsygankov enquired of the Chairman's PA if she and the Chairman were in good health.

The PA, a woman in her late fifties beamed at him. "We are fine and it is so good to see you Brigadier General Tsygankov, it's been far too long." She cocked her head with a shy glance at Polyakov. "And you General, will find the Chairman's humour much improved since your last visit. He does listen and has some thought of reform of his own now. So never fear, you are appreciated." She gave him a beaming smile that lit up her face. "Take a seat I will get you coffee and for the meeting I have made a Russian multi-layered honey cake – his favourite and sure to sweeten him up a bit." She had a well-made body that carried its sinuousness into her fifties. She was smartly dressed in a two-piece Sherwood green tailored suit over a silk blouse. Her matching green high-heeled shoes made her hips sway as she went and opened the door to the Chairman's office. Her hourglass figure was emphasized by the bounce jacket she wore and the two generals looked at each other and smiled.

"I wonder if she would like a holiday in my dacha, she would add to my street credibility in no small measure," Tsygankov whispered to Polyakov.

Polyakov feigned astonishment. "My God Carl, am I hearing you correctly? I always thought of you as a confirmed bachelor," he whispered back.

"Truth be told, I am mellowing in my old age and can see the advantages of being paired off. Especially I think on a cold winter night."

Polyakov slapped the Brigadier's thigh. "Now that, Carl, cannot be disputed." Tsygankov lips turned up in a smile.

The PA came back for them and waved them into the Chairman's office. He had been there a long time and the room was cluttered with his life's memorabilia collected over the years along with two massive bookcases overflowing with books and files. In striking and complete contrast his desk and square abutting conference table with its six chairs, three either side was clear.

The Chairman stood at the edge of his desk and came forward to meet the two men.

"My old comrade Tsygankov, good to see you are still with us. And my dear Polyakov. Please be seated." The Chairman retuned unsteadily to his desk chair, his myopic limited vision evident to both men. Polyakov was suspicious of his welcome, had the Chairman forgotten that the last time they met he was virtually thrown out of the office?

They sat in silence as the PA brought in the coffee in a silver pot and the refreshments including the cake. She fussed with the Chairman's drink and slice of cake, serving it in front of him on the desk, not to risk the Chairman making a mess of pouring his coffee in front of his guests.

"Pour yourself some coffee and help yourself to the cake," were her parting words, as she left the men to their meeting.

The Chairman was in an affable mood, a rare occasion for him at least. "You will be wondering why I have called you in, especially you my Polyakov after I balled you out last time you were here." Polyakov nodded. "Well it's because I have three matters that need to be aired so I hope you think your journey was worth it." He took his coffee and sipped it before putting it carefully on the desk top. He squinted towards Tsygankov, his thick-lenses glasses flashing in the process. "Now Tsygankov, I have read the file on your mission in the UK. Normally my preference and speciality as you will know is to spread disinformation to confuse our enemies, this direct action of yours is bold and risky. Tell me I am wrong."

"Mr Chairman, the risk has been mitigated in the context of tracing this planned action back to us. We are facilitating albeit in country but the act itself will be carried out by the IRA. Our people will be gone before the action takes place."

"Very well, in that case you have my blessing which is not lightly given. Make sure we are in the clear whatever happens on the ground. Tell me Tsygankov, are you retired or not or between the two states of being?" his lips smiled but the eyes held Tsygankov.

"I am between."

"Good, good, we old soldiers never really retire do we? My second point is: in my observation of the British, who by the way I admire greatly as a nation who are it seems over the years to be as we, defenders of their borders against all comers, it struck me comparing our economy with theirs that they seem to be enjoying far too good a time. I would like you to come up with a plan to do just that. Think you could think of something, Tsygankov, from that dacha of yours if you had a free hand and the support of General Polyakov?"

"Interesting propositions my Chairman, and a great challenge to which I will do my best."

"Make it your very best!"

"Of course sir."

"Let me see, this operation of yours should be wrapped up by the end of June. Come and see me with Polyakov on the first of October with your first thoughts and a draft proposal. Feel free to consider anything, no matter how outlandish at this early stage. Can we agree on that?"

"Agreed." Tsygankov inclined his head to Polyakov.

"Of course. We will supply whatever economic and infrastructure intelligence is required."

"So be it. Now to my third reason for calling you in today. Last time General Polyakov came to see me about reorganisation I sent him away with a stinging rebuke." The Chairman looked from one man to the other and paused. "I was wrong." He pushed himself away from the desk and opened one of the desk drawers, withdrew a file and slid it noiselessly across the desk onto the conference table. "After you left I had a rethink, and on reflection had to come to the conclusion that we need to do something, or they, our masters, will force changes on us." He took off his glasses and polished them on his tie. "My life's work has been to argue for our existence and to strengthen it in order to protect Russia and her borders. Now in doing that, as General Polyakov's file pointed out, we have become hide-bound by our bureaucracy, there is duplication and in general a moribund organisation. That takes nothing away from the hard work we do and achievements of our staff. But I want us to be lighter on our feet, quicker to react, not just on the front line where the man on the spot has to take a decision but all the way through the organisation. Streamlined is what I want, that's the word, and accountability at every level. Decisions must be owned, and taken at the lowest level, and monitored. This will be a massive change and of course a consequential training liability thrown in." The Chairman looked at Polyakov. "What can you do for me in this regard, General?"

"I would be happy to lead on this for you; there will be resistance which is to be expected. I think the first step should be for you to call heads of the Directorates together for briefing. The next step I see will be a task team set up with representatives from each of the Directorates so no-one feels they are being side-lined."

"Good that mirrors my thoughts."

Tsygankov interrupted. "Was there one matter that bought this to a head?"

The Chairman looked away from Polyakov to Tsygankov. "Not an individual occurrence, more a set of circumstances and a few reflections. Polyakov's paper, the change agents in the Duma, Mikhail Sergeyevich Gorbachev is a reformer and wants us to change. I also thought about my time as a commanding officer in the last war and the way individual tank commanders worked by themselves and then worked with others as was needed. It is time to change. I am not sure I am the man to see the changes through, as I feel my tenure is almost up and my eyesight and health uncertain," he added truthfully. "And I have tested Gorbachev's temper at times on funding. I may not see the reorganisation complete but I want to be the man remembered for starting the process at least."

It was a startling revelation from the Chairman and both the men facing him were unsettled, the whole concept of change was so out of character with him, clearly he was under enormous pressure and financial constraints to even consider the possibility, no matter how he had now convinced himself it was the right thing to do.

The Chairman sighed. "General Polyakov, I want you to champion this review and I agree to the meeting with the heads of the Directorates. Set it up for tomorrow please, an hour before lunchtime. No excuses from anyone. I will try to get Gorbachev to attend. Make it a social occasion. My address followed by a meal served in your Directorate large conference room."

"Of course it will be my pleasure to host."

"Very well let's get to it. But first let us spend a few minutes together to talk of these matters, the immediate strategy and you can tell me about your dacha, Tsygankov, and let's enjoy the coffee and the cake together." The Chairman beamed at them and saw them visibly relax.

Chapter 46

MAINTAINING THE ZERO

Major Rodney Brown lolled in the chair at the small conference table in the middle of the operations room, staring through the blast-proof curtains and bank of large casement windows. The air-conditioning fed into the room was on full blast and ruffled his unruly mop of fair hair. He luxuriated in the cool of the over large operations room as his office was hot and stuffy today.

His mind wandered, to his left, 40 feet away, he glanced at the finance team and the animated exchanges between Andrew and the Banker while the others looked on. They had made great progress and identified half a dozen money laundering pipelines which had been handed over to the FBI to close down with their massive resources. A myriad of business run by the IRA in the Republic of Ireland and the North which were being investigated by the Irish and the Fraud Squad. "And," he thought, "they were still going, finding new targets. Andrew had set up and sorted a marquee company premises and the vehicles and kit was on its way." He looked at the ops deck 20 feet to his right at Graham working with the Royal Signals Captain Freire Howell-Speed and the green phone which was the current link for anyone calling the marquee company. It had rung once when Vasily had tested its function. He switched back to the windows and his revelry really needed his team back from Ireland now to get the marquee company manned and functioning. It was his hope that they would identify and roll up the IRA teams before the marquee was drawn and used but he doubted it.

He felt like a sniper who was 'maintaining the zero' outwardly showing the patience of a saint waiting for that one-shot kill. He would hold this outward appearance of calmness until the operation was over, no matter what was thrown at him. He thought of the great snipers of the past and their special gifts of concealment and deception. He must be like them as the mission rolled into its critical phases as possible drawing on the strengths of those men. And women for some inexplicable reason, perhaps it was the Russian connection; he thought of Senior Sergeant Roza Shanina, Soviet Red Army he remembered Shanina was one of the more well-known female snipers in history. He remembered it was written she had joined the Soviet Army after her brother was killed in 1941. As a marksman she amassed 59 confirmed, by the age of twenty, kills in her very short career. She rose to command the 1st Sniper Platoon of the 184th Rifle Division. She had by then been awarded the Orders of Glory and Medal of Courage. She was killed all too soon while shielding a commanding officer during an artillery attack.

Rodney tried to bring to mind male snipers. There was the famous duel in Stalingrad between the Russian and the German but he suddenly brought to mind Herbert Hesketh-Prichard, a big game hunter and adventurer who revolutionised the British sniper effort in WW1. Herbert had been turned down for a commission in the Black Watch and Guards, because of his age, 37. So undaunted he obtained a post as Assistant Press Officer at the War Office, and first sent to the front lines in France in February 1915 as an 'eyewitness officer'. By 1915, open warfare on the front had ceased, and had stagnated into the trench warfare that characterised much of the conflict. He witnessed there the victims of gas attack and the unnecessary losses to well-trained German snipers. Rodney remembered the German snipers could not be located, leaving them free to continue shooting from their place of concealment.

Herbert had been, Rodney remembered, dismayed by the poor quality of marksmanship amongst the British troops. Herbert had set about improving the quality of marksmanship, calibrating and correcting the few telescopic sights that the army possessed. He borrowed more sights and hunting rifles from friends and hunters back home, and funded the acquisition of others from his own pocket. He investigated the quality of German armour plate, he retrieved a sample from a German trench. He discovered that their armour could only be penetrated by a heavy cartridge, such as Jeffery 333, while British plate could be easily defeated by a Mauser, a much smaller gun.

Rodney, when he had read about Herbert, had marvelled at the man's deductive and observation powers. Herbert had recognised German skill in constructing trench parapets: by making use of an irregular top and face to the parapet, and constructing it from material of varying composition, the presence of a sniper or an observer poking his head up became much less conspicuous. The British in contrast trench practice had been to give a military-straight neat edge to the parapet top, making any movement or protrusion immediately obvious.

So it meant an observer was vulnerable to an enemy sniper firing a bullet through his loophole, but Hesketh-Prichard devised a metal-armoured double loophole that would protect him. The front loophole was fixed, but the rear was housed in a metal shutter sliding in grooves. Only when the two loopholes were lined up – a one in twenty chance – could an enemy shoot between them.

He used dummy heads to tempt the enemy sniper and periscopes. To increase the realism, a lit cigarette could be inserted into the dummy's mouth and be smoked by a soldier via a rubber tube. If the head was shot, it was dropped rapidly, simulating a casualty. The sniper's bullet would have made a hole in the front and back of the dummy's head. Clever, thought Rodney, and as Churchill was fond of quoting about the, "The genius of the British for deception and guile."

Rodney smiled to himself as he imagined how the head was then raised in the groove again, but lower than before by the vertical distance between the glasses of a trench periscope. If the lower glass of a periscope was placed before the front bullet hole, its upper glass would be at exactly the same height as the bullet had been. By looking through the rear hole in the head, through the front hole and up through the periscope, the soldier would be looking exactly along the line the bullet had taken, and so would be looking directly at the sniper, revealing his position.

"So bloody clever of Herbert to work that one out." Rodney remembered, and how Herbert had set up the first training school in the village of Linghem, Pas-de-Calais for snipers, starting with small groups he taught them everything that was known of the craft and broke the former German superiority in the sniper practices. "He well deserved his military medal for conspicuous gallantry and devotion to duty, especially as he continued the training of his snipers into the trenches and the dangers and his promotion to Major before his illness took him home in 1917," he thought. Rodney marvelled that he done so much in the two years for the British army saving many thousands of British and allied lives.

Rodney wondered where his two unruly sniper reprobates Mould and Sharky were and what they were doing, until he realised they along with Mr Reid were on their way to the marquee company real-estate.

He stirred himself still with his, "Holding the Zero" focus and the pictures of Major Herbert Hesketh-Pritchard crowding his mind, as he imagined him along with his snipers mentoring and cajoling them in the trenches and in no man's land. Herbert's achievements motivating him, he picked up his long-cold cup of tea and bounced over to the operations desk feeling rested and invigorated.

"Freire and Graham, it is time to get to work!"

"I thought that was what we were doing?" retorted Freire slightly affronted.

Graham rolled his eyes.

"Well you are, but I want my work done now." Rodney had a half smile on his face but his eyes narrowed. "Stroppy."

"Well sir why didn't you say so I thought you meant we were skiving."

"Heavens no, with slave driver Graham that could never be."

Graham sat straight in his chair and looked attentive.

"First thing, Freire, please call up the marquee company site and see if the boys are there yet and if there when, the situation."

He turned to Graham, "Can you bring me up to speed on where we are re. Ireland, the Russians, and our people?"

"Well the latest from Avery is that he saw the two Russians Carla Kazimira and Vladimir Servo leave from Dublin for Heathrow about four hours ago and he was getting his men and himself over to the UK. With luck they should be back in a couple of hours." Graham scrutinised his log sheets. "The watchers picked up the Russians at Heathrow and they were met by another Russian we now know is known as Vasily Vladimirov. The watchers report Vladimirov had a motor-home parked at an offsite location and they are following. They will get back to us later with an update."

Freire interrupted, "Sir, the team is now on site and the kits arriving and they will need help to sort it out."

"Good, message please Graham to Avery ask him to get himself and the Fred and Lewis Jones to sort out themselves out, pack for a few weeks and get down to the marquee company location for first thing in the morning."

"Freire, wander down the room and ask Andrew to join us for a moment please."

"And how would you like some tea and biscuits too, to follow, Major Rodney?" Freire teased.

Rodney looked up about to tick off the Captain until he saw her face. "Very good, you almost had me going. And yes please."

Andrew joined Rodney and Graham and looked grey and tired. "Bloody hell mate, you look knackered." Rodney was shocked.

"Price of working my bollocks off, but satisfaction oh yes. We have just cracked a major Channel Island bank fraud worth several million. And it's something we don't have to hand to the FBI to sort, we can do it easily ourselves. What a coup, the IRA are now leaking funds all over the place. We have hurt them already in the pocket, of that I have no doubt. They are going to be scrabbling for pennies and new sources of funds before long."

"Well done. You are going home to get some sleep and in the morning you report to the marquee company location to help the team sort out the kit and practise putting up the tent."

"But we are hard into the finance map and they need all hands on deck."

"No buts my friend, Brigadier Robinson no less is going to take your place and you need a good night's sleep and some fresh air. If you don't believe me go and take a look in the mirror."

"But..." Andrew began.

"No buts, just get it done. Sign off from the team and if you are not out of here in ten minutes I am personally going to throw you out."

"Oh all right." Andrew grinned, accepting the situation and secretly relieved. He sloped.

"My God, does the rest of the team look like that?" Rodney thought shocked. He had left them to their specialist task busy with other matters and not noticed their slow descent into fatigue. He got up from the operations desk and walked over to the finance team. He studied them carefully and was pleased to see Pat and Jane were fine. Only the Banker looked a little stressed. Andrew waved goodbye.

"Hi boss," said Jane, noticing him for the first time standing there silently watching them. "What's up?"

"Lots, but I just saw Andrew who looked all-in so I thought I should make sure the rest of you were holding up."

"We're fine. Andrew decided to spend the night and worked through analysing some new data. I told him he was mad but you know him once he has his teeth in something he will not let it go." Carol replied and Pat nodded his head in agreement.

Turning and addressing the Banker directly, Rodney asked, "And you sir, how are you doing?"

"Just fine Rodney. It has been and continues to be an Aladdin's cave of discovery. I will give it you and Robinson, you have more than met my expectation. I spoke to the Brigadier yesterday when we gave him some more files for him to pass on to the FBI to chase and gather, he is going to sit in."

"That's the plan. I need to borrow Andrew for a day or two but I will get him back to you as soon as possible."

"That's fine, we have plenty to get on with to close out this phase. We will be putting together the plan for the next phase to lift the IRA treasurer and get a look at his books. Say in a few days from now."

"Hmm I would like with the Brigadier to be present once the plan is formalised. Not to interfere but to make sure you and the team are resourced and protected."

"That's fine but we hope there will be no rough stuff and we will get what we want by deception, we will see."

Rodney wandered back to the operations desk.

His tea awaited him and a plate of digestive biscuits arranged carefully on in a fan shape. He thanked Freire but the truth was he was suddenly hungry. His eyes looked over the operations board and the way it was organised. It reminded him of his service days. Signals in and signals outs, spent log sheet all backed with bulldog clipboard backings. The maps were marked up with enemy and friendly forces. Trays marked in and out and pending and for various eyes only were clearly marked and stacked. On the ops board were the telephone lists and contact details of the key players. Clip files also marked up, clearly held the mission plans and details of received intelligence from named sources. He grunted. "You have done a good job here Graham."

"Can't claim all the credit, Freire since she and her operator have joined us have made shall we say a few adjustments. And I am the first to admit I have learnt a lot from them."

"Well that's good. I have been thinking how is the flow of intelligence and communications working now Freire is here and not at GCHQ, is it still working as well?"

"Truth is it's better. Not to tell stories but the GCHQ team found you two men a distraction." She laughed and so did Rodney.

"No change there then." He fluttered the log sheets. "What's the news on the close recce team."

Graham took the log sheets gently from Rodney and tidied them. "Well they are in place and will be going in tonight to start the recce of Q's estate. By tomorrow they have promised to have 'eyes on' via mini cameras and sound from both inside and outside the house."

"Great news. Anything come in overnight that I missed?"

"You signed off the night log sheets so there is some interesting stuff you have not seen yet and a transcription of a conversation between Q and another. It is an important call and I could kick myself for not getting you to listen to it when you came in."

Rodney smiled the omission away it was as much his fault as anyone's for not going through the routine of catching up and signing off the log and said so, and then, "Let's hear it then."

Freire pulled out the tape from the stack and inserted it into the play-back machine and waited for Rodney to put on the headphones before she set the tape off. He listened to the one sided conversation between the IRA Quartermaster and Brigadier General Tsygankov.

Rodney listened to the tape, stony faced. When it had finished he rewound it twice more, and a smile played on his lips. "Graham, please ensure Brigadier Robinson hears it next time he is in. By the way, what did the analysts make of it?"

Freire found the report in the file. "In conclusion they say that the IRA want the Russians out of the way when the mission goes down and that accords with what they believe the Russians want too." She looked at Rodney and Graham expectantly.

"Then they and I agree with that assessment. Good it makes things so much better for us." He didn't explain, and Graham and Freire didn't press him.

"So Freire, how are you getting on here – is it what you expected?"

"More and it is an eye-opener. I am impressed."

"And how is Graham looking after you?"

"Great, he is an amazing cook, did you know that?"

"Well there was a rumour but no more than that."

"Believe me; we could not have been better looked after. And what a lovely house."

"Hmm, good, pleased. Thank you Graham."

"My pleasure, I am thinking of having everyone over for a meal when this is over. Do you think it would be a good thing to do?"

"I do, very much so and I will insist you allow me to contribute to the food and drink bill." Rodney put his hands on the shoulders of Graham and Freire. "I am delighted with the work you are doing to keep this part of the ship running so smoothly, without your efforts the mission would soon descend into a morass of chaos. Well done." With that, he returned to his small conference table to write up his notes and plans for the future. He wrote a title on the top of the page to remind him of the importance of focus and the need to maintain overall observation of the mission, it read, "Holding the zero." Pleased with himself he decided taking his eye of the ball was simply not going to happen from now on.

Before he left, Rodney got Graham to find the latest report from Bernard Gérard the French Intelligence Officer and head of the Direction de la Surveillance du Territories. Rodney scanned the latest report, which indicated that Saied and his boat with its load on the Canal du Midi were about four to five days from Toulouse. He just hoped Bernard never found out that Saied was carrying enough explosive to do serious damage to the canal and any surrounding environment. Bernard was, as far as he was concerned, keeping an eye on a person of interest for the SIS.

Chapter 47

GAME

Rodney's mood was sanguine as he threw his briefcase onto the sofa along with his jacket and tie. The Malayan chicken curry and rice he had put into his slow cooker before he left that morning was ready and filled the flat with that special coconut peanut butter aroma of the distinctive Malay curry.

It would wait; first he needed a shower and to change into something more comfortable than his business suit. Picking up his jacket he went into the bedroom, undressed and hung his suit. Minutes later he stood under the power shower and let the jet massage his body. Still-muscled as he soaped his frame, he as ever gingerly soaped the puckered skin of the leg bullet wounds he had taken in Borneo where he had been left for dead by the traitor Lawson.

He stood under the shower trying to dispel his jumbled thoughts that still persisted. They were like a tune that takes hold, consisting of the snipers he had known and respected in his time; the almost mythical and revered Hesketh-Prichard and the young Russian woman Senior Sergeant Roza Shanina, killed at such a young age saving another.

He called the operations centre to ask for an update of the Russians' location. The watchers had followed them to the safe house and were standing off but believed they were there for the night at least. Satisfied, Rodney began to relax.

It was not until he had devoured his first helping of curry and was well into his second glass of Merlot did his mind turn to the Russians. He wondered what they were doing and if in another life they would have been comrades not enemies. He thought about his meeting with

Vasily and his plea for the members of his team. Certainly he would like to talk to Saied about Tsygankov and meet Servo, a brother in arms. The thought made him smile.

***

For their part Vasily, Servo and Carla had arrived at the Wallop safe house a couple of hours ago. Vasily had first given Servo and Carla weapons and ammunition before he had shown them round the land and facilities before Carla and Servo went to unpack and Vasily prepared the evening meal. Vasily was looking forward to having some company after his enforced time alone. He was not sure if it was the thought of safety in numbers or it meant another phase of the mission was over. He set the table and poured the wine. He had prepared a simple meal, stir-frying vegetables and chicken breasts with plenty of spices and garlic. A rice dish made up the meal.

Vasily heard Servo descending the stairs followed by Carla. Servo was the first into the kitchen. "So Vasily, I can see that you have not been idle, the food smells great. How about a beer if there is one?"

"In the fridge to your right, help yourself, no Guinness – regrets – but try the John Smith, it is a great beer. The food is ready so I am going to serve up." He carried in the rice and followed with the stir-fry.

They sat round the table, drinks poured, Carla proposed the toast. Clinking glasses they dug into the food bowls.

"Tell me of your adventures in Ireland," Vasily began.

"We had a most interesting time and it was for the most part enjoyable. The IRA liaison man Liam I did not warm to but he probably thought we were a little strange in our own way. We will give you the whole story from start to finish, but tell us where we are with everything here and Saied?" Servo wanted to get the latest news so they could plan forward.

Vasily started with the core items he felt important from his past experience. The core items were the safe house's weapons and the vehicles at their disposal. He had prepared the maps and atlas and showed them the locations and the target area to the front of the officers' mess. He explained where the marquee company was and that the marquee was to be erected the week before the ball.

Carla sat back sipping her wine and held up her hand to interrupt Vasily. "I see two imperatives coming out of what you are telling us and one mega issue."

Vasily and Servo looked at her. Vasily asked Carla to tell them what were the issues that concerned her. "As I see it we have little over three weeks, if that, before we have to get hold of the marquee. Then we have to hold the marquee company men captive for possibly a week! Some will have families and they will want to know where their men are if they don't come home. The IRA will need time to prepare the explosives and get their men into place. We need to get over to France and back and soonest. Where is Saied now?"

Vasily nodded. "I can see where you are coming from now and you're right we need to motor."

Servo contributed. "Let's give Saied a call right now, we need to know when and where we can meet him and transfer the contraband. Once we have that knowledge we can slot the rest in and then work through the other issues."

Vasily hit the encryption icon and then the speed dial and Saied picked up after a few rings. Vasily put the phone on speaker and placed it in the middle of the table. "Good evening Carl, I have you on speaker phone and am here with Carla and Servo. So how are you?"

"I would be fair to say whilst I am enjoying this trip it will be good to get on dry land." They all laughed. "But it has been a great experience and some of the views of the vineyards in Languedoc and the bridges etc. are outstanding. One point I would like to see at my leisure some time was when we came over the highest point of the canal, 90 metres above sea level by the way, Seuil de Naurouze, it's absolutely amazing. But I can tell you all this when we meet as I am sure this is not a social call?"

"Regrettably this is not a social call as you say. The fact is, Saied, time is not with us, we have lost a week. So we need to know when we can meet and where so we can plan."

"We are making good progress, but wait out a moment just going to consult. Stay on the line." Saied was away for a couple of minutes. "Okay, this is the situation. We are three maybe four days out of Toulouse. Four nights from now we will be at this location just to the North of Toulouse and to orientate you, it is about 3 kilometres northeast of the airport. Do you have a pen and paper?" Saied waited until they confirmed they had the means to take a message. "We leave the Canal du Midi at Toulouse Centre and enter the Canal Latéeral à la Garonne going north. We will meet you four nights from now, excluding tonight, at this grid 43667144 1410615. Repeat that grid back please?"

Carla read the number back and asked what was at that location.

"The location is the second lock out of Toulouse on the road D64 leading to an area of Toulouse called Lacoutensourt. This lock has on the west side of it a hard-standing area where you can park and we can cross load. Note at the western side just before the entrance to the lock is a berthing shoulder that will enable us to tie up for the night and there we will be waiting for you."

Carla replied for them all. "That's just fine Carl. We will stay in touch but until we meet, stay safe."

Servo took the lead. "Let's work it back. The target night is 23 days away so I made it 16 days before we have to turn up with the marquee at the target, maybe 17 at push. Let's work on 16. In 5 days from now Carla and I need to be at the RV. Give us two days to get back that leaves 9 days for the IRA to work the explosives. It leaves 9 days to recce the marquee company and put a plan together to capture the staff, take it over and steal the kit and trucks etc."

"My understanding from Tsygankov when I spoke to him this morning was that the IRA executes the plan, our task is to facilitate and be away before the night of the attack," Carla stated looking at the men.

Vasily wanted to confirm his understanding on a point and raised the question about the marquee company. "Does that mean do you think that the IRA is to hold the staff hostage as well as prepare and set explosives and erect the marquee?"

"See your point." Servo was annoyed with himself that he had not had more time to discuss the situation in more detail with the IRA. On the other hand it was only now that they had all the pieces of the jigsaw. "I think I should speak to Liam and discus the timetable and what he wants to do."

Carla fished out her phone and scrolled to Liam's telephone number. She hit the number and laid the phone on the table with the speaker enabled. "Vasily, think you should remain silent okay?" Vasily nodded.

Liam answered, "Hello?"

"Liam, its Servo and I have Carla with me so we can both listen in."

"Go ahead."

Servo gave Liam the timetable and the issues and waited for Liam to process the information. A GCHQ device phone was flagged and the recording of the conversation started. The analyst on duty began to transcribe and concurrently routed the call to the recording devices in the operations room in London. The lights flashed on the recording device and Captain Freire's operator went to alert Pat who was on sleeping night duty in the next room. The operator had little trouble getting Pat up and went to make a brew for them both.

Liam, after some thought, came back to Servo. "Tell you what I am going to do, I will be with you tomorrow morning and we can sort this together. You are at the address you gave me?" Servo confirmed that was the situation and Liam asked, "Do you have a room for me and one other to use?"

"Sure, no problem."

"Good, is there anything you want me to bring over?"

"Don't think so unless you can carry some draught Guinness," Servo answered.

"I really don't think so, sunshine. Until tomorrow then, boy." Liam was curt and harsh and he cut the call.

Vasily commented, "Don't think he likes you all that much."

Servo smiled. "He is a professional at the end of the day and so am I, so it will work out. We can't choose our relatives or our workmates, but we can choose our friends." He raised his glass to the other two.

"That's very philosophical of you Servo, so terribly Russian, my Miska." Carla reached out her hand and grasped Servo's arm. Servo coloured and Vasily hid his smile.

Servo recovered. "I would not mind having a drive past the marquee place tomorrow some time, we could take Liam too. What do you think?"

"Don't see why not," Vasily answered to Servo brightly. He crossed his finger in the hope that Major Brown would have the place up and running by then.

"Where is this place anyway? Is it near to here?"

"It's not too far on the back road between Basingstoke and Reading at a small industrial complex in the country. There is not much there apart from the company and a couple of small units, so I was informed when I called them."

"Sounds good, if it is slightly remote that will help us I think." Carla was thoughtful. "I had better get us booked on the ferry to France. Vasily, I will need the vehicle registration etc. Do you have the vehicles keys?"

"Yes and as it is still light, why don't we fill our glasses and take our drinks to the vehicle. I will show you both over the motor-home. It really is pretty impressive as you will realise what's on offer and we need to decide where you are going to stash the entire explosive load."

***

In the operations room, Pat and the operator listened to the conversation between Liam and Servo. Pat wrote a few notes, got the duty driver stood up and got him to drive over to Rodney's before he called Rodney.

"Pat, what can I do for you. Just washing up my dishes it is hell living the high bachelor life."

"You realise with Carol, Graham and yourself you're the only ones who don't have to wash up for two. I will swear my other half uses every utensil we own to cook an egg. Anyway, I am sorry to call you but we have had a conversation between our two parties over the water and here at home and think we need to discuss it." Pat waited. "I have sent the car for you and it should be there in two."

"Groan. Well done Pat see you soon." Rodney put the phone down and finished the washing-up, collected his keys and briefcase. He looked around the flat. "Bollocks, could have done with a night in," he said. But he knew Pat would not have called him if it was not important. Outside the flats the car purred and a sleepy driver had the window down. When he saw Rodney he struggled out of the car and went to open the door for the boss.

"Thanks Fred, had a busy night?"

"Naw, you're the first call, boss." Fred, close to retirement, was white-haired and fat, his jowls nestling in two rolls of fat that squeezed out of an over-tight collar. His black driver's suit was worn and shiny, his shirt yellowing and Rodney thought Fred was a mess but understood and sympathised with the man's attitude who was so near to his retirement after a lifetime of dull employment.

"Can't be long now before you retire can it?"

"Three weeks and I can't wait to fit this suit on the scarecrow at the allotment. They said I could keep it."

Rodney laughed. "Don't see it fitting anyone else."

Fred chuckled. "Right there you are, boss." His east London accent strong tinged with Welsh.

"What will you do when you finish?"

"Do? I will do as little as possible. I have my pigeons and the allotment and the club and a wife who loves me so I am set for pleasant retirement. You know the first thing I am going to do is learn to sleep through the night and not get up before nine. That will be heaven. No more tube, no more fighting the London traffic, no more hot, sweaty London for me. Hurray."

They were both laughing as Fred pulled down into the underground garage and tipped Rodney out. "Call down when you want to go home," Fred called, wandering over to the duty driver's room at the back of the garage.

"Hi Pat, what's the gossip?" Rodney asked as he entered the operations room.

"Listen to this. Want a cuppa?" Pat switched on the play-back machine.

"Yes, coffee I think. White, one sugar please."

Pat nodded to the operator who went to make the brew and then sat beside Rodney.

"Well, well, we have the timetable now and another player to trace whoever the other man coming over with Liam is."

"I made a few notes and some what ifs. For example, what if, they want to do an early recce of the marquee company location."

"Should be okay, the team is on site."

"What if they do a recce in silent hours? An established company would have some paperwork and invoices and signage, a PC etc, teacups, posters, pictures of the tents up etc., etc."

"Deception and disinformation," Rodney thought out loud.

"What did you say?" Pat asked, not sure he had heard Rodney correctly.

"It is the little things. It is always the minutia that is missed and gives away the game, always. Pat, thank goodness you were on the ball. How the hell do we get that sorted in no time?"

"Thought about that. I can get the signage done overnight and down to the site before nine; don't ask, it will just happen along with some magnetic banners for the vehicles. Design the Managing Director's business cards and print a few dozen, got some blank sheets around in the stationery stores. Same with invoices and with the help of the operator create some past ones and a few letters from clients etc. Plus we will design a full colour brochure and posters taking examples from other like companies. It will be a push but we can get them printed downstairs when the printer and design team comes in and should pack up the office stuff for them and to site by midday."

"Who's the MD, what name will you use?"

"Reid."

"He will like that." Rodney looked at Pat's notes. "Could you put Andrew in the picture? He is leaving in time to get on site for nine. Don't think we need to wake him up, he looked wrecked this afternoon."

"No problem."

"Are you sure there is nothing I can do to help?"

"Think it would be best coming from you if you alerted the duty officer for the watcher teams."

"I will do that now, it may be with more people arriving at the safe house he may want to put another team in the area." Rodney also made a mental note to speak to the Brigadier in the morning. It was close to the time when the anti-terrorist branch SO13 and the regiment needed to be briefed so they could make and lay their plans to counter the enemy mission.

At the time Andrew was arriving at the marquee company to rendezvous with Mr Reid, Rodney was entering the Brigadier's office and found him feeding the pigeons.

"Are you sure that's wise sir, they make a hell of a mess out on the pavement below?"

"Not really but that's the point don't you see, I do enjoy seeing the occasional senior civil servant arrive with a dollop of the unmentionable on their immaculate shoulder."

"You are looking a bit immaculate yourself this morning, a meeting perhaps?" The Brigadier was dressed in a dark navy lightweight pin-stripe suit and highly polished shoes with his guard's tie carefully knotted.

"Well yes you're right. Two of the five wise men have asked to see me with their ministers."

"That's would be the permanent undersecretaries for Home and Foreign Office I take it?"

"Exactly but I am a little phased if not surprised that the PUS from the Ministry of Defence is not attending. The other two have little relevance to this meeting. Anyway, you have something for me?" The Brigadier shooed the pigeons off his ledge and closed the windows.

Rodney relayed the intelligence gained from the conversation believed to be from Tsygankov to the Quartermaster and from the calls later last night and latest developments and analysis and why he felt the need as he felt it, to bring in the Regiment and SO13 for briefing.

Robinson listened in silence to the younger man's analysis and requests. "It would seem things are moving to a head and we need to stay ahead of them." He packed some files into his briefcase. "You are right of course Rodney in your thinking, and the need to bring in extra resources at this time. I nevertheless want you to hold off until after my meeting, which should be over well before lunch; meet me in the operations room at midday."

"Thank you sir."

Robinson turned back as he strode towards the door. Rodney, should we not have a name for this operation by now?"

"The team thought OP Dove-Cot or OP Maze might be appropriate as there seem to be so many different pigeon holes to fill."

"Ho, ho, very droll Rodney, OP Dove-Cot is fine thank you."

At the marquee company Andrew was meeting with Mr Reid. Sharky and Mould with Avery and the two Welshmen were in the yard sorting out the marquees.

Reid sat at one of the two desks and Andrew the other who was putting the last plug into the computer connecting it to the printer/fax. "There done, you are set up with the usual packages and a simple account based on XL that Pat cobbled together. You need one of the team to play with it and create some past history. He looked round at the filling cabinets and the near empty bookshelf apart from a dozen box files all empty, behind Mr Reid's desk.

"Done well here Andrew, this place is ideal, this big wide front office and staff room, showers and toilets behind accessed through this room; now let's get back to Pat's concern."

"He is right you know if they come visiting they will be looking at more than your trucks and tents. If they come at night you need enough paperwork to convince them this is a legitimate business."

"Pat's sending down basic stuff as I understand it and the signage is here and up, and the vehicles have their decals. How he got that done overnight is a mystery."

"Not really, one of his many brothers has a sign-writer's business and I think Pat leaned on him."

"Well what I propose is we get Avery and you, when the printed material and the rest arrives, to spend the rest of today turning this office into a believable business." Mr Reid looked at Andrew who shrugged his shoulder and nodded.

"How is your finance team doing?"

"Forging ahead and hurting them greatly in the pocket." Andrew rubbed his hands together to emphasize the point.

"Good. Let's hope we can take a few of them out too."

"What concerns me, Mr R, is obvious risk to the team here. If you and the team are held as hostages for say a week, that's a long time and you know as well as I that that is more than enough time for something to kick off especially with the lot out there."

"Yeah I have been thinking about that a lot. I have a few ideas which I need to pass over to the Major. Rodney is planning to come down late afternoon so we can chew my ideas over with his, as knowing him he will worry about the situation and will have some thoughts."

"Want to bounce them off me now?"

"Why not? Come and get some fresh air and we can talk about them. I have to say Andrew you look as though you could do with some sun."

"Too right, I have been closeted for two weeks now and it's been the most difficult task I have handled for a long time. The Banker and Pat bless them revel in the stuff, for me and Carol it's been full speed ahead accumulating and interpreting data. Then we have to find where the data fits into the jigsaw. Initially it was a black vertical wall of jumbled figures, now patterns are beginning to emerge and repeat themselves. Even though I had to run my own companies and have a better understanding of finance off and on shore than most; the complexity of their finances astounds me. I can't wait to meet the IRA accountant; he must have some brain on him and one I reluctantly have come to admire."

"Still your work is paying dividends. Now my thoughts, they are based on divide and conquer."

"What if they simply go for the nuclear option?" Andrew let that phrase hang in the air. "Simply shoot you all, after all they are going for a big one and a few more dead men are not going to worry them overmuch." Andrew looked at Reid with concern. "Or even transport you to some other location where they can control you better."

"That's not going to happen."

"How can you be so sure?"

"Look around, what do you see?"

"A Dutch barn for your vehicles and three containers for the stores and tents tools etc. The security fence line and of course the office building is all there is."

"What about the office building?"

"Pitched roof. Rear windows where the facilities are have security shutters. The office is open but with roller shutters. Why?"

"Hear the plan, but first the options open to them."

***

While Reid explained his options and plans to Andrew, Liam the Quartermaster's enforcer called ahead that he would be arriving between ten and eleven and would turn up at the Wallop safe house with two men not one.

Servo had been waiting in the woods keeping an eye on the gate. When he saw a battered black Toyota four-by-four truck pull up, he emerged from the foliage and opened the gate to let Liam in and waved them forward toward the house.

Trotting behind the Toyota, Servo wondered again about the mission. The more time he spent trying to convince himself it was a legitimate mission the more he felt it irrational and the feeling persisted. The only winners he could see might be the IRA teams involved.

The vehicle pulled in front of the house and Liam O'Neil and the two men dismounted in time to greet Servo.

"Joe, Ian – can I introduce you to Servo."

Servo shook each of the men's hands scanning their faces, reading the eyes. He saw no flicker away from his gaze as they returned the scrutiny. "They would be confident men in their own world." Servo thought. There was strength in their handshakes and Servo was surprised by the men's deep tans. "These must be the two Saied had met in Libya." Of the two men Servo picked out the leader of the two, he thought probably Joe, who seemed open without guile while he thought the other, Ian was the quiet one, possibly unpredictable and the one to watch out for.

Servo led Liam into the house while the other two grabbed the bags and followed them in. Vasily and Carla waited in the kitchen for the party to assemble and for introductions to be made.

"Quite a reunion," Liam said. "We'll get ourselves and our kit stowed away and then let's eat and drink and talk the mission through. How's that?"

"Sounds a good plan, give me your vehicle keys I will move the Toyota round to the garage. Vasily seems to be our cook and Carla will show you to your rooms." Servo held out his right hand for the keys and his sleeve rose enough to show the point of the spring-fired Spatnez Special Forces knife. It did not go unnoticed by the IRA man.

"Do you have any arms here?" asked Ian.

"Enough for now, I will show you our small armoury later."

"Good enough."

"Come on grab your things, I will take you up. We managed to rearrange the rooms so you are all in the same one." Carla led the IRA men out. Dressed in jeans and a fleece covering her blouse, the IRA men were nevertheless appreciating her as she led them upstairs.

The meal when they had reassembled in the kitchen was eaten mostly in silence. Except for Liam whose caustic remarks did not endear him to the others. "They say your boss is a freak of nature is that true?"

"Not at all, admittedly he is different – exceptionally tall. You would have to go a long way to find anyone taller," Carla replied.

"Is that right? Will he join us?"

"It is not planned. These days he lives in the shadows," Vasily responded, with a vague hint of warning in his voice.

"Pity, I would like to have met a man like that," Liam said offhand.

"Think yourself lucky you are not. You probably wouldn't enjoy the experience." Servo laughed and poured another drink for Liam to shut him up. "He is not called the Spymaster for nothing. They say he can look into your soul and smile while pulling out the heart out of your chest with his hands."

Vasily shivered.

"Someone just walked over your grave?" asked Joe grinning, looking at Vasily.

"Not sure I understand?" Vasily looked puzzled.

"It's a saying." Carla looked at Joe. "Am I right you say that to someone who shivers for no reason?"

"Quite right Carla. I have to say all of your English is excellent. Did you know we met Saied a few weeks ago, I thought him very professional. Will he be here?"

"Servo and I will bring him back with the product he is minding. We should all be together in five days."

Joe finished his meal. "Ian and I will clear up and if you would be good enough then to bring us up-to-date we can begin to plan." He brigaded the plates and Ian collected the glasses and bottles. "Vasily could you come with us and show us the kitchen." He called out to the room. "A large pot of coffee for all is it?"

It was late in the afternoon when they broke up from the planning meeting for a breath of fresh air and a look round. The IRA men were particularly interested in the large garage that had been suggested for the technical bomb preparation work.

As Liam expected, it transpired that he had the hardest task. He needed to get a team to control the staff at the marquee company while still giving the outside world the feeling of normality. He needed a couple of flying teams to erect the marquee and set the explosives. He had to decide when to let the Russians go. Joe and Ian for their part needed to collect the items they needed to construct the bombs and the accompanying electronic control and initiation devices where they were stashed north of London. "If their Russians were not going to be back once they left tomorrow for four to five days, it would give the IRA time to get their men and equipment sourced and set," Liam thought as he followed the other outside.

Joe looked round the garage. "This will do just fine for making up the parcels."

"Parcels?" Servo asked.

"Yes Servo. What we want to do is create parcels of explosive to go into the floor panels of the marquee. With a detonator and mini radio receiver embedded in the explosive."

"Where will the transmitter be?" Carla asked.

"Ian and I have not decided yet. The transmitter will either be mobile phone to receiver of a base station located here or perhaps both." Joe looked round for Liam. "Liam, Ian and I need to go and get our kit tomorrow. But we also need on the way to have a good look at the target site"

"Take the Toyota. I for one would like to have a look at this marquee company site. Do you mind driving me over tomorrow Vasily?"

"I can do that no problem, when would you like to go?"

"I want to see it in daylight and have another look at it at night. Could we go late afternoon? We can have a meal locally and wait for dark. I want to have a close look at the ground and buildings"

"That is not a problem for me."

"Good."

Servo and Carla excused themselves they still had some more preparation to do on the motor-home and packing for their trip which they intended to start first thing tomorrow.

***

At the marquee company Major Rodney Brown was arriving at the small complex along with Commander Robert Coveney of SO13 the anti-terrorist branch and bomb squad. Rodney's initial impression of the yard was it was big enough to erect the marquee unobstructed. The office he scanned Dutch barn and containers. What really interested him more was the surrounding area. Apart from a few other dispersed units in their own fenced compounds and others under construction, the units were isolated through a long pull-off from the road and the site was forest-bound on three sides. As far as he could see the forest on three sides of the site was at least a quarter of a mile thick.

Rodney shut the door to his car and walked over to the team with the commander who had been working around the canvas and pile of marquee poles. "Heh guys, what's it like working as a rigger?"

They looked up and laughed. "Better than working," Mr Reid called out walking over to Rodney.

Andrew joined Rodney asked what the situation was.

"We have sorted the office and created a history that should fool anyone providing they don't chase references," Andrew informed him.

"The team has put up the marquee; another practice tomorrow and they could get a job in the industry."

"Well done guys. Have we seen anybody nosing around yet?"

"We have been keeping an eye out and seen nothing out of the ordinary."

"Good location. Pretty isolated but the wood could be useful to both sides so we had better dominate it," the commander commented and got a sidelong look off of Mr Reid who smiled.

"Got some ideas on that and when they take us as hostages," Reid said.

"Let's hope that's what they do; what if they decide to silence you, they may see that as a better option? Collateral and hurting the innocent is not something they baulk at," Rodney warned.

"I have a plan that may help," Reid put in. "Want to come in the office and have a tea while I take you through it."

"Sure." Rodney turned to Andrew. "Done a good job Andrew, not sure we could have pulled this off so far without your help. But now the finance team want you back. They have the word that the IRA accountant is on the move and will be flying into his Guernsey residence tomorrow so it has been decided to lift him as he comes through customs." Rodney looked down at his feet. "Unfortunately or fortunately depending on your perspective, it has been decided that your work output is to be shared with the Fraud Squad. It is their job to carry on the investigation once we are pulled out. The team knows and now I am telling you. On the plus side, the Brigadier has made sure that your team leads on the Accountant's interrogation tomorrow, although there will be a senior office witness from the serious Fraud Squad and SO13." He paused and tapped his head. "There was something else. Oh, the Fraud Squad officer has a warrant, so will allow you to enter his residence and search it. Right off you go

Andrew, the Banker wants to see you tonight. I gather there had been a major breakthrough, don't ask me what, but the Brigadier is pretty pleased with himself."

Rodney and the commander watched Andrew collect his things and wave him off, while Mr Reid busied himself getting those cups of tea and some biscuits.

"What you got for us?" Rodney opened his log book ready to take notes.

"Before I start where are we with resource permissions?"

"Good question. I asked the Brigadier for SO13 and Regiment this morning and he has got the OK. I thought it important re. the legal side to get it sorted and now we have the permissions we can get any of the cover we need and I suspect you want." Rodney had a smile on his face as he could almost guess what Mr Reid was going to say.

"Excellent. I have considered as many courses of action the enemy may take and what we can do to defend ourselves and counteract. The main problems I see are where are they going to get riggers to do the job professionally. Our experience today is that you need to practise. Handling the heavy kit is a knack as well as knowing where everything goes. So if I was them I would take some of our men and keep the rest hostage for our good behaviour. Regardless, they could keep us as hostages either in the back room or one of the containers."

"What if they have the skill?"

"They will still be going to need to know our kit and how it goes together. No I think there will be dialogue. Plus they will need someone to man the office and take calls about where the men are when they don't arrive home as expected, if it were a normal company, so I think that's something they will want me or someone to manage. They will after all need someone here who knows the families of the men and can explain for example we have a job up north and will be away for a week. I thought that would give you an opportunity to phone here, and we could agree a few key words linking to action, all is well, help, or things are kicking off standby." The commander nodded. "What I want are a couple of armed men in the roof space with eyes on with hidden cameras and microphones. And some good shots camouflaged and dug in, in the woods, with eyes on us. 24/7. Thought we might secrete some arms in the containers and in the roof space in the rest room next door, so if they put us in any of the location we can defend ourselves as and when. What do you think?" Mr Reid wanted Rodney's view.

"Not disagreeing with anything you said but let's go back a step. We agree that if they want to take some of the team to help put up the marquee we going to allow that to happen. We agree that our aim is to roll up all the IRA men involved in this caper. One thing you should know is that we are going to let the Russians run for cover. It's complicated but essentially with Gorbachev's open policy toward the West. The Soviet Union is in a poor state and in the early days of Gorbachev's reform programme striving for democratization of the Communist Party. This is being promoted by himself personally as Party Secretary Mikhail Gorbachev's and his policies of *perestroika* and *glasnost*. The last thing the West needs now is four dead or captured Russians upsetting the cart sent on a fool's mission by an ageing spymaster. Not saying the spymaster is not alone in this mission but God help him and his confederates if Gorbachev finds out." Rodney could see Mr Reid was sceptical so he added, "It is thought keeping the spymaster in play may be to our advantage in the long run. That's all above our pay grade," Rodney sipped his tea. "The boss thinks the IRA may give the Russians the job of guarding the hostages. It makes a sort of sense. As it has been agreed that the operation at the target is the IRA remit and the Russians are not to be around at the target or seen in any way to be part of it on the day."

"I can follow you just."

"Good, now time and space." Rodney made sure he had the attention of both men. "I have been thinking about when we should strike." He flicked through his notebook. "There are three IRA positions to strike at. The safe house located in Wallop and the rear garden of the officers' mess where the marquee will be being erected and this location."

"Could simplify by hitting this place when they arrive to pick up the kit and the safe house?" the commander contributed.

"I thought about that but we don't know if all the explosives will be at either location. And I may add all the IRA members. I rationalised that the explosives may be on a vehicle even another truck with the explosives pre-prepared in the floorboards for the marquee, I don't see them trying to fix the explosives as they erect the marquee. It risky either way if something goes wrong."

"I can see that and agree with you. Let's go for the three location option." The SO13 commander got out his pocket book and began to take notes.

"Timing then," Rodney said. "D Day, the trigger is when the marquee and all its kit arrives at the mess. We have to make sure that the floor is there too. Our long-term friend Major James Collins who is going to be the officer on the ground posing as the mess committee representative to make sure all is well. So James, when he is satisfied he has seen all the kit in place and the IRA team working, will call it in. Commander, we need the three sites hit at the same time. Can it be done?"

"I will take overall responsibility for the raids. But I am going to get the Regiment to take out the safe house. Even so I will have one of the bomb squad teams with them and a squad of my officers to search and seal of the area. As Mr Reid has indicated, we will salt this location and add to my people here on the day to support and as before same detail to seal off the area after the event." He sat back thinking. "The marquee site is a difficult one. I see the regiment taking out the IRA men on site. But supported by my teams to search and seal off the site. I will make sure I put my bomb squad commander and two teams there and one from the Army EOD regiment." He laughed. "You would be surprised of how jealously my bomb squad guard their patch from the Army EOD even though most of them are ex-services and EOD to that."

Mr Reid had his hands on his knees, head down. "My concern all along is the bomb trigger, it takes a second to press it or dial up the number to the initiator and that trigger could be anywhere."

There was silence for a long minute.

"Noted," said Rodney. "In an effort to try to track the trigger amongst other matters, the Regiment is preparing to do a close quarter recce of the safe house within the next 24 hours and an SAS team is going to dig into the field opposite the house main entrance and they are doing that tonight."

The commander, seeing the two men had finished, put in, "I am going to set up three forensic teams for the three locations and they will be under the command of the SO13 Senior Officer at each of the sites. The other thing I am going to do with my opposite numbers the day before D Day is ensure the emergency services respond. I will have my deputy begin the planning of this when I get back to base, what we don't want is the roads kept clear for fire and ambulance services should they be required. I hope they will not be needed. Like yourselves, we have to plan for the worst and hope for the best."

Rodney finished writing in his log and closed it. "Commander, thank you." Turning to Mr Reid, Rodney asked, "Is there anything you want to add, take away, or generally comment on?"

"Apart from my concern about the trigger, I will feel happier when we are armed-up and the commander's men are in place. Apart from that we need the game to play out. I would like a lady secretary to give the place an air of normality."

"Hmm, leave that one with me for a day. I am reluctant to draw off Carol from the finance team as they are about to tackle their target and our lady captain on secondment to us is worth her weight in gold in the operations room."

"In the interregnum, boss, I thought I would ask Mrs Reid to step in?"

"Not sure a civilian on an active site is a good idea," Rodney replied, knowing he would get a retort from Mr Reid.

"Agree with you on that boss, one hundred percent, but don't anyone ever suggest to Mrs Reid to her face she is a civilian. Notwithstanding how about this, she mans the desk until you get me a replacement."

"All right, if you feel it's the thing to do. And it does keep the pressure on for me to get you someone."

"Tell you what," the commander chipped in, "I will get you one of my ladies from SO13 to you, day after tomorrow for the duration. I will make sure she doesn't look or sound, like a police officer and is able to chip in." He looked at his watch. "It is a bit late now but I will have two ex-regiment men to you by midday tomorrow to live in your roof and kit out the place for what, 8 to 9 days at most. And you will not see them. If you do, I have failed; two sharp shooter teams dug in to your front left and right by midday. They will be there for the duration. All communication and pictures will be relayed back to my centre and Rodney's operations room." He turned to Rodney. "Once the close target recce goes in tonight at the safe house would you relay voice and pictures to me?" Rodney nodded and opened his book and noted the commander's request.

"My arms?" Mr Reid persisted.

"We will take Mr Avery back with us and he can draw whatever you want tonight and bring it down in the morning. I take it you only want small arms stuff?"

"Of course boss, just in case they find a catch they need to seem innocent enough for a gun club fanatic to have in his possession, perhaps." The commander and Rodney chuckled.

"Gentlemen, and please call me Bob, drop the commander stuff, if there is nothing else we should be getting back." He took Mr Reid's hand and shook it warmly. "Great to meet another professional like you. When this is over if you want a change of career come and see me."

Rodney said quietly, "Sorry Bob, he is spoken for."

The commander shrugged. "As they say never say never." He smiled and made his way to Rodney's car.

Chapter 48

RENDEZVOUS

Carlo and Servo got an early afternoon car ferry from Portsmouth to Caen and arrived at nine-thirty local time. They laagered overnight at a camp site off the A28 to the north of Le Mans.

In the morning they continued their journey to Toulouse coasting down the E5 to Tours and on to Poitiers on the E62 leaving the city for Limoges on the A20/E9 which took them south past Brive-la-Gaillarde to Montauban where they quickly joined the E72 into Toulouse.

They had looked up a couple of small hotels almost on top of the canal lock but decided on a hotel within 500 metres of the lock, the Hotel de Etats-Unis in the road of the same name. It was good choice as it turned out with plenty of parking for their motor-home and more anonymous than a smaller hotel and the food was good, Servo ate the house confit du canard at every main meal time they were there.

With a night and a day to wait, the first night they took a walk to the lock gates. The approach down the narrow road Impasse da la Glacière was bounded on each side by a mixture of a row of old houses all adjoining with various small businesses in the row. The area was typically Napoleon, red-brick, poor and run-down. As they came to the canal, the area opened up. The towpath on the left looking south had a well-kept double-storey house overlooking the lock. Walking over the bridge and looking down in the lock they could see the hardstanding area on the right of it. A white painted slip pole barred their way onto the hardstanding but it was not locked and there was space for pedestrian access. They slipped past the pole onto the hardstanding and walked its length to the southern lock gate and the area behind it that Saied indicated he would tie up to.

Servo noticed the hardstanding where Saied had indicated they would transfer the product continued as a towpath past a few moored barges and to the right of what appeared to be an off-loading area. Together they followed the short path, some 20 metres, to the off-loading area which turned out to be a large, close to 200 metres square, concreted area and it was not only empty but derelict. They cautiously tramped the northern edge of the square, bounded by overhanging trees and found a road leading off it that linked back to the Impasse de la Glacièere. They would use the square as a standby if the slip pole at the entrance to the lock was in some way compromised.

Arm-in-arm they made their way back, stopping at a French bar for a drink and some tapas on offer. The locals kept to themselves and they found themselves talking about the amazing welcoming Irish and the British Vasily had met on his travels. They rationalised it was the language that could be the problem. They both knew the French preferred to speak French and let strangers struggle. Servo didn't mind, he was happy to talk to Carla. "Do you know that when they asked, I think it was Napoleon, what his religion was he said, French!" Carla laughed and Servo grinned.

"You know, Servo, you continually amaze me with your knowledge. That is for a Russian." Carla teased him.

"Are you not Russian?" Servo asked in mock seriousness.

"Maybe?, I mean I used to be Russian but now I think I have more in common with the Irish or the Brits." Carla looked down at her drink and a tear rolled down one cheek. "Servo, I don't want to go back." Carla brushed the tear away and smiled at Servo. "Crazy huh, as if we had a choice?"

Servo looked at the woman he now realised he loved, he was torn – how could he desert a Spatnez officer with all his training behind him targeted on defending Russia. But he said, "There is always a choice Carla. You can simply step off the merry-go-round and defect."

Carla was silent. Servo said gently, "We Russians are a complicated people because of our history stretching back to the Mongols the Tartars, 1200 something, until Ivan III kicked them out two hundred years later and all the other people who have had a go at us, all the way up to Napoleon. Now, I wonder when we could we expanded all the way into Siberia thousands of miles away from Moscow and the Crimea, the Caspian Sea and into the Asian lands to our south and not forgetting Persia. Alexander wanted riches of India wrenched off the British and Constantinople to be the centre of the civilised world. All this has left us with an irrational fear of being surrounded and attacked. It is not going to happen; who would want to take on our debts and the teaming millions of every creed and colour. With all that baggage and paranoia don't think Russia is at risk. If you truly want to stay here in the West I will help you if I can."

Carla put her hand on his arm. "Thank you Servo. Forgive the tears it's just a mild depressive regret mood I am in at this moment and that's very Russian don't you think?" Carla brightened. "But if I do decide to stay and I am not saying I will, will you come back for me when you have done your duty?"

Servo looked at Carla she knew him so well. "On my honour I will come back."

Carla leant over and kissed him. "Good. Now new subject to discuss, where are you going to keep the product when we get it? I have racked my brains but I still don't know where you will stash it?"

"Well there should be 250 kilograms and that's a lot to hide so I thought we wouldn't. We'll hide it a little. The seats in the saloon have detachable cushions on the seat. Once free of Toulouse we will stop at a rest area and ditch most of the stuffing of the cushion and refill the cushions with the product and put some of the stuffing back on top so if you sit on them they will feel relatively as they should."

"Clever."

"What I am not so happy about is Saied. He will stand out like a sore thumb if he travels with us in the van. I don't know how good their computer program is, but if they know two people left for France in this motor-home and it flags three on the return it might seem suspicious."

"Hmm, perhaps we drop him off at the port and he travels as a foot passenger and we pick him up on the other side."

"That would work."

"Settled then." Servo grinned. "Come on let's celebrate, liven up these French people." There were half a dozen men and women in the bar, obviously locals. Servo told the barman to buy everyone a drink, whatever they wanted, and a bottle of champagne for himself. The French toasted the couple and went back to their conversations. Servo and Carla shrugged shoulders and laughed and toasted old Tom from the marina in Ireland.

Servo and Carla checked out of the hotel next morning and spent the day in Aras looking at the bishop's palace and his cathedral Saint Vaast, the museum of the son of Count Alphonse de Toulouse-Lautrec-Monfa – Henri. They had a late lunch in the Palestinian restaurant opposite the museum up a side street which was interesting after eating the comparatively bland French food for a few days. They just had time to visit the miniature museum of rooms before they had to travel back to the meeting point. They were armed with leaflets from the hotel and Aras as well as books on Henri for window dressing, so that if they were stopped they could appear at least as ordinary tourists collecting the dross that tourists do, when they get home they would never see the light of day again.

It was still light when they got to the target area so they parked under the trees on the north side of the square, positioned so they could see any approaching river traffic. As the evening drew on them, another car with two men parked on the square. The occupants were looking at the canal.

An hour later the boat carrying Saied came into view. Servo watched the added interest of the men in the other car. They all watched Saied's boat moor up for the night. Servo could see the men make a call and then drive off. He was relieved but his six senses told him the men were following the boat. If they had worst case gone for food they would be back. They needed to do the transfer quickly and get out of the area.

Servo moved the motor-home to the edge of the square so there was only the short 20-metre path separating them from Saied. "Carla, stay here; if anything goes down drive off." He was out of the vehicle and running to the boat. Saied and the captain were on deck and saw Servo coming.

Servo didn't give them time to call out, he was in the boat dragging them inside. "There was a car and when it saw you it drove off. We need to do the transfer and get off. You captain will need to backtrack to the last lock you came through, with luck if they come back that will delay them long enough for us to get away." Servo shook hands with them. "Sorry about this but gut feeling means we have to move."

In silence the three men worked furiously and in ten minutes had the product on board to the rear of the motor-home and covered loosely with a bed cover. Saied grabbed his bag and thanked the captain, but not before agreeing to meet again after the mission was over for a reunion."

Five minutes later Servo had the motor-home on the motorway heading for the north.

"Carla, food and drink for us please; we are not going to stop apart from refuelling and sorting the product until we hit Caen again," Servo looked over his shoulder at Saied. "We are better than a hotel with all facilities on board. Hope I wasn't panicking but better safe than sorry."

"Great to see you again both of you, and no Servo don't think you were wrong as I saw the same car, not sure if it was the same as yours, from time to time on our trip up. The trip by the way was amazing. I will tell you all about it as we travel, but first let me help Carla get the food, I am now an accomplished cook, not that I wasn't before, but having cooked for the captain and myself during the trip my skills are honed, I even cooked for the odd lockkeeper. Most of them appear to be ex-wounded or partially disabled French servicemen."

Servo was working the satnav. "Got a rest area, Cahors north, that will be our stop to eat and sort the product, but until then a snack would be welcome and a coffee. Please."

"Two minutes," said Carla and Saied together and laughed.

Around an hour and a half later they pulled into the rest area. At eleven o'clock the rest area was lightly populated, only the lorry parking area was busy with truck drivers. Servo found an isolated area to the rear of the car park and work of sorting the Semtex bars began. Carla stripped the detachable cushion covers in preparation. Saied made a study of the cushion padding. It was in two parts. Two thirds of the padding was dense hard-sprung sorbo type, the padding where the top third was softer. Saied carefully separated both fillers. Discarding the hard filling he began to pack into the cushion base the 5 kilogram packets of Semtex. He managed to load 12 packs into one cushion and replace the top third layer of softer filler. He zipped the cushion up and bent it into shape. It looked exactly like it had before the stuffing had been removed. Saied replaced the cushion on the seat.

"Good job Jean," commented the watching Servo.

"I need three more cushions; that gets rid of 48 or the fifty 5 kilogram packs. I will split the last two up. I am sure I can get them in the cushions without distorting the shape. It is better I do this as only one of us will have, if any Semtex residue on our hands. Odourless it may be, but a swab would still test positive and be a problem. So leave it to me."

"On the subject of detection and security, do you want the good news or the bad?" Carla asked Saied.

Saied looked up at Carla and Servo, pausing in his task.

"The good news is we will give you a lift to the ship and pick you up on the other side. The not so good news is you have to go on board as a foot passenger. It will reduce the risk, as two people left the port with two on board and will return with two. It is probably overkill but there is just a chance the exit and entry custom authorities may ask questions where we picked up a third passenger. Sorry, but we feel it will be safer for all and the product."

"Is that all? Don't give it another thought. It will give me a chance to get a cabin of my own as I really do need to wash the grime accumulated from my travels and sort my kit out. We can still meet in the bar by chance." He returned again to his task. "In the meantime bring me up to date on everything while I sort this."

Servo told him of Vasily's adventures and the safe houses and their travels in Ireland and the appearance now of the three IRA men at the Wallop location. Servo told them of his visits to Split and Libya and what he had seen at the Libyan terrorist training complex and who he had met there including the two IRA men, Joe, the bomb maker and Ian, the radio electronics expert.

Servo wanted to give Saied an appreciation of the timescale they now faced and the fact that Tsygankov and the IRA chief had agreed they would be out of the area when the bomb went off so the Russians were not implicated.

When Saied had finished, Servo gave him a hand to take the discarded stuffing from the four cushions out to the rest area fence line and toss them into the undergrowth they found there.

When they got back to the motor-home Carla had set the table and put the food on the table in the galley. A large pot of coffee was the centre-piece. While the three ate, they continued to discuss the last few weeks and the next two ahead.

It was nearly midnight when Servo climbed into the driver's seat and they set off. Carla spelled Servo every two hours. They stopped once to refuel and arrived at the port just before six in the morning. Saied dismounted and went to the ferry terminal to get his ticket and Servo and Carla went through the ticket filter and parked up on the dock. Leaving the motor-home they also made their way to the ferry terminal and the café for a big breakfast.

They were due to board at eight and were back in the motorhome well before and waited, nodding in the front seats until they were called forward.

Once on board they went to their cabin and got their heads down until lunch. They went to the restaurant and asked for a table at the window and watched the sea rolling by while they studied the menu. Jean Saied, in a smart tropical suit and polished shoes joined them.

"Wow you clean up well," said Carla.

"Need to keep up standards, Carla."

"So I see. Will you drink wine?" asked Servo.

"Let's do that, a good red if you please. I feel hungry now." Jean called over the wine waiter and chose a wine from the card.

After lunch Jean disappeared and the other two walked the open decks to get some air and calm the nerves which were beginning to build up as they contemplated the hurdle of passing through customs with the explosives.

As it was, the customs officer only looked at the passports with a cursory look and swiped them into the computer. He kept his face neutral as he passed the passports back. He had a flag come up that indicated the two of them were not to be held, but the customs officer was to call two numbers immediately which were for the SO13 and Rodney's Operations rooms.

Rodney got the news half an hour later that the motor-home had returned to the UK and as far as he was concerned carried the explosives. The French had told him earlier in the morning that the boat they were watching was on its return journey and that only one man was now on board who they believed to be the captain.

While Rodney worked through his notebook in the operations room that evening he had just put an action in his book to get Major James Collins down to the marquee site to meet all the crew so he would recognise any of them that turned up as riggers with the IRA team when he got a call from Jersey.

Chapter 49

THE ACCOUNTANT

The Accountant was looking forward to getting back to his house. His driver and minder, Mahoney, should be at the gate to meet him as soon as he cleared Jersey customs. He had flown direct from Dublin after a week with his associate, a partner in the Dublin firm. The Accountant was weary, not only did he have to present his books and workings to the IRA internal auditor but he had had a difficult meeting with the IRA Chief of Staff. It was familiar territory for him but it didn't get any easier.

The Accountant was only too aware that the IRA had 300 part or full-time members on the pay, and to retain them and their loyalty they needed funding it was true. The Army Council continually griped at the Accountant for transferring money into the Sinn Fein political coffers and he would each time request that they take the matter up with Adams. To make matters worse, as far as he was concerned there were pensions, so called, to pay out to.

Unusually he was stopped with a few others in the green lane of customs but as he was not alone he waited patiently for his turn. When it came he placed his attaché case on the table along with his carry-on bag.

The customs officer spun the case toward him and tested the catches, it was locked. He spun the case back to the Accountant, "Open your case would you please sir."

The Accountant thumbed the combinations and opened the case turning it back to the officer. The officer gave the case's contents a cursory look before looking directly at the men in front of him. "Would you go with the officer behind you please sir?" The

Accountant made a move to close the case but the customs officer stopped him.

Andrew, watching from behind a one-way screen nodded to the Fraud Squad officer beside him. The officer made two calls which triggered an entry to the Accountant's residence and the detention of his driver who was waiting at arrivals.

While Andrew and the Fraud Squad officer waited for the Accountant to be brought to them in one of the interrogation rooms, Pat, Jane, the Banker and the senior officer from SO13 followed the Jersey Police into the man's residence.

The Accountant was led in and made to sit opposite Andrew and the police officer. The Accountant was relaxed and sat silently, it was not the first time various authorities had detained him but not usually in the Channel Islands. Andrew took his time summing him up. Andrew hit the switch of the recoding machine, "Would you state your name for the purpose of the tape?"

"Don't think so, you have my passport – work it out," the Accountant smirked.

Andrew struck a hard lightning-fast slap to the man's face and it stung bringing tears to his eyes and it shook the man mentally. Before he could regain his composure, Andrew slapped him again on the other cheek which bought more tears and a groan.

"Shall we start again? State your name please." This time there was compliance.

The Fraud Squad officer going through the attaché case found two discs in the lining of the case. He got up and left the room. Andrew waited for him to return, doodling on his notebook, sighing to himself now and again. When the officer returned he shook his head, the discs were password protected.

"Your password, please?" Andrew demanded. The man looked at his feet and said nothing. Andrew rocked him again with a left and right slap. "I can keep this up all day, can you," he pushed his notebook forward a clean set of pages face up, "write it down."

The Accountant leaned forward and wrote a password on the left page. The customs officer studied the series of numbers that made up the password and left the room again.

"You can't do this you know," the Accountant started. Andrew put a finger to his lips.

"Yes I can and this is nothing. You can expect the worst if I don't get your full cooperation. There is a rendition request for you to travel to the USA issued by the FBI." Andrew paused. "Of course that unpleasantness can be avoided if you help me. You do understand the consequences of a trip to the States. It would be a one-way trip?"

"What do you want?"

"Now that's the attitude I like. We will leave here shortly for your residence; we have some people there who have some questions for you, they have a jigsaw puzzle and although they have most of the pieces there are one or two they are having trouble fitting in to complete the picture. Simple things really for instance; how much did FARC (*Fuerzas Armadas Revolutionaries' de Colombia*), in Colombia pay the IRA to advise them on how to turn their agrarian terrorist activities into an urban one?"

"It was close to two million pounds sterling as makes no difference." Andrew made a note. The fraud officer hunched his shoulders for something to do.

"Which of the, have I this right, 90 or so banks you use from time to time around the world did the money eventually end up in?"

"I would need to check but probably here in Jersey." The customs officer entered the room quietly and had heard the exchange and raised his eyebrows; this was all news to him and he realised for the first time that the Fraud Branch had to pay catch-up. He nodded to Andrew. "The password works and I have taken two copies of each disc, one for your team and two for the Fraud Squad.

"Fine, let us then retire to the residence and continue this conversation with the team. Cuff him and bring his driver too."

"What about my rights? I want my lawyer."

"What rights are you talking about? As far as I am concerned you forfeited them when you got in bed with those murdering employers of yours. You are as guilty as for example the FAAC who dismember people and destroy lives and for the innocents and disappeared in Ireland and elsewhere where the IRA's fingers have a part. Do I make myself clear?" Andrew showed his anger. "No rights, no lawyer of any kind at this time. It is simply not going to happen, unless you convince me during the course of our time together you are an innocent victim of circumstance. Clear?"

The Accountant nodded, head down as he held out his scrawny wrists to be cuffed. Andrew was not naturally a bully and it gave him no pleasure to dominate this frail grey-haired man, who Andrew judged must be in his middle to late sixties. "Perhaps they should have gone for the Accountant's company in Dublin too at the same time?" Was Andrew's' idle thought, as they left the airport confines. They could now leave that to the Fraud Squad and the like, perhaps.

"Probably to do that would have been too difficult for us, still it was a thought that they might have to at some time if the man didn't come over with enough to enable the Banker and now the Fraud Branch to freeze and seize the funds that made the IRA and Sinn Fein activities possible." At this point in time Andrew could not mentally separate one from the other.

When they were underway Andrew asked the police driver how far to the residence. "Be there in five sir. We are heading due north from the airport heading for the La Grave de Lacq. We will turn of west just before we get there and less than half a mile on is a nest of houses which is where we are going."

True to his word the driver got them there inside the five minutes. The house, like so many on the island, was built in the grey stone of the island surrounded by a six-foot dry-stone wall. The house was substantial; the interior was impressive, high ceiling and rooms all over-size; five bedrooms, each with their own shower bathroom and three receptions with a large kitchen and utility room. In the half acre of ground Andrew could see a low building split into five modest apartments for either staff or guests. A swimming pool led via a wide stone flagged patio to the French doors of the house on the east side of the main property.

Pat met the party on the driveway, shook hands all round and led them to the main reception room. Sat in a high-winged chair was the Banker with a grin on his face. When the Accountant saw him he gave an involuntary cry of anguish. "You!"

"Who else could you have expected, one of your friends from Inland Revenue or the treasury?" The Banker waved a sheaf of papers at him. "Just because the old *Dail General* Tom Maguire, God rest his soul," the Banker crossed himself, "before he passed on, ruled the Provisional Irish Republican Army was the legitimate government of Ireland not the Dublin democratically elected parliament. Why even you're too good to be true Sinn Fein refused to recognise them early 1986. So how come boyo, the IRA and Sinn Fein are getting tax relief and money laundering favours from the British Government?" The Banker's voice took on an Irish lilt and it was only then did Andrew understand the Banker was Irish and after some sort of revenge for an outrage to himself of someone close to him.

The Accountant had overcome his initial shock at seeing a ghost from the past and replied, Andrew thought bravely. "Michael it's complicated."

The Banker went after him. "That is not an answer."

"For God's sake Michael, will you not let me sit down at a table. I will answer your questions calmly and in full. Come on man, we were once friends let us at least be civil."

"You killed any love I had for you when your masters raped and killed my daughter."

"It was not my doing and I fought against them, give me that at least I tried to stop them."

"Maybe you didn't try hard enough but it did not do any good did it?" The Banker sat back in the chair suddenly drained. "You and your hypocritical bastards took away my only child."

"I am so sorry. It was such a long time ago now I sometimes forget. It tore me apart too, you know that. But once you are in you are in. God forgive me."

The Banker was unremitting in his anger. "God may but I never will."

The people in the room were spellbound by the exchange between the Banker and the Accountant. Andrew for himself felt for a moment he had been as all of them had manipulated by the Banker but at least he understood now why the man was so driven and that would not be a bad thing if kept in check. The immediate task was to regain focus and momentum.

"Pat does the dining room have a large enough table for the Banker, you, Jane, the Accountant and the officer from Fraud Squad to do your thing?" Andrew took control.

Pat, already now in front of Andrew, sparked. "Easy. I will get them in and we can begin the debrief." He addressed the Banker, who was clearly upset, as gently as he could. "Will you please lead, sir? The officer from SO13 will be able to tell you what we found here." The Banker nodded and rose from his chair

"Give me a moment I need some air." The Banker's eyes were brimming

"Thanks Pat." Andrew left when the Banker had left the room. Andrew left the others to organise themselves and went to find the SO13 senior officer.

There seemed to be police in every room of the house and in the kitchen the housekeeper and cook in his whites were sitting with Mahoney. They sat glum and silent as the police organised them for interviews.

Andrew eventually found Carol and the SO13 senior officer in the master bedroom, which was divided into two and big enough to double as the Accountant's office. In the office, half of the room had probably been a dressing room in a past life. The walls lined with shelves full of files and international bank and law reference books. Three filing cabinets were open and a floor safe was exposed. On what would have been a partner desk with kneehole to both sides, Jane and the officer were shifting through files. The Accountant's laptop had been run up, the same password used for the CD worked on that. A local fraud officer was downloading files onto external hard drives as though his life depended on it.

"Carol, gentlemen, the Accountant is about to be interviewed by the Banker and Pat in the dining room." Andrew had their attention. "Judging from the Accountant's mood which is now very co-operative your job should be easier. With the expertise here and downstairs I am now surplus, so I am going back to base to talk to the Brigadier and the Major. Carol please help these two officers as needs be and tell Pat he is responsible for the Banker and the Accountant. Two more matters, I think it would be a plus if you could find anything related in the books about the operation going on, on the mainland. If you do, fire them over to me in the operations room back in London. Secondly I think it would be useful as you come over stuff new to us that you get a note to Pat ASAP so it can be covered in the debrief before it begins."

Carol said, "No problem, Andrew. There is a mountain of stuff here and Tom," she indicated the senior fraud officer who put his head round the door, "is going to fly in a team tonight made up of tax and international banking specialists?"

Tom took up the conversation, "This is going to take many weeks if not months to unravel, not sure this is the best place to do it. But I will consult your team before I request we move the data."

"Don't think we have a problem with that. The plan is that you are to take the investigation over long-term anyway but we both need to clear this with the Brigadier as this a ministerial and Central Intelligence driven task and they have ownership." Andrew responded. "Our mission was to open Pandora's Box and give it a shake but we seem to have gone further than was intended."

Carol was concerned at what they had unearthed. "What worries me is the possible complicity of some government departments." She was addressing Tom. "There is anecdotal evidence that the IRA are being allowed to launder money from, for example, some high profile bank accounts. There is the case of the revolutionary taxes." Tom looked blank. "This is where small businesses, in many instances builders, whereby the builders hand over relatively small amounts of money to the IRA and fiddle the books and claim the tax relief. Large business, and there is one that's into revolutionary tax for a couple of million. There is even some evidence that those businesses suffering from revolutionary tax are being paid to make up the losses by Inland Revenue. These are all shady tax schemes from both sides and it's costing the UK billions. The point at the end of the day is the UK tax payer is funding the IRA for Christ sakes." Carol was incensed.

Tom ran his hand through his hair in exasperation. "Wow this is all new to me. What on earth is going on?"

Andrew grinned. "Spend some quality time with the Banker and all will be revealed. He has been working on this for years and I expect you are going to need him."

"We know about some matters like the Euro Pig where they drive cattle backwards and forward over the border and claim EU subsidies on both sides, but we are on to that now. We are even making progress where their schemes rely on buying cheap on one side of the border and selling high on the other – be it alcohol, cigarettes smuggled in, fuel etc., etc., then claiming the products are business purchases and claiming back tax. As well as their expanding control and manipulation of Belfast dock and port. It's a nightmare and if as you infer basically the Treasury is compromised, it's the biggest case we will ever have worked on."

"It gets worse; this is costing us billions, trust me. And a great chunk of the population is part of the multi-tentacle beast. Don't get me wrong but I caution the IRA as you squeeze them they will move the emphasis to pure crime," Andrew added.

"Crime, what have we been just talking about? It is all a crime," Tom said.

"Yes and no. What many people fail to understand is that the IRA learnt over time that intellectual and victimless crime is far more palatable to the community and the payback is higher. This funding stream has made the IRA political arm one of, if not the wealthiest political party in Europe, with an income of millions every year. And they need funds to employ people and money from banks, robberies etc. This money is seen by some senior and older hands as pension money. We all get old. They need money to keep people loyal. Don't get me wrong, the IRA have some morals; they don't traffic people, at least not yet and tend to steer away from drugs and punish those who are in the trade but that could change if the revenue earning potential outweighs the moral imperative. Their Gaelic Catholic policy based on peasant particularities rejects the liberal democracy we aspire to, for example. Well most of us. Their policies have an appeal to people unable to improve their status and get recognition in this 'ho-ho', modern metropolitan country of ours. That's it in a nutshell, pay me later." Andrew had them all laughing which at least lightened the mood. He made his excuses and went downstairs to see the Banker and Pat before he left to catch a late flight back.

Chapter 50

THE WALLOP SAFE HOUSE

Vasily and Liam, left alone at the safe house as the others dispersed to their various activities, soon realised they didn't particularly like each other. Vasily thought Liam was brash and ignorant, and also a man willing to override anyone else's point of view that was not in accord with Liam's personnel agenda and opinions. Liam for his part resented the younger man's position and Vasily's intellect. Liam, used to pushing his own men around, found Vasily could not be manipulated or easily managed. Whereas Liam found it difficult if not impossible at times to show his growing distaste against Vasily. Vasily found it easy to hide his feelings toward Liam. That Vasily appeared to completely ignore Liam's more overt feeling towards him only served to wind up Liam more.

It almost came to a head when on the afternoon drive-by of the marquee company Liam wanted to stop and go into the company and pretend to be a potential client who wanted to hire a marquee. Vasily was not prepared to accompany Liam as he thought it would risk exposure if the site had CCTV and they had not prepared a proper cover legend if they were asked difficult questions. Instead he insisted they do a drive-by giving the appearance of visiting one of the units adjacent to the marquee company and purchase something, while they took the opportunity to observe the target site.

Liam had, with bad grace, reluctantly agreed. In the event it was a good decision as they were able to see the site clearly and the men working on the tent-age and trucks. They counted five men outside and two people, a man and a woman, in the office. While Liam went into the neighbouring unit, an electrical equipment supplier to buy an item without raising suspicion Vasily sat in the car, facing the company and sketched the key details of the facility, making notes as he went along.

Liam returned to the car and threw a box onto the back seat pleased with himself. "Electrical ties, they may come in useful for cuffing people. They make great plasticuffs," Liam explained vindictively.

Vasily looked over at Liam and handed his sketch and notes over to him. "Food, now I think and wait until dark before we come back and have a good look round. Is that what you want to do or have you seen enough."

"No don't think so. I would like to have a closer look at the place. Find us a pub. I think we passed a place a couple of miles back on the run up from Basingstoke so I did."

"Could we consider going a bit further out? Think we should consider that after the event and the police will be questioning around the area. Think two men one, with an Eastern European accent and an Irish man, may be remembered. What do you think?"

Liam gave a sidelong look at Vasily and seeing no sign that Vasily was putting him down he agreed and suggested they go back to Basingstoke and find somewhere in the town.

Vasily may not have bothered if he had known that the SO13 team had noted the registration of the car they were in and the fact that the passenger seemed to be paying special attention to the company area and the staff.

It was ten o'clock that night before they returned. Vasily dousing the car lights drove them slowly into the small industrial estate. The unmade road with its stone chipping crunched under the tyres. They drove to the end unit and parked. Only a single light on the entrance doors to each of the units blazed and there were enough shadows to hide themselves in, or so they thought.

The SO13 team in the forest had "eyes on" and followed the two progress through their night scope. The two made their way to the rear of the company unit and climbed over the chain-link fence with little difficulty. The SO13 team called in the two men now settled in the roof space of the office to alert them they may have visitors and got an acknowledgment with two clicks on the radio back.

Liam led the way round the back of the building, noting the grills on the windows along the side and stopped at the corner looking and listening to the front. When he was satisfied all the area was deserted and quiet he slid round the corner and along the front to the office door. A quick inspection convinced him it was alarmed and he didn't try to open it. He could look through the window and make out all the clutter and paraphernalia that he would have expected in a blue collar business. Unwashed cups on the desks and foul-weather clothing hung over one of the chair-backs. Liam gave Vasily the thumbs-up and moved quickly towards the Dutch barn and inspected the trucks parked under it. He tested the truck doors which were all locked but hopped up on each one to check the cabs. As he had tested one of the truck doors he noticed the decal was magnetic. The trucks themselves were clean and business-like. Shrugging, Liam moved into the yard, listened and then went over to the three grounded containers and checked the locks. Vasily joined him. "Found any issues?"

"No, looks as it should. Bit surprised the decals on the truck doors and these containers are magnetic."

"Perhaps they lease the kit and it's a way to save expense when they hand it back," Vasily said helpfully.

"Yeh you could be right. Come on we have been here long enough. We don't want to run into a mobile security van which I am sure they will have out here." Liam again led the way and they exited the compound the way they had come. Liam spent a moment making sure the fence looked undisturbed and the ground immediately outside they had used by kicking some loose debris around. When they got to the car Liam shivered, he had a feeling they were observed. He listened carefully and looked round slowly the industry site and forested area. He used his night vision to look out the side of his eyes to help detect movement.

In the forest verge the SO13 men put their heads down. It was a truism that if you and the target were looking at each other, even in the dark, some primeval instinct often kicked in and likely as not you would be spotted.

Liam saw nothing. "Come let's go." They climbed into the car and Liam calmed.

The SO13 men watched the car drive out of the estate, before it switched on its lights and joined the carriageway. "Well looks like a hit. That second man was pretty alert I thought he might ping us, wonder what he heard or saw that made him stop and look round."

"It was probably nerves or just adrenaline running riot. Better get this contact intelligence back to base."

Vasily and Liam were back at the safe house not long after midnight. They had a glass of whiskey in the lounge and watched the late news before turning in. Liam expected his two men back in the morning and he needed to get the other men he needed stood up and moving down to the local area so they could carry out their own recce of the two target areas. Until he had all his people and the kit in place he was reluctant to settle on a date and time he would ask the Russians to leave.

In the farmer's field a hundred metres from the front fence line of the house the special air service two-man team were dug into the field and picked up the first pictures and the conversation between Liam and Vasily as they had sipped their whiskies. The conversation was automatically rebroadcasted to SO13 and the operations room where Rodney listened and watched. While the pair were out, the specialists had been in and fitted devices into the house and the garage. The team in the field had eyes on the house and another two-man team, closer, to the left had eyes on the large garage workshop.

Rodney was late, he and Brigadier Robinson had had a couple of days intense briefing off and on from Andrew. Earlier that evening Robinson handed out Andrew's technical report on the team's findings to the gathering in the Treasury's meeting room. He had a bad-tempered meeting with the Senior Civil Servants of the Treasury, the Home and Foreign Office, and their ministers, along with the head of the Fraud Squad and his deputy. Robinson had pulled no punches and the report said it all, along with the possible complicity of unnamed members of the civil service and possible rough elements of the UK and Irish governments. The outcome of the meeting was that fraud branch with the help of the Banker would now lead the investigation into IRA finances going forward. Robinson's team with the guilty congratulations of the meeting could be relieved from their task and return to their other duties. The Foreign Minister caught Robinson's eye before he left and joined him in the corridor while the others streamed by, most heads down.

"Brigadier, your boys have done an outstanding job as I would have expected but nevertheless I am personally delighted they cracked the nub of the issue. Would you please thank them from me personally and assure them I will be keeping a close eye on the progress of the Fraud Squad as they move forward." Robinson nodded cold and distant, and shook the minister's hand.

"Of course, Minister. I will see the PM possibly tomorrow to tell her this phase as far as we are concerned is closed out, as I will the Joint Intelligence Committee." He spun on his heel, not without seeing the concern on the minister's face and headed for his own office. "Hypocrites," Robinson mumbled to himself. "I wonder if Mrs T knows what they have been up to. Goodness knows what will happen if the other lot get in. They might even bend over backwards to placate the IRA for a peace settlement but at what cost."

Rodney packed his case, casting his eyes around the operations room and smiled at the Brigadier and Andrew who were chatting. "Well Rodney, what is next?" Robinson asked, also making his move to leave.

"Truth is I need to be nearer the action for the next week. I am going to ask," he indicated, "Andrew and Pat to bolster the operation duty desk to support Graham 24/7 now we have the IRA in our sights." He clipped up his briefcase. "We need to get Carol down to the marquee site to take over from Mrs Reid tomorrow latest and prise Mrs R out of her desk which I hear she has become attached to before the game goes hot." Robinson and Andrew laughed. "But that's for tomorrow morning. I think it's time we all got a good night's sleep. Andrew can you get Pat and Carol in for say nine in the morning?"

Robinson indicated the finance team's corner of the room with all the data on the boards and the files in the cabinets and safe. "I suppose we should get that lot over to the Fraud Squad tomorrow too?"

"Think a word with the Banker from you sir would not go amiss before we disturb any of the work." Rodney suggested and Andrew nodded his agreement.

"You're right to say that. I will call him tomorrow if he is not in." Robinson hefted his old leather and battered attaché case. "Until tomorrow."

Vasily was up early and went out into the grounds to get some fresh air and look over the views laid out before him. Some early morning flight training was already happening on the airfield and he envied the young men, their simple if not demanding occupation, firing up their helicopters. He watched a few helicopters come into the hover and then spin the tail before lifting off into the sky. He pulled the BMW's key from his pocket, time to put it away.

In the safe house Liam was also up and working through his list of things to do before he would begin his round of calls to the men he would use. Another matter, apart from when the Russians should leave, was the marquee company's location and manning it during the week before the attack.

The problem had been created and complicated by the client's dictating that the marquee was to be up a week before the attack. What he had decided was that he would use a couple of the staff from the company to help his men erect the marquee and guarantee their compliance by holding the rest of the company's men hostage back at base.

He was fully aware that holding the staff quiet for a week at the unit was going to be a challenge. He considered the alternative of eliminating the problem by killing the staff. On balance he chose to keep them alive, at least that way they could talk to their family members by phone and bluff that they were on a job up north for the week. Decision made, he did the analysis of how many people he would need to manage the staff. He thought four and a woman receptionist, unless he used the woman there depending on her circumstances. He would only know that when they took over the site. From the visit the night before it was evident that there was a front office with a room at the back and ablution facilities. He would hold them in the back complex behind the office.

Vasily entered the house and called out. "Going to do breakfast, Liam do you want some.?"

"Thank you that would be good. Full fried for me please." He returned to his notes. He would bring over young Shaun and Sheena just in case. Sheena could carry out the reception duties if needs be. Time to make his calls, no point in holding back any longer. Back at SO13 Graham, in various operations rooms, recorded and listened to the calls as Liam made them from his mobile which were picked up by the microphone in the room. Clever men in SO13 would listen to Liam's key strokes on the mobile phone pad and work out the numbers he was calling for follow-up later.

After breakfast, Vasily told Liam he was going for a walk round the country lanes. Liam was not happy about that but there was little he could do to stop him. He wanted to do a reconnaissance of the area where the marquee was to be erected before Ian and Joe arrived in the afternoon and wanted Vasily to drive him. "I'll be back in less than an hour, finish your calls and I will drive you then, how's that?"

"Fine, don't get lost."

Vasily ambled down the drive to the gate and unlocked it and turned left up the road to check on this option for a route out if needs be. A mile up the road the minor road hooked left and he could see it joined an arterial road running north-south half a mile away. This was what he expected and knew that the arterial road if he went north would cross the A303 and he would then be away and just another vehicle on the busy road. He scampered back, feeling the muscles in his legs tightening. After the few weeks of little physical activity it felt good.

At the safe house he got the BMW out and left the doors ajar. The reconnaissance would not take long and he would lock up on his return. He drove the BMW to the front of the house and went to get Liam.

"All well?" Vasily asked Liam, as he got into the car, more for the sake of making conversation with Liam, not expecting to get an answer.

"All done, the men should be in the area from tomorrow night. Now let's get this show on the road shall we?"

They turned right and down the hill into the village and then right to the crossroads at Wallop. Here they went south on the Salisbury road passing the officers' mess on their right and the main camp on the left. Liam noted the officers' mess car park to the road side of the mess. "Turn around when you can. What I want you to do is, when we get to the mess turn into their car park and do a circuit and then drive out again. I believe I will be able to see the front of the mess and where the marquee is to go. The rest I can do from the map."

Vasily nodded and saw the air museum coming up on his left and spun the car round in the museum car park. They drove slowly back up the road until they got to the entrance to the mess car park. It was deserted apart from a few cars and tree-bound for the most part. Vasily drove to the far end of the car park where tennis courts were in use by a couple of off-duty officers. At this far end of the car park, between the tennis courts and the mess lawn was a gap in the trees so large vehicles could drive off the car park onto the lawn. The officers looked up and saw the BMW manoeuvring awkwardly taking its time but ignored it as it finally reversed and went out the way it had come in.

"Did you get what you wanted?"

"Yes I think so. The back of the mess has a patio and a set of wide steps down onto the mess lawn. That must be where the marquee will be sited. Happy with that, let's go home. I will get lunch and we could break open a bottle or two." Liam was happy now he had his men on the way and had seen both target areas and they had not thrown up any unexpected difficulties as he now saw it.

"Good. As soon as you have your team ready I will make a call to the officer in charge of the event and tell him what day and at what time to expect the marquee to turn up. Then I will tell the marquee company to have the kit loaded for a start on whatever day that is and that someone will be arriving to accompany them to the site," Vasily responded.

"It's a plan. But I need to discus with Joe and Ian where and when we set the explosives into the marquee floor panels. Be that on site or off. Not got that detail yet but watch this space."

They drove back to the safe house. The day was warm but dark rain clouds were appearing from the west and the clouds scurried overhead. The light breeze that had kept the temperature down was beginning to bluster. At the house Joe and Ian had not yet turned up. Liam went straight into the kitchen while Vasily put the car away out of sight. Liam busied himself getting lunch. The act of preparing the meal helped Liam to clear his mind for a while. Vasily arrived and went to fridge to get out a few beers and poured them into glasses.

"It seems to me, Liam, that our involvement will soon be at an end when the Semtex turns up," Vasily said starting up a conversation.

"Rest assured I don't want you under my feet any longer than I have to. I was thinking when your other three members turn up and the explosives are unloaded we might send them on their way. But you will need to stay to make the calls before you bomb out too. Think that would be tidy and free up space for my crew in the house."

"That should work. Cheers!" Vasily for his part carefully raised his beer glass to the Irish man.

Liam took his glass and drank it down in one. "A Guinness this time son, not that milk water they call beer over here."

Vasily reddened but smiled all the same. "Certainly."

Rodney listening in to the conversation was thoughtful. He still had the motor-home under surveillance and that would remain as long as he wanted it watched on its routes. He needed to pick up the other vehicles the IRA were and would be using and gave the instruction to Graham sitting by him to make it happen as they were identified. He glanced at the roster and saw it was already populated with Pat and Andrew in the silent hours leaving Graham with the core day hours with his now tame captain in support. Rodney would need to take the captain with him to help set up an operations centre at Wallop. But that could wait. He didn't want to upset Graham's day just yet.

In the far corner of the operations room Pat and Andrew were helping the Banker pack up the finance team's records. The Banker and the records would be transhipped to the Fraud Branch offices later this afternoon. He went to join them. "Can I buy you all lunch?"

"Good of you Rodney, but my old friend and sparring partner your boss is taking me out. I can say without reservation that I have enjoyed working with you and this team. My every hoped for expectation has been met so I am grateful to you all. No doubt we will meet again."

The Banker held out his hand and Rodney took it. Rodney now knew about his daughter and the loss and discerned in him another human being that had, like he, lost something very special. The Banker held his gaze and Rodney felt fullness in his eyes and fancied he could see a glistening in the Banker's. Rodney looked away quickly.

"I will avenge your daughter, I promise. Until we meet again sir."

"Happy to part we are and happy to meet again," was the Banker's farewell as Rodney took his place at the operations table.

It was close to three o'clock when Joe, the IRA bomb maker and Ian, the IRA electronics specialist turned up in their four-by-four. The Toyota truck-man was weighed down with kit. Liam and Vasily helped them unload the vehicle into the garage. Joe wanted the BMW out so they had the whole area to work in unimpeded. Vasily moved it out and hid it as best he could in the trees just off the driveway leading to the out gate. He checked it was not easily visible from the road and rejoined the others systematically laying out the bomb-making materials and the electronic equipment around the garage. They were filmed and recorded. At SO13 and the Rodney's operations room they could hardly imagine another operation where they had such good intelligence of the enemy.

The men finished and the garage was locked up. The four men went into the house and sat at the kitchen table. Vasily offered drinks but the IRA men would only take tea and coffee, as far as they were concerned the operation was in play and no alcohol would be taken until it was over. Vasily duly produced a pot of tea and coffee and plate of biscuits and as he had no part to play opened a bottle of Merlot, a soft red wine.

"Well Joe, did you and Ian get everything you wanted?" Liam wanted to know.

"We got plenty and some over just in case," Joe told him. "What's the situation on the Semtex and the men?"

Liam looked over at Vasily. "We expect the Semtex to arrive tomorrow afternoon. The exchange from boat to vehicle should take place tonight."

Liam looked away from Vasily to Joe and Ian. "The men are sorted. Here is the plan as far as I have got. I will have a crew of four good men to manage the hostages at the marquee company site, plus Sheena to possibly act as the receptionist and Shaun as a runner for whatever. I will have eleven men for the marquee erection. Some have worked as riggers before so there will be some experience in the team. Plus I intend to take two men from the hostages to work under close supervision with our boys, just so we don't look complete amateurs.

They will behave themselves as we will make it plain what will happen to their mates back at the company site if they don't."

"Big team you have for this, Liam, where will you be while this is all going on?" Ian wanted to know.

"That depends on you two boys." Liam sipped his coffee. "The way I see it, and interrupt me if I have this wrong, I see the team erecting the marquee day one and laying the rails to take the floor. I took some time out before I came over and spent a day with a marquee company in the south, so I've some idea how it all goes together and how the floor suspended about three inches off the ground is constructed. On day two the floor gets put in. During both these days I will be on site with the marquee as it goes up. Now the big question for you two is are you going to doctor the floor panels at the marquee site of erection or before it is loaded on the trucks?"

"We have been thinking about that too and what is for the best. It is interesting the Semtex is in five, not two, kilogram blocks the way we normally get it supplied in. For preference we, or rather I, would like to fix the blocks and radio wave activated detonators as each floor plate goes down. The tent will be up so we will be screened and we can be on the lookout for any curious onlookers. One man can keep them out pointing out they cannot come within the curtilage of the marquee for health and safety reasons until it has been inspected and passed as a safe temporary structure. Give Shaun a millboard and he can be the HSE manager for the company." Joe finished.

Liam laughed. "Good idea. Okay, that's the plan we will go with. What preparation do you two need to do before the day?"

"Well we need to prepare the detonators and set in the frequency to them and the radio transmitter and the hand held phone which will also be able to detonate the bombs. To set the explosives off you will need to dial in a six figure number to the phone or the radio and then hit any key and it will send the signal. The phone device will only have a range of a couple of miles or so for the initiation, but with the radio we can also trigger it from here."

"Guess I should have the phone as I will be on site. I think for the second day we don't need the two men from the marquee company. It would be less risky if we only use our own men."

"I agree. I don't want to be identified later as one of the men working the marquee. Ian will stay at the safe house as we may or may not need to do some last minute tests between him and myself if one of the antennas is damaged."

"Then it seems we have a working plan," Liam was about to conclude before he added, "One last thing I want to add. After the completion of the marquee all the men will come back here to collect their kit before they disperse. Shaun will stay as he and I will go to the target once a day to check the marquee's safety and to see no-one has meddled with it."

They spent time going over resources and logistics matters and what they had to do the following day, before Vasily excused himself to prepare the dinner.

The following day Vasily saw little of the three IRA men as they worked away in the garage workshop, apart from the lunch meal until late afternoon when Servo, Saied and Carla arrived.

It was a great reunion for the three Russians and Saied, the Palestinian. Although they had kept in touch on the phone they had much to catch up on and stories to share but overriding all that was the need to help the IRA men move the Semtex to the garage.

In the operations room Rodney was conflicted. A low-risk option would be to roll up the mission now. They would get Liam and the two top IRA specialists Joe and Ian. What to do with the Russians was still a niggle in the back of his mind. Should he do as he was minded to, let them go or capture them? The higher risk option was to let the mission develop and capture or kill an additional 20 active IRA fighters as well as the damage they would undoubtedly do to the IRA Q and Tsygankov in particular for a spectacular failure. He had discussed his options with the Brigadier Robinson as was proper and had gotten from Robinson that whatever decision Rodney came too he would support him no matter what the outcome. Conscious that a decision delayed was a decision denied, as hammered home to him by his instructors at Hereford, he took the decision to let the mission run its course. His next task was to communicate the decision to Robinson and the team.

In the field to the front of the safe house the two SAS teams were listening and watched the events unfold. They were fascinated and were mentally planning and preparing how they would attack the targets when the time came. Having ears and eyes on the key areas of the safe house they hoped would ensure there were no surprises. They were stiff and did their best to keep the circulation going with regular tensioning and relaxing muscles, it was boring but necessary. With three or four days to go they were sanguine and resigned to the wait.

The SO13 teams at the marquee company in the forest fared better; they could move around, exchange shifts, and eat and rest off-site. The team in the roof space were comfortable if a little bored.

Filtering into the officer's mess at Wallop over the next forty-eight hours would be men from SO13 and the SAS with their weapons. Their task would be to take out the IRA men working on the marquee when Rodney, with the agreement of the minister and SO13, gave the order.

The Russians and Saied sat in the sitting room of the safe house with Liam. Liam sipped his tea but the others were drinking wine and beer. For them the mission was over, bar getting back home. Liam was explaining that he needed room for his men and was proposing the Russians less Vasily left next morning. Servo leant forward and said quietly to the surprise of his colleagues, "We stay together; when we go we all go together."

Liam was not expecting this pushback and had to backtrack. "I don't see that would do any harm for Vasily to stay for another day or two. Don't you others want to get on your way?"

"It is not going to happen. We leave together," Servo said again firmly but without threat.

Liam could see he would not move him but he had thought of a solution, he realised he just needed Vasily to make the call and it may as well be tomorrow. "Okay, how is this for an idea? Vasily makes his call tomorrow to the officer IC the event and tells him his men will be on site in two days first thing in the morning. That will mean the marquee goes up as they wanted a week before the ball. Everyone is happy."

"That is acceptable. We will leave once you have heard Vasily make the call."

Vasily spoke up. "Good, the officer was expecting me to speak to him and it may or may not have been suspicious if someone else spoke to him."

Carla got down to practicalities. "You realise Liam we need to take the safe house weapons with us and get them back. They were there for us to defend ourselves in an emergency, not part of the deal. We cannot afford to have them traced if they are captured or turn up somewhere."

"We were hoping you would leave them for us, they would have been useful but under the circumstances I fully understand where you are coming from. So be it."

"And lastly Liam, you will be one single mattress short."

"Oh?"

"We need to re-stuff the pillows that held the Semtex," Carla explained with a smile.

Liam smiled back, his craggy face for once friendly. "No problem. Anything else."

The team looked at each other and shook their heads.

"Good, my men will begin to arrive after lunch tomorrow so I suggest you get on with whatever you need to do so once the call is made you can get off." Liam left them to their own devices and drinks.

Vasily put out his hand to Servo. "Thanks Servo, you did me a great favour. I have little liking for Liam and more than once I could have hit him."

"Welcome, now come Carla let's get that mattress sorted and the cushions stuffed." He stood and offered his hand to Carla to help her out of the easy chair. "What are you two going to do?"

"Saied and I will pack the guns into the boot of the BMW and then Saied has promised to show me how to make a couple of great curries for tonight's dinner." That brought a laugh from the others.

Carla asked. "And just how are we going to get rid of the armoury?"

"Now we are all leaving together. You three need to follow me in the motor-home to the North London safe house. We will lock them up there and leave the BMW there to. We all then head for the place I have arranged for us to catch our breath before we head home." Vasily took care to explain to them.

Servo grunted. "We will need to tell the General what is happening so he can arrange for the roll-up of the house vehicles and kit. I will do that tonight."

Rodney, sitting in the operations room listening to the interchanges, was making notes. For sure he knew the intelligence services would want to know where the safe house was and who visited it once Vasily and the Tsygankov team left it. He still needed to re-confirm with the Brigadier that the powers that be were of a like mind in letting the Russians leave unmolested. He wanted to talk to Vasily one more time in person and he had an idea how he could do that with the help of SO13. Last but not least he needed to ensure Major James Collins was in the officers' mess office to take the call next morning.

The last night in the safe house for the Russian team and the newer occupants was not unduly tense but it was clear the IRA wanted them gone so they could get on with their task. The Russians read the atmosphere and made a great effort to make it as easy as they could for the IRA men. They maintained a serious and friendly manner towards the Irishmen, trying not to show that in their minds for them it was over, their job was done and that they were demob happy. In many ways Saied carried the day as he had met Joe and Ian in Libya and related his experiences in the hotel and the ruins, which neither Joe nor Ian had had the opportunity to visit and they were genuinely interested. Liam was, at the beginning of the evening and the meal prepared by Saied and Vasily, up tight and at times bad-tempered so it fell to Servo and Carla **to** bring him round with stories of the people they had met in his native land and the fun night at the marina. Liam eventually came round and apologised for his mood; it was he explained the responsibility of the coming operation that was distracting him and he found it difficult to relate to or to think of anything else outside of the mission. Servo understood and entertained Liam and the others with some stories from missions he had planned and executed in Afghanistan that had not always turned out as he had wished.

Next morning the Russian team were ready to leave shortly after nine o'clock. Vasily fetched Liam from the garage where he was working with Joe and Ian, reading the detonator and explosives.

The garage doors were open to allow any fumes from their bomb-making work to escape, giving the left-hand located SAS team good views of the bomb making and devices the IRA had inside. They took a series of pictures and fired them up to the operations rooms. In the SO13 operations room, bomb disposal experts studied the pictures coming through.

In the sitting room the other members of the Russian team and Liam watched Vasily dial the officers' mess and ask for Major James Collins. The room was tense and silent while Vasily waited for Collins to come on the line. Vasily hit the speaker button and placed the phone on the coffee table.

"Collins – can I help you?"

"Major this is the marquee company. Just wanted to assure you that all was well and we will be the mess ready to erect the marquee in…" Liam held up two fingers, "…first thing two days from today." Liam nodded.

"That will be Thursday morning then," Collins returned. Liam nodded to Vasily.

"That's correct. We aim to have the tent up on the first day and put in the floor on the next."

"That's great, it gives us comfort to have the marquee up in plenty of time for the main event and the opportunity to use it for a few small events leading up to that, as well as time to dress out the tent and get in the furniture people etc."

"Until Thursday then, Major," Vasily cut the call and looked at Liam. "Satisfied?"

"Yes satisfied." Liam added joking, but it didn't show in his eyes. "Now get the hell out of my house I have work to do." He offered his hand, which they all shook, but no-one felt like wishing him success.

They had agreed between themselves that Vasily would lead in the BMW and the other three would follow in the motor-home and that if either were stopped the other would go on to the next services, but in any case they would RV at the services on the M11.

All was going well until they both saw a blue flashing light in their rear mirrors. The police car slowed as it approached the motor-home, its light still flashing but overtook it and pulled alongside Vasily's BMW a hundred further on. They had just passed Junction 6 on the M3. While the police car pulled Vasily into the side the motor-home went on. Carla forwarded the satnav and picked out Fleet Services for the next service ten lines on and indicated to Servo who was driving to make for it where they would wait for Vasily.

Vasily slowed to a stop and waited while the police car came to rest behind him. Vasily watched as the policeman got out of the car and adjusted his hat over his eyes. For a fleeting moment Vasily was tempted to roar away and try to outrun the police but he knew he didn't know enough of the area to lose them so he waited patiently for whatever would come.

The policeman strode up to Vasily's passenger door opened it and climbed in. The policeman put his finger to his lips and took off his hat. Vasily instantly recognised him as Major Brown and almost blurted out.

"Now sir, can I see your licence and insurance please?" Rodney was enjoying himself.

Vasily handed them over to the Major, almost mechanically. Vasily was still in a mild shock and some confusion.

"Thank you sir, please come with me while I check these out." Rodney indicated Vasily should follow him.

Rodney and Vasily walked back towards the police car and the driver got out and walked to Vasily's car. Sitting in the police car, Rodney explained to Vasily why he had stopped him. He wanted Vasily's opinion of the enemy and to tell him he and his team were to be allowed to leave the UK unimpeded provided they left in the next forty-eight hours and took no further part in any matter that would compromise or hurt the UK.

"Vasily, what I also need of you is two of the weapons and the ammunition for them. Say a machine gun and a pistol, from the stash in the BMW boot."

"Can I ask why?"

"It is better you don't know. But be rest assured they will be wiped and none of your party's fingerprints will be discovered. Not sure how well you wiped free of fingerprints in the safe house just hope we don't find any."

"Don't think you will find anything. Saied and I cooked and washed up and wiped down the kitchen and dining room. Front and backdoors and bedrooms, hoovered hairs up etc. We are pretty good at it. Plus by the time you get there a dozen or more of Liam's men will have obliterated anything we missed."

"Good. Now let's get you back on the road." Rodney reached to the back seat and pulled a large bin liner and waved it. "For the guns and ammunition?"

Rodney and Vasily left the car, and the police driver a member of SO13 left Vasily's car and returned to his own. Vasily hit the fob and the boot lid opened slowly. Vasily stood to the right of the boot to hide the contents from the rushing traffic feet away. Rodney whistled. "Good job you and the rest were stood down from the actual engagement." He scanned the boot's contents. He chose a VSS Vintorez a GRU and Spatnez issue weapon 9 mm and ten shot and a KEDT PP 91 9MM 20 shot and three mags per gun. There were some RGD5 hand grenades so he took one for interest. Rodney slid his hoard into the bag. "You will need to cover the loss of these arms when you unload so I suggest you do it."

"Not an issue, I can engineer that. So, Major goodbye." Vasily held out his hand and Rodney took it firmly holding the younger man's gaze.

Rodney smiled, "Never goodbye, the world is too small for us not to bump into each other in some place or other. But I do say good luck Vasily and wish you well until then."

Vasily climbed into his car and Rodney with his bag settled into the police car. The exchange had taken only seven minutes and Vasily was soon reunited with the others at Fleet Services.

Back at the safe house the first of Liam's team was beginning to filter in and as Vasily had predicted their comings and goings soon obliterated any residual finger print smudges and any other signs of the recent Russian occupation.

Chapter 51

SET

For Major Rodney Brown the next two days flew by, and suddenly it was the eve of the mission. Mr Reid, Robert Coveney from SO13 and Rodney were in the marquee company office talking what ifs and checking the SO13 marksmen were ready to respond if anything went wrong. The hidden cameras and microphones in the ceilings were checked and found working at their optimum. Between them they agreed a code word for 'help now'. Mr Reid would give his men on the team the code word so any one of them could make the call if others were in trouble. The feeds from the marquee company office and the other locations electronic equipment intelligence being relayed to the London operations rooms was now being fed into a temporary operations room in one of the back bedrooms of the mess. Captain Freire Howell-Speed and Andrew supported by a sergeant from the regiment and a SO13 senior policewoman were checking the feeds and getting themselves organised for a long wait.

SO13 had a backup squad of a dozen men arriving to stay at Basingstoke police station overnight. They would move up to the rear of the forest for 0700hrs next morning and finesse their way into the electrical supplier unit via a back window once the terrorists had left with the marquee. The owners of the electrical supply business had been alerted and he and his staff had taken a fortnight's leave on the state, out of the country.

Rodney reached into his briefcase and gave Mr Reid the VSS Vintorez 9mm special forces pistol. "This is for you to use." Rodney had held his deputy's eye as he spoke. The SO13 man looked away and shut his ears to the exchange between the two secret service men.

Reid had a slight smile on his lips. "Confuse and deceive. I understand, Rodney." He hefted the weapon and the magazines. "Always wanted one of these but they are as rare as chicken horse. Now you two had better get off to the mess as I am sure you have a stack of things to do."

"Expect them as soon as you open and for goodness sake be careful. No heroics, tell the men too." Rodney put his arm round Mr Reid and whispered in his ear, "That means you." And then to Reid in an almost inaudible voice, "But I do need a Russian bullet in one of them, dead or alive."

"Trust me, now go away." Reid waved them off before returning to dismiss his crew after a final briefing to them. Waiting patiently in the backroom when Reid entered, he could sense the excitement overlaid with concern. He knew each felt that they would not be good enough to hold up their part of the mission facing them. Reid understood the kaleidoscope of mixed feelings men experience the night before the battle. The adrenaline would be running and he looked for signs of stress and fear as he gazed round the room. What he saw pleased him. His job was now to lay it on the line and remove fear at the same time. They were well prepared and protected. If anything went wrong it was because they didn't listen to him and he made it clear as always he would deal with any situation and if they followed his lead and did what he told them to he would see them safely out of the other side. He finished and told them to get a good night's sleep and to be in at 0730hrs. He held Carol back. "Have you thought how you are going to behave when they come?"

"I thought afraid and compliant."

"That will do. Don't arrive before 0830hrs. It would be unusual for the secretary to be in too early."

"Will do, boss, see you in the morning."

In the operations room in the mess, the sergeant from the regiment said, impressed, "He is some piece of work your Mr Reid."

"He should be, he was one of yours. Let's hope this generation of your men is as good as him," Andrew said, winking at the men from SO13. Behind him working up the operations board Captain Freire snorted. Andrew looked back at her and laughed.

"Time will tell." The sergeant returned to screens in front of him.

Reid locked up after checking the canteen supplies of food and drinks of which there was plenty. He said goodnight to the men in the ceiling and wished them well.

Liam, no less busy than Rodney, was giving his final briefing to the hostage team and the attack group.

"Sheena," he began. "You are in control of the marquee site and have Shaun as a runner and general factotum. Billy here and his three men will secure and guard the marquee staff. You will take the blue Ford people carrier for your team. After you release the hostages you drive up to Basingstoke and park it in the Anvil car park, switch the plates and all of you catch the first train to anywhere. Drop off at different stations if you can and after that you sort yourselves out and get back home. Any questions?

"I know we have wigs and beards etc, for disguises. I would be happier with a balaclava for my men over that period of time," Billy said.

"Up to you, use both or none for all I care. Remember the plan is to get the staff in the back room so when you are not watching them you can wear what you like in the front office, but you can't wear a balaclava in there because it might look a little suspicious if a punter or salesman visits up and see you dressed up like the man in black on a blag." The room laughed.

"Point taken, we will mix and match. So we will."

"Anything else from your team, Sheena?"

"Just to confirm the hostages are not to be harmed unless they play rough and then they are only to be subdued," Sheena said to Liam but as much for Billy's ears and his boys.

"Exactly!" Liam looked at Billy who was looking disappointed. Billy nodded and folded his arms across his chest. "Sheena, take your team away for some food and sort them out. I want them on site for 0730hrs waiting for the marquee staff to arrive. They are to be secured and in the back room before my team arrive. Got it?"

"Yes Liam, and I minded to tell my team the hostages are important to us all." Sheena looked round the room before she led her team out of the room.

"Right me boyos, the main event. Gather in and find seats where you can." Liam still stood. He had a map on a board and with his pointer began. "This is us here and here is the marquee company and here is the mess. The route from here to the marquee company is this way." His pointer picked out the route to the company and back to the mess. "First day there will be twelve of us in all in the other two people carriers to the company and leaving plus two riggers from the marquee company. We use the two trucks from the company to carry the kit day one, and one people carrier with the two hostages who are going to help us, or else their mates get hurt. I will drive the people carrier and the trucks follow me. We must complete the erection of the marquee on the first day and put in the floor rails. Day two, we leave the two hostages with the others and pick up the flooring. Joe will join us and place the charges. Clearly we don't want onlookers either day but certainly not on the second day, they might want to know what the lumps are we are attaching under the floor." The room laughed at Liam's joke.

"How is the attachment of the charges going to work?" one of the men wanted to know.

Joe stepped forward. "Simple. I am going to staple them to the back of the floor plate through the tape they are wrapped in. I have prepared twenty 2.5 kilogram packages and sandwiched in them each are two charges of nail gun nail packs. So with some 2000 embedded nails and the explosive that will rip the wooden floor into thousands of flying splinters, it should suffice." There was a low whistle from a few men.

"Now it's important we are co-ordinated on that second day you three are to form a screen around Joe and whoever he chooses to help him and look natural while you are making the screen. The rest of us will be lifting in the floor panels and placing them to Joe's instructions. Any questions so far?"

The room was silent but a hand went up.

"Yes Maguire, you have a question."

"It's just, I think we would all like to know what the plan is if we are bumped. You know, if someone susses us out?

"Yes good question. Let's put it like this, you keep your day bag close. So it's seconds to reach in and get your arms out and working."

"Okay, but what do we do then?" Maguire was insistent.

"Whatever you can on foot or in one of the vehicles you fight your way back to here. Ian and Joe will be rigging this place and the grounds tomorrow with a few surprises. It will take more than they think to winkle us out of here."

"And then how do we get away?" Maguire again, and Liam could see he had the room with him.

"You heard me tell Sheena I wanted the hostages unharmed, well they are our insurance policy. Sheena and her boys will bring them here as soon as she hears we have an issue."

Andrew was covering for Rodney in the hastily set-up operations room in the officers' mess, listening in, sat back in his chair and was relieved that the IRA had a sound reason for keeping Mr Reid and the men alive and in good health.

Liam was talking again. "Any other questions?" There were none. "Off you go, get yourselves ready and have some supper, there's plenty of food in the kitchen so help yourselves to whatever you want and a can, but only one. Breakfast at 0600hrs and we leave at 0630hrs on the dot. Find somewhere to kip down wherever you can."

Liam, Joe and Ian were left in the room. "What do you think?" Liam asked Joe.

"What I think does not matter. They look keen enough but many are new and mostly untried. You are going to have your work cut out keeping control of them that's for sure."

Ian said, "Don't want to break this up but I still have some work to do on the explosives detonator receivers and the two transmitters."

"I thought we were ready." Liam was annoyed.

"Yes well we are, but I need to double check. It won't take me long now, another hour and I can join you for supper. By the way, I will keep what Joe and I need to rig this place but I am going to take the bulk of the explosives and kit to a nearby dump first thing in the morning. I've alerted the key holder and he will meet me there. I should be back around ten to help Joe. You okay with that, Liam? Thought I could use the Toyota four-by-four."

"Sure makes sense."

"I'll be off then. See you later."

Joe and Liam wandered off to join the noisy group in the dining room. "Keep it down, boys, don't want the neighbours calling the fuzz because they think there is a disturbance here." Liam got the noise level down to something like acceptable immediately.

Andrew in the operations room picked up the remark by Ian intending to take the bulk of the explosives and spare kit to an IRA dump. He was on the phone to Graham. They needed the watchers to follow Ian and note the location of the dump and identify the key holder if they could. Graham agreed to get the watchers out on the road. Andrew turned to the senior SO13 man. "Once we have identified the dump and the balloon goes up, do you have the men to secure the site and relieve the IRA of whatever is there?"

"Sure, may need to get a bomb disposal specialist to open the dump anyway as they may have booby-trapped it."

"Do whatever you need to do, as long as you can deprive them of the load one way or another." Andrew was suddenly hungry. "I am going to have supper, can I get you anything?"

"I would like sandwiches, egg and bacon, lots of them and a flask of tea and coffee and a tea-making kit for the night," said the sergeant.

"Same please, sandwiches and chips and tea," called out the two SO13 officers in unison.

"Same," said the captain. "And cakes and biscuits too."

"Oh my God. Think I have just been had," said Andrew feigning a miserable countenance, which brought a laugh.

"Allegedly," added the captain cheekily, which bought another burst of laughter including from Andrew.

"Far too much joviality going on," said Rodney entering the room. He had the head of SO13 Robert Coveney with him; Major James Collins, the SAS Major in charge of the men from the squadron that had been deployed at the targets.

Andrew came to their defence. "My fault boss, I was just going to supper and made the mistake of asking what I could bring back."

Rodney smiled. "Supper, now that's a good idea, what say Robert and James – shall we join Andrew and he can bring us up to date. Major will you join us."

"Certainly, be with you in three, just need to have a word with Sarge."

"See you downstairs."

Much later that night Rodney sat in the operations room checking his notes, which was his way of getting focussed on the issue at hand. He had promised to talk to the Brigadier before turning in and needed to order his thoughts before he did so. He had walked the mess corridors with the others and viewed the disposition of the men inside the mess. It had been agreed that for the first day the men would pull back from the front rooms of the mess and only Major Collins as the liaison officer with the marquee company would be in contact with them. They had reviewed where the supporting forces would be on the second day and the police plan to shut off the roads and evacuate around the mess for a distance of a mile once the terrorists had arrived to set in the floor on the second day.

They had reviewed the similar arrangements for the safe house and the marquee company. Having exhausted all the things they could think of and a dozen what ifs, they had parted for the night.

Rodney smiled as he remembered his interview with the General, his Chief of Staff and the Camp Commandant earlier in the day when he explained what was going on. Expecting rage at being kept in the dark, he was surprised when the General an ex-gunner had been concerned and supportive after being momentarily stunned. "Good God, you mean they were going to blow up the entire summer ball, all our people, all our guests? The Army would have been affected badly,

I don't know how long. It beggars belief even for them." The General was furious with the IRA, not Rodney. "It is difficult to take in, can you imagine the retribution our troops would want to wreak on them and what would follow it could alienate the whole of Ireland when we seem to be moving on to a new phase there."

"That could all be part of their thinking. I myself was to be a guest with the Brigadier."

"We have a glittering guest list of the great and good including your boss. I just can't get my head round this." The General was still in shock but this last outburst seemed to clear his thoughts and he but quickly rallied. "Do what you have to do."

His Chief of Staff was silent thinking of what if? The Commandant swore, "You get the bastards every one, Rodney."

The Chief of Staff asked the difficult questions. Like why not roll them up now to lessen the risk. Rodney explained had to take out the whole nest not just a few and how now he had the additional bonus of seizing a major IRA arms and explosives dump. His last question was how Major Collins had become involved. Rodney explained briefly James' close and supportive association over the years with the Brigadier and his SIS section. He seemed to accept that and the premise for not rolling up the IRA earlier and finally asked what if anything they could do to help.

"I don't think so, excepting on the second day if you could somehow ensure the civilian mess staff was called away after breakfast without alerting them. Some of our people will take their place so it all looks normal. Of course any mess members also need to be away by 0800hrs latest."

"I will fix that with the commandant after this meeting." The Chief of Staff looked at the commandant who nodded.

"Now Rodney, I would appreciate it if you and the force didn't do too much damage to the mess itself. I know it's showing its age and needs a makeover but I need it for the ball, end of next week." The General was half joking half serious. "On the other hand a little damage would enable us to twist the arms of the powers that be for some funds."

"Do what we can sir. Just sorry the thing is happening on your patch."

"Don't think you could have done anything about that. Positively I think we should thank you and the others involved for being ahead of the game. It is not often in my experience that happens enough. Good luck to you all." The General stood and held out his hand.

"Thank you for that sir. I will let the team know that you wish them well, I know it will mean a lot to them on the eve of the battle, for that is what this is."

Robert the head of SO13 had sat silent during the meeting after initially being introduced. "Just so you understand, General, apart from my teams I will need to formally hand over from the civil power through Rodney to the SAS Major so the military can play their part."

"All very complicated but I am sure you have it all in hand." Turning to Rodney, the General said in parting. "See you and the Brigadier after the event."

Rodney smiled and nodded. "I look forward to that, General."

Rodney cleared his mind of the meeting and put his notebook flat on the operations table he was using so he had it in front of him as he picked up the phone and dialled the Brigadier.

As Rodney called, Servo and Carla stood on the cross channel ferry looking back on England. "Wish we could have stayed you know, Servo." Carla looked into dark at the fading port lights.

"In a way so do I. But on the other hand it looks like the General has something else for us to help him with. That we are all to go back to the dacha is for me a bonus as it means we are together." Servo leant on the rail; it was probably the first time he had opened up on his true feelings for Carla.

Carla put her arm through his. "Not sure that's adequate compensation."

Servo grinned. "I can do better."

"Maybe so, but not on this deck, it is cold wet and slippery," Carla complained.

They left to meet up with Saied and Vasily in the bar. Saied greeted them and offered to get them a drink. "Guinness," they said together.

Vasily held Carla's chair out for her to sit down. "You can't quite believe Tsygankov is allowing us to drive down to him in the motorhome. I have looked at the route; it's close to 5000 kilometres give or take, a few hundred."

"What route have you decided on?"

"Amsterdam, Hanover, Berlin, Warsaw, Kyiv in the Ukraine, Voronezh to Borisoglebsic then pick up the E119 to the dacha. Say average 1000 to 1200 kilometres a day, sharing the driving, that's close to 5 days maybe 6 or 7 if we are held up at the borders."

"Maybe a little longer if we do some sightseeing and shopping," said Carla, reminding them she was the senior officer present, which brought a laugh.

Robinson was on the line, "Rodney that you, all set?
 "All set sir."
 "I am with Graham in the control room, so speaker on, tell us all."

Chapter 52

MATCH

Dawn broke over the marquee company as Mr Reid arrived early ahead of his team. The dawn was cool and grey and Mr Reid thought, "Miserable, with that light rain mist too fine to be rain but you got just as wet." It was barely seven o'clock and he had not slept well, deciding to give up and get up. Mentally he was prepared for whatever the day would throw at them. He shrugged, took out his keys and made entry into his office. Put on the kettle, called to the men in the roof space to shake a leg and get ready.

The team filtered in and by seven thirty they were doing what they could to look busy.

The IRA when they arrived drove slowly into the company yard and parked alongside almost with enough room to open the doors between the people carrier and the office door. Sheena and Shaun were out the vehicle first and entered the office. Both held a gun on Reid who sat up straight in his chair, arms on the desk relaxed.

"You are wasting your time, love. We don't keep any money here," Reid said to Sheena.

"Is that right? Might be you have something more valuable, like your life!" Shaun spat at him. "Don't do anything stupid but go to the door, and call the men outside to the office. Do it now."

Reid sidling away from the guns went to the door and called his two men outside in. "Fred, Sharky, get yourself in here sharp like." He stood by the entrance of the door to watch Fred and Sharky double over to him. As they came level with the office door the four IRA men led by Billy tumbled out of the vehicle, balaclavas on. Billy pushed Fred and Sharky into the office unnecessarily roughly.

"What the fuck!" sparked Sharky.

"Quiet Sharky, you too Fred, settle down." Reid took control. "I don't think this is personal."

"It could be," said Sheena. "Move into the back office, be quick now."

Reid, Sharky and Fred shuffled into the canteen where the others, Avery and Mould were drinking tea. Reid was suitably impressed by the acting skills of the team as they did second takes as the IRA band filled the room.

"You three sit with the others." Sheena waved her gun to give effect. "And I will let you know what this is all about." She turned to Billy. "Go and call the rest in will you."

Sheena now faced Reid and his men. "You are now hostages. Nothing will happen to you if you behave. If you don't, these men behind me will hurt you. You will comply with what we ask you to do. You will stay in this part of the block, for up to a week, so get used to that fact quickly and live with it."

"People will come looking for us; wives, girlfriends, clients when we don't turn up," Reid said reasonably.

"I agree so we need to neutralise that eventuality. However, first things first. I want two volunteers from your team to work with us." She waited. No-one moved. "For a mature woman, slightly chubby," Reid thought, "she moved quickly," as she pistol-wiped Avery across the head who crashed off his chair onto the floor groaning, holding his head. The others tensed, and those IRA men that had not done so pulled their weapons.

"Whoa, whoa, whoa slow down, slow down." Reid put his hands out, palms down, waving them to emphasise the need for everyone to keep calm. "Fred, Sharky you are volunteered. Agreed?"

"Yes boss."

"Alright love, what you want the men to do?"

"Help us erect the marquee without us looking as though we haven't done it before which some have, but some haven't and it is your kit so you know it."

"And then?"

"You spend a week in our company here in the canteen, until we leave and you release yourselves.

She turned to her men. "Plastic-cuff those two, and the wanker on the floor. Hands in front, or you are going to have to cuff them every time they want to use the bathroom, drink or eat. Then you two watch them, and keep them quiet, no talking." Turning to Reid, Fred and

Sharky, "If you three behave, nothing will happen to your mates in here. Run away, compromise us, they are dead – understand." She got nods of understanding. "Come with me." She led them out of the canteen with her men covering them with their guns. In the office she ordered them to sit.

"Riley, get yourself outside and see if the others are here yet." Riley took off his hood to reveal a long dark wig that covered most of his face and went into the yard. Liam had arrived with his vehicles parked to the side of the Dutch barn. Riley waved him over.

Liam, after meeting Riley and getting the latest on the situation, went into the office. Reid had briefed his men well, reminding them to keep their heads down and avoid eye contact. Instinct told Reid that this newcomer was the leader. He could only see the lower half of the man but his stance was confident and his voice commanding. "Who are these three?" Reid recognised the harsh Bogside accent. Sheena explained and Liam once he had understood turned to Riley, "Take those two over to the boys and get to work. I want the trucks loaded and out of here in fifteen minutes."

Reid raised his head. "To get this over I have copies of the plans to erect the marquee in the box file over there." He pointed to the bookcase. "It will make your life easy."

Liam reached for the file and brought it over to Reid who sat still, hands in the open behind his desk. "Show me."

Reid opened the box file and brought out a series of documents. "Here are the loading lists. Small truck one is for ladders, poles, ropes and pegs. Truck two the larger one the canvas. Once the canvas is off the bigger truck and it's empty it returns for the floor panels. I would normally rent a third truck but I can't get one immediately."

"Not an issue, we will come back for the floor tonight. Next."

Reid opened a large format document which showed the construction detail for the marquee and order of build. "Notice all the poles are colour coded and the canvases numbered. If you lay the kit out in order, your job will be straight forward. But the kit is heavy so you will need caution." Reid opened out a third document also in large format showing the details for the poles and guys. "The process is simple, get the skeleton up and raise and place the canvases on it. My guys will manage the roof panels for you, with the muscle of your men."

Liam studied the documents before folding them away. He studied Reid for a second. "It is always good to do business with a professional. Where are the keys to the containers?"

"The men have them. The truck keys are in the key press behind you, it's open."

Liam gathered the keys, leaving Sheena with, "See you later," and he was gone. They heard the trucks start up soon afterwards and leave the site twenty minutes later.

Reid drew Sheena's attention to him, "My secretary will be in, in about half an hour. What I would like to do is this. Explain to her we have a job on in Scotland and will be away for two weeks so she might as well take two weeks to be with her kids who are on summer holidays. Tell her it is a good job and the holiday is gratis above her entitlement and she will be paid for it. Can we go for that, it would prevent a manhunt for her if she doesn't get home tonight and I don't think we want that?"

"You can try it, but if I think she suspects anything then we will need to think of something else. Do I make myself clear?"

"Very clear." Reid's Scottish accent was heavy.

Sheena smirked noticing the tightening of Reid's jaw. "Don't get heavy with me, boy. I said we would try it."

"I would like to talk to the men in the back please to ensure they keep quiet, the walls are not that thick. And I would appreciate it if you and your men were in the back room too when she arrives."

"Okay, but we will be listening. Now make the calls to your man's partners and spin them the same story." Sheena nodded to her men and they walked into the back room leaving the door open. Reid followed her in.

"Listen in. Carol will be here shortly and I am going to send her on holiday. You will hear what's going on. So keep it silent in here or she will end up with you and that will just raise the risks to us all. Got it? Good." Reid went back to his office to make the fictitious calls. First call was to his wife for real in case they checked. "Hi love, listen we just got a dream job come up in the Scottish highlands. It's a quickie and the boys are on their way already and I am following in a few minutes as soon as I have locked up. It's a rush job and for a fortnight. Think it is following a party of rich people round a number of shooting moors." His wife obviously asked him something. "Not an issue, I got plenty of spare kit and no you can't come. Listen love I really am up against the clock, could you phone the wives and Avery's partner Rodney for me. What Avery sees in him I can't think. And tell them we are away, and I will get their other halves to call them tomorrow night latest. Yes, yes, there will be bonuses. Love, got to run."

In the operations room in the mess Rodney laughed.

Sheena put her head round the door. "You should be on the stage Mr Reid, well done it was. Now do the same for your secretary."

Five minutes later Jane walked through the office doors. "Don't take your coat off and turn round."

"What's up boss? Want me to do some shopping?"

"No you're on holiday. The boys and I have a job up north for a fortnight. They have already gone. Your kids are on holiday and so should you be. There is no joke, it's a good job with premium rates and a performance bonus for being able to respond immediately. So your bonus is a gratis holiday, you get paid, and it will not come out of your entitlement. So off you go so I can lock up."

"But are you sure? What if there are clients trying to contact us?"

"My mobile number is on the website and in the Yellow Pages; I'll take the calls. Now's here's fifty quid, take little Rodney and the other one to Lego land or something. I know young Rodney likes to play with his bricks."

In the operations room Rodney and the others burst out laughing.

"Go on out of here, enjoy the break, I have got miles to go." Reid eased her gently out of the door.

"Thanks boss." Reid waved it away and came back into the office and sat watching out the windows as Carol drove off the site.

"Okay she's gone, you can come out now," Reid called to the backroom he reached into his desk drawer for a pen and at the same time palmed a small set of nail clippers which he slipped into his waist band.

In the control room Andrew turned to Rodney. "Good tradecraft to get Carol out of it."

"Yes I agree. Can you get hold of her, I would like anything she saw or heard or noted?"

"Sure. Do you want her in here?"

"No I don't think so, she needs to get back to the base operations room, and support Pat through the night, taking your place and we need to keep the men's blood pressure down eh Sarge?"

Sergeant George SAS agreed."You may be right there, sir." His East London accent was to the fore and his grin infectious. "Perhaps you could get me a date when this is over."

"Join the queue." Andrews's caustic put-down didn't faze the SAS Sergeant.

"As you say, but when she sees me, I will be going to the front of the queue." Rodney doubted this long-haired ripped-eared broken-nosed veteran, was Carol's cup of tea but you never could tell.

"Another good performance and I owe you one for that." Riley smiled and clipped Reid about the head. "But how do we know you didn't slip her a note with the money?"

"Simple. I have a responsibility to ensure my staff are safe, it is called loyalty. Secondly Sheena or you were watching me from the crack in the door so I could not have written anything even if I had wanted to. Thirdly my only motivation now is to see this thing through with the minimum fuss. If we are going to be together for a week let's get grown up about it. You have the guns we don't."

"Smart man," said Sheena

"Too laidback by half if you ask me," Riley said, and Shaun stared at Reid weighing him up.

"Just bowing to the inevitable. Now if there is nothing else, I thought we might get something to drink. This acting is thirsty work." Reid went into the canteen to the kitchenette there and filled the kettle and busied himself with the cups. He collected the dirty cups from the table and saw Avery give him a smile and thumbs-up. Lewis sat head down dozing, and Mould was stretched out sleeping. He looked at the IRA guards who shook their heads in wonder, they had not expected the hostages to be so compliant and had relaxed in the chairs they had set against the wall so they could watch from a distance.

One held his gun loosely in his right hand resting on his thigh. The other two men had holstered theirs. "Amateurs, they have not even searched the room," was Reid's take, "But not that Sheena or Riley or the younger man Shaun?"

Reid eased the tea towel off the radiator and only because he knew it was there; saw the comforting butt of the gun given to him by Rodney. It had a full magazine and was made ready, safety catch off. The night before he had driven to his local gun club and fired off a magazine to get used to the weapon. It kicked right and up if you didn't control it. Mentally he was already preparing to kill the three with head-shots one, two seconds max, three bullets. They would have no time to react. One bullet for whoever came to investigate from the back office. The rest he would make up. He rehearsed it over and over in his mind while he made the tea for everyone.

Liam led the trucks into the officers' mess car park and through the break in the tress and hedges onto the front lawn of the officers' mess. The day had brightened. A slight breeze ruffled Liam's hair as he climbed down from the vehicle. The other vehicles parked alongside him. Liam scanned the front of the mess, the early morning sun reflected black windows back at him. He could see a few windows open and their blast net curtains fluttering in the breeze. The mess was the typical "H" structure. The two uprights of the "H" jutted out and where he had been told were the officers' accommodation, bedrooms and ablutions. The bar of the "H" extended was the public rooms downstairs, dining rooms, ante and quiet rooms and bar. Upstairs were senior officers' suites and more bedrooms.

Liam stood some 40 metres from the mess but even at that distance he found it difficult to take it all in without turning his head. It was a big old mess by any standards. Bringing his gaze down he noted the large double doors and their stone pillars holding a large stone canopy over the entrance. Three wide stone steps led off the mess lawn onto a wide and deep patio with its centre of focus, heightened by the balustrades leading to the entrance. On either side of the patio were stone tubs of plants and a number of metal tables and chairs and at one sat an officer reading the paper.

Seeing Liam arrive he carefully folded the paper and placed it on the table before advancing to meet the IRA man.

"Good morning. Good day for it. Not too hot and dry for the rest of it I fancy. James Collins." James extended his hand to Liam.

Liam looked at the man in front of him, just over average height wide shoulders and a face that had the look in the eyes that had seen much. "Good to meet you Major." Liam took the offered hand and shook it. The hand that gripped his was that of a powerfully built man and Liam hoped he would not have to go against him, one on one.

"I just wanted to meet you and welcome you. I'll get tea and a snack sent out around ten, and sandwiches say 12:30, afternoon tea 16:30 if you are still here. How's that?"

"Very welcome thank you."

"How many for?"

"All up, fourteen of us."

"Good, is there anything else you need?"

"May be the men will want to use the facilities from time to time."

"Ah yes." James didn't think they had thought of that. Thinking quickly on his feet, he knew there were a bank of portable toilets stacked in one of the hangers on the camp for air shows and the like. "Give me ten minutes. I will get a couple of temporary toilets over for you. Don't think the mess manager would be happy with fourteen men tramping in and out his clean mess with grass all over their boots." James grinned.

"Happen your right, Major. That would do just fine."

"Anything else?"

"No."

"Right, I'll get off and get the toilets organised." Liam watched the Major jog over to the mess in his polished high-ankle boots and take the three mess steps together in one high stride before disappearing into the darkness of the mess entrance.

Liam turned to see his men milling around the trucks. "Come on, boys, let's be having you. You two," he pointed at Sharky and Fred, "get the teams organised or do you want to be here all day?" He marched off to his truck and got out the construction plans and drawings.

Under Shark's and Fred's urging and direction they had the IRA sweating within minutes. They worked together like demons running between the IRA men helping and correcting as they went. By the time the tea arrived they had the skeleton of the marquee up. Spare rope needed later, ladders, floor rails and pegs were neatly stacked, and the canvases were dismounted and laid in their piles ready for use.

A couple of silent waiters arrived just before ten and put two of the metal patio tables out on the lawn, then went back into the mess to bring out trays with pots of tea and plates of biscuits, which they left on the tables and then departed.

Liam led the men to the tables. "Jesus boys you two are a find, never seen a work rate like it."

"The hard stuff is just about to start, the canvases weigh a ton and are stiff and difficult to handle," Sharky grunted, chewing on a biscuit. The men around him groaned. "Not wanting to tell you your job but I would send two men back with the truck to get the floor plates. They will take time to load."

Liam glanced at Sharky. "Okay, which two would you send?."

"Those two, they are not used to this work. The rest are naturals," Sharky said.

"Okay, you two, can either of you two drive a truck?"

Both could and they were told to get back to the site and with the help of Sheena's men get the plates loaded and then get back here.

Liam was secretly delighted. "Sharky, what's your take on the job going forward?"

"Hmm, we should have the roof panels on and some if not all the sides on by lunch if the men don't fade on us. That will give us the afternoon to get the floor rails in and level them up on the spreader boards. They can take time if the ground is rough, depends – this area looks pretty flat to me so we might get lucky, even get a few floor panels down by close."

"We will see about the panels when the time comes. Better get on." Liam got the men moving.

Sharky and Fred took five men each and rigged the lines to draw up the roof panels. An hour later the roof was on. Breaking the team up again in to two they masterminded the putting up and hooking on the side panels. By 12:00 it was complete, including a ten-metre double wide canvas tunnel that met the mess patio steps. Sharky called them all together. "Right, well done, everyone. We now have half an hour before lunch so let us get the guy ropes tensioned and pegs checked. You four, pegs with Fred you four, with me, guy ropes and the toggles on the side and top sheets. Let's go." It was a good call as they found errors and loose kit, all of which they corrected.

Major Collins led out the waiters and the luncheon chunky sandwiches with bottles of water and paper cups. He left them laying out the food while he walked over to see Liam. "Your men have done well." He noticed they looked tired except for two men, one he knew Sharky and the other must be one of the new men Rodney had recruited. He ignored them. "You have lost two men." He looked round before his gaze rested on Liam.

"They're off to collect the floor panels, they will be back soon. Don't worry, Major, we will save them a sandwich or two." Liam thought, observant bastard we need to watch him.

"Do you mind if I have a look inside?"

"From the door maybe but we need the safety officer to check it out before we release it. Insurance requirements. And for that reason we will need to tape it off tonight before we go."

"Sure understand, maybe later then." James made his way back to the mess and lunch. The men with the panels didn't arrive until nearly two o'clock. By two o'clock Sharky and Fred had the rails sorted and laid close to half the floor rails. Liam went out to the men in the truck and ordered them to bring a floor panel with them.

"Sharky," Liam called him over to where the two men had brought a floor panel in to the marquee. "Show me how this panel goes on the rails."

"Sure it's pretty simple. See the hinged plates on the back of the panel, they are spring-loaded and clip over and catch in the rails. The only trick is you start at one corner and work across the floor before you start the next row. If you don't do that you will get out of sync and end up with a problem and have to start over again. Follow that simple rule I just told you, and you can't go wrong. One last thing there are clips to lock in the end of the runs so the panels don't slip. They are in a bag, come on I will show you."

Liam told the two men to put the panel into the double-width entrance tunnel they had put up. The canvas tunnel leading all the way to the mess steps meant they had to load the floor panels from a canvas door at the rear of the marquee. "And get the rest of the boards stacked there too. Do it now." Grumbling, the men went off to get on with the job. "I'll get more help to you when we finish the rails." Liam called after them. The men shrugged. "Wasters," mouthed Liam to himself as he left and went after Sharky.

Liam was satisfied just after four that they had done all they needed to apart from fix the floor panels the next day. He got the men to tidy up and reload all the unwanted kit back onto the lorries. He kept back a few mallets, pegs and ropes, in case they needed to replace or re-adjust anything in the morning. The staff again served tea and biscuits to the IRA man as promised. James joined them and poured himself a cup, found Liam, and thanked him for the work and enquired what was to be done to complete the task.

"Well Major, we have the floor panels to put in tomorrow and then we should be out of your hair."

"Looks pretty good, any chance I can have a look inside now?"

"Still rather you didn't till tomorrow when our safety manager gives it the OK. Insurance will not kick in till then, for the third party liability." Liam felt quite proud of his response. "Sounded well," he thought.

Collins toasted Liam with his teacup. "Until tomorrow then."

"Until tomorrow, Major." Liam walked away and called the men to. "Mount up, time to go."

The lorries drew into the marquee company site shortly after six and while the men parked the trucks in the barn and got their personnel bags packed in the people carriers, Liam walked to the office.

He was surprised to see Reid still at his desk but didn't remark. "Well how is it going?" he addressed his remark to Sheena.

"It's been fine. No issues. Mr Reid there has been very cooperative and helpful."

"Good, good, well Mr Reid, seems I was wrong about you – I had you down as a trouble maker. Let's keep it that way." There was a threat in Liam's voice. "Now do you have safety check sheets and anything else that would be helpful for us to sign over the marquee tomorrow to the clients?"

Reid pointed to a drawer in his desk. Liam pointed his pistol at Reid. "Open it slowly."

Reid opened the drawer to its full extent and Liam peered in and lifted out a box file which he laid before Reid. "Open it."

The box file revealed a series of forms and Reid fed the relevant ones to Liam. "This is a safety check sheet." Reid held it up and passed it to Liam. "We would normally invite the client to accompany the safety officer and get him to counter sign. Don't suppose you will want to do that?" Liam shook his head. "This form is for the local council reference permission to erect a temporary structure. Don't expect that that will be necessary as I believe the military still have crown immunity." He passed it to Liam anyway. "This form, you log the kit on site so you can check if anything has gone missing." Reid rummaged to the bottom of the box "This one is the most important one as far as I am concerned and it's in triplicate. It's the indemnities form that you need to get the client to sign. Give him a copy and bring the other two back." Liam looked at him. "It is for the insurance. If anything gets damaged or lost it enables me to claim."

Liam took the indemnity form and a smile played on his lips. "If you only knew?" he thought. He ran through the sheets and picked out the kit list. "Take this into Sharky and get him to complete it while I have a cup with my boys here. Sharky did well today," Liam meant it.

"I would have been disappointed if he hadn't." Reid got up from the desk and took the kit list paperwork and a pen.

Sharky was still in the yard, ordering the IRA about, and getting them to stash the spare kit in the appropriate locations. "Hi boss," he greeted Reid.

"Well done Sharky, seems you are a hit. Fill this in for me, will you?" Reid leant his back on one of the containers and watched the IRA men clearing up, and then mounting the people carriers.

Sharky took his time filling out the form, talking quietly under his breath, telling Reid how it had gone and Major James' masterful performance with Liam. He broke off from time to time to go and check the returns, whenever anyone showed any interest in Reid and him. Fred joined them, declaring all was sorted. When they had finished Reid followed Sharky and Fred to the office.

Riley was waiting for them while Liam talked to Sheena. Shaun was collecting his kit.

Riley called Fred forward and patted him down before applying plastic cuffs and sending him into the canteen. He called forward Sharky and did the same. Reid went to his desk and closed the box file and put it back in the drawer and opened the top drawer and put in the pen while palming a second small set of nail clippers. He turned to Riley, "The kit list fully completed for your boss." He handed it over to Riley. "Going to get the dinner for the men, do you and the others want any food?"

"Go ahead I will join you shortly just to make sure you are not going to poison us."

"Be difficult, tonight's special is all-in stew," Reid responded, closing the canteen door.

The team looked up at Reid as he entered. "Time for supper, you just sit there I will get it." He grinned. "And you will like it."

"Starving," called out Mould.

"Shut the fuck up!" one of the IRA watchers hissed.

Reid busied himself in the kitchenette. Opening cans of stew and peas and peeling a small mountain of potatoes. He drew out two large pans and put them on the double rings of the cooker. He filled one with water and tipped in the potatoes. "Tea, everyone?" He got nods from everyone including the IRA men.

Later when he served the tea he inspected his men's hands to ensure their circulation was not cutting off. He found them all fine except for Avery's. His hands were swollen and blue. Reid held out Avery's hands for the IRA men to see. "Can you please re-do this cuff, it's stopping the blood to the hands and he will lose them if you don't."

With bad grace, one of the IRA men got up and inspected the hands. He drew out a workman from his inside pocket and slid open the saw blade. Avery winced as the cuff was cut through. Working his fingers to get the circulation going he groaned.

"Give him a few minutes please to sort himself out before cuffing him again."

"You get on with the food. I'll cuff him when he is pink again so I will." The man laughed and his fellow guard smiled.

Riley arrived and wanted to know what was going on. Reid, back at the cooker, told him. Riley shrugged. "How long before the food is ready?"

"Ten minutes if that," Reid responded, his back to Riley. Reid searched the cupboards and found a packet of curry powder, jars of herbs, and other spices which he added to the stew. The smell was soon overpowering and the men salivated. He set the table, placing bread and butter on the canteen table, followed by the stew and potatoes. He served each of his men's share into a bowl and passed it too them with a fork. He then served the IRA guards and carried three steaming bowls of food into the office for Riley and his man and Sheena.

Reid made himself indispensable, washing up and making tea or coffee until late into the night until he declared he was going to get some sleep. He had become invisible to the IRA, just part of the furniture, which was his aim. He slumped down, still without his hands cuffed, by the side of the radiator next to the kitchenette but not before checking the comforting sight of the pistol stashed there.

***

While Reid dozed, Rodney held a final meeting in the operations room in the mess. The large room, part of a senior officer's suite on the second floor at the back of the mess was nevertheless getting crowded.

There were three desks against the longer wall; the first held the SO13 operation duty officer working to London, the second desk, the sergeant from the SAS and a technicians from SO6 and SO7 listening to the safe house and its environs, and at the third sat Captain Freire with an another SO13 officer concentrating on the marquee company. The traffic volume to each of the desks was turned down and the three duty officers had earphones on their heads listening to the incoming traffic and keeping their eyes on the video screens that fed pictures of the activities at the sites.

The rest of the people in the room sat at two tables pulled tighter to form a working platform, strewn with the location maps, signals and other documents. Rodney sat at the head of the table with a junior Minister from the Home Office, who had suddenly appeared late afternoon and was to Rodney as welcome as a spare man at a party and possibly bent on disruption. To Rodney's right was the SAS Major and to his left the head of SO13 Robert Coveney and Major James Collins. To the Minister's left was the Chief of Staff from the Air Corps and the Camp Commandant and to his right a non-descript woman with jet black hair that fell about her face, Rodney guessed she was in her late forties and from MI5.

The meeting had become heated when the Minister prevaricated over handing over jurisdiction to the military where it was required at the safe house and the marquee company in the context of Reid and his men. Robert the head of SO13 calmed the Minister and cleared the air when he told him he already had the authority to bring in the military and for them to act at certain locations. The SAS Major who had begun to show signs of frustration with the Minister who he thought was a waste of space sat back in his chair and breathed a sigh of relief. Rodney felt for the Minister and thought he had had too much information to process in too a short time and he was confused; the woman from M15 he had bought with him had an agenda to make sure nothing stuck to them if it all went wrong.

Rodney was very patient and explained the dangers several times and the havoc these IRA men could wreak on the capital or elsewhere on the mainland if the Semtex was allowed to be used. The Minister was visibly shaken. His remit had been to limit exposure and he had found himself in a complex and nightmarish situation.

"Let me understand this. There are four operations and they are going to take place simultaneously?" The Minister straightened his tie.

"That's correct," Rodney confirmed back. "Would you like me to take you through them slowly?"

"Very slowly, if you please."

"Let's start with the simple one. We followed one of the IRA men who transferred the unused Semtex to an IRA arms magazine where it was handed over and locked away by the keeper of the store just north of London using MI5 watchers." Rodney acknowledged the woman from MI5. "The watchers have now been withdrawn and SO13 is keeping it under observation. The men from SO13 will only move in to capture the keeper and the stores but only when the IRA mission here, and at the safe house, and the marquee company, have been attacked simultaneously. Okay with that?"

"Fine." The Minister smiled for the first time.

"What if the magazine is booby-trapped?" The woman from MI5 wanted to know.

The head of SO13 gave the answer. "Along with my arrest containment force there is a bomb disposal pair who will check it out and if it they need resources they will call it in." She nodded.

Rodney continued. "Secondly when the action is taken here against the IRA, two other locations have to be attacked simultaneously to save lives. The first is the safe house which our intelligence reveals will be occupied by the IRA electronics expert who will have his finger on the remote radio trigger if he hears anything has gone wrong. We simply cannot let him trigger the bomb at a time chosen from there, so he has to be taken out. The SAS have this action." He paused, the Minister gestured him to continue. "Okay, just so you can picture the action here." Rodney gestured to the operations desk behind him. "When the action starts here, the SAS desk will radio through for the SAS team at the safe house to take action. At the same time the SO13 desk responsible for the arm magazine raid will call their team up to take immediate action. The second SO13 desk over there will call up the teams at the marquee company to do the same." He paused again and pulled out the area map of the marquee company. He pointed out where the SO13 teams in the forest were and the men in the roof space. "At the marquee company, six of my men are currently hostages. They are posing as staff of the marquee company. They are plastic-cuffed and IRA men are guarding them. At this moment in time the IRA at this location number four men and a woman. The hostages have to be rescued before they are shot."

"My God Rodney, that's risky, can we not negotiate their release afterwards?"

"I am sorry Minister, that is not going to happen. My men know the risks they were taking. The woman Sheena and a man called Riley are ruthless killers, and will not hesitate to execute the hostages. Let's face it, we don't have capital punishment in this country, and they don't fear prison. It is like a holiday to them with their mates in the Maze. And they know that they will get out sooner than later and be looked after for the rest of their lives by the IRA."

"I see, and you make your point well." The Minister was coming round unlike the MI5 woman who still sat po-faced and uncommunicative.

"I take it Rodney, you are now going to talk about here." The General's Chief of Staff was interested in his part of the ship, as he would be, and wanted to hear about it.

"To the main event, then. At least I hope so. We are expecting, according to our maths and observations of the IRA team, fourteen men to appear tomorrow. And they will be armed. Importantly they are led by a man called Liam, who is the Chief of Staff and Enforcer for a senior member of the IRA, and one, we believe wants to break away from the traditional IRA that may be looking at a permanent ceasefire and peace. Success here will make that easier for those that want to continue to murder and bomb their way to a united Ireland, and to get recruits, resources, and funding." He went through the pictures and showed the minster a picture of Liam. "We believe he personally executed one of our own, earlier this year in a most horrific way." He let that statement sit, before picking up a picture of the bomb maker. "This picture is a man called Joe. He's dangerous and like the electronics man at the safe house, recently arrived after nearly a year in the main Libyan terrorist training facility south of Tripoli." The woman from MI5 now showed interest.

"He would certainly be a catch if he could be captured." She looked at the Minister soliciting support and then at Rodney.

Rodney stared her down, and the SAS Major next to him raised his eyes. "We will see at the time, no promises and no disappointment. So then, let us move to the main event, and some matters that you need to know. The bomb maker Joe has plans to place 20 parcels of 2.5 kilogram odourless, and hence undetectable Semtex below the floor panels of the marquee. The Semtex parcels have wrapped round them, hundreds of nails, in total thousands. Liam the Chief of Staff will have with him a hand-held detonator, built into an ordinary mobile phone. We understand they have to enter a code of six figures, before they press any button. So we plan a subterfuge by drawing Liam into the mess, and overpowering him and getting the detonator off of him."

"And if you fail?" The woman wanted to know.

"The front of the mess will need re-decoration," the Camp Commandant said dryly.

"I don't think that remark is helpful," the woman cut back. "What if you fail?

"We have tried to mitigate the risk to our people. In the matter of a premature explosion, should it occur, we have marksmen external to the mess as well as inside, covering from the wings. Any explosion will be almost certainly show damage to the front of the building, where our presence will be limited to a few essential players."

"You have thought it a possibility then, so why haven't you taken them out before now?" She was relentless, and she even got the Minister's attention, and both she and he now looked expectantly at Rodney for an answer.

Rodney was quite calm, he expected this question and it would be one he felt he would often be asked. "It was not convenient."

"Not convenient?"

"That's correct, it was not convenient." Rodney looked at the minster not at the woman.

The junior minster shifted in his seat. "I think we may be missing something here and I think we will move on. Please continue Rodney." The woman huffed, clearly put out but the minster simply smiled and again gestured for Rodney to continue.

"There is not much more to say, Minster, except to assure you we have the full support of the police and the areas around the targets will be secured, people evacuated on the receipt of a command from Robert, Commander of SO13 here. Further we have the emergency services on standby for what they of course don't know yet. The other sites excepting this location will get a ten-minute warning before we act. We have tried to take every precaution we can think of to ensure civilians are not caught up in this operation. It would be facile to say everything will be alright on the day. No plan however credible will need to be modified on first contact with the enemy. We would hope with the experience around this table we will prevail no matter what is thrown at us."

The minister stood. "I can only wish you all well and good luck. Rather you than me I think. We will meet after this is put to bed." He turned to his woman minder from MI5 and said rather ungraciously, "Would you like a lift back to London or will you make your own way?"

Dawn was coming up and Liam and his men had been up long before working their weapons and day sacks, getting ready for the mission. For all except Liam, Shaun, Joe and Ian they would be on their way back to their homes or bolt-holes. Liam with the two specialists expected to be confined to the safe house for another week until they pressed the button.

"Liam, your hand-held device, it's all set up. You remember the six numbers?" Liam nodded. "If anything goes wrong today, or thereafter, just punch them in. All you then have to do is press any button on the phone and that will set the bomb off." Liam looked at the remote; it looked and felt like any other mobile phone. He tossed it in the air and caught it deftly in the other hand. Ian frowned. "It is not a toy, Liam."

"Sorry." He put an arm round Ian. "You have done a good job, mate. I was just letting of a little nervous energy. It is a big day for us today. Pity we will have to wait a week to press the button."

"We will get through it I am sure." Ian left him to go back to his workshop.

Liam stood for a moment in the doorway of the house. Nothing for it but to get the job done. He went in to get the men moving. "We leave at eight fifteen. So be ready, my boyos. Sooner done, sooner finished and you go home."

The IRA men climbed on board the people carriers at the allotted time. Some showed nervousness, others were sanguine accepting this was just another job. Joe appeared calm and once seated closed his eyes. Shaun was excited to be playing a part in this venture and had prepared a mill board with his safety check sheets and looked the part. Liam was tense, hyper aware of everything going on around him.

Ian came to see them off and spoke to Liam again. "Remember, Liam, the circuits are live so do not go testing the phone, it will work when needed to be sure." He took the phone and punched in the six figure code.

"What are you doing Ian?"

"I am arming the phone; I need to run some tests, handshakes when you are on site. So don't touch the finger pad unless its for real, You remember if anything goes wrong you all you do is press any button press your button, you understand how careful you need to be with the phone till you bring the phone back and I disarm it?" Liam nodded affirming he had got the message. "Right see you later. Make yourself, useful and open the friggin gate and close it, after we have gone," Ian grinned and doubled down the track.

The convoy swept out onto the road and turned right to the village and then at the crossroads took a right. Shortly after they were at the second set of crossroads and turned right onto the main road leading to Middle Wallop Army Base. Liam was feeling palpitations and had to breathe in and out slowly to calm himself. He looked over at Joe with his eyes closed and thought. "Cool bastard."

A mile on they bumped into the officers' park and made their way to the gap in the hedge and drove onto the grass making for the entrance tunnel of the marquee.

In the mess Rodney stood with the SAS Major, the Commander of SO13 and James protected by the shoulders of the corridor that opened into the wide, high, mess entrance. Rodney looked round the corner.

The IRA were just pulling in and parking nose into the tunnel. Rodney pulled back. He thumbed his two-way radio and called up the operations room. "Send to all, ten-minute warning, confirm back over." He and the others waited.

"Text to Reid and message sent SO13 and received and understood at the marquee site, roger out," Captain Freire reported.

"Message sent and understood at the safe house, roger out." The rasp of the SAS sergeant was comforting.

"Message sent to the arms magazine, received and understood, roger out," reported the SO13 duty officer calmly.

"Police and EMS ready, message sent and understood." Captain Freire reported. In effect this was a warning to the police and other emergency services, fire and ambulance, that the operation was going ahead. The police had been working on traffic control for an hour with the exception of the IRA route to the camp. Before dawn the population for half a mile around the mess had been silently evacuated into one the hangers on the airfield.

The IRA had by now dismounted and was to a man with their day sacks over their shoulders entering the tunnel into the depths of the marquee. One man stood out, he held two large holdalls straining at the handles and waddled into the depths with the others. "The bombs," Rodney guessed. A moment later two of them re-appeared with long handle mallets and their day sacks.

Rodney turned to James. "You ready for this?" He got a nod. "Are you sure, Major, it's not too late to replace you."

"Not a chance." James picked up his powder-blue beret set on his head and smoothed it close to his skull and marched out of the mess calling for Liam.

Liam appeared in the tunnel entrance. It may have been a sixth sense or he saw something. "Yes Major, what I can do for you?"

"I need to get off; can you come up to the mess now so we can sign off the paperwork?"

"Sure, give me one minute to hand over and I will be right with you, just wait there." Liam hurried down the tunnel and got hold of Shaun, . "Shaun, hold on to this if anything happens hit a number. Don't fuck about with it otherwise. Don't touch a button or anything. Do you understand?"

"Sure Liam. No problem."

"Right, be back in a moment." Liam retraced his steps breathing hard.

As he emerged, Rodney gave the executive order to all satellite operation targets to 'go' and got immediate confirmation that others were activating their part of the plan.

James let Liam come to him and turned to go into the mess. "This way sir if you please." James held the large door open for Liam to follow him in.

As Liam got just inside the mess and the double wood latticed glass doors driven by the springs closed slowly on Liam. James launched himself at him.

***

A full minute before James' attack, Reid making breakfast slipped the two nail clippers to Sharky who had dozed upright propped against the radiator with Mould on the other side of him. He quickly snipped through the plastic tie and passed it on to Mould while Reid distracted the IRA men. "Eggs and Bacon alright for you boys?"

"Right there sir."

Thirty seconds had passed.

He reached down into the cupboard and heard movement in the roof space above him. His right hand wiped into the space behind the radiator and bought out the Russian pistol. Mentally rehearsed he calmly took aim and he got off two quick shots to the heads of the terrorists. Both went down in a liquid movement, sliding of their chairs.

Free of their cuffs, Mould and Sharky scrambled for the two dead men's weapons. Mould threw the nail clipper over his shoulder to the others who quickly released themselves.

Reid called out the code word. "Help me!"

Reid was instantly covering the door holding the gun with two hands and his legs in a strong stance when the door was flung open by Riley. Reid shot him in the head. The force of the bullet drove him back into the office. He could hear a scramble as the remaining IRA man and Sheena sought to escape. The men in the roof space had waited patiently for this moment and crashed through the ceiling tiles onto the last IRA man. Sheena was at the door screaming, fumbling for her gun and mobile phone. As she brought up her weapon to empty the magazine into the office, Sharky following through the door shot her with a double tap in the chest. Sheena was already dying, her finger tightening on the trigger of her automatic tightened sending half a dozen shots high into the office before she was tumbling backwards over the step onto the tarmac of the working area of the site.

***

At the safe house, a minute or so before out of the side of his eye Ian caught movement in the field to his front, "Was there something out there in the field, a bit of black plastic perhaps or something more sinister?" he thought, or had he imagined it. He reached for his phone nevertheless and after a moment of hesitation punched in Liam's mobile number. He watched horrified as two shapes detached themselves from the earth and another two to his left began to emerge. SAS, as he hit the green button to warn Liam he was ripped apart by well-aimed shots. He sank to his knees the phone slipping from his fingers. His head fell forward on his chest and he slowly toppled over onto his right side.

"Right listen in," the leader of the SAS team called out. "Sort out your shit. then secure the track. No-one enters. until the bomb disposal boys give it the all clear."

He called up the operations room and reported, "Job done, send Felix. Roger out." Felix the cat was the old-fashioned name for the ammunition technical officers.

***

Shaun looked at the phone in his hand as it began to ring. Without thinking he pressed the green receive button before he remembered Liam had told him not to touch any buttons. "It was an automatic reaction and Liam would understand." It was Shaun's last conscious thought.

Joe setting the bombs into the second row of the floor panels heard the phone ring. A premonition perhaps but he said, "Oh fuck!"

James looped his arms around Liam, trapping Liam's arms to his side. He rammed Liam back against the mess doors, heavy though they were, were slowly opening out onto the mess patio pushed outwards by the weight of the two men's bodies. Both heard the ring of the phone and Liam with superhuman strength forced James to take a step backwards into the mess entrance hall and the doors swung closed on Liam's back when the explosion happened.

Rodney and the SAS Major had just come out of cover, to help James, and were blown back, partly sheltered from the explosion by the corners of the corridor.

Liam took the full blast of the explosion as the doors blew inwards. The glass was shattered into a thousand shards by the flying nails wrapped round the explosives. The wood of the door that framed the glass panels were driven from the frame that held them, and were driven deep into Liam's body peeling open up his back. His blood gushed over James. James, although protected from the worst by of the blast by Liam's body, was blown upright and flung backwards, limbs out of control. At high speed he slammed against the heavy solid mess foyer table, itself upturning and on the move. James, with his arms round Liam, had seen a blinding flash, an almost physical blow, and then felt himself hurtling backwards. As he hit the foyer table with Liam spread on top of him, he felt a crack as his head was brought to a stop, and an intense pain spread through his body. He drowned in that moment and blackness enveloped him.

Most of the IRA men were blown apart and dismembered in the explosion. The few that survived were maimed for life. The two men outside with the mallets were blown off their feet for many yards. Some of the flying nails and wood splinters released from the explosion claimed one of them. The other, blooded, staggered to his feet hands over his bleeding ears. He staggered to the nearest day sack, stumbled over and reached inside for a gun. Waving the gun around blindly, he was cut down by a burst from Rodney borrowed Russian machine gun. Rodney, who himself shaken, deafened and bloody, and had emerged from the mess ready for a fire fight. "One for the Banker's daughter, you bastards!" He screamed the adrenaline coursing through him.

The marquee was shredded and down. The bloody mess that met Rodney was a lot of body parts, most of the IRA were missing limbs. The horror of the aftermath of the bloody explosion would return to him over the years ahead in his dreams. A few weak groans of the maimed, reached him. The carnage was for others to sort out; he had to refocus, and find out the situation at the other locations.

He would leave the SAS Major to sort the immediate mess and for him round up his scattered soldiers. A few of them and the SO13 team in the mess wings, had been cut by flying glass but otherwise they were suffering from the deafening noise and pressure blast of the explosion, and that would soon pass. One or two had been bowled over and were concussed and bruised and there was the odd broken arm and torn tendon. They had been lucky.

The SAS Major caught up with Rodney as he was picking his way through the debris on his way back into the mess. "Sir, messages, other sites all secure. Police and EOD (Explosive Ordnance Disposal) are taking over." And almost as an afterthought, the Major gripped Rodney's arm, holding the Russian machine pistol. "Might be better sir, if that weapon was made to disappear."

"Yes thank you." Rodney released the weapon, to the Major who then called one of his men forward and told him to lose it, permanently.

Rodney turned back to the mess, he needed to find out how James was, and get back to the operations room. He looked up at the once proud building for the first time. "Bloody hell, what a mess." The front of the mess had hardly a windowpane left and the patio was a jumble of ripped up concrete. The mess entrance was door-less and the interior in that area was in total ruins. Rodney suspected the public rooms would also need a makeover.

James was being attended to by an SAS medic who declared to Rodney, James would live, and the injuries were in no way life or limb threatening but, he was going to be in pain for a few days. The SAS medic hit the morphine jab, wrote a big M on James' forehead, broke the syringe needle and pinned the syringe to James' bloody uniform. "He was lucky, not a broken bone, unlike this one," he rolled Liam over. "A lot of broken bones some collapsed his ribs cage and he caught a shit load of flying nails and debris, they tore his back open."

Rodney thanked the medic. As for Liam, his feelings were mixed, he was his opposite number in many ways, and he would not wish that form of death on his worst enemy, but at least it had been quick.

***

He found the operations room busy with incoming communications from all parties involved in the operation. Captain Freire saw Rodney enter the room. "Boss, got Mr Reid on the phone waiting to talk to you. That green one over on the table please."

Rodney slumped in a chair and took the phone. "Mr Reid, give me some good news."

He heard Reid chuckle. "All well, not a scratch. The targets are all dead."

"What about the site?"

Not a lot of damage, a couple of ceiling panels to replace and bullet holes to patch. There are some blood and guts to clean up. But we can't do that until SO13 give us back the site, which they have now declared a crime scene. That will not be until tomorrow at the earliest. What do you want me and the boys to do to help? I take it you destroyed a very venerable officers' mess."

"Well it's certainly a mess." Rodney laughed for the first time since the explosion. "James caught a package but will be fine eventually, a few weeks at most I am told." Rodney thought about the mess. "I want you and the team over here soonest and get Andrew down; I sent him back home last night, a mistake. Don't know how we are going to do it yet but this mess has to be invisibly mended by the time the Corps hold their ball in a week's time."

"Got it, we will be there in an hour."

"Thanks, I had better phone the Brigadier."

In the event, Robinson was waiting on another line to speak to him. Rodney took a deep breath and got him switched through. "Good morning sir, how are you?"

"Think that's what I should be asking, Rodney."

"We're physically good, a few bruises and scratches." Rodney wiped his face and saw blood. He had been so adrenalized up he had not felt the cuts and damage to himself. "So where we are sir is, the enemy is defeated, and as far as the tally goes no-one involved that we had been watching got away. Many of them are dead. Most of them are dead, and some are maimed. The police will give us the précis breakdown latter. Everyone did their job, a few broken bones and bruises. Quite a few of the SO13 and SAS ended up with cuts from flying glass and the odd nail. And a lot of us are suffering hearing loss. James took a beating but should be okay in a few weeks. Reid as always played a blinder."

"Good I will wait for your report. Any immediate issues I can help with?"

"I need some money to get the mess repaired; it is in a hell of a mess from the blast. And I need to get it put back together for the Corp's ball next weekend."

"I will make sure you get it now, what about the people to repair it?"

"Reid's team are coming over and I have sent for Andrew. We will move heaven and earth to get the repairs in. Money talks and it would be immensely helpful if you could get the MOD departments responsible for buildings and works, to work with us, and not against us. We will generate the impetus but we need their engineers to carry it through. Talking about engineers, any chance we could have a Royal Engineer Combat Squadron with their plant and earth-moving equipment and a troop of pioneers for a few days? We need to re-profile the mess grounds and turf them. We also need to re-build the mess patio, balustrades and door pillars etc."

"Stop, let me get that sorted and I will get back to you. Your difficulty will be getting the police to let you have access to the crime scene I think."

"Thought about that and have an ace up my sleeve."

"Good man."

As it happened Robert Coveney from SO13 arrived in the operations room. He came over to Rodney and sat down, calling for one of his duty officers to get some tea for them both. "Make us big mugs, hot and very sweet." He turned to Rodney, took his head in his hand and turned it this way and that. "You got a few cuts, my old friend, some quite deep and you seem to have the remains of a nail sticking out of your scalp. Captain Freire, get a medic in here to sort out your boss please."

Rodney ignored his injuries. "Bob, I need to ask a big favour. I want to get the mess restored to its former glory. Is there some way we can clear areas and let my team get people in to fix it up?"

"Don't see why forensics and your own investigators cannot clear areas to let you do that. Say the wings of the mess first then the public rooms then the foyer and patio. Think the marquee scene itself will take a few days to process though."

"Thought about that; supposes we clear a marquee-size area, say to the right of the one we put up, and erect a marquee there, once that patch of lawn is cleared of blast fall-out."

"We can do that." Robert called over his second duty officer and asked him to get the senior forensics officer in here as soon as possible as well as the officer in charge of the crime scene and the military police colonel on the scene. "Consider it fixed. Now drink your tea Rodney, as you will shortly be facing the General and his Chief of Staff not to mention the Camp Commandant. They are waiting at the barrier I set up for you to collect them at the back of the mess." He had a wicked smile on his face.

Rodney, taking a deep breath and with a smile on his face, left the back door of the mess and went to meet the General's party.

"Rodney, I hear you got the lot and more from your Brigadier Robinson. A job well done." The General was amiable. How long that was going to last once he had seen the mess, Rodney was not now sure.

"Thank you sir. I can't take you everywhere but we could review mess front from the foyer area. I am afraid it is a bit of a mess. But we will have it back in shape and a new marquee in time for the ball. Trust me."

"Don't know about that, the last person to say that to me was my wife before she wrote off my pride and joy – an old MG. The mess has at least the same attachment for me."

Rodney groaned silently. "This way, please General."

On the remains of the patio the General and his party stared up at the ruins of the mess. "Good God Rodney." To everyone's surprise the General laughed. "Forgive me gentlemen, but despite the look it is only superficial and I have seen almost as much damage done on a young officer dining out course night. Rodney, if you say you can get the mess back in time for the ball I believe you. No-one could create this much havoc in such a short time without having some idea on how to put it right. Mind you, if you don't I would hate to be the one who presents you with your mess bill this month. Come on, chaps, back to work as you can see Rodney has his work cut out."

The General had thrown down the challenge to Rodney. The General paused with his aides and looked at the bloody shredded remains of the marquee and the bodies and body parts being recovered. He looked at Rodney. "Thank goodness Rodney you stopped that happening to us and our guests. Well done indeed." With a wave of the General's cane he shepherded the silent Chief of Staff and the Camp Commandant ahead of him. He turned to Rodney with a wink. "The place needed a makeover. I know a couple of TV interior decorator personalities who owe me a favour or two for free rides, in our expensive flying machines that they have enjoyed from time to time. I will have them report to you, and you can use them as you think fit."

Rodney was back in the operations room as soon as the party had developed to write up his notes and get himself up to date. "What's the situation on the IRA magazine?"

Robert bent over the desk with his duty officer and responded to Rodney. "A massive finds, thank you Rodney, the list is still coming in but there was everything there from rockets to grenades. Enough on first sight for men there to claim it would have outfitted a small army. And yes we got the key holder who appears to be a retired member of the IRA and a fairly senior one at that."

Rodney did the sums. An IRA electronics specialist had been killed. Five IRA at the marquee company killed. Fourteen here including Q's Chief of Staff and the bomb maker killed or maimed. Twenty IRA personnel in all removed from active service and a magazine captured. He considered that score met the original mission statement and wondered how the IRA would treat this home goal and if Tsygankov would survive this failure.

Chapter 53

ALLEGRO

It was August and the dust had settled. The mess was ready for the ball and as good as new, better in fact some had claimed including the General to Rodney.

The Brigadier and Rodney attended the ball. Along with James who had recovered enough to limp into the ball helped by Mr Reid. The internal SIS enquiry had exonerated and gone as far as to commend the section for its part. The police closed the case. Only the Banker and the Fraud Squad soldiered on. Rodney had got out of Robinson with the blessing of the PM a block leave for the team and had taken this week himself.

What had driven him to decide on his holiday destination he didn't know? When the Brigadier asked him why, Rodney told him he didn't have an answer but it was something he had to do. Robinson cautioned him to be careful and told him he was off the books for a week.

Rodney sat on the boat's side watching the great river rushing by as they forged up country. The landing area Rodney had chosen came into view on the left as they passed round a corner of the island. The time was ten o'clock in the morning of the 31st of August 1987.

The boat, a clinker built fishing boat, while showing its age was wide and comfortable sluing the current close to shore and it slowed and gently nudged the high bow onto the sandy beach. The boat was at an oblique angle to the shore and the current tugged at the long poled tiller which the captain was skilled enough to hold his position steady, while Rodney, his stick in his right hand and his day sack on his shoulder, swung himself onto the sand.

The captain got back off and called out he would be back in two days same time. Rodney waved to him.

In the garden behind a high wall a man was tending his grapes. They were ready to harvest. The grapes were ready early this time of year, a full fortnight, but nature has its way. The man listened to the boat arrive and leave. Curious, he went to the gate in the wall and swung it open.

A man stood on his beach looking out across the river to the other side. Shading his eyes against the fierce sun gaining in strength as the day wore on. He was broad shouldered, brown to fair hair somewhat awry, longish. He stood silent and still in a crumpled cotton suit leaning on a stick.

The man at the gate initially felt his heart go to his throat and weakness in his legs. He steadied himself and a smile played on his lips. "Major Rodney Brown, it is him, as I live and die?" He was astounded but felt compelled to call out to Rodney. "This way Rodney."

Rodney turned slowly to face Tsygankov; a mixture of emotions crossed his face until he suddenly smiled. "General. Good morning to you." Rodney waved his stick and then picking up his day sack, using his stick for support he made his way up to the walled garden.

When they were both inside the gate they stood looking at each other. Tsygankov was the first to speak. "Why?"

Rodney broke eye contact and looked at his stick. "In truth General I still don't know why I came. It was just something I needed to do. I haven't come to harm you, of that I am sure. Or take revenge for the loss of a woman I came to love, that pain is now quiet. And I haven't come to gloat either. I am just here and I don't know why."

"In that case Major Brown, Rodney, welcome. Walk with me a while round the garden and let's just talk of matters past and experiences."

Rodney followed the tall man round the garden and Tsygankov told Rodney about the plants and the plans he had for his estate when he had finally retired.

Rodney for his part found the General likeable. It may be that the older man reminded him of his own Brigadier Robinson. The two older generation individuals he admired but for different reasons, but both were without a doubt the two most clever and venerable spymasters in his life.

They eventually circled the General's small lake. "You know, Rodney, your timing is perfect. I have other house guests who will be fascinated to meet you as you will them." He hailed Mac who had appeared from round the dacha with a tool bag in his hand.

"General, you have a guest; I didn't hear him drive up."

"He came by boat. I would like to introduce you to Major Brown of the British Secret Service, but who was once like you Special Forces. What do you think of him coming here unannounced, to see us, socially?"

Mac put his head to one side. "Think he needs feeding. I will have a word with Tamara, food in ten." Mac held out his hand. "Welcome Major."

"Just call me Rodney, Mac, I don't stand on ceremony." Rodney's Russian was rusty but he got his point over and Mac slapped him on the shoulder.

"Good man." He disappeared in to the house.

"You've made a friend there Rodney. Now come and meet the guests."

On the patio behind the dacha, sitting with papers on a large patio table, sat the guests. Seeing Rodney appear, they put away their papers into a file and stood to welcome this unexpected guest.

"Can I introduce Major Rodney Brown to you who has come to stay, as a guest, for a day or two to see us."

Rodney took up the theme. "I am pleased to meet you. Servo, I think?" Rodney offered his hand which was taken and Rodney felt the physical strength of the man. Turning to the man on his left he said. "Saied, it has been a while." Saied smiled and took the proffered hand. "Vasily." Vasily shook his hand but his eyes never left Rodney's face, which betrayed no sign of having met him before. "And of course Carla, I am very pleased to meet you all."

"What are you doing here in the lion's den?" Carla wanted to know.

"If I knew I would tell you. The truth is I simply don't know, I just needed to come."

"Could be, General, he has heard you have the best vodka in Russia and needs some help harvesting the grapes," Servo said with a twinkle in his eye.

Rodney laughed. "All of those things, Servo, and now I am promised food too."

The next two days passed in a blur for Rodney. For two days he helped pick and process the General's grapes into large stainless steel drums and was promised a box of wine by post when the wine was ready. At night he ate and drank and listened to Carla play the violin on the dacha patio and watched with delight as the Russian sang and danced Ivan Larionov's circa 1860 famous Russian folk song, the Kalinka. He listened to the stories from history that Tsygankov told of the great game and the battles for spheres of influence in Afghanistan, Turkey, Persia and Central Asia between the British and the Russians in the 18th and 19th century. He told them of the young and daring British officers and their pundits, and brave Russian officers whose task it was to spy and survey the lawless empty zones, and of the deceptions they used to penetrate the lands of the fierce Khans of every shape, taste and hue to bring back the intelligence on each other and the local Khans' depositions and intentions. He told of the Russian advances to its new east, west, and southern boarders, and the resistance of the British in order to defend India and its wealth. "It was claimed where the Russian flag was hoisted, it was never taken down. There were of course exceptions. We sold Alaska to the Americans, for one."

Carla finished off the last evening playing several Allegro pieces.

Saied asked Carla what Allegro meant; she explained to everyone that the only meaning of this music term in Baroque times was when each piece of music was associated with one specific mood or emotion according to the then powerful Doctrine of Affections. Unlike some specific tempo-markings Allegro was not perceived as an indicator of a specific tempo but much later it becomes associated with fast. Carla entertained them with a series of Allegro pieces to demonstrate. She chose gipsy and mood music. The men were enchanted with her.

With something like regret, Rodney was surprised to find he gathered his belongings, he knew he could not delay his departure even if he had wanted to; he had to get his boat. He had, he realised, had a great time and was tanned from the sun and felt fit and had been completely relaxed in the company of his newly made friends, if that is what they were, he was not sure?

On the morning he was to leave Tsygankov called Rodney into his study. "Well Major, time to say goodbye. I seem to remember we probably both swore to kill one another next time we met. Well it didn't happen. If we had I would not have enjoyed the last two days as I have. I regret to say this but you can't come back here, ever." The General held Rodney's eyes, looking down from his great height.

Rodney held the gaze. "I know, General, perhaps when we are both out of the game we can meet. We were well met I think this time, perhaps one day we can tarry a while in some quiet place and sit a while. Take a dram of whisky or vodka if you prefer, smoke a pipe and talk of battles won and lost and battles, we only dreamed of."

"Well said, Rodney, but not yet. Remember what I told you, you can't come back. By the way, your ruse using Russian weapons caused me some embarrassment, fortunately the IRA scoring an own goal outweighed any comebacks. On balance I probably am in your debt."

Rodney laughed. "I do understand General. And so you know, I still don't know why I came." Tsygankov laughed then. "You British, what can I say?"

They saw him to the beach when the boat arrived and Vasily carried his bag and Servo helped him board. Vasily threw Rodney's bag on board after him as the captain chugged out into the current.

"God speed," cried Carla, and Rodney waved from the boat to them all.

It took Rodney two days to make his way home. When he unpacked his bag he found a page of paper tightly folded into an impossibly small parcel. He carefully unfolded it so not as to tear it and read it twice.

Next morning in the office Robison paged him.

Rodney took his notebook and went to see the boss.

"Morning sir."

"You look pretty chilled out, had a good time I suspect and how was Tsygankov?"

"The perfect host. I even helped to harvest his grapes and have been promised a box or crate of whatever the Russians do."

"Yes Rodney but?" Robinson had worked with his deputy long enough to know he was holding back on the mother lode.

"Well sir." Rodney opened his notebook and took out folded note he had found. "We are in trouble, of that I have little doubt."

The paper simply read:

"Mission. The mission is to undermine the British economy by attacking its energy infrastructure. The code name for the Mission is be Acceso Armageddon."

Robinson leant back in his chair. "Will it never end? Rodney, this is my very last task." He waved the paper at Rodney. "After this you are on your own and God help you."

"As you say sir." Rodney paused, "I was wondering if you might have a word with the minister and the PM. Why can't we short-circuit this one by going straight to Gorbachev? I am sure he would never have sanctioned such a blatant attack on us."

"We will see what we will see, but I will see the minister."

"Good enough for me sir."

"Where is Mr Reid and the others? The place is like a morgue. Apart from Secretariat and Christian, thank goodness. I have been rattling around this place like some lost soul."

"Mr Reid is due back from Somalia tomorrow. Mould and Sharky took their wives to Spain. Andrew, Pat and Jane, the Jones boys plus Avery and their families are having the time of their lives being looked after by Graham in that monstrously large house, and seeing London as tourists. I take it from Pat the group holiday has been a massive hit with everyone and Graham is the host and cook to die for, aided by his able assistant Captain Freire who keeps order."

"Good God, Graham, I would never have thought it."

"Anything in the in tray, to sort out, so when they all get in tomorrow, they will be gainfully employed. I take it we will be keeping the Jones's?"

"Oh yes keep them. As for the box it is full, apparently MI5 and 6 are having one of their all to frequent spats with the minster and passing stuff to each other and back again. So I have managed to get us a couple of juicy morsels to keep the boys and girls entertained. But more of those matters later. Talking of morsels I am taking the Banker to dinner tonight at the club and wondered if you would join us. He seems keen to talk to you."

"Can't wait sir, time?"

"Seven for seven thirty, do you?"

"Perfect."

Book Three

SPYMASTER

ACCESO ARMAGEDDON

CHAPTER 1

London, Thursday the Early Summer 1988

Major Rodney Brown sat with his knuckles on his knees outside the secure conference room at Thames house, the new home of MI5 and his own section. Rodney was the Deputy of a semi-autonomous Special Operations section, tasked to serve where the Secret Intelligence Service, commonly referred to as MI6 and Security Services MI5, needed a third agency to resolve an issue neither of them wanted nor felt that they could take the responsibility for, or a task that simply fell in a black hole that neither of them covered.

He was not worried that he had been called to a meeting of the Joint Intelligence Committee, JIC. True his boss, Brigadier Robinson, would normally attend the Committee but he was away on leave. The Committee did not normally meet at Thames House. Rodney was curious but more than that – annoyed – at being kept waiting for over an hour. He looked at his watch. Eleven forty-five already.

Five minutes later, Sir Percy Cradock, the Chairman of the JIC, opened the door and nodded to Rodney and walked off down the corridor with his briefcase swinging. Rodney stood and stretched. Perhaps with the Chinaman, as Rodney thought of him, gone his wait would soon be over. He did, nevertheless, think it odd that the Chairman had left the meeting. Cradock, Rodney knew, had spent time, a lot by most people's experience, in China in various roles, including as Ambassador. People he knew thought Cradock too close to the Chinese and too quick; it was reported, to compromise if matters got difficult with them. Rodney shrugged. It was not his problem and way above his pay grade.

Rodney got his summons to join the JIC meeting as he saw the Chairman disappear round the corner, heading for the lifts.

As he entered the room, Rodney glanced round and acknowledged everyone. At the head of the large oval table sat Sir Christopher Curwen, the head of MI6 in the chairman's seat. The Director of MI5 sat alongside him on his left. To their left and right were the other members of the Committee, most of whom Rodney knew or had a nodding acquaintance with. He knew the military intelligence man and the representative from GCHQ. He was surprised to see the minister, sitting to his left and the head of special branch on his right.

"Rodney, welcome." Sir Christopher with his grey eyes studied Rodney. Rodney, for his part, summed up the head of MI6, a Knight's Commander, and who like him was an ex-soldier, but 4th Queens Own Hussars, not ex Special Forces. Rodney had heard whispers of Sir Christopher's recent coup, who with the help of John Scarlett and the Viscount Asquith had spirited the KGB case officer, Oleg Gordievsky, out of Moscow, under the eyes of the Russians. Rodney waited.

"We understand you visited General Tsygankov at his dacha. Why did you do that?" the Director of MI5 asked smoothly.

Rodney thought for a moment before answering. "After the tidying up of Tsygankov's mess in Wallop, I felt I needed to see him. At the time I was not sure why, but now, in retrospect, I think subconsciously, I was going to rid the world of him for good. The Old Russian Spymaster has been a particular thorn in our side and mine, in particular, for a decade or more."

The head of MI6 took up the questioning. "But you didn't, Rodney?"

"No, in the event, I didn't. I had no authority to, although I did think my visit could be seen as an extension of the task."

"Did you have authority for a meeting with a hostile agent?" MI5 demanded.

"Not sure where this going, but I think we should wait for the Brigadier to return from leave." Rodney smiled as he pushed back, which drew a smile from Sir Christopher.

"Quite right, Rodney. It is an internal administrative matter." He shuffled his papers and drew out a single sheet. "This is the mission statement you bought back after your visit to Tsygankov about a serious threat to our country. I read, '*Mission. The mission is to undermine the British economy by attacking its energy infrastructure. The code name for the Mission is to be ACCESO ARMAGENDDON.*' Am I right?"

"That's correct."

"Do you think that the threat is credible, Rodney?" the Special Branch man wanted to know.

"Good question. I think Tsygankov, with what seems to be his immediate team, all of whom I met at the dacha are capable, with resources, of doing us serious harm. More so, if Tsygankov is backed in this exercise by General Polyakov and the KGB Chairman."

"What is he like, this Tsygankov?" The minister wanted to measure the man.

"Physically, near seventy, I would say. Still very fit, broad shoulders at least six foot nine inches if not more. A skull-like head with thinning hair, near colourless eyes, now. His left hand is claw-like from a knife attack by one of my team that cut through his tendons, more than a decade ago." The room stirred with interest. "As for the man, he is mission focussed, with a ruthlessness which only an amoral man can aspire to. Clever very, intelligent certainly. Well regarded by his peers for his past achievements and loyalty to Russia and the KGB. A sense of humour. I did see another side of him at the dacha. He never married, did have a love in his life for a while, no children but he had transferred his parental feelings, if he has any, to his team and they, more than once, drew a wry smile from him. The smile did appear genuine but with Tsygankov you never know. He was the perfect host, during my two days, but as I left he called me into his study and told me I could never return, ever!"

"No love lost there, then," the Director of MI5 mumbled.

"He holds me personally responsible for the damage to his hand, quite apart from any success we have had against him. He was a skilled, if not brilliant violinist, and has a collection of valuable violins by most of the famous luthier. The damage to his hand means he is unable to indulge, which I would judge to be his vice."

"What of the others at the dacha?" Rodney had the room spellbound, and he suspected this diversion was as colourful as it got for them.

"His house is run by a retired nurse called Tamara. Tamara's husband, Mac, is the maintenance engineer and general keeper of the property, which is extensive and sits, exclusively, in several high walled hectares at one end of a small tear drop shaped island, bordered on all sides by the River Volga. It is served by solar energy, a diesel and water turbine and mains power, as well as a butane bullet. From the satellite dishes and other antenna I saw, I suspect he is in direct contact with Moscow and anywhere else he wants to call up. Hence Mac and Tamara live at the other end of the island.

"The brigadier followed your advice, Rodney, and saw the minister and suggested we speak to Gorbachev directly, to short-circuit this mission. Your suggestion has merit, but the JIC determined that we needed some more proof. What if the KGB denied such a mission existed? They easily could do that." He shuffled his papers again and brought out Rodney's post-visit report. "We studied your report. In it you say that you found the mission statement in your bag, when you got back. Clearly, it was placed there by one or more of the principals you met on your visit. Who was that?"

Rodney didn't blink. "I am not at liberty to divulge that, at this time. To do so would compromise an asset in play."

"One of yours?"

"No."

"One of ours?

"No"

"But someone you have access to."

"That's probably correct."

"How deep is this individual's cover?"

"Very."

"They must be a very brave man or woman, then. Rather them, than me." Sir Christopher paused, thinking the problem through, while the others looked at him for direction. At last he said, "Rodney would you mind? Wait outside for a moment."

Rodney left the meeting and stood in the corridor, cursing himself. He was summoned, again, after a few moments.

Sir Christopher took up the reins. The rest of the room had their heads down, Rodney noted. "We are all grown-ups, here, and we are going to respect this person's anonymity for the present time. We need to look, elsewhere, for evidence and this side of the table will do that by coming at the issue from other angles. So saying, Rodney, what we would like your team to do for the present time is work on this threat to the country, exclusively, to the exclusion of all other matters. As always, you will have the support and resources of the members of the JIC to back you up. How does that sound?"

Rodney smiled. He knew he was supposed to be grateful. "It sounds fine to me. However, you are all aware that we are working on a number of files for you, at this time. Here is what I want to do. The team will close as many of the files out as we can by close of play, next Thursday, and you will, as appropriate, have the files back with a situation report on each, hopefully closed, but as a man used to say to me in Belfast; *no promises, no disappointments, sir*. My report will summarise the work on the files, to date, and a further report from me 'for your eyes only', on the strategy and tactics the team will use to execute this matter. An appendix will detail the budget and likely resources we will need to make headway. Finally, I am going to fly out to see the brigadier very early, Saturday morning, and I will be back, late Sunday. It is important he knows what is going on, in his absence, and I will seek his good counsel at the same time. He will, no doubt, direct that we observe Mossad rules"

"Mossad rules, what's that?" the Minster wanted to know.

"Mossad rules, Minister, is the mantra of the Israeli Intelligence service, which simply states that you will not waste public money on intelligence that is already contained in reports of the newspapers. As an example, and in the context of the task we have been given, we will seek to review the special branch and MI5 visit, and other reports, on key installations and other vulnerable energy sources, rather than go and see them for ourselves. For instance, the energy services being supplied by the Channel Tunnel. I am sure that will have been reviewed, time and time again.

"I can see, Rodney, you have been puzzling this threat through, since you received the message. That's all to the good. Where is your esteemed leader, by the way?" Sir Christopher asked.

"Working, as ever, on his motor yacht, the *Harlequin*, in Guaviare Marina, Corfu. I have an open invitation, work permitting, and this gives me an ideal opportunity to go and see him. Mr Reid will run the section and be in contact with me at all times."

"Thank you, Rodney. Now, does anyone have any questions before we release Rodney back to his team?"

Rodney gazed round the featureless and windowless room at the personalities. He watched them shake their heads, one by one. "Looks like I am free to go, Sir Christopher." Sir Christopher stood and walked Rodney to the door.

In the corridor, Sir Christopher asked him, again, about his contact. "You know, Rodney, you are going to have to have a file on this person at some time."

"There will be a time, Sir Christopher, but it is not now. I promise you, if the contact dies away and, or, he or she has the crown jewels and needs to come over, you will be the first to know. I do caution, though, that the person is in the game for the long term. That has to be good for us, don't you think."

Sir Christopher held out his hand. "Like your style, Rodney. Come and see me if you need fresh fields to play in. I think you, and your special operations team, are safe, as long as you have the confidence of the JIC and the PM. But now you are in Thames House with the dreaded MI5. They will be politicking to have your special operation subsumed into their organisation."

"I am sure you are right, sir. We will just have to see, and fight the battle, if and when." Rodney waved goodbye and followed the corridor to the lifts. As Rodney turned the corner, he could see Sir Christopher still watching him, apparently deep in thought?